Sunetra Gupta was born in 1965 in Calcutta and spent much of her childhood in Ethiopia, Zambia and Liberia. In 1987 she graduated in Biology from Princeton University. Now living in London, she divides her time between researching infectious disease at Imperial College and writing.

'Refined sensibility and a graceful style . . . she shows an intelligence, wisdom and judgement rare in so young a writer' *Independent*

'Gupta's talent is of a rare quality' *Oxford Times*

'Gupta's poetic and figurative language, springing abundantly from free association and allied to continuous timeshifts, is reminiscent of Virginia Woolf's *To the Lighthouse*' *Independent on Sunday*

BY THE SAME AUTHOR

Memories of Rain

# The Glassblower's Breath

SUNETRA GUPTA

PHŒNIX

To Adrian

A PHOENIX PAPERBACK

First published in Great Britain by Orion in 1993
This paperback edition published in 1994 by Phoenix,
a division of Orion Books Ltd,
Orion House, 5 Upper St Martin's Lane, London WC2H 9EA



Second impression 1994
Third impression 1994



A CIP catalogue record for this book is available from the British Library.

ISBN: 1 85799 029 3

Printed and bound in Great Britain by
The Guernsey Press Co. Ltd, Guernsey, Channel Islands.

It's the old rule that drunks have to argue
and get into fights.
The lover is just as bad: He falls into a hole.
But down in that hole he finds something shining,
worth more than any amount of money or power.

Last night the moon came dropping its clothes in the street.
I took it as a sign to start singing,
falling *up* into the bowl of sky.
The bowl breaks. Everywhere is falling everywhere.
Nothing else to do.

Here's the new rule: Break the wineglass,
and fall toward the glassblower's breath.

*Jelaluddin Rumi*
1207–1273

# THE GLASSBLOWER'S BREATH

# I

# *Sparrow, Seldom Shaven*

That night, you dreamt, that instead of dying fresh as a blade of grass, last year, one winter afternoon, your sister had lingered, until her flesh had blackened so that the moonstone on her finger stood a monstrous white against her charred skin, and the whitewashed walls beside her bed, where, in your dream, she fought grimly with death, the whitewashed walls, in your dream, spread with stains of old blood at the touch of her fingers, as death sliced into her gums like the sharp thread with which the two of you would floss your teeth after a meal of rubbery mutton. Yet, in truth, she had left you, smiling, joking of the smell of dead rats in her urine, she had settled peacefully into the arms of death, she gasped once, in mild surprise, and then the fingers fell loose upon the starched sheets, it was the image of her upturned palm that had haunted your dreams, until this night, the faint stains of turmeric upon the fingers that stretched into the tropical winter stillness. You had waited, as the smell of whitewash deepened around you, wanting to be alone in these last moments, while her blood slowly released its warmth, you waited before you woke the household, staring upon the newly lifeless palm that you did not dare touch, you were as awed by death as you had been by life, when, eight years before, your sister had held up to you her newborn child, and you had hesitated to lay your hands, teeming, as they were, with life, upon the child's uninitiated flesh. And so you had waited, as the shadows deepened, mute shadows, fresh evening wind scattered the steam that lingered upon her lifeless lips, parted in half-smile in the heavy dimness, you dreamt, that night, that those lips were compressed in terrified resignation to death, and you woke, remembering that you had begun to write of her death long before it had become a reality, long before you were drawn back into the shadows that had been your home, to watch her die, smiling, on a winter afternoon, her palms streaked with the dark mockery of her long lifeline, carved against the contours of her exaggerated mound of Venus, she would be lucky in love, the hoary soothsayer had told her, dragging his filthy nails across the cushion of flesh into the sallow valley where her heart line dipped and dispersed, but her health, he had said, gravely palpating the bony hollow, her health would always trouble her.

You dragged the tendrils of your dream across the mirrored hallway, a mirage of plaster icing, ghostly dim in the early morning light, and pushing gently open the door of the room in which he lay, Jonathan Sparrow, lips parted in dreamless sneer, you walked in and buried your eyes upon his thin arm, stretched across the sumptuous bedclothes, this has never been your home, this voluptuous hostelry, this ornate parody of Victorian opulence that fills the inflexible spaces of your existence, you smother your mirth upon satin pillows, yet within you, that sudden sharp hollowness, like the inside of an eggshell, of living within the walls of a joke, the sort of hollowness that Teddy Ginsberg must have lived with, at least that was why you had pitied him, for having turned his life into a bald statement, garnished plentifully with inedible Americana, he had given you toilet seat covers for your wedding along with a pair of iguana earmuffs and several copies of *The Plain Truth*, where was he now, swallowed by that vast mass of land, deep, thick, heavy land, that you left, five years ago, promising never, never to return.

You buried your sleep-curdled eyes upon Sparrow's thin arm, flesh you had never desired, although you had coated it often with parched salt tears, under false Gothic arches, watching the narrow light from the window where your faithless beloved lay deep in the arms of another. You had dragged Sparrow, through sour midnight cold, to witness the laughing shadows behind the bare window, high high above, you stood clawing at cold stone, and your tears froze upon Sparrow's worn cuffs, last night, over thimblefuls of cognac, you laughed long at these recollections, it has been many years since you have felt such pain as that which had numbed the sharp fangs of the North American winter upon your bare fingers, a chorus of icicles in your hair.

Sparrow, you whispered, you will miss your flight, get up now, I'll come with you to Heathrow, get up, you laid your hands on his head, grey hairs already pepper the back of his skull, slowly you turned his head onto your hand, and felt the leaden weight of dead dream, Sparrow, whatever happened to Teddy Ginsberg, do you know?

He stared up at the invaginations of cold plaster upon the ceiling, a bony ear upon your palm, I think he died of sorrow, he said, his grey eyes hovering aimlessly. He died of sorrow when his favourite drag queen wandered out into the New York sludge in ballet shoes and got a bad case of frostbite, and a small voice whispered within his skull, this is the last day of your youth, Jon Sparrow, make the best of it, did they cut them off, Sparrow, cut what off? he asked, rubbing his eyes, the toes, Sparrow, did they amputate his toes? You can see them, flaming red and blistered, under sodden nylons, the nails painted a diseased blue, he shrugged and threw off the covers, give me that sweatshirt, he commanded, his back still sunburned from the tropics, you picked the shirt off the writing table, under the window, and threw it to him over your shoulder, you pushed away the rest of his clothes, draped over a typewriter, a half-typed page bounced up as you lifted off a cap, have you been typing Alexander's book? you asked incredulously, why not, he answered, I have abused his hospitality for over a month now, you turned around, page in hand, his hospitality? what about my hospitality? you haven't typed anything for me.

You haven't asked me to, he said, lifting himself wearily from the bed, he padded away into the bathroom, you read in the morning light, filtered blue by heavy curtains. On the Immunological Origins of Aggression, and the first subtitle, Blood: The Ultimate Medium of Communication, and there his interest had faltered, for under the heading only a single word appears, BEFORE, the rest is virgin page, deathly white, you tucked it into the obese Medical Dictionary beside the typewriter and walked out, down the stairs, into the kitchen, the only honest room in this house, although gleaming copper pots march gaily, unused, against the walls, and jars of unknown spices fill the shelves, for dinner always arrives from your brother-in-law's restaurant, under heavy metal domes etched with Persian roses, still the butcher block has an honest dullness to it, and the wood of the vast kitchen table is the only surface you can lay your hands upon with love. You found your niece pouring from a heavy bottle of full cream milk into a bowl of cereal, she was to take it to Alexander, she explained, in his study, your husband's mirrored retreat on the top floor, across from the room which has been hers now for almost a year, ever since, after her mother died, you brought her to live in this strange land. She balanced the striped blue bowl in her hands, thin shoulders rocking sharply against the back of her dress, you watched her move cautiously towards the door. In a year she has grown taller and more fragile, you remember, last winter, gliding like a ghost from the room where your sister lay, death still soft upon her lips, you had found the girl, sitting at the head of the stairs, stroking the rabbit, Andropov, who lay like a furry slug upon the marble floor, chewing violently upon cinnamon sticks that she held to him, the sounds of his chewing echoed down the darkened corridor, magnifying as you approached, you knelt beside her and trembling, drew her to you, she prised herself gently free of your embrace to retrieve a piece of cinnamon that had fallen down a few stairs, and once more the shadows were filled with the fury of chewing, a smell of wet cinnamon.

The child halts in the doorway, there is a letter from Calcutta, she says, turning her head slightly towards you, I have put it by the fridge. The twisted stem of her narrow pale neck catches a few flecks of autumn light, and then unbends like a river of porcelain, will her beauty ever cease to fascinate me, you wonder. Holding the letter to the light you can tell by the regularity of its pages that it is one that your father has written in tranquillity and therefore must be read without haste, unlike the uneven scraps he will employ when writing perfunctorily, merely to maintain the ritual of weekly communication unnecessary now,

now that you can afford to telephone every few days, but he cannot accept that the letter must only be a luxury of spirit, although the rich but infrequent tomes you will send please him more than the regular stream of uninspired missives that you sent from college. You tuck it into a pocket of your nightgown, you will read it later, on the interminable underground ride back from Heathrow, perhaps.

Sparrow, seldom shaven, walks in, his chin glistening, you smile, that even he, your beloved iconoclast, should capitulate to the absurd ritual of grooming himself for air travel, he even wears a clean shirt, and the Portuguese maid has patched his sweater, perhaps between bouts of hungry lovemaking, you wonder. He holds a large teddy bear under his arm, of the most expressionless kind, surely, Sparrow, with your vast imagination, you could have done better than that, but my favourite toys, he explains, were the least interesting ones, why must we impose our oak-barrel-aged humour upon children? I remember being devoted to a plastic ark, no animals, mind you, a plastic ark that you would have consigned immediately to the garbage heap, one that I, myself, have considered the single worst impediment to the development of my spatial skills.

Eat your cereal, Sparrow, we will be late. Why 'we'? You, my dark beauty, will stay behind in this susurrating amnion of tasteless drapery. He crammed the bruised caverns of his mouth with the glutinous mass of sodden wheatflakes, I'd like an egg, he said, a boiled egg.

We don't have time for an egg, you said sharply, I'm going upstairs to change, hope you're all packed.

What have I to pack, he called after you, what indeed, the heavy journal of his travels, a hardback of Mann's *The Holy Sinner* that he picked up at a second-hand bookstall in Calcutta, which he somehow considered an omen, although of what, he did not know, and apart from what he wore, he did not intend to take any other clothes back, detritus of his travels. And he tells Sparrow, it's fucking cold in New York, I don't wear it anymore. Sparrow puts it on and surveys himself in the mirror, this house of false mirrors, it sits heavy on his bony frame, it does not flatter him but it will do, in New York he might throw it away, or sell it, it will do for now, thank you, he says, it's very comfortable. In the dark shadows behind him, in the mirror, Alexander's eyes glisten, they always glisten, is that why you had loved him, first, many years ago, you had woken Sparrow at dawn to tell him you had finally met the man of your dreams, is he rich, he had asked, foul with sleep, very rich, you had replied, but I love him not for his wealth, although he does have a house in London. London, city of your combined dreams, in the first spring of college, you and Sparrow had ventured across the Atlantic, on pennies saved from hard labour in vaulted dining halls, mincing rat gristle to feed the sons and daughters of the nation's leaders, while others crept southwards to roast their flesh under plastic palm shadow, you and he had taken your Spring Break in London, begging floor-space in a house of disgruntled students, one of whom was tenuously connected with Sparrow's chaotic past, and there had been nights, when you had been forced to wait, your limbs croaking, for a party to fizzle out before you could find sleep upon the alcohol-sodden carpet, anxious not to let precious hours of daylight creep past while you lay insensate upon the soil of Great Britain.

And here you are now, in the city of your dreams, in a houseful of mirrors that each scream your story, some with the grainy tenderness of crumbled silver, the speckled benevolence of ruined mercury, some with the cold clear passion of polished glass. Some fissure your gaze into a thousand threads, others curve your smile to cruel rainbowed horizons, the odalisque-sized mirror that guards your bath still steamily flatters, but the glazed portals of the broom closet remain relentless in the examination of your features, surgical, under harsh kitchen light. Somewhere, among these, hide the lineaments of your destiny, that you will always search. Yet every one of them, my love, down to the last looking glass, will tell your tale differently, as we will, my love, all of us who have loved you.

Your niece moves the teddy's arm in farewell, she is going to a birthday party this afternoon, she has told Sparrow, eyes dancing in her delicate face, as she poured him more cereal, this morning in the kitchen, it is the first party she has been invited to, since you brought her back with you to these unfamiliar shores, you tell Sparrow, outside the house, stopping to tuck the unopened letter from your father into your handbag, children are so insular, but she is a contented child, happy for long stretches in the company of her toys, endlessly she will chatter to her one-eyed bear, Hookahface Greedyguts, this new faceless creature will never displace *him*, you assure Sparrow, her attachment to Hookahface is stronger than any of her human relationships, you tell him, a little bitterly, her mother's death has passed her by like a shadow, she has not mourned her, strangely, perhaps she will later, perhaps the enormity has yet to settle upon her.

And even in you, although you have seen those hands limp in the steam of death, that part of your consciousness that has become used to her absence in these long years, that cruel part of your consciousness refuses to believe that she is not alive, her laughter smoothed by guava shade, her tears swallowed by hot concrete. Many afternoons, as a girl, you had tugged impatiently at her afternoon dreams, and she had remained encased in fast sleep, death had been closer then, than it is now when the concrete reality of her nonexistence rubs like grains of glass against the familiarity of her absence. A few words across the static of an international telephone like, every other month, that was all it had been, these past years, across the painful gulf that had been sealed that first summer, home from college, when you returned dry of that dense passion for which you had forsaken her, the love of your cousin Avishek, who languished in green England. Your sister had spent nine months dreaming of your doom, nine months, she had carried her pastry-faced husband's child, and wallowed in the sweetness of your impossible passion, your sister had stuffed herself with mango ice cream and prawn crackers, and let her mind swell with the tamarind tang of your incestuous love, the image of his thin young hands reaching in the moment of farewell for your hair, when she had averted her eyes, standing in the bedroom doorway, she had turned her tearstained face to the cloudy sky and prayed that he would kiss you, even though the arrogance of this gesture must have rushed through her like a river of ice, even so, your sister had turned her fearful eyes to the sky and then to the length of the empty corridor, praying that no one come to interrupt the grave farewell, she had stood sentry, while he crushed your hair under his aching palms, but he had not dared to touch his lips, even to your head, instead, he had walked out, his eyes, black mud, pressed your sister's hand, without words, he had walked out, down the long corridor, ignoring your father, who had suddenly appeared at the foot of the stairs. Avishek had rushed down the stairs, and left a trail of honeyed thunder that came to haunt your sister, two years later, as she lay, listening for the pulse of the child within her, two years later, as she folded each remote eagle-marked letter, sighed, and wondered what had come to pass between you, she unfolded your letter, for the tenth time, and searched helplessly among the indifferent passages for mention of your cousin, some cryptic reference to the fulfilment of your dreams. Her heart had leapt when you wrote that you were to visit England, the child had kicked rudely at her liver, irritated at the sudden gallop of blood, and yet, it had remained a mystery to her whether you and he had at all met, and then, finally, the summer had come, and the child had struggled, madly, painfully, into the world, you returned, and she knew at once, lifting the helpless infant to your happy eyes, your sister knew at once, that those wonderful troubled winds had died a deep death, that the inky spaces beyond your dark eyes were dry and chipped now, a new cold light bathed them, did you see him? your sister had asked desperately, lowering the baby onto the bed, I saw him, you answered, I saw him, but it was not the same.

Long summer days followed, with the child finally asleep, you whispered above her quiet sighs, fanning the fine locks that clung to her sleep-damp brow. Eagerly you had whispered together, but never of love, and as you submitted slowly to delicious afternoon torpor, you would study wistfully the gulf that separated your experiences, your sister, overcome with new motherhood, swilling the unimportant dregs of a dull marriage, and you, in your first summer, home from college, full of raw despair, for he, who had eased from your blood the dark steam of unbidden passion, he, your first lover, David, who had blotted with fickle kisses the shadow of your cousin's eyes, he, now lifeguarded upon sandy Midlantic shores, and drove, every evening, across to the dusk rose sunsets of Valley Forge, Pennsylvania, where his new love waited, in tigerskin shoes, to taste the sweat upon his deep shoulders that had once been your privilege alone. Of him you could not bring yourself to speak, to confide in your sister, of the cruel fangs of desire that had shredded you to pitiful fragments over the winter, lingered like lumps of glass into that strange spring, come like a wall of torn paper between you and your once beloved cousin, in the streets of London, driving you to despair over the emptiness of your forgotten passion. You could not bring yourself to tell her of the ugly pain of wandering through dark corridors in search of David's shallow laughter, waiting under frozen arches with a grumbling Sparrow to watch his shadow mingle with the form of another woman, the demeaning comfort of his false arms, sweeping rich memory into distance, lips that had laughingly coaxed your trembling mouth to open and taste of the confidential thrust of his tongue, stirring vicious New Jersey vowels onto your palate, white shoulders, thick from rowing, pressed you to the wall, of this you could not speak, any more than your sister could tell of the nightly exertions that had brought about the birth of the wondrous being that breathed happily under your gaze, you dared hardly dream of the furious fingers that had pushed open your thighs and had bound you in the thralldom of a first fulfilled lust, the first gentle explosions that buried blood into your brain, burning all memory, and thickening the need to beyond curiosity, you longed to despise the cry of possession that came so easily to his lips, when it was you that longed to possess, so utterly, that which you could never bind, that which was not worth binding, between the slow circled syllables of the languorous ceiling fan above your head (as a child you had always feared it would swoop down upon you and shred you to pieces) you strained, wordlessly, to cultivate a disgust for the formless lust that had been born within the first few weeks of your acquaintance, and died a protracted death over the length of spring. And so, when you returned that autumn, you returned to the torment of a more dignified desire, one without ends and beginnings, where it was you that sharpened the whip, and one chill evening, you left him, your first lover, David, you left him chewing the shards of a styrofoam cup that you had ripped apart with your pencil, cowering in the landscape of your renewed ambitions, he was too small for your dreams, and undimensioned he drifted from your life, took his delightful shoulders elsewhere in the fog.

David, your first lover, battered by the once unwelcome force of your desire, you left him, huddling among the inglorious memories of your painful tryst, for him you had betrayed your sweet cousin, lost to you now forever, your sweet cousin Avishek, you returned the following summer to the city that had shaped your tender doom, you returned brimming with grave resolve, stern desire that led you to walk for hours, sandal-footed, in the stark heat brine, you were determined to experience all that you had been shielded from in the marbled halls of your grandfather's home, where you spent the most crucial years of your life, for it was the inadequacy of your relationship with the city that you had begun to blame for the death of this love. One hot gecko-specked evening, behind the carved grill of the long veranda, you accused your father of having neglected your education, ensconced in his own dreams, he had allowed your aunts to take charge of your life. Your mother had died giving birth to you, her dust-rimmed portrait hung upon the wall, alongside others in your family who had died before their time, the only testament to her existence, apart from a few heavy silks in your wardrobe, rotting at the creases, she hung, haloed by withered flowers, next to an uncle who had fallen prey to typhoid, in the years before the War, three months before your father was born. You envision your grandmother, grieving her oldest son while another writhed within her, it is an image that returns often to you, and never so tenderly as it did, three years ago, at a Royal Society lecture on Epidemics when you heard the Wise Man tell how remarkable it is that we have grown to take for granted, in the developed world, that we will live out the full course of fourscore and more upon this earth, that all our children will thrive, how hard it has become for us to accept that we have not perfected the art of war against the invisible nasties that burrow so often into our blood, eat us from within, and you and Alexander had walked home silent, and after dinner he drifted in a dream to his study, not yet chequered by alternating tiles of cork and glass, that evening, he began to form his thesis on the immunological origins of aggression, an exercise that has held him in total captivity for many months now. Even on the afternoon of your sister's funeral, last year, on Christmas Day, you woke from guilty exhausted sleep to find him scribbling on yellowed grocer's foolscap, upon the pillow beside you, writing furiously of the effects of tropical pathogens, the fascinating tension between the richness of immunological strategy that came about from living in a veritable broth of disease, and the dulling of the memory of blood in the tropical heat. But you had been distracted from his excited discourse by the penetrating tones of low argument next door, where a young cousin insisted that she be allowed to accompany her friends to the Christmas disco at the Park Hotel, yes, even on a day like this, what did it matter, what difference did it make? the girl demanded, you heard the short sharp sound of a slap behind thick walls, muffled wails, you rose from the bed and moved quickly out into the corridor. Come back, he called, I have not finished. You had stonily commanded your aunt to let the girl have her way, and returned to find him admonishing the rabbit, Andropov, for having consumed a page of his work that had drifted unawares onto the cold stained marble under the heavy bed.

• • •

Sparrow, hyperactive as ever, rocks back and forth on his heels on the fermented cement of the Underground platform. Suicides are most frequent, you tell him, catching his eye upon the cold clean edge of the Third Rail, suicides are most frequent on the Northern Line. His eyes jerk back from the tracks, of course, he says slowly, the caverns of Mornington Crescent would drive anybody insane. In the distant spring when you had come, penniless, to this city, you had stayed with a group of students in Camden, but no, you protest, apparently, the suicide hotspot is on the other end of the line, where its spidery jaws cleave again after embracing the City, south of the river, I don't like cities, he says, where the river flows from west to east.

You lie, Sparrow, you love London as much as I, years ago, from the plane window, the two of you had wistfully watched the city fade, you had not considered then that one day you might live among the ruined streets, and even in this past month, basking in the niche of the Royal Borough that you call your home, there had been between you the familiar complicity of exploiting the hospitality of solvent acquaintances. During that fortnight in London, you and he had endured on several occasions, to break your otherwise steady diet of plastic-wrapped steak and kidney pies, the company of a fellow student whose family controlled much of the finance of a certain Far Eastern Island whose imminent umbilicotomy became the inevitable topic of conversation at the dinner table, last year, you ran into him at Heathrow, a Portuguese passport tucked between his sallow fingers. This past month, on many evenings, you had reminisced within the vulgar plushness of your own home, insulated by the distant click of the typewriter, two floors above, Alexander, long footfalls upon the stairs. He comes down for a glass of milk, pokes his head in briefly to announce quietly how much he longs for real orange juice, the sharp shadows of his regal features fall against the silk paintings of the elaborate gardens that had fed the lust of his Persian ancestors, his mother is English, a touch of elderflower in the dusky rose wine of his blood, an endearing insanity that the fruits of his ancestor's plunders permitted him to cultivate, amid the chiaroscuro of cork and mirror, in his study above, while you and Sparrow wallowed in nostalgic conundrums, feeling ever that you were guests of some absent-minded emperor, cavorting in the carriage houses of an oblivious king.

∘ ∘ ∘

Born in the cusp of the Lion and the Maiden, a confluence that Sparrow held in mysterious distrust, Alexander had found his way into your life at midnight, during a tedious shift at the departmental library, under harsh lights that numbed your mind to all exercise of thought, you would sit knitting behind the counter, dark colours so that the library ink might leach through without much damage, socks for your niece, a warm woollen cap for the gardener's new baby, a waistcoat for the rabbit, Andropov, getting on in years, but waiting to outlive you all. You waved the absurd garment under his liquid eyes, and they rose, enchanted, to your face, and leaning on the counter you had talked until the clock struck one, and then, you had wandered out into the warm night through the seminary woods. Hickory leaves had swept your hair as he lifted your face to the stars, not to kiss you, but to feel the nodes under the smooth curve of your neck, in the hollows where, if you were a fish, you fancy, you might have had gills, those nodes he explained were reservoirs of defence, filtered from the blood, he was one of the rare University Scholars who pursued unlikely interdisciplinary combinations, which, in his case, straddled physiology and politics. Years later these interests would merge again, as he walked back with you from that fateful Royal Society lecture, heavy with thought, he had sealed himself since, in his room of cork and glass, to uncover the intricate links between the wars fought within the blood and the wars fought without, the immunological origins of aggression, for this exercise he needed seclusion, he declared, more peace than was afforded by the wood-panelled warmth of your shared study, and so he had gathered his papers and books and moved into the old nursery, smothered the Andy Pandy wallpaper under helices of corkboard and mirror, evicted the wonderful old rocking horse, sole relic of his childhood, it has found a new home in a corner of your niece's room. The child has not dared confess that it gives her the oddest nightmares, of being ground slowly under its monstrous oscillations, even though it is too small even for her, a wisp of a girl, little Rima, light as a bird, bones that feel as though they might crumble under heavy arms, a thin cloud of glossy hair hangs over her pale brow, fine as milk thread, an elven light shines in her eyes. On summer evenings, tucking the child in bed, you read in curtain shadow from *The Lord of the Rings*, but Rima shifts restlessly among the smooth sheets, and you close the book with a sigh, and with a hand upon the silky head, you sing instead, as you do, every night, the same song:

> the clouds whisper sweet adieu, night bids farewell
> the ocean roars, the shore has come upon me, I am no more
> love proclaims, I will wake through aeons for you
> death sighs, I sail the vessel of your life

Your voice wavers upon this last line, you smooth her sleeping brow and wonder at how little she resents death, her own gray death, untasted, and her mother's death, a faint punctuation in the unnerving continuity of her existence, where the peace of her first English summer merges seamless with the stiff tropical silence that had muffled, in her grandfather's house, the pain-filled sobs of her dying mother. Your sister had been removed, in the last year of her life, to her childhood home, so that death, when he came, might find her among spotless sheets, spread his wings softer upon starched stretch of pillow than upon the rancid tumescence of her own marriage bed, that she might die in the comfort that she had enjoyed before your aunts had thrown her into an unfortunate marriage, to a man who did not have the means to keep her in the style that they had expected, who had never moved out of the dilapidated flat that they had thought was merely a temporary inconvenience on the road to far better circumstances. On the day of her death her husband was away on business, for two days he had not performed the tired ritual of coming in from the office to sit by her side, wash in the bathroom, eyeing with awe the multitude of medicinal phials on the chipped marble rack, then sit to eat his evening meal with his daughter, hurry to catch the last bus home, you have always found him pitiful, a cipher, that sad man. Sparrow had nodded his head in watery sympathy, the widower had made the painful journey to his father-in-law's home to meet him, Jon Sparrow, prestidigitating protagonist of so many summer tales, strange tales that had sent his wife into windy paroxysms of delighted laughter. He would smile sitting beside her, more out of overwhelming affection for the prostrated form upon the bed, the thick sea of hair undulated with laughter, now a bed of ash, he had reached to touch the writhing mass, smiling hesitantly, for he had not mastered the meter of your humour, never, that pathetic man, had he looked upon Sparrow with the same sorrowful curiosity with which he had scrutinised Avishek, two years ago, when your cousin came with his new wife to pay his respects to your family. He had gazed then upon Avishek with strange choked compassion, as if the shadows of your legendary doom still hung vine-veined about him, this was the man then, from whom those thick letters had arrived on Wednesday mornings at his address, letters that his wife wrapped carefully in the folds of her sari, before any other eyes might fall upon them. Once he had asked for the stamps and been met with stern silent reproof, had she not told him, his lovely wife, had she not told him, before a night of love, under moonlit mosquito nets, had she not told him, her voice, thick with tears, of the desperate passion of the grim youth, their cousin Avishek, incarcerated in moated boarding school in distant England, for you, her beloved sister, the ponderous letters that pressed the weight of your desire into the hollows of her palm could never be mutilated by his philatelic fancies. So this was the man, no longer the pale boy whose bulging missives his wife would transport under her blouse, for in that large house, your father's home, many were apt to rifle her handbag. This was the man then; he had lifted his beaten eyes to the gaunt face in pathetic wonder, and memories had come swiftly, gently to you, of waking, long ago, from an afternoon dream of death and wet marigolds, your sister, hovering above you in the ambrosial half-light, tucking under your cheek a heavy letter, a happy tear, vestige of dream, would drop silently upon the envelope, you might have waited long, until the shadows creased at the edge of the door, the passing of the delightful twilight, your cheek upon his letter and your fingers tracing circles upon your sister's palm, those hands that you have seen outstretched in mystified welcome to death. Her husband was away on business on the day she died, in cruel confirmation of his peripheral role in her life and in her death, you opened the door to him in the morning, he stood shaking uncontrollably, his eyes blanched as they met your scornful, pitying gaze, a sad, sad man, Sparrow had said, shaking his head, remembering how he had shuffled out of his sandals outside the swinging doors, and shuffled across the marble floors, bare calloused toes curled shamefully inwards. Your father reluctantly interrupted his vivisection of post-Structuralism to introduce him, Sparrow had risen from his chair to shake a feeble left hand, the right clutched a wrapped parcel, a present for his daughter that Sparrow had faithfully transported across the seas. Confused, much too late, the man had transferred the parcel to his left hand, much too late, for Sparrow had fallen back once more against the old leather, and the conversation had resumed, your father ignored his son-in-law with familiar ease, the man perched stiffly upon the divan, fingering his ragged parcel, his hare eyes darting back and forth from Sparrow's blistered lips to his father-in-law's wagging pipe, and then resting in disgust upon the tranquil rabbit, Andropov, munching his way through the moth-eaten Persian rug. When your father was called away to answer the telephone, Sparrow had attempted to converse with the forlorn man, a sad man, Sparrow had said of him, he asked me for Siamese stamps.

Sparrow, strangely sorrowful, picks at the hem of the ragged upholstery, sucking in the Underground air through harp-strung teeth, at Baron's Court, the train is disgorged into the wine light, a lovely autumn morning, must he leave then, must he leave the sad shadows of green, the wilted garden sheds in the frequent backyards that steer their narrow and inevitable course towards the train tracks. How he would love to sink his tired head upon the ugly ribbed blue, drown in the murmurs of the morning tabloids, the quiet rustle of diseased paper, and yet the stations streak away, he is rushing inexorably towards Heathrow airport, and beside him, wonderfully awake, you fidget with an unhealthy energy, excruciatingly unaware of his doom.

For him, it has been a long, long journey and yet at its end, there is no home, it has been a long, weary journey, and yet he is not to rest his head upon childhood down, and you, to whom he has imparted the ease of solitude, while his own solitude has come to gravel beneath his tongue, you rest lightly upon the edge of the seat, the smile that churns upon your lips drags from within him memories of untold pain. It is the same smile that his mother wore on the train to his grandparents' where he was to be left, to grow into a man, in a yardful of waxed dandelions, where, as his myopic ancestors rocked upon the porch, he would adroitly masturbate, his Latin book open in front of him, writhing upon the weeds to the rhythm of his grandmother's incessant and oblivious chatter. Tears would gather in his eyes rather than the dim clouds of laughter that would fleck them later when, while making love, his pleasure would become so disjoint from that of his partner that he might well be, once more, groaning among dandelions, slapping his flushed face against imaginary insects to mask his final gasps, tears had gathered then in the back of his parched throat, rather than the honeycombs of laughter that piled within him later, when during the act of love, his pleasure would suddenly divorce itself from the presence of another's flesh, only in climax would he reach for an image, not always of the face before him, in fact, almost never.

After a point even an image was not enough, and he invoked concepts, like Post-Impressionism or Neo-Plasticism, and favourite of favourites, the Lyapunov function, he seized upon an idea, a theory, a searing flame of thought, to match the jolt of bloodlessness between his ears, he told you and you laughed, perhaps you should cultivate blankness, you advised, that perfect blankness essential to any man's happiness.

He presses a cold cheek to the greasy glass, and lifts his eyes to the section of Underground map caught between two unamusing advertisements, both pathetic puns, we take it personally, claims a courier company, and wings of pastry gild the brand name Upper Crust, perhaps a creation of your cousin, he wonders, the mysterious Avishek, erstwhile partner in a rapturous and incorporeal incest, now professional baker, he focuses in onto the map. Oh, to be caught eternally within the yellow vein of the Circle Line, to describe forever, within the shuddering cage, the hapless ellipse that embraced the innards of this despised city, the inevitable locus from which the astronomer Keppler had sought refuge in the oval, the banality of the ellipse had repelled him, and the oval offered itself, a suitable aberration, a degeneration of the ellipse that eluded its triviality, and yet the rabbit, Andropov, had shown no regard for its asymmetric beauty – for when Sparrow had mentioned that Nabokov had once observed that rabbits were among the most oval of animals, the creature had snorted, and then proceeded to defy all geometry by reaching down to lick his tail.

You smile as his mother had smiled on the train to his grandparents, where he was to be left, ten years old, to the mercy of their Midwestern sensibilities. His mother had smiled, a smile of love, and yet, on her lips danced a vast excitement at the thought of a life unencumbered by his presence, and in your smile today, so many years later, there is an echo of that small sense of relief at his departure, mild comfort at the thought of your life slipping back into its sheath, although how he might have altered your unstructured existence, he did not know, there was a time when you had vehemently deplored his filthy habits and often had been distinctly glad to be rid of him for that reason alone, there was a time when he would burn holes in the hallway carpet outside your room with his banished cigarette, reading poetry to you through the open door, there was a time, in the dead of winter, when you had cruelly thrown open his windows to air out his room, he had taken revenge by signing his name in urine upon the thick snow outside, and while you had cringed at this insufferable violation of the seamless white, it had been a source of unending mirth, for even then you would suspend all your inhibitions for the sake of the absurd.

In your smile, there is a small flutter of that same ghastly eagerness to be rid of him that he felt upon his mother's lips as she kissed him goodbye. All the women with whom he had shared this memory (and you were not among them, for it was, of nature, an adjunct to the act of love, it had its niche in the orifice of confession that separated climax and arousal, resplendent with cigarette smoke) invariably attempted to convince him that he had misread the situation – childhood resentment surely had interfered with his interpretation of the simple kisses, a mother's sad kisses as she abandons her child, in spite of herself, for after all the death of his father in Vietnam must have gouged deep into the chalky substrate of his child mind – and he would lean over to stopper the clichés with his serpentine tongue, drive deep into the flesh as if to arrest the stream of sugary reassurance that boiled forth from within, remembering with fond grimace the wisdom of a hockey player, whom he had overheard, while showering in the gym, explaining to his friend how a woman must on no account be allowed to speak during or between intercourse. For good measure he would begin to slide his fingers between the cheeks of his partner's backside, soon, his pleasure would rise beyond her, but until then, he must make sure that no element of her individuality escaped her flesh.

Your lips brush his chin, so seldom unbristled, in lingering whispers of content that your life will be as it was before he came, that you might settle down in the evenings with your well-worn typewriter, and continue to write the story of his life. He had received the news that you were writing his biography with indifference, even distaste, but, last night, overcome with the tenderness of farewell he had asked to read it, and you spent a good part of the evening in Alexander's study, painstakingly xeroxing the unruly manuscript, page by page, and then, at your insistence, his own heavy travel journal, by curious coincidence, complete but for the last page. In the middle of the night, the child cried, in the room across, you rushed to her succour, and never emerged, you must have fallen asleep, next to the girl, and he was left alone, to photocopy his entire journal in the lurid cage of cork and mirror, and wonder who would have heard the girl's nightmare shrieks if you and he had been buried deep in laughter and reminiscence, downstairs in the garish parlour, as had been your usual manner of spending the evening, punctuated by forays to the cellar for wine. As he watched the light gnash beneath the last page of his journal, vomiting collated copy,

Alexander returned, he had been with his mother to the opera, the music had served, apparently, to orchestrate his musings on the ramifications of cell-mediated immunity. He was still dressed in his opera clothes, for he had raced up to his study to jot down his thoughts before their logic fractured, for indeed, whereas, before, his ideas had condensed and consolidated within him, now, at best, if left overnight, they might congeal. If he was lucky, then he would have the day to unglue them over, if he was lucky, most often, they would melt into the fabric of his dreams, when he awoke, it was the dream that would lie clear before him, in excruciating detail, wonderful dreams that he could not savour for fear they would engulf the last traces of the urgent insights that had come to him in the last few seconds before dipping into sleep, wonderful dreams, for instance, last night, he had dreamt of being sentenced to eternity within *Last Year at Marienbad* and had only managed to escape when the main character, the one who kept losing the match game, decided to take a trip to India, and Alexander was allowed to accompany him, out of the film. In dreams such as these were entangled, and often lost forever, his precarious thoughts, and Sparrow, horribly jealous, for he did not dream at all, anymore, had asked, how he came, in the first place, to be searching in immunology for the roots of our deepest desires, and holding his opera scarf about his neck like an untied noose, Alexander began to speak, a voice that trickled like thick honey in the mirror-studded darkness, his preoccupation with life processes, he claimed, began with an awareness of the recurrent confluence of clinical and poetic metaphor. Consider the lily, he said, and the lily-livered, consider the ether that prostrates the evening upon a patient's table … Later, that night, he found himself, armed with a medical dictionary, his fingers poised upon typewriter keys, ready to search the sanguinous roots of aggression, he had become, for this night, at least, his last night in your home, he had become scribe to his host, mesmerised by the curious marriage of politics and immunology. Whether the tract was to secure a seminal position in the history of science he did not know, but there was little doubt in his mind that it would be a great work of art, which, as with his dreams, Alexander would never be able to bring himself to enjoy, for like his dreams, the beauty of his work would distract from its logic, and drown, like his dreams, the fine meshes of scientific principle.

Sparrow had heard the hallway clock strike three as he sat down to type the manuscript, but the turgidity of Alexander's prose rubbed heavy on his fingers, he surrendered to the urge to inscribe these mysterious visions in a more familiar idiom, and so he had broken off to scribble upon the last page of his journal the detail of the day's events, the last day in his travels, the last infinite arc of the inexorable circle, the journal that he began, last year, on a bumpy flight to San Francisco, his first stop on his long limping tour. His journal would have run out of pages long ago, but for the stagnation of his teaching duties in Thailand, those six heavy months that had robbed him of dream, he is at his journey's end, journal's end, he wrote in pencil, and on his last question mark, for he had to end upon a question mark, he broke its lead. The last page, upon which he lamented the painful contradictions of xeroxing and distributing an exercise as private as a journal, and ruminated upon how in his journal entries, he had always been slave to the muse of posterior scrutiny: after all, it is the future self that I most seek to please – he wrote – for a long time now, I have pared and pruned, and retained only what I might like to read, years from now. And then he wrote of the vision of Alexander, in a smaller, finer hand, and still, was forced to abbreviate his comments, for lack of space, the final question, the graphite cracks, it is the end of his journey, you have disappeared already, behind glass doors, with one last look of fond regret, too fond, regret that you will savour through the day, nurse into the night, hoping perhaps it will acquire the shades of sweet inspiration, a few more pages to your endless novel, to arrive at his New York address (for he will have one, yes, once again, next week perhaps, for now, he will stay with Vladimir), together with the Weetabix and the Branston pickle. He feels the weight of your unruly creation as he lifts the sheaf of papers out for inspection, will he ever read it, he wonders as he watches you wander out into the crisp autumn morning. A red-haired youth prods his underarms, routine security, he explains, sucking in his lips, I haven't even checked in yet, Sparrow protests, I may, yet, decide not to take this flight.

That's up to you, sir, I've got to do my job.

If he were not to take this flight, if he were to violate the finality of his journal, the portentous crack of last night's lead pencil, if he were to change his mind, and not leave at all, not until tomorrow, what would it matter to the world, who would notice, if he were to inflict upon his much abused American Express card the cost of a night's hotel, which is about all it could bear. There was no question, of course, of returning to your house, such bending back upon itself his fate would never stand for, besides he is tired, all he wants is to be alone, alone among the scurvied masses, alone, to gather his thoughts, before jumping the small arc to full circle, alone, upon that uninspired bridge across the Thames, where yesterday, at noon, a man in a bowler hat had demanded of him, are you from Yorkshire?

Schleswig-Holstein, actually, he had replied, spitting into the Stygian depths.

I've just written a book on Michelangelo, the man told him sadly.

I'm terribly sorry, said Sparrow, genuinely moved.

They had stood, side by side, until the silence that held them together was scattered by the sky, if he were to turn now, snatch his bags from the grubby claws that close over them to pass into X-ray machine, and run, he might find himself again upon the bridge with his friend of yesterday, for Sparrow has a feeling that he is a man of habit, that he has frequented that very spot since the days of brave Churchill, perhaps, perhaps. His bags slither into the fatuous aperture, on the faltering screen, he catches a glimpse of their innocuous entrails, he recovers them, and walks out, past the probing post-pubescent red-head, towards the city, in search of silence.

Schleswig-Holstein, another part of the world whose existence has always seemed to him to have been evoked merely to lend topological consistency to the earth, geographical counterpart of the neutrino, why had it sprung to his mind, perhaps in anticipation of sumptuous non sequitur, and the sublime silence that came after, only to be scattered by sudden sardine clouds in the newborn afternoon. Silence, sorely lacked, in these past few weeks, sorely missed, come to think of it, in the entire span of your relationship, you have never let him rest, whenever he read, you would pout, kick against the twin chests you had inherited from a banished room-mate, had he not already read all that was worth reading, you would demand, the rest of life was to be lived, you insisted, in the stench of laughter, you would grab at his book, command him to make you laugh, and not with the vile whiffs from the canister that bulged low in his coat pocket, nor the magic squares of paper he kept folded within Flaubert's Sottisièr, he must tickle your brains with his own. You gave him no peace, you would not let him sleep, creeping into his bed in the smallest of hours to cry over the untold cruelty of that wretched athlete who had claim to your limbs, for him you had dragged Sparrow, sleep-sunk, into the moth-eaten New Jersey cold, to sharpen your sorrow under the sordid light of one pale window where he lay, your beloved David in the arms of another. And it had not even inspired poetry, as he had half hoped, climbing out of nicotine-sodden warmth to pander to this painful whim, he had half hoped that your wild eyes, your anachronistic tropical love would weave the essence of a new poem into his barren veins, a letter-poem that he hoped to pry from his dream depths, yours, in abstraction, instead hours later, numb with cold he had fallen into leaden sleep, exhausted by your sorrow. All that winter you had deprived him of silence, of poetry, and all this for a woman whose lovely eyes inspired not a hint of desire.

Sparrow, chalk-veined, watches you, for you are still visible, from behind thick glass, faltering at the entrance to the Underground. He watches you realising he will not be able to rush to you now, as he might have if he were, or ever had been, your lover, to rush to you and hold you from behind, and tell you he cannot bring himself to leave, not today, not yet. The tunnel engulfs you, he longs suddenly to call you back and scream, as he had done, many years ago, across midnight fields, blue is the colour of death, and you had speared this hallucinogenic aphorism with moonbright scorn, pitched it soundly into the luminous snow, at the foot of the snow woman the two of you had built earlier that evening, until bored by the exultation of her firm snow breasts, he had left you, still intent on procuring twigs with which to fashion the comely maiden's hair, he had left you to seek other crystalline pleasures. He had scoured the campus for the generous Teddy Ginsberg, for that winter he was particularly penniless, that winter, when he saw, in your beautiful and undesired eyes, the end of adolescence, as today, in your morning caresses he had uncovered the violent death pangs of youth, a small voice had whispered against the hard baked bone of his skull, this is the last day of your youth, Jon Sparrow, make the best of it, let it not end as did your sorry adolescence, when death, deprived suddenly of its blueness, became unbearably real.

Teddy Ginsberg, infamous supplicant, had attempted to soothe his loss of blue with a mammoth mushroom omelette, as a result he spent a tortured night in the infirmary, in the morning, you came to see him, with you the penitent athlete, David, your lover. Reaching to smooth his brow, you uncovered, under his vomit-streaked hair, an unhealthy rash, which the nurse promptly declared to be chicken pox. Your fish-brained lover backed away nervously, he had never yet succumbed to the avian scourge, he appealed, scared still to leave lest you should find it cowardly, he who had driven the knife so deep now that its edges had risen to meet his own teeth, he who had toyed with your affections for an entire miserable year, now, since summer, your slave, you told him to leave, which he did quietly. For three weeks you would use Sparrow's ignominious condition as a refuge from the athlete's rancid devotion, his confinement gave you seclusion. In the overheated sanctuary, between incessant television game-shows, you would smooth calamine over his limbs, and when you were gone, within the heavy darkness, he would see death, shorn of blue, but distant, even forlorn.

Teddy came to see him, pockets bulging with hash, and ecstasised for an hour and a half over some obscure East European poet he had just discovered, Sparrow, distrustful of any vehemence of opinion, had found his gush unbearable, finally he told him to shut up, told him that his tendency to either strongly like or dislike any work of art suggested to him a miserable sluggishness towards other realities, for you, he said, itching his burning testicles, for you something is great only when it strikes a chord within you – yes, when it resonates with your own limited sensibilities – why, then it is sublime, simply fucking marvellous, and otherwise, it's a piece of shit, totally – you see, my dear Theodore, mine is the cult of ambivalence, which is only how you can be when exploring realities that are not your own. He fell back exhausted, your calamine smeared fingers fell cool upon his forehead. Teddy smiled good-naturedly, you're even more of a bastard when you're sick, he said, picking up his hat, but his voice trembled, the passion punctured. Feel better, he said, and climbed out through the window. Sparrow closed his eyes, there, he thought, you have had your revenge, you have avenged your loss of blue upon an innocent, poor Teddy Ginsberg, whatever happened to him, you had asked this morning, he did not know, the last time he had seen him, he was on his way to Peru, armed with a sheaf of xeroxes from a Machigenga-to-English dictionary – did you know, he had asked Sparrow excitedly, was he aware that the very same string of syllables could mean sleep, sing, expectorate, or crucify?

Were there differences in inflexion, Sparrow had asked dryly. No, not that he knew of, he said, perplexed by the question. Was he lost then, for ever, in the Madre de Dios, gnawed by leishmania, foul with fever, or carved up by the Shining Path, or had the project been indefinitely shelved, as were all his other plans. Did Teddy Ginsberg still languish on the Upper East Side, spilling sad tears for the frostbitten toes of his favourite drag queen, pasting excerpts from the *National Enquirer* over his parents' Picassos, Mother Sells Ugly Twins to Circus, Woman Turns into Washing Machine, and crème de la crème, the caption that had saved him, after three weeks in the infirmary, from certain suicide, Drunken Mortician Mistakenly Cremates Sleeping Janitor, photographs of the mortician, rather anxious, and the unsuspecting janitor (forty winks that turned into a lifetime!) had drawn from within his poxy lungs a dry hacking laughter, and you had been relieved, oh Sparrow, don't go all glum on me now, you had pleaded, now that I'm back to my senses, it would seem that while he battled the unseemly virus within the toothpaste walls, it seemed that you had finally taken command of your life, severed all links with the miserable athlete, the ridiculous David, life now stretched limitless before you, how could he be so cruel as to besmirch it with his gloom?

Sparrow, drawing his sheepskin collar high against his chin, decides he will not leave, not today, not yet, he will take the bus into the city, lest he should bump into you in its serpentine bowels, you have an uncanny sense of his presence, you may smell him out as you did, on campus, follow his spoor into the dungeons of the rubber-baron-bequeathed library, the forgotten dungeons where volumes, out of print since early last century, crumbled to the touch, there you would find him, among the quiet feastings of silverfish, chewing a pencil, poemless. For many years now he has been a poet without poems, those sweaty couplets that had drawn you to him in the first place, between the plastic rattle of the Fooseball board, that miniature soccer game where the skewered players are manipulated by side handles. Between the shrieks and the laughter, between the thunder and the defeat, he had muttered his poems, standing back, behind you, against the wall, and you had abandoned your position to other eager hands, and edged your way past the pinball machines, to where he stood, fat felt over his eyes, belching syllables of stewed shark, the foul portion you had eased onto his plate a few hours ago, across the counter, you had noticed him then, for the first time, six weeks into the semester, you had noticed between his soiled fingers the Thomas Mann that he stuffed between his teeth as the place was returned, slopping shark stew, your eyes had followed the pale back, the T-shirt that hung from the bony shoulders like a thin sheet of dough, and impatient fingers had drummed on empty plates. Broccoli, I asked for broccoli, not peas, you know, he said. I wouldn't be surprised, the cook told you, if, when they see you on the serving line, the boys and girls don't just give up and head for Burger King. How did they expect you to do your job well, you who had never so much as poured a glass of water for yourself in your life, no that was not strictly true, in the five years you lived alone with your father in Birmingham, you had, on occasion, dried the odd fork. You are such a princess, Sparrow would tell you, such a bloody princess, he would tell you, as you drew on your gloves on an egg-scorching day in New York to avoid contaminating your shapely hands with subway sweat, how did you survive in the suppurating tropics?

# II

# *Bread and Butterflies*

At Hounslow Central, you remember your father's letter, and hurriedly pry open the partitions of leather to recover and read it before the Piccadilly Line dives underground, and the lavish foolscap is stained sordid lemon. The letter is brief, not at all what you had expected, it is a short wooden note to the effect that your family home is finally to be sold to Marwari developers, the very same who had, three years ago, purchased the back lawn and erected a thirteen-storey monstrosity. Anger and grief are frozen in the clipped sentences, his prose, shorn of metaphor, is bitter slate to your tongue, although the condensation of nostalgia that the news incites is not unwelcome, for since the death of your sister, the past has gradually encased itself in the delicate violence of glass, a forbidding lacquer has smeared the memories of rich summer dark, your sister sleeping beside you, the quiet tide of her breath has ebbed, in these past few months, into some unchartable region of your memory, the waves of summer moonlight that once brought such sweet insomnia, shrink back from the probing tendrils of your grief, the mind floods instead with the healthy roar of the vacuum cleaner, the over-zealous Portuguese maid, Alexander shifts and curses, having just drifted into the nether reaches of REM, you might rise to chastise her, or close your eyes and wait for the din to fade to resume your half-hearted courtship of nostalgia.

So the family mansion is finally to be sold, the gilded halls that undernourished your adolescent passions are about to fall, as one by one you had watched your neighbours' houses collapse, to be ground under rusty caterpillars, and from each devastation a stodgy phoenix would rise, columns of pigeon cage, the solemn confetti of strangled television aerials cowering over your darkened patio, where once the only ghost was the ridiculous shadow of a life-size mannequin of a dispossessed zamindar turned tabloid tycoon, on which his progeny lavished more solicitude than he had commanded in life. Seated on his favourite rocking chair, with his favourite woollen muffler about his moth-eaten neck, he would survey the street with bright gouache eyes, ignoring blithely the insects that swarmed to the untouched sweetmeats and mug of tea at his side. He had been fashioned in Kumartuli by the same craftsmen who supplied the household with their goddesses of Wealth and Learning, for they had maintained their long-standing rural tradition of worshipping Laxmi and Saraswati, whereas in your family, only the latter found a following, the goddess of learning, Saraswati, swanborne, to be worshipped in the colour of spring, a young yellow, edged with blood red, crisp new cotton, catching, in its stiff folds, the last sweet chill of dying winter. All morning, you would sing, you and your cousins, plead with the divine to descend into light, hide not in mysterious mind shadow, beloved being, seduced by the magic of the subconscious, and the children next door would crowd upon the veranda to hear your choruses, the circle of voices that rose from your courtyard. The mannequin, freshly groomed, a Kashmiri shawl upon his shoulders, would rock in approval, cossetted by his curious grandchildren, for there had been no music in their house for many years now, not since the loss of their fortune with the Partition of Bengal, when the music room had been converted into a printing press for smutty tabloids. Even that did not do so well at first, and the portly patriarch began to shed his paunch, in desperation, he began to take up all manner of jobs – his opportunities, from lack of education, were limited, he was once seen, much to the delight of your father and his brothers, to be conducting traffic at Chowringhee. But then his fortunes reversed themselves, the silver screen and its idols came to his rescue, the press graduated from the abandoned music room to gaudy offices on Central Avenue, but the music room itself was never rescued from its desuetude, the wailing musicians and the heavy bells of dancers were no more to be heard. No, the last music that graced their opulent halls came from the lungs of a recalcitrant cuckoo, whom they adopted and tortured to death in the summer of '48, squeezing its belly to persuade the hapless bird to call beyond springtime. They had installed a microphone system, ancestor of the intercom, with which the family were called to meals, much to the annoyance of the neighbours, and eager to demonstrate the talents of their mute pet, they would, every afternoon, position it in front of the microphone and convince it, by no gentle means, to reproduce the muffled quadrisyllabic, one morning, your father found it, dead, in your courtyard, flung over the garden wall, its striped belly, so oft palpated by rough hands, overrun with small red ants.

They were the first to sell their house and mango grove to the developers, one of their own kin, more kine than kith, your father had exclaimed, for your neighbours had been cheated, taken roundly to the cleaners and back by one of their own sharp relatives, and meanwhile, as the public turned increasingly for their blood surrogates to Bombay, their tabloid press had started losing money, and the old mannequin had ended up in a dusty corner of a poky Shyambazaar flat, where you imagine he raises more wrath than respect, occupying precious space, and yet impossible to discard, with only his toothless wife to soothe the chipped elbows, brush the flakes of plaster off his rotting pate.

The train slides into the musty gullet, and the letter in your hands is splattered with unholy fluorescence, you detect a scrap of writing overleaf and fold it over, to see that your father has written: I enjoyed immensely the tape of your conversation with John Sparrow, except every now and then, I was overtaken by an irresistible and fruitless urge to intervene. You can see him reclining in his old leather chair on the veranda, fiddling with the earphones of the Walkman you gave him three years ago, tongues of soot begin to climb the slim neck of the kerosene lamp at his side, the neighbourhood is in darkness, an interminable power cut. It was on such a night, in your second summer home from college, that you had stood against one of the capricious Corinthian columns and accused him of having taken no real interest in your lives, neither yours nor your sister's, whom he had seen pushed into a sterile marriage, without protest. But I never seek to impose, he had said quietly from within the dark, summer insects wreaked havoc with your bare arms, but surely it was your duty to protect, where does one end and the other begin? You had interpreted his reluctance to mould the mind as indifference, and he had answered that he did not know, perhaps it was a disregard for your fate that underlay his philosophy, who was he to say, the still air was rent by a child's scream, and your year-old niece stumbled forth on unsteady feet, pursued by the jealous rabbit, Andropov, who, anticipating censure, had stopped dead in his tracks.

That summer, armed with a black-and-orange umbrella, molten tar bubbling at your heels, you went forth into the city that you had never really come to know, that you had left two years ago, convinced that it was for the love of your cousin, Avishek, you were ready to abandon these beloved shores, ready to throw up your life in this city, a life that you had painstakingly built from rude beginnings, from when you had returned at the tender age of twelve to its difficult embrace, the stone and the blood moss that you had let clasp you, you would rip once more from your breast, for him, only him. That summer, your love ruined, you stood face to face with the city, and conceded that there had been no blood and no moss, and the fetid winds that had once fuelled your desire were no more than perfunctory cosmetic, why else would the love that had swelled in the humid tropical afternoon shrivel so suddenly in more temperate climes? You stood before the city that had once celebrated your passion in sudden strokes of foxthorn and pale purple madder between cracked stone and betelspit, circled warm wet winds upon your neck where his lips might have strayed if he had dared, the city that had wept with you after he had gone, on winter evenings, the stars muffled with heavy dung smoke, and in the raw cold of a winter dawn, when sleepless, you had tiptoed to the bathroom, a jagged cold would rise from the rough marble floors, what delicious suffering, like the little mermaid, the pores of your feet would revel in the sublime agony, and throwing open the bathroom window, you would watch the sun rise, blue and hard, from the pondside slums, the wails of frozen children would bring a rush of tender tears, you would return to your bed, and reach under your pillow for his letter, bury your face under the cold quilt and surrender once more to the splendid discord of your impossible passion.

Two years later, your passion spent, you ventured forth once more into the winds that had not sustained your desire, declaring that your acquaintance with the city had been hopelessly inadequate, the monsoon rain had churned your blood only in the vast marbled halls of your home, when you should have been knee deep in bilge, struggling with a recalcitrant umbrella, only then would the sad poetry of your love have soaked deep to your marrow, only then, if you had glutted your desire upon the rancid fumes of smoked fish and old diesel, rather than the anonymous perfume of disaster that rose and mingled with the green blood of marigolds upon the veranda where you sat late into the evening, alone with your dreams. Two years later, you scoured the city for those sombre shadows that might have secured your passion, the fields of death where you might have wandered instead of the antiseptic green of the Tollygunj Club the insulated verdure of your own lawn. In a clay forest of idols your quest came to an untimely end, the pujas were to come early that year, and the potters' quarters in the North hummed with activity. Within a clay jungle of broken limbs, your camera shutter jammed, and its fierce final rasp ran like a shiver of cracked glass into the pit of your stomach, you hurried outside and solemnly you threw up your lunch into a nearby drain, felt a hand upon your back, a distant cousin, you had seen her last, waiting nervously in the hallway, clutching a sheaf of soiled medical bills that she needed help to pay, you felt her hand upon your back, your hair tumbled out of its unstable knot and fell over her fingers, she wiped your sweaty forehead with a corner of her sari, I thought you were in America, she said.

I'm home for the summer, you said, and fainted into her arms. When you came to, you were between clean sheets, worried faces around you, the kindly family doctor thumping your chest, and what troubled you more than your fever was the sense of alienation that your disease made complete, your illness, which would last for weeks, became an immediate metaphor for your isolation from the city that you had longed to love. Mocked by its pathogens, you languished in your sterile prison, with only the rabbit, Andropov, for comfort, and long letters from Sparrow, he was to travel the length of France with Vladimir, he proclaimed, without spending a red cent – the gas would go on Vladimir's father's credit card, they would sleep in the car, and food would have to be procured rather than purchased, strictly no cash transactions to be made, these were the rules of the game. Vladimir Ivanovich, the wealthy Slav who had befriended the scabby Sparrow, in the difficult weeks that followed the remission of his chickenpox, Sparrow had followed him to Paris, where your friend would spend an uncertain and perilous summer, struggling to maintain his sanity upon bacon rinds and stolen fruit. Vladimir, the heavy tide of whose desire you had held at bay all spring, lest it break too violently upon your new freedom, for finally unencumbered by David's narrow presence and his confused, mistimed devotion, you sought to resurrect that solemn communion with yourself that had always been the source of your strength, you wished to regain that divine containment that had sweetened the acrimony of the most unrequited of your passions. Vladimir, the fruitful curve of his lips would prey upon your dreams for a time to come, but this you did not know then, and when the swollen stealth of his unformed kisses began to fill your fevertorn reveries, you dismissed them as the agonies of an unanchored soul, a rootless being, spurned by the very city of her birth.

And although Sparrow held the breadth of his desire in deep scorn, your friendship would weather Vladimir, as it had survived David, and the growing multitude of peripheral lusts on his part. It was only under Alexander's most equanimous presence that the bonds slackened, a strange unease crept into your relationship, I'm sure you will like him, you had told Sparrow, and he had snorted and said: someone born in the cusp of the Lion and the Maiden? But that was not all, certainly that was not all, what it was you would not know, but he avoided Alexander, all spring, and so came to see less and less of you, the trip that you were to take together to Calcutta that summer was less and less spoken of, became a carcass of a fevered undergraduate project, to be fondly remembered, and never accomplished. You saw him once before you left for the summer, walking out of the Visual Arts Building, he was taking a course in candlemaking, he told you, he would be spending the summer in Greenwich Village, with a woman he had met at one of Vladimir's mother's parties. Helga Schnabel, he said. She had a small curiosity shop of sorts, where they sold fruit-shaped candles, and the like, though he had other ideas, if Helga would allow him to experiment, he would be making candles all summer, rolling and dividing wax, punching moulds, and twisting cottonwick. He, who was to have come with you to your festering city, would endure instead the tragedy of a Manhattan summer. Six years later he would make the journey, in your absence he would visit and violate your home. Violate? he had asked, reading from your diary, gladly offered, how do you mean, violate? Did you not wrestle with a tropical lust, between the sheets of my very own bed, you demanded. Never, he answered, what tropical lust, the tropics left me cold, there was only a dusty sadness in all I saw, the faded skies and the fickle festival lights, the tawdry darkness, and the tired faces of men, what tropical lust? You smiled, a little disappointed, a little hurt, but determined to cling on to your notions, and this sharp obstinacy raked within him a faint irritation, I enjoyed your city, he told you, but only because it clings like a cadaver to that wise and filthy river, hoping forever to reach the sea, which it will never do, it is like a stranded cadaver, on the banks of that strange, powerless river which, even a hundred years ago, was not fit to make ice of, did you know how the residents rejoiced when in 1834, the first shipment of Boston ice was brought to Strand Road, the Harmonic Tavern fair burst its beams in celebration, no more Scotch on Hoogly slush. City of Joy, indeed! It is the City of Pain, said Sparrow, and much the better it is for it.

You remembered how in the first hours of your acquaintance

he had drawn you a map of Calcutta, faltering only briefly in the southeastern quadrant, digging his pen thoughtfully into his representation of the Lower Circular Road. So where do you live then, he had asked, I hope it is not to the south of here, although I am assured it is still very fashionable. You are lucky, you had told him, rather taken aback by the depth of detail, you are lucky that my home is within the confines of the Circular Road, which, by the way, was once a war trench against the Portuguese.

The Marathas, he had corrected you, without scorn, it was called the Maratha ditch, don't you remember.

But at least he has never been there, you had consoled yourself, I may muddle my history, but it is I who knows the scent of bubbled tar, the death rattle of the dry guava, the texture of the autumn sun, as it frees the wind of the anguish of summer, none of this he has known, and his erudition hangs almost pitiful without experience, the taciturn Sparrow, entangled in the city maps of exotic, impossible dreamlands, as your father too had once pored over the edges of Mediterranean coastlines, while his family's fortunes sank, and the more privileged cousins took their last trips abroad, the laundry returned from its final voyage to Paris, and your father had bent over maps of lands he might never see. It was only in his later years that he had come, ostensibly in the pursuit of higher education, to Birmingham, leaving behind your sister safely settled at school, he had arrived with you, his younger daughter, to these long sought shores, lands that he never might have seen save in the shifting moods of Hardy's moors, Wordsworth's impoverished clouds. And you, his daughter, had inherited this horror, that others affectionately dubbed wanderlust, it was this horror, rather than the love of your cousin, you had reasoned later, that had driven you from your city, compelled you to rip away the bonds of stone and sweat and travel heedlessly into the unknown, lest you too become trapped in that disgrace of knowing more than you had seen: a madwoman in the attic, furiously scratching tales of vicarious misfortune.

You have come a long way, my love, a long way from home, you have found your way into a housefull of mirrors that each tell your tale, but none as well as you might have, if you had looked within, instead of among your myriad reflections, for the shape of your destiny. For mirrors have their own memories, my love, old shadows that fill new outlines. And in your life, my love, do not old images still struggle to service new metaphors, old anecdotes totter upon arthritic feet, and audacious kisses still hover, unsavoured, settling thick at the base of your tongue, old wine fills new bottles, even your obsession with butterflies, once a shameful concession to romantic superstition, is put to good cause at the Institute of Frenatology, where you make the pretence of earning your daily bread. There was a time when you would sit late into the evening, in mirrorless, mothstrewn, tropical dark, courting the brush of butterfly wing upon your limbs, for even the dullest variety were veiled prophecies of love, you would hold your breath as one alighted upon the lantern lip, sigh in disappointment as it overbalanced and fell into the unholy fire, and the terrible perfume of its charred flesh filled the evening air. Butterflies, those nicest of insects, in adolescence you had been at their mercy. To avenge this you took to trapping them in swirls of cotton net, as they scoured the New Jersey fields for nectar, as they tumbled upon a breeze among the tangle-veined flies, trapping them as they joined in disinterested fulfilment of fate, you had sent them into sweet stupor, and pinned them mercilessly onto pale sheets of wax. On the night that you had first wandered with Alexander into the seminary woods and he had lifted your face to the stars to press his fingers against your lymph nodes, you had seen, beyond a cloak of hickory leaves, a young white-lined sphinx moth, and reaching beyond his head, you had caught it in your hands, it struggled against your palm as you brought your arm down against a startled Alexander's back. I have caught a moth, you announced, but he had not heard, his lips, throbbing with desire, had come to rest deliciously upon the curve of your neck, he kissed you, and your fingers clenched over the desperate moth. Your distraction fed his lust, he clasped you in consuming embrace, and still your fist remained clenched against his shoulder. He kissed you again, and finally you released the subdued insect, and spread your fingers across his chest. Later, when the dawn came, you found mothstreaks upon his shirt, in your college room, he watched you as you impaled the rescued moth (it had fallen to the ground without the energy to recover, and by some miracle had escaped being trampled under arduous feet). Alexander watched in deep fascination as you shook the hickory dust off the delicate wings under the lamps, and then when the dawn came, sticky and swift, you looked up and saw the moth trails upon his blue striped shirt, saw the unshaven cheeks curled in smile, the dark eyes, bright with liquid sleeplessness, he slipped down upon his knees to kiss you, you waited for the arms about your neck to slide to your waist and lift you out of the chair and guide you to the narrow bed under the window, but he drew away and smiled, and said, I have a plane to catch in four hours, he had to be in London for the weekend. I'll be back, he promised, reaching for his overcoat, piled upon your bed, I'll be back on Monday, and then he was gone. You sat for a while, inspecting your insects, trying to nourish the small flame of hope in the pit of your being, you picked the phone off the floor and dialled Sparrow's number, a sleep-thick voice answered, what is it? I have met the man of my dreams, you answered, I have the man of my innermost, my most profound dreams.

Good for you, princess, now is he rich?

He's just gone to London for the weekend, if that's any indication.

I hope he comes back.

Actually, he's fabulously wealthy, you said laughing, but that's hardly why...

When was he born? Sparrow interrupted, you told him.

In the cusp of the Lion and the Maiden, Sparrow remarked scornfully, and suddenly you were tired of his sinister speculations, once a source of endless amusement, really, you said, you could be somewhat more enthusiastic.

The cusp of the Lion and the Maiden, Sparrow continued, the confluence of the terrible and the graceful, the clash of fire with earth.

You hung up, and laid your face upon the cold wood of the desk, the sweet smell of dead insect wing and wax, these memories crowd thick now, amid the vinegar and the alcohol, and against grey skies, as you bleach the butterfly wing, lifting with small silver tweezers the clear membrane from the bath of Clorox into the water dish, the veins appear, the imperturbable geometry of the universe, you drag the floating wing corpse upon a glass slide, and gently blow, this is your job, you tryst with society, it has been so, now for four years, you, who are fed and clothed and cossetted by satin sheets, are to repay these debts by blowing on butterfly wing, and watching your past coalesce upon the paleness of the weak discal cell, crossed by dead vein, you will remember the stiff hum of bees, on a Sunday afternoon, as you sat upon the sill, reading *Anna Karenina*, and the door blew open in a vast rush of wind, and there he was, a day early, Alexander, different, darker in daylight. Gravely, he shut the door, I brought you a piece of wedding cake, he said, extracting from his pocket a mass of napkins. He sat down beside you, while you uncovered the rich mass under the soft linen, I found it very hard, he said, contemplatively, to be away from you, very hard indeed. You lifted a sticky morsel to your mouth, and offered him the rest, he lifted the white nest out of your palm, kissed your crumb-strewn lips, and buried his wet eyes upon your shoulder. I was almost afraid, he told you, that you were a figment of my untrustworthy imagination, and what is to say that you have not remained a runaway dream, you have wondered trapping discoloured moth wing under glass, what will tell you that you have not been, all these years a delectable mirage, an abandoned myth, emerging from childhood to garnish the future, for why is it still that when his hands weave upon your hair, it is still as if he were stroking dense night, the billows of dream, and when his lips meet your eyes, closed in feigned sleep, there is yet upon his lips that awe that had once, long ago, stirred unfathomable desire, his lips will touch your brow, dewed in the dawn, with a reverence that is boundless, a reverence accorded only to fantasy, only to the image of flesh, and never to flesh itself, against clean porcelain his fevered lips will falter, clasp your sleepless form in grateful embrace.

Your love of Lepidoptera has served you well, your bread and butterflies, Avishek has dubbed it. Your cousin lives now with his wife in pretty Berkhampstead, from where he journeys to London, a few times a week, he will call for you at the Institute of Frenatology, take you to long lunches, on summer days, he might insist that you take the afternoon off and drive out with him to the country, or simply laze in some London park. Last month, on Primrose Hill, during a sudden afternoon interlude, your olives and Brie had been snorted up by a pig on a leash, that is the rhythm of your relationship now, one that feeds upon the convolutions of language, and the wordless spaces of mature memory. Last month, a soft afternoon, he had padded across the library floor and surprised you, poring over an army of tent caterpillars, tempted you with a bottle of Chilean Cabernet Sauvignon, you thought of driving to Hampstead, gave up near Primrose Hill, and settled yourselves upon a grassy height, the clarity of the atmosphere had been distracting, and you had spent long staring at the haphazard London skyline, until a pig, a leashed porker, no less, had snaffled your picnic, much to your merriment, that was the last you had seen of him in a while, his long absence, conspicuously coincident with Sparrow's visit, has irked you. Where is he today, you wonder as the Underground train rattles into Piccadilly Circus, perhaps you might drive out to visit them tomorrow, no, but tomorrow you have promised to help your friend Karin with her wedding gown. She is to marry next week, sweet Karin, your closest friend on these shores, Karin will wed Joshua, the pompous Manhattan Levite, and will she not turn once before the wineglass breaks, turn once to you and smile in wondrous pain, before raising her eyes to the falling wineglass, icicled between her Norwegian childhood and her death in new Hampshire, fifty years hence, suddenly clear in the anticipation of cracked glass, for she is to be engulfed by that torpid continent, that vast mass of land, that you had left five years ago, vowing never to return. At the end of the year Joshua will return to New York, and she will go with him, fade from your life, as others have, so many others, and perhaps, years later, she will die in New Hampshire, her hair taut steel, grandmothered back from her creased forehead, will you have no place in her last thoughts, will you not bisect the last grand vision of the bloodfilled autumn, years later, when her life, thin glass, is swallowed, in its last frail shards by the robust New England autumn, and her sons bending to kiss her dead lips, will taste just the trembling outline of your love, more precious once to her than her youth.

Next Saturday you are to wake, earlier than usual, pull aside the window drapes in the hope of sunshine, your niece already knocking timidly at the door, for she will be bridesmaid at the syncretic ceremony, dressed in small silk, flowers in her soft hair, she will be beautiful, a delicate blossom against Karin's fullblooded bloom, almond white against old ivory, they have chosen the colours carefully, and you will be in luxuriant black, for it is the colour that Karin thinks suits you best, silverbordered black, rescued from the half of your mother's trousseau that had gone to your sister, last year you had returned with suitcases full of her clothes, loath to surrender her garments to hands that would not recall the softness of her skin at every touch, lest the silk, invested still with traces of her breath, weigh heedless on other limbs, you had brought her whole wardrobe with you to these shores, suitcases of swatheful memory, stacked under the eaves of your splendid home.

Next Saturday, Alexander, unslept, will grumble into his long embroidered shirt, the heavy kurta that he had worn at your own wedding reception in Calcutta, the loose drawstring pantaloons, a style of clothing his own ancestors had once brought to your land, brought to the multitudes the obscenity of stitched cloth, taught them to sully the purity of uninterrupted weave with needle and thread, so that cloth might be chopped and shared, and not merely wound to sculpt a sheath for the body, Alexander will struggle sleepless into such travesties of cloth, next Saturday, to take your side, you, bedecked in moonlined night, rushing at the sound of the doorbell down the stairs, where your cousin, Avishek, will be waiting behind pillars of icing, your beloved cousin, the cream curlicues glistening upon his most correct shoes, and behind him his ashen wife, in extravagant goldshot silk, you will smile compassionately upon the excesses of her dress, command the maid to relieve Avishek of the cake, take care with its height, you will warn her, your eyes resting anxiously upon the Tree of Sefiroth, for it is the Qabalic Tree of Life that will crown the cake rather than some graven image of the bride and groom, the cake is to be Avishek's wedding gift to Karin, for your cousin runs a business in exotic bakes, your humorous cousin, where is he now, you wonder. Does he still linger in his suburban bed, morning desire quenched, flicking through TV channels and waiting for his dutiful wife to bring up the toast and tea? Or has he got an early start on the kitchen shelves, morning desire unfed, does he swiftly slap gloss paint onto wood, bewildered wife attendant with paintcan? Or is he buried in some voluminous novel, morning desire distracted, his voracious appetite for literature, which you had never suspected in the days of your youthful passion, when you had struggled to elevate his dreams beyond the substrate of popular song, oh, can't you see, you belong to me, how my fool heart aches, every step you take, where is he today, your cousin?

• • •

In the mail, that morning, a sachet of salt had arrived, and he, unwashed, swathed in the afterbirth of dreamless slumber, had languidly released the grains from their plastic prison and raised a fingernail to his tongue, a handful of salt fills the mouth of a garrulous slave. His wife drew a sharp breath, could be poisoned, she said, some harmful chemical, perhaps it is not salt at all, in her mind, a row of phials on sticky school laboratory shelf, perhaps it is a curious plot, she had suggested, in the guise of an appeal for donations to an oral rehydration programme. But it is a registered charity, Avishek had protested, helping himself to more, the thick grains taste of old brass, a handful of salt fills the mouth of the garrulous slave, you had written in restrained desperation, many years ago. He licked the weak metallic encrustation upon his lips, he must see you, today, a handful of salt, a young girl bent low between heavy feudal bedboards, a tropical winter, oh not so many years ago. I must go to London, today, he said slowly, some business, and his wife's face darkened, a mist of melted ash upon smooth billows of cloud, he had chosen her for the large dark eyes, even though she had been low on his mother's list, included only out of politeness to the friend who had suggested her, he had chosen her over the countless convent-educated porcelain nymphets that his parents had forced him to scan, he had chosen her, gentle Mrigaya, for the large lacustrine eyes, though the brow that curved gently to meet them was of sombre, dusky hue that his mother had not favoured, he had chosen her, Mrigaya, of the dark eyes and the Master's degree in philosophy, Mrigaya, and now he watched the damp clouds in her eyes turn to chalk, I must go to London, he told me. A handful of salt, raking rough against raw palate, the slave tongue numbed under the acid weight, or was it a tongueless slave, once garrulous, of whom you wrote, ten years ago, on a winter afternoon, your sister sleeping beside you, your sister who now slept the sweet dream of death, you wrote upon onionskin of exile and the kingdom, a tap might have dripped in long beats upon the stained marble of the bathroom floor, its slow cadence modulating your thoughts. Those early letters had betrayed hours of revision, when you scratched out a word, you would obliterate with a solid layer of impenetrable ink, or dig through the thin paper with your furious pen, and later you would scribble several other words over it, so that it was lost in a mesh of entangled syllables, for you knew he would hold it to the light, hoping to penetrate the recesses of your soul, the pentimento of spontaneity, obscured among the pages of careful poetry, misty girlish desperation. He had devoured them between classes, reading them over and over again under naked dripping trees, among wet leaves, on daffodil banks, and over the summer in Monrovia at the end of Fourteenth Street, in the road of a ferocious Atlantic, he had read your childish reassurances – if you can, imagine I am there with you now, that the wind within your hair is the caress of my unhappy fingers – for it was that summer that you passed through England on your way to the United States, and he stood cursing his luck throwing rocks into the ocean froth, five thousand miles away, on his summer vacation with his suspicious parents in humid West Africa. He had mistakenly left your letters in Monrovia that painful summer, and two years later while they were exchanging desks, his father found the lot in a drawer he had forgotten to clean out and threw them furiously across the floor of his room. Avishek shook his head and smiled, knelt among the strewn wreckage of faded correspondence, gathered each swollen letter and then very deliberately walked out through the dining room, past his grim father buried in his *Guardian Weekly*, to stuff the lot into the kitchen garbage. Later that night he felt a twinge of remorse and tiptoed in to rescue them gingerly from among the eggshells and fish livers, but they were sodden with barracuda curry and three days later, unable to bear the smell, he threw them into the Atlantic, bitter in his surrender of the last crumpled shards of his childhood dream, bitter that he had ceased to care for you, the smell of salt-soaked faeces drifted up from the littered beach and he was engulfed by a thin raw resentment that you had not permitted him to sustain his desire, for in your letters from that vast land, you had become increasingly familiar, unrestrained, a confidence that irritated his passion. He had longed for your careful letters from the tropics, brimming with dignified sentiment, dark and secret, he had imagined you laying a hot cheek on his hidden photograph in the seclusion of your bedroom, running soft fingers through his untidy letters, locked in your drawer. Now in your new, removed existence, you pinned his pictures on your bulletin board along with your class schedules, your riding lessons, and your international lunches where you hobnobbed with dark Middle Eastern princes and romantic Italians, you had written, teasingly, and he crushed the lined paper mercilessly into his waste-basket in his college room, wiped a few bitter tears with an edge of rough mustard curtain. In the spring, he had seen you in London, with an odd, whimsical friend, Jonathan Sparrow, you were not lovers, you told him curtly, as the two of you guarded a commercial driveway where Sparrow had decided, quite abruptly, to relieve himself, you were not lovers, and yet you walked arm in arm, and Sparrow kissed you upon the lips when you dropped him off at the Wallace Collection so that he might wallow in Fragonards while you gathered the rotting tendrils of your past about you, your past, buried under dead seaweed. You put Avishek on the train to Sheffield, and that was the last he saw of you, boldly he reached down to brush your lips as your friend Sparrow had done, and instead he touched a dry cheek, tasted of the deadness of spent dream, that was the last he saw of you, until, two years ago, you had appeared, at his wedding, decked in dark silk, thickened with womanhood, diamonds in your ears. You had walked into the frenzied crowd with your sister, you came straight towards him, and many eyes had frozen upon your form, those that had scorned, those that had shed tears for your adolescent passion, watched with wistful disbelief as you seized his hand with a voluptuous smile, and he said to you, I'm so glad you could come, and then he had turned to the broad radiant face of your sister, no shadow of death had lingered within the bright eyes, the gold that gripped her neck had not sunken under the corpulence of death, nor had the silver upon her finger turned ashen, as it would later, but the murky moonstone glared ominous as she raised a hand to his cheek, how you have grown, she said tenderly. His mother came to whisk you away, come and see the bride, his mother said firmly, patient Mrigaya, painted ghastly chalk, enamelled eyelids drooping with fatigue, he pushed his way through the crowd to where she sat, upon the flower-filled throne. Beside her, you stood, swathed in elegant olive, diamonds piercing the pale hollow of your neck, you turned to him and said, your wife is returning to England with me, since you must leave so soon, I shall be here for another month, we have arranged that she will come back with me, a handful of salt, once again you have my won, my lovely, a handful of salt in the mouth of a slave, but for once the slave tongue will moisten the harsh grains, perhaps with fresh blood, until the salt mass melts and slithers down a parched throat. The bride's eyes open in sudden swift inchoate comprehension, the air between them is already thick with lies, he nods and smiles, an admirable arrangement, he says, I have to go back, for the smell of baking bread calls, the mounds of warm naan pounded by machine, squeezed flat under heavy irons, the wheat chapattis, cut into thin circles, flighty puffed puris popping onto the conveyor belt. He must return, that he may stand, when the day's work is done, against the tall cylinder, hermetically sealed now against the invaders of the night, the unbidden bacillus, he will stand, in his fresh white coat, with his back against the warm metal, womb of dough, he will feel the warmth seep out into the weak evening. In his white laboratory coat, he will watch the sun fall gently through the raw fingers of the winter trees, and think, instead of his new wife, of you, as he had done, years ago, in the seclusion of more spiteful substances, when the privilege of possessing a key to the organic chemistry lab was his alone among the entire Upper Sixth, for Mr Charlesworth had proclaimed him a genius, a rare mind, he told the proud parents, a rare intelligence, his father had reminded him, tears in his eyes, and will you waste it all then, Avishek, will you throw it all away, baking bread?

The supple silence that carved vacuum into the wooden corridors, rushing through stone into the sterile laboratory to form an impalpable umbilicus to the rest of the world, where other boys smoked quick foul cigarettes under perilous eaves, or thrashed their tight limbs upon the ice currents of the swimming pool, far far beneath, submerged in old stone, and others, his friend Nicholas Butterfield among them, pelted frigid walls with hard balls, a gloved hand that would sometimes softly turn the knob, or whistle outside the heavy doors, but more often there was simply silence, and lowering the hood upon some foul preparation, he would muse upon the angst of the chemist Berzelius, he who had believed that an organic compound could never be synthesised by mere mortals, he who had imbued all organic compounds with the essence of divine creation, and then, overnight, simple inorganic ammonia conspired to transform itself into urea, distillate of human sin.

And now, on a still evening, alone within floury vaults, his mind would writhe still in the delicious agony of experimentation, organic naan for the wholesome epicure, Persian alphabet pasta

(Alexander convinced his brother to introduce it on the children's menu of their lesser restaurants, but it never caught on), and his last pet scheme, one he had cherished ever since the days he and Nick Butterfield had first conceived of their avant-garde bake factory, like Sue Bridehead, companion to Jude, the obscure, he would craft the spires that he had aspired to, like Jude, that had rudely and inexplicably rejected him, it's that grudge that you are still playing out, his father had spat out, unable to bear the thought of his son, good Brahmin stock, engaged in the fine art of kneading fat dough to variations of the wholesome daily, don't come crawling back to me, he had screamed into the tannic New Jersey dark, don't come crawling back at the end of the day, and turning his face to the flat disks of luminous cloud, Avishek had dreamt of spongy Oxford spires, his first dream, his last dream, for all other schemes have slowly petered out, and their steady income is now in plain white loaf, microwavable chapattis, stacked thick, like limpets, and endless tangles of elastic spaghetti, Japanese delicacy, Nick called it, last week, scooping up a handful that had fallen foul of the inspectors, Japanese delicacy, plate of raw nerve. The high interest rates had hit his partner hard, and he, himself, now and then, would let his eye drift down a column of job advertisements, in hesitant guilt, but, no, he would never leave a sinking ship, less out of principle than perhaps this new feeling that had overwhelmed all his senses, these last few years, that nothing mattered, nothing mattered at all, that supreme paroxysm of indifference that had frozen within him since the day of his wedding, when you walked in, lithe olive, dewed with diamond, you, whom he had loved since the days when he still thought he could hide behind glass.

To shaft flimsy cake batter into medieval university spires, his last dream, he placed a hand upon a sallow palm and told his patient wife, this morning, that it is for this purpose he must take the train to London, that he must see about the specifications for the intricate moulds they had commissioned, smooth labyrinths into which the thick mass must flow, and then harden into cake-flesh. And who will eat your Gothic arches, she had asked once, nervous with grief, who will glut their fantasies upon the sugar-dusted gargoyles. Who indeed, when none had patronised the marshmallow Taj Mahal, the marzipan Möbius strips had left the scientific community unamused, this much was true, and this she had not bargained for, colouring vague blood purple under the thin cloak of tropical twilight that hid her from her mother's anxious eyes, two years ago, when a worried voice had commanded her to powder her face once more, before taking out the tea, the firm fish cutlets fat in oil, to the scrutinising trio, whose voices she had heard from within, the pompous rasp of the father, tired impatience in the mother's curt syllables brought tears to her large eyes, and the fledging Bengali of the son, that peculiar translucence that infected the optimistic consonants of those that had stopped speaking the language long before their voices had broken. The child-man voice had made her anxious lips curl in sad smile, what futile exercise was this that her parents had set for her, she rubbed the powder puff harsh upon the dusky cheek, if only the grains would embed themselves into the invisible crevices, mingle with the murky melanin, if only, and yet, more than ever, her complexion took on the shades of spent charcoal, so that when she emerged, they were her eyes alone that shone in the farewell rays of the sun. Yet the look that met her as she drew aside the curtain and stepped in with the laden tray was one of gentle wonder, he smiled, and when they were alone, he asked her, what does your name mean, Mrigaya, the royal hunt, he closed his eyes in strange satisfaction, that is wonderful, he told her, and there had been a quiet madness in his voice, like the smell of wet earth after the first rain, as there had been an insane calmness in his love-making, three weeks later, on the night of their wedding, the frightening metronome of his gentle fingers circling within her thick hair. But it was the eccentricity of his trade that disturbed her now, more than the sudden fits of delinquent passion that drove him, in search of the absurd, to the gaudy halls of his cousin's home, more than the lunatic meshes of incomprehensible emotion that kept him in your hold, more than anything, she feared the conception of another gastronomic travesty, for in the twisted multicultural creations, she saw, where no one else did, an undisguised contempt for mankind, a mockery of its most basic need, bread.

In an aging copy of *The God That Failed* that she had found at a relative's funeral Mrigaya had underlined much of Stephen Spender's essay, and on the plane with you, two years ago, she had tried to quote, in a flush of excitement, the last few lines, the solemn disjunction between a need for bread and a desire for freedom that had given backbone to so much of her thought, and you, instead of contemplating these precious words in heavy silence, had burst into rich laughter. A chill had gathered in Mrigaya's blood, was it her English pronunciation that excited such tactless mirth, for there was no call at this juncture in their conversation for laughter, indeed, moments ago, she had seen you tremble in bitter recollection of being ordered to tip a tray of scrambled eggs into the garbage, your first day at work at your American college, and with you, she had trembled, in disgust and fascination, the ugly reptile, surplus, and charged with emotion, she had invoked Spender, the need for bread and the desire for freedom. In bubbles of delight, you murmured that she might suggest that to her husband as a motto for his business. Bewildered, Mrigaya had attempted to laugh, with an affectionate squeeze, you had said: Mrigaya – such a lovely name – guard it well against the wooden-tongued English, and for that matter, your echolalic husband. And it was true, although he repeated her name often, even now, in tantalising delight, the resonance of the first syllable was squandered upon his soft palate, as would have been the *ri* in the first syllable of *brishti*, rain, those lips that trembled upon the valley of her palm would have taken the edge out of hard tropical storm.

Her name, walnut wine upon his tongue, he whispered again, this morning, between grains of salt, trapped in the cruel fence of his teeth. Her name, he whispered with the same wild ether that sometimes pervades his spirits on the banks of a river, on small summer picnics among happy, inconsequential crowds, when his eyes mist suddenly with secret laughter, and the summer happiness within him dies as the wind might die, a sudden, absolute death. Oh often, has he turned his face suddenly upon a warm sky, a prawn sandwich still safe between his fingers, and been snatched from her, from their friends, by an aimless curve of cloud, and how often, has young grass blood upon his nostrils buried him under heavy seed sacks of memory, while she has sat at his feet, entertaining his friend's wives. Why, even when apparently absorbed in some heated debate, she, Mrigaya, only she, has seen the greater part of his consciousness rise to mingle with the lofty choir of incestuous desire that floats ever above him, and crowns, like a mellow halo, his efforts to love her, his wife, dark Mrigaya, of the doe eyes, whom he has brought across many murky oceans, to grace the empty halls of his home.

Tipping back his chair, he told her again, I must go to London today, he told her, staring up, beyond her to the wall of books that had propped up his life for so many years, wood splinters driven deep into her troubled fingers. Behind her, the walls of books rises, shelves he had crafted himself, in those first few months after their marriage when Saturday would pass in foul indecision, dare he present his trembling self, unannounced, at your London fortress, should he telephone, and if he were to interrupt your weekend slumber, mid-morning love, hammer blows would harden a portcullis of uncertainty, and a patient, bewildered wife waited with a handful of nails at the foot of the ladder – no, in those days, when he would tell her, he must go to London, there was none of the firmness of the mature lust that now imbued his very being. Nervously, he would beg her to accompany him, as if she needed coaxing, his wish was her command. The first time, she remembers, the day was spent in waiting lounges, under harsh neon, flicking through endless assortments of magazines, until towards the afternoon, he took pity on her and dropped her off, between appointments, at the Holborn Public Library, and of course, he had not appeared by closing time, she stood for half an hour in the crisp February cold, he will never forget the piercing sadness that overcame him upon the sight of her huddled in the doorway. Yet it became a habit, to drop her off at some museum or library while he went about his business, until one afternoon, in the darkened room of the National Gallery that sheltered Leonardo's *Cartoon*, she found herself, sobbing silently, from the nameless conviction that while she wandered alone through these all-too-familiar halls, he was not in some musty office at all, but cavorting, somewhere, in the wide imperious city, with you, his cousin, and indeed, that evening, on the train, he mentioned casually, although the words fell from his lips beaded with wax, in those early days, before the ease of a mature lust had infected his actions, he told her, with studied casualness, that he had indeed dropped in on you and Alexander. Your husband, however, was in Florence, and you, he told her, you had been in bed with a cold, so he had not stayed long. Long enough, she had caught herself thinking, long enough perhaps to ravish your cold-swollen lips, and indeed, the half hour that he had spent at your bedside, that afternoon, was the most tender of times that he can remember, save the excruciating moments of your adolescent passion, a few sheets of spring light condensing upon plaster curlicues in the ice-cream ceiling, the room, not your bedroom. Far too cluttered, you told him, I need peace, in the bare, almost sad, little room where you lay unfamiliarly defenceless, in antihistamine haze, eyelids lipid, languorous he had dared, once more, to press ardent fingers against the fever of your cheek, touch them to your pale forehead, your turgid lips, and this crescendo of your new passion had driven it, once and for all, into the realm of the incorporeal, a limpid chorus of angels pierced with copper light was to play in his head, forever. His fingers had strayed onto a fevered chin, undimpled, and the firm parchment of your neck, where, you had told him, many years ago, in a curious letter that marked the onset of the self-indulgent absurdity that was to replace the careful poetry of your earlier letters, you had told, you had felt there, often, the presence of gills, the faint painful lines where gill covers, beloved opercula, had cleaved to flesh, sealed, now, for aeons, and that afternoon he had run fingers back from your chin along the edge of where the gills might have slammed shut, like those of a diseased mermaid, against your jaw, and then, in satisfaction, his hands had fallen in a slow sweep down the length of your neck onto the eiderdown, and smiling, he had said, I must go now. Upon the stairs he had encountered Alexander, just returned from Italy, who greeted him with the words Vitzli-Putzli, warrior god of the Aztecs, they fashioned him out of dough, Avishek, Vitzli-Putzli, that's where your future lies, and without waiting for a response, he had rushed up, past him, to the room where you lay, in sweet rheumy haze, would he drink richly of your inchoate distractions, the enigmatic Alexander, whom he would never envy, save upon that fateful day when he burst in upon you, packing a suitcase, you were going home to watch your sister die, odd worms had crawled into his viscera then as he watched Alexander wrap you in a monstrous black cape, and later that evening, while the two of them drank whisky in your study, an imperceptible tension had strung the winter air, it had seemed to Avishek, only this once, that Alexander was cautioning him to know his place, recognise the limits of the overlap of their territories.

A few weeks later, visiting his parents in New Jersey, he had borrowed one afternoon his father's car and driven fifty miles to your alma mater, to wander among the snow-caked Gothic arches where you had ceased finally to delight in your doom. Last winter, while you watched your sister die, he had walked upon the snow fields of your youth, the frozen stream, the empty bridge over which you and Sparrow had sailed upon trays, on icy nights, he had found his way into the deserted Hall of Residence, a converted inn, where, behind some aquamarine door, you had squandered your purity upon some worthless womanising athlete, who meant less, oh far less, to you now, than he, whom you had lost by stripping your passion of the gentle membranes of secrecy that kept it moist, impaling his photograph upon corkboard, here, within these halls, you had laid out your love for a generation of young Americans to trample over. Walking slowly back to his father's car, he wondered whether he would tell them where he had been, and watch their eyes rise from their dinner plates in embarrassed surprise, memories, shovelled away, dragged back like dead animals onto the dining table. His wife's eyes would tremble in sad despair, for it was she that had declined his offer that afternoon to come for a drive. He had planned, originally, that they would go together, wander together through the snow-covered campus, he, ensconced in his private memories, she, in her private despair. He had imagined this irony, in hapless detail, from the day that his mother telephoned to tell him they were finally leaving West Africa to realise their ultimate dream, Somerville, New Jersey, rejoice, my son, for you too shall gravitate, in due course, to the land of milk and sunny nirvana, crisp winter, and cold grass, from that day onwards he had begun to fashion his intrusion into that side of paradise. Turning for a last farewell glance, he had been hit by the pastry texture of the snow-dusted spires, and this gentle vision had resurrected his desire to craft in cake flesh the spires of Oxford, his first dream, his last dream, his one enduring fantasy, Balliol in bakemeat, a gingerbread Christchurch. It was for those precious moulds that he needed to go in to London today, he told his wife, this morning. She attempted to smile, and he resolved to release himself swiftly from her presence, before the burnt black of her eyes tampered with his mood, before he was expelled from the recesses of lingering dream into the sparse reality of the sad suburban autumn, the nauseating green of the garage door, she stood in the doorway, shivering as he turned the handle, and with his free hand, motioned her to go in, but she waited, framed in cheap wood, until the trusty Vauxhall Cavalier had disappeared into the trees.

And now he stands glaring at the Portuguese maid who resolutely blocks the doorway, repeating over and over again that you are out and Alexander is busy, finally the footsteps of your niece, and her joyous whoops give him the strength to push past the maid, and lift the girl into his arms. He carries her into the living room, and there she begins excitedly to demonstrate her newly acquired skill in cartwheeling, don't break anything, he warns her, but the child is extraordinarily nimble, landing perfectly always between the Attic Wedgwood and the gilt-edged Coalport shepherdesses, the spindly chimney sweep. She has been invited, this afternoon, to a party, she tells him. Yes, Sparrow has indeed gone, he must see his lovely gift to her, she rushes away. He locates the telephone under the plush fringe of an extravagant armchair, has set up an afternoon appointment with the craftsmen of his moulds, when Rima returns with a large stuffed toy, and her uncle. While he inspects the bear (it is of a particularly unimaginative expressionless kind, he cannot see how it will compete with the snark he had offered her on her birthday, this summer, admittedly it was chosen more for the pleasure of her aunt, the baker had found a snark and it was no boojum) Alexander confesses that he has no idea when you will return, you had gone with Sparrow to Heathrow, but had also mentioned something about Foyles, you would be back, certainly, in the afternoon, in time to take the girl to her party, would Avishek stay for lunch?

No, not today, he kisses Rima and promises to return. He has four hours to kill, should he try Foyles? Why not, it is not as if he has no reason to go there himself, he could check to see if they had procured the monograph on bread making in Mohenjo Daro. Admittedly it is too early to make the inquiry, and the staff could be surly, it is not as if he will go to hang stupidly about between shelves, hoping against hope for a chance encounter, those are tactics of the past, long abandoned.

He has to change buses at Hyde Park Corner, if he is to try and find you somehow among the seething masses, a ludicrous idea, but something urges him on, something akin to premonition, that he dare not explore, instead he turns his eyes to the green expanse, and remembers how, many years ago, you had eagerly shown him a letter, pressed flat in a folder, a yellowed letter from your maternal grandfather describing the pleasures of walking in Hyde Park on a clear Sunday morning. Avishek remembers, among the mush of unfamiliar script, one clear English word – Serpentine. You had read aloud the rest, the brave unadorned prose of your shared progenitor, homesick student in this friendless city, the man whose crooked left thumb appears now among Avishek's otherwise comely digits. Your mother's father had returned to India to take up a post with the Forestry Commission, and his daughters spent their childhood in vast stretches of tree-thick silence, silence that had clawed its way into your mother, she had merged with silence, no one remembers having heard her speak except in monosyllables – to you, her absence is like the negation of a dense whiteness, that ceased to be as you took your first breath, and it was the dimming of that blank light that had plunged your father into his first nervous breakdown, even though he had never loved her, his translucent bride, unravished silence. In Avishek's mother, the long tryst with silence had left her eager only to deny it, she talked incessantly, afraid that a pause in conversation would suddenly balloon into an overwhelming soundlessness. You remember when she first arrived with your eight-year-old cousin at the university flat in Birmingham, you looked hopefully across the ceaseless stream of his mother's monologue to your cousin, you had been very lonely, those few summer months since you and your father had arrived in England, lonelier than you had ever been, even though back in Calcutta you had always been cruelly ignored by your cousins, your sister, all those you had left behind in the vast house of your birth. You knew how to fend for yourself certainly, for you had played alone, so often alone, while the rest of the children engaged in energetic games from which you were excluded on account of your inexcusable size. You knew, unlike them, how to amuse yourself, perhaps that was why your aunts had agreed that your father take you with him to the lonely chalk shores, to grow alone into adolescence. But you were lonely then, three months of friendless summer, school had yet to start, you did not know how you might approach the small clump of children that played under the trees outside your window. You sat at the sill and wrote stories in a beautiful white exercise book, and sucked endless lollipops, a story in English and a story in Bengali, on alternate days, that was what your father had dictated, he had suggested that you write the English stories in the front half, and to write the Bengali stories, to simply invert the exercise book, and write from the back, and somewhere they would meet. But somehow you had been disturbed by this reversibility, besides the margins would all be on the wrong side in the Bengali part, he insisted that that did not matter, but you divided the book in half by drawing a thick blank line down the middle page, colouring carefully in between the yawning jaws of the staples, it was your first experience of felt tip, you loved the smell. You were lonely then, desperately lonely with a child's broad loneliness, when your cousin arrived from mysterious Africa, and a voluble woman, your mother's sister, you examined her in awe, was she anything like your mother? no more than you resembled your sister, surely, your child mind reasoned. You gazed across the deepening swirls of her endless prattle to your cousin, smiling nervously, they were only to stay for a week before he was packed off to boarding school, and his mother returned to Africa, but a week stretched endless then in your small frame of time. You took his hand and led him to your room, proudly you showed him your bunk bed, replete with possibilities, the ladder, you declared, could be gangplank of a ship, and the top bunk, scattered with your toys, a populous deck. You put a bare foot on the cool tubular rung, he grabbed your arm, wait! the whole structure seemed terribly precarious to him, he was sure that the ladder would slip. Many years later, he dreamed that you were about to escape from a terrible crisis, the last ship waiting to take you all on board, everyone has boarded but yourselves, you are about to climb the ladder, in a moment the ship will depart, but he pulls you back, suddenly, he pulls you back, the ship sails without the two of you, you are left alone, with your love, you are left alone to savour a few unfettered moments of passion, before the flames spread or the waters rise, to drown you in fire, in water.

# III

# *Tigers Must Taste Like Peanut Butter*

Outside Foyles, you saw him, a statue of alcohol-sodden marble, an unwashed child at his arm, he was pointing through the stale air towards the bookshop, one hand on the back of the boy's head, Foyles, he was saying to the child, is the largest bookshop in the world. You would have passed him by, if the child had not in answer to his father's comment coughed a fearful long low cough, and you had turned to meet his deep eyes, broad hands steadying the trembling cage of bones that held the tortured lungs, is he all right? you asked.

Just a bad flu, he said, rocking his quivering frame gently in his blistered hands, very kind of you to ask, hollow cheeks creased in smile, such a smile as you have not seen in a long time, his lips meet as pleasure might meet with pain, the enigma of all existence is in the curve of that smile, whose corners reach dimly to his eyes like distant spasms of darkness. You have searched long for this smile, a smile that swells now with meaning, without sound or fury.

The child breaks again into a fit of terrible coughing, the man kneels down and encases him in his long wiry arms, he looks up at you, it's the damp, he complains, I keep telling his mother it's too damp in his room, but the woman won't listen, the bitterness in his voice is dry like dead flowers between the leaves of a heavy book, the child squats upon the pavement exhausted by his fit, gulping in the syrupy air, you steady his head, that has slipped from the circle of his father's arms. You feel the sticky tufts of hair between your fingers and are drowned with sudden affection, let's get him something hot to drink, you suggest. His father takes the boy's arms and lifts him to his feet, he looks up at you, you're being very kind, he says, and again he smiles, seen from above, the fullness of his lower lip is a ledge for the weak English sun, sensual and sarcastic, the corners curl in the ecstasy of some exceedingly private dream, seen from above, it is the smile of a disturbed entertainer, bowing before an adoring audience. He stands up and the smile climbs the length of your body, hovering about your waist as he straightens his arms, then shooting rapidly up, it lingers upon his lips as you walk slowly to the nearest tea shop on Charing Cross Road. The boy falls heavily onto a chair, wheezing badly, what would he like? Cocoa? A big slice of chocolate cake perhaps, to get back some of that energy he has squandered in coughing, and what would his father like? Some coffee? Please let me get this, you say, and from behind the cash till you watch his grave face, wondering if you have made a mistake in offering to pay, have you insulted him? But when you return, he smiles like sudden quiet lightning, by the way, he says, my name is Dan, and this, he thumps the boy on his back, you are afraid his tired ribs might crack, this is Kevin, and this, he says, gesturing to the world in general, is our Saturday together, isn't it Kev?

The boy scratches at the plastic table cloth with his knife. You remember a piece you read at an elocution contest years ago about ill-mannered children who combed their hair with cutlery, as in forks, at the dinner table, you had bagged the first prize much to the consternation of a precocious rival who had read from *The Wasteland*, HURRY UP PLEASE ITS TIME. Can I call you Daniel? you ask.

He shrugs, a new smile upon his lips, one that consumes his lower lips, and still exhilarates, nobody ever wants to call me Dan, he says, at the hairdressers where I worked last year they wanted to call me Hansel, I suppose Dan isn't a very exciting name.

So you cut hair? you ask, you cannot see him, fiddling about with scissors, long snake-toothed combs, you cannot picture him shaking a grass-wet head, brandishing a blow drier like a surgical instrument.

Not really, he replies, the beverages arrive, overfull, syruping down the uneven china. The child attacks his cake with the unsatisfying rapidity, that is to say you find little satisfaction in the speed at which he consumes it, knowing that the rich crumbs will not have lingered long enough upon his tastebuds to produce the sensation of deep thick sweetness, what he will have enjoyed, at the end of it all, will be the concept of chocolate cake, but then, perhaps, like all children, he is more comfortable with abstractions than adults.

Not really, he says, I thought I'd have a go at it last year, my wife, ex-wife really, Kevin's mother that is, thought there might be some money in it. I used to cut her hair, you see, but I didn't like it, I went back to my old job, working in a butcher's shop.

That's more like it, Daniel, no, Dan, beast blood on your chin, those restless fingers, dancing upon the coffee cup, thick in blood jelly, the dirt under your nails is black pudding, you can see him sawing gravely through heavy bone, spreading butterflies of cold flesh upon steel counters, you can smell the penetration of old blood within his skin, and the scent, like dry smoke, pours into the caverns of your consciousness, you long suddenly to feel his breath upon your hair, the agony of his smile rubbing upon your neck.

In his eyes, a bemused desire flickers, dances upon his smile. How would your father feel, you wonder, if you were to walk out now, with this man, an acquaintance of half an hour, if you were to walk out with him, and his son, and take a taxi to his miserable home, or even to the palace of kitsch that was your abode, where, perhaps in the very room where this morning you had buried your eyes upon Sparrow's limp arm, in that very room, unbeknownst to all, you would indulge in amused love-making, how would your father feel if you revealed such an incident to him in one of your ponderous letters, that you had indulged this shallow fantasy within the padded coffers of your very home, what would you have done with the child?

Would it be some sort of delayed revenge for those restless nights in Birmingham, when you waited to hear the door shut upon the sounds of a woman's laughter, Erika, his German tutor. For dinner, he would have warmed two days' portion of the curry that your aunt brought over, twice a week, from Northfields, and the next night he would come back with fish and chips, newsprint dripping fish oil upon the doormat where his sad shoes scraped, and you would be glad that it was to be an evening alone with him. On other evenings, you would listen, from your room, stroking your pet ladybirds, you would listen for the sounds of their laughter, for you had unwittingly adopted the role that your aunts had hoped you would play, a sentinel. They had hoped that in the process of falling prey to the allures of white flesh, the flesh of your conquerors, your father's large eyes would come to rest upon you, his child, and he would shut the door upon the temptresses that gathered outside. Would it be a sort of delayed revenge if you were to reach out now, under the table, allow your aggressive fingers to knead the rough fabric that sits upon his eager thighs, or if you were merely to distill the essence of his smile, his smile, turned now upon his child. In a series of liquid images you see him bent in a paroxysm of lust over plastic flesh, strands of bleached hair between his lips, you see him hold the chipped hands of a woman convulsed in childbirth, pacing disinfected corridors, and then the wizened caricature of himself in his young hands, his child, you feel a strange envy as he reaches to move the thin locks of her hair plastered in sweat upon the boy's pale forehead, I made this, his hands seem to say, between scooping sheep brains from narrow sheep skulls and grinding diseased sheep gut to feed to hungry bulls so that they might dance in rare madness, between the splaying of ox kidneys on old bloodsoaked marble and the washing of goat livers in frigid metal tubs, cowspit in my hair, I drove my flesh into another and I made this.

Sparrow said that a man was distanced from his creation in the same way that he was distanced from reproduction, a man, he purported, therefore, could be more critical of his own work, and why it was then that he had given up writing poetry, could he not bear the concept of dragging his medieval metaphors into middle age, why instead did he surrender his soul, his precious time upon this earth, to making candles for his lover's boutiques. A sorry lot you were after graduation, you, in London, learning to live in the vulgar absence of the need to work, and he, in the basement of his lover's boutique in Greenwich Village, moulding surly wax to satisfy the unimaginative, and then, when he left her, she was too old, his Helga, and so very New Jersey anyway, so when he finally lifted himself out of her sagging bosom, he had offered his services to the Blue Toad, a sex shop that specialised in animal fetishes, and there he fashioned, out of wax, the organs of luscious beasts, and occasionally those of *Homo sapiens* too, judging from the grotesque element of his handiwork that he sent you at Christmas, that year, Jon Sparrow, candlemaker. Then, one afternoon, in his workroom behind the blow-up ferrets and pumpkins, you like to imagine that he ripped, in sudden overwhelming frustration, he ripped out the wicks from a pair of wax udders, coloured with oil of wintergreen, he ripped out the wicks before the udders had set, and then he left, to see the world, not as you had tried to see it, but in the guise of a teacher of English, in far-away Siam, where, finally, after many long years, his deep desire for destiny died a slow, slow death, and packing his bags, he set off, once again in his Angkor Wat T-shirt, to navigate slowly towards the land where he was born, and this had been the last outpost of his imagination, Jonathan Sparrow, you have sent him into a screaming abyss, the beginning of the circle of his dreams, which the geometry of existence decreed that he must meet.

You say to Dan, today, I said goodbye to a friend and I am afraid I will never see him again.

Where did he leave for? he asks, his eyes still upon the boy, wrestling with his plate for the last morsels of chocolate icing.

New York, and at the sound of these magic words (had he expected Chipping Campden or Tunbridge Wells) his eyes come darting back, misted with keen fantasy, have you ever been, he asks quickly, have you ever been to New York?

Yes, for four years, you lived within fifty miles of New York, amid spurious spires, on banks of sterile green, smeared with geese pellets. I have a terrible feeling, you tell Dan, that I will never see him again, my friend, Jon Sparrow.

I've always wanted, he replies dreamily, to see New York, I've an uncle who married an American lady, in Yonkers, they live, far from New York City, he asks shyly, is it?

not far, the ragged tip of sleepy Westchester, the dull the Hudson, and dreams of old Dutch farmers, whose d coursed slow in their veins, too slow to quench a s thirst, and one of them, many many years ago, had wandered into the Catskill Mountains and slept long, sliding through some insignificant wormhole in the space-time continuum, to emerge, in a new time, where nothing had changed at all.

Not that I would ever be able to afford to go, he says wistfully. Oh, Daniel, the crust of your dreams rakes rough against my palate, my desire falters, only to waken again as those lips, bent like a wick under weight of dull flame, curve suddenly, the first fearful notes of a severe toccata, a dry, smoky lust wraps its tendrils about you, born of an older flame, now quenched.

I wonder, he asks you, his fingers moving close to your hand upon the table-top, but not daring to touch, I wonder if you'd know where we could get some nice books for Kevin. He likes to read, you know, and I promised I would get him some books, but I can't, for the life of me, remember what I read as a boy, and I'd like to get him, you know, what children ought to read, the right stuff, that improves their minds, perhaps you know.

Along this very road, there are bookshops where you have spent many a blissful hour, and so often your eyes have rested fondly upon the stacks of *Boy's Annuals*, on clothbound volumes, peppered with the dust of many years, *Last Term at Hickory Towers*, *William the Blasphemous*, books written for children of another age, and you had fed fondly upon the idea that you might crowd your children's shelves with such treasures, and now, you contemplate often that you might bring your niece on an excursion to these caves, but the child has not developed an interest in books, not yet.

I know just where to go, you say.

And so he saw you, your cousin Avishek, he saw you emerging from a nondescript coffee shop on Charing Cross Road, a man and a child by your side, and instead of calling out to you, as he might have done if there had not been a peculiar radiance to your face, the sudden steam of a delicate lust that drifted towards him, twenty feet away, through a crowd of stale tourists, and if, within him, there had not darkened, suddenly, an overwhelming, perverse desire to follow you, without you knowing that he was just minutes behind you, to follow you, as he had done, ten years ago, through the perspiring streets of Calcutta, his sandal soles caked with burning asphalt, he had followed you from the gates of your school, hanging back in the shadows, his face obscured by a pair of oversize sunglasses he had borrowed from a cousin, he had followed you into a crowded bus, he had watched you with your friends, where are they now, your friends, how you must have loved them, laughing you had descended in College Street, utterly familiar terrain to him, intoxicated he had followed you as you and your companions hunted for textbooks in the second-hand stalls that lined the street, tropical bouquinistes, he heard you haggle, argue, the one boy among you told an irate vendor that his manner befitted a grocer more than a bookseller, and he smiled, behind dark glasses, incognito in the tropical sun, you thumbed through a book of Eliot's poems that you decided you could not afford and he had ached then, to tap you on your shoulder and pay for the book. Instead, after you moved on, he bought it himself, intending to give it to you, but he never did, for how could he tell you, though you surely would have comprehended his thrill, how could he tell you, that one hot August day he had followed you up the dusty stairs to the College Street Coffee House, that he had sat and sipped cold coffee at a corner table, erecting his parcel of books to bifurcate your field of vision, a beverage that would severely compromise his digestive faculties in the weeks to come, that he had followed cautiously, once again, as you left with a smaller group of friends, taken the same bus to the Esplanade, and sat two rows behind you in the Globe Cinema, watching *And Justice for All* for a second time. It was he who had, the night before, urged you to see it, and though he had toyed with the idea of catching you at the end of the film, feigning surprise, he had not had the courage, he had sneaked out with the credits, taken a taxi home. And so, ten years later, on a Saturday morning on Charing Cross Road, seeing you, he halted, pulled up his collar and wrapped his scarf over the lower half of his face, followed you and the unfamiliar man, whose child shuffled tiredly by his side, he followed you cautiously, from a distance, until you dived into a bookshop, and he lingered outside behind the 50p shelves, rummaging aimlessly through the rack of inconsequential printed matter, until his eye fell upon an old Dick Francis book, of the sort that he had devoured in his youth, the Liberian summers, the air-conditioner dripping, in every heroine, he had seen you, a faithful obsession. Four o'clock would strike, and he would draw on a shirt, seize his squash racket, and saunter down the Tubman Boulevard to the covered courts to meet Joe Dinkins, son of the Dean of Faculty at the hilltop university. Joe would always beat him silly, they would walk down later to Joe's sprawling home, and he would stay to share their fried Spam and cornbread, and his mother would be irritated, once more, by his lack of appetite at dinner, the multitude of dishes she had so painstakingly prepared, while he had gorged himself upon fried Spam. To escape her indignation, he would seal himself in his room, with his unfinished book, all those summers, and yet how little he seemed to have read, when he burst into your life, grown from skinny boyhood into tall pale youth, on his way to university, how easily you had put him to shame with your vast command of literature, how skilfully you tried to instill within him the love of books, and yet, the obsession with literature had come much later, to replace rather than feed your youthful passion, it was only after he had seen your love a sorry carcass that he took to devouring the written word.

You stumble into the basement, eerily lit, a smell of book damp strong in the air, inhaling the mystic odour, Dan remarks, I worked in a shop near Tufnell Park once, just for a few weeks, Pilkingtons, purveyors of nostalgia, they called themselves, this place has the same smell. And what did they sell, you ask, laughing, running your finger along the spines of a shelf of Biggles books, these purveyors of nostalgia?

Oh, this and that, old furniture mostly, and some old books, clocks, weird little boxes and things, he has moved very close behind you, his hand resting upon the shelf beside where your own has come to rest, there was an old chess set I really fancied, almost thought of nicking a piece of two, but . . .

But, like any true artist, he could not violate its wholeness, his breath falls warm upon your hair, beyond the cloak that is gathering round you, you hear the flap of pages as his son flips listlessly through a large coffee-table book of dogs. He would have liked a dog, perhaps, his son, because, behind those pale bones, there hides the essence of an English boy that occupied so many of your childhood musings, of hay and apples, and cool green brooks, and a faithful hound nosing after rabbits, and your trance is interrupted by the thud of a book falling to the cold floor, and a long low cough that would seem to tear his guts out, this frail child. His father rushes to hold his head, it's too damp in here, he says irritably, far too damp, perhaps it is an obsession with him, in his otherwise unfettered mind, damp, too damp, he says, picking up the child, let's get out of here.

And so, the book-buying venture indefinitely suspended, you sit, the three of you, upon the bruised lip of a fountain basin in Trafalgar Square, here you once grovelled among the pigeon shit with Sparrow, in that shiftless spring, for a fallen contact lens, was it yours or his, you cannot remember now, both pairs were caked with sleep, and peering through the murky film, you had wondered whether it was not just the notorious London fog. The boy insists on feeding the birds, still sucking in the harsh air into his fragile lungs in low whistles of pain, never more palpable has it been to you, this struggle to breathe, a struggle for life, for although last night you dreamt that your sister fought long and close with death, in truth you had seen her capitulate with the grace of a slave girl, smiling in her chains. Between tortured gasps the child voices a request impossible to refuse, can he feed the birds, and so father and son rise from the fountain edge and move off in search of feed, and you feel suddenly that all might end well if you were to get up now and creep away, the book sale at the Institute of Contemporary Arts that you have been meaning to visit for weeks now beckons invitingly, and from the crowded steps of the National Gallery, Avishek senses your agitation, sees you glance quickly about, shift yourself to the edge of the basin lip, he thinks perhaps that he might intercept you finally, if you rush quickly up into the street, but then, the stranger is back at your side, once more, and though you remain perched on the edge of the rim, he leans well back and stretches out his long arms in a wide arc about you, his fingers lurk once more in the delicious penumbra of your being, caressing wet stone. The eyes that turn to you colour suddenly in cloud shadow, eyes that are like tight lids on deep coffers of new pain, drops of light shine where his head has caught some of the diseased fountain spray, the thick luxuriant locks, blackened, no doubt, painstakingly, over chipped porcelain, if some of the strands were to stray onto your tongue, there would be a taste of cold ink, a metallic infusion of death that still lingers, from last winter, when, in final farewell, you had kissed your sister's frozen feet, cold beyond death, for they had kept her, through the night, upon large, trembling blocks of ice.

* * *

Is it worth following you, your cousin wonders, after all your lives are full of secrets, best left unshared, as in any mature passion, and beside him, a gaunt form, scarcely noticed, throws a burnt rind of bread to a passing pigeon, Jonathan Sparrow, fleetingly familiar, easily ignored. Sparrow fixes his eyes upon the mass of humanity below, and sees you not, nor your curious companion, Sparrow stares vainly at the simpering fountains, hoping to resuscitate, by suggestion, his utterly inactive salivary glands, for the pallid pumpernickel that he had hoped might be lunch has left his mouth in a state of fearful desiccation.

The Bloomsbury hotel had not found his credit good enough, the battered American Express card, he had not used it at all in the time he had been here, and in the meantime the bastards had stopped his credit, how did they expect him to pay if the bills were still going to his address in Bangkok, perhaps he should have asked you to send them a cheque, anyway they would not accept his card at that hotel, nor at the next, and with thirteen pounds eighty-three pence and three hundred rupees, he was left with little alternative but to park himself upon a bench in Russell Square and contemplate the situation, but the racing of clouds in the rare blue above, the mellow rhythm of cloud and shadow, had convinced him to postpone the decision. There was always the National Gallery, if it rained, and even if it did not rain, it had been your first refuge on that spring trip to London, when you and he had punctuated your fascinated forays with frantic phone calls to the students whose mangy living room carpet would eventually be your bed, there was never an answer. Towards the afternoon, you began to get worried, perhaps they should just take the coach to Birmingham, where you had an aunt, but he would not hear of it, he had not, he told you sternly, come to England to languish in the maggoty Midlands.

To the maggoty Midlands, you had taken him, this time, on one of your frequents forays into the fabled verdure of this sceptred isle, in your feisty little Midget, your trusty steed, it had served you well until rear-ended by a British Telecom van, two weeks ago, on Earl's Court Road, and now recuperated in some appropriate sanatorium. Would it ever recover from the ignominy, your applecheeked pegasus, that had borne you to Ashby de la Zouch, you and he and the curly-haired Karin, who had undoubtedly found him most humourless, for when you had stopped for coffee at a picturesque church hall, Sparrow had refused to share your mirth over the handicrafts that were on display in sunken glass cabinets. Little cards accompanied each item, bemoaning the unfortunate life history of each artisan, the lace kerchief that cowered against the wooden cross, you learnt, was crafted under eyes so feeble that within them the moon never shone. This old lady, despite her failing eyesight, the caption explained, had read all of Jane Austen. You and Karin collapsed in each other's arms with laughter, while Sparrow stood grimly by, turned away to read that the railway linesman who had knit the scarf that cascaded into the diffracted dark, when it was finished, felt robbed of life's purpose, and used it to hang himself, the scarf survived, into the latter half of the century, found its way to Leicestershire, found its way into this glass cage, where it would spend the rest of its life, manacled, mothspit. Sparrow had caught himself wondering how much of his paraphernalia would outlive him, but he had not given the earth any reason to remember him, Jonathan Sparrow, poet and mathematician. His one contribution to the theory of numbers, Sparrow's Lemma, gathers sock sweat at the Illinois State Penitentiary. Don't cry, Jon, the Professor had pleaded, time, time, without responsibility, that's what I need, the burly mentor had exulted in his sentence, near life, for mixing mercury in his wife's cod liver syrup. This is my freedom, don't you see, Jon, he had told the seventeen-year-old Sparrow, this is what I have been waiting for, for this peace, you wait, Jon, before the year is out, I will have finished the manuscript, you wait, he said, tucking the folded piece of paper into his sock. There, he said, pointing to the bulge on his ankle, your contribution, I want it next to my skin, Sparrow's Lemma. This was the man who had given him the world, this man was to spend the rest of his meagre time left on earth, striped and caged, his mind slowly dissolving under the weight of his useless erudition, until they commuted his sentence and moved him to an asylum, rubbed away the stripes and padded the cage, so that nightmare became resilient rubber, impossible cocoon, and Sparrow's Lemma still strains against ribbed wool, in the stapled enveloped that no one may claim.

Jon Sparrow, poet and mathematician, child prodigy, so much for mathematician, doom had discoloured differential topology, squalid courtroom drama, the keen, laughing eyes of the helpless Professor, his delighted submission to forces beyond him, had he really spilt the silver liquid into his epileptic wife's cod liver oil, the truant metal, mercury, dancing through globules of piscean fat. The only thing that disturbs me, Jon, is that I would have hoped they would credit me with more imagination. After all, in his prime, the Professor had been a regular contributor to the 'Perfect Murder' series in the local paper, a habit which had not aided the counsel for his defence, Sparrow had heard the lawyer whisper angrily, why didn't you tell me? why? and the

Professor had shrugged and smiled, I wouldn't have thought it mattered. But later he told Sparrow, it's a good thing they dug out the 'Perfect Murder' stuff, I was hoping all along that they would bring that up, it shows me as a man with an infinitely more sophisticated repertoire of strategies, and makes them look like petty fools. He had not expected a conviction, not then, not yet, not until that fateful morning when a red-faced sophomore in a ROTC uniform climbed into the witness box, and stammered that the Professor had indeed made advances to him, yes, slipped 'perverted' poetry between his homework sheets, really disgusting stuff. The Professor refused to comment, and Sparrow saw settle upon the cataract blue a deeper gleam of utter despair, of final capitulation, as if he could distill from the sordid events an Oedipean grandeur of disaster, but Sparrow saw instead the raw chasm of laughter that separated the mind from the horror of incarceration, the mind that had been fettered for so many years now by the laws of numbers and spaces, refused to recognise the jagged finality of prison wall. In the lurid half-light of the No Name Motel where the man had moved during his trial, he saw, through thick tears, wilted yellow fingers folding the foolscap, Sparrow's Lemma, and tucking it into thick sock. Three days later Sparrow left for the East Coast, cured of his precocious mathematical genius, where, in the four long years that he spent at university, he would never once touch a single book upon the subject, never once venture into the concrete wilderness that housed his once beloved abstractions, sticking strictly to the trembling arches and the elm-lined courtyards, hoping to exorcise the demon of presentiment that hung heavy upon him since the trial, if this light turns, he will be proven guilty, if the milk sours, or the duck stirs. Once he had even taken a pack of cards, and interpreted their order, the heart spelled victory, the diamond, uncertainty, the club, sure defeat, and the spade, hard labour. So uncertainty had fed upon uncertainty, draining him of logic, draining him too of poetry, Jon Sparrow, poet and mathematician, he had had engraved in a fit of narcissism, on visiting cards that his mother insisted upon, in one fell swoop, nothing.

And yet it had been the bedraggled corners of his verse that had poured into your ears over the din of the Fooseball machine, later that autumn, his first year at college. It had been the tattered syllables of his soured dreams that had drawn your black eyes away from the plastic rattle, the strawberry muffin breath of your companions. You turned towards him your hungry eyes had pierced the rim of his recently rescued Homburg that shielded him from the multitudes, you came and stood beside him, pressing your back, like him, against the panelled wall. He juggled with his forehead to lower the hat further onto the bridge of his nose, but still your presence filtered through like sharp dust shadow. He fell silent, you begged him not to stop, or was it more of a command, it was more of a command, and although he did not obey, he pushed back his hat and turned towards you, stunned by the relaxed authority of your plea. He had seen you before, in the dining hall, in your flowered skirts and eyelet lace blouses, you had pieced perfectly into the conventional collage, he had never given you a second glance. If he could place you at all, it was in association with a rather handsome youth in whose company he had seen you often, somehow the boy had caught his eye, that curious combination of classical Mediterranean with immigrant American that sharpened the curve of his worriless brow, the tanned shoulders that he had loved to leave bare in that warm autumn, David, your first love. So are you sleeping with him, Sparrow had asked you, later that night, as the two of you watched him stagger, beer-blind, towards his room across the hall, and as you rose to follow him, you had explained with pride that you had pledged to preserve yourself for a young cousin, a love that was not of this earth, a love that had been conceived in the bowels of childhood and risen sharply to confront you the year before, after curling sinuous silent through your beings, treacherous spine-fingered roots, burrowing deep into the soil of your existence, for him, you would remain intact, unsoiled, you had whispered, as you eased open the door to the drunken youth's lair, shut it resolutely upon his face, leaving him to wonder how you would nurse your dreams among the tawdry vapours within, how ethereal incest might conspire with a mineral lust. He sat through the early hours of the day where you had left him, facing the door, the erasable message board, hamburger-coloured, sporting his name in thick lustrous black, for an hour Sparrow attempted to construct anagrams from the long line of letters in his name, INVADORS EDEN, ENDORSE DIVAN, DANE DROVE SIN ... and then he slept, sprawled upon the ash-bitten carpet, until you emerged, woke him, and convinced him to accompany you to a solitary Saturday breakfast. Your love, your cousin, you told him over scrambled eggs and cottage cheese, lived across the ocean – Sparrow had stiffened at the mention of demi-paradise – in springtime, you would have saved enough to make the trip to see him. And he, Sparrow, surely, he too, might surrender himself to the rigours of the college kitchen, the humiliations of scraping fish flake from fellow inmates' platters, and burning blue fat for berry pancakes, tipping cigarette ends from spittle-smeared juice glasses, surely, he, too, would put up with as much for the pleasure of a London spring? And indeed on Monday morning, he was there, the sad Homburg tilted over sleepy eyes, the breakfast supervisor had developed a deep gulping passion for him, and he got away, in the four brief months that he gave her his service, with the minimum of work, lounging in the deep freezing cabinets, grovelling for poetry among the frost flakes, the frozen pizza crust, gelid pancake dough, searching among the groin-vaulted cellars, the vats of insipid cola. Fill the cups half with ice, the supervisor advised him, panting with lust, fill it half with ice, like this, lipsticked fingers closing upon the cup in his hands, shovel in the ice, and then fill up with soda. At the slightest opportunity he would abandon his post to hunt among the caverns of styrofoam and plastic cutlery for hook, line, and sinker with which to bait his dissolving emotions, and there she would stalk him, your anorexic supervisor. Behind dusty metal shelves she would, without any preliminaries, unbutton his trousers, while he stood, gazing up at the cobwebbed vaults, until in perfidious rapture he would seize her orange hair, and realise happily in climax, that poetry must be postponed until after the trip to London, the pilgrimage that filled all crevices of their existence, that winter, your first winter in North America. As he watched you submit to the exhausting temptation of your athlete's lovely shoulders, paling now in the winter sun, he had been glad that the trip to London had acquired a significance of its own, for the charms of the sweet cousin were fast fading from your memory, the black-and-white photograph of the bulletin board hung stiff, ignored, but you were still to go to London, and your cousin was to come down from godforsaken Sheffield or whatever provincial seat of learning had been his alma mater. He had hoped to go to Oxford, you told Sparrow, it had been mightily close between him and some other apple-fed youth, and having no other means of distinguishing between their abilities, the authorities had invited them to a game of cards, not Bridge or Hearts mind you, you said, but what we call Donkey Bashing in Bengal, who knows what it is in English, a game of miserable chance. Sparrow never knew whether to believe you, nonetheless, he could not help, on first encountering Avishek, he could not help but picture those unsettled eyes watching his pile of cards diminish, the spires crumble sad upon his palate, confound Christminster, where Sparrow's Lemma too had failed to enchant, for he had long thought of dragging his hopes and dreams across the mighty ocean, though the Professor had never approved, the British, he claimed, were haunted by the meagreness of their seas, one can console the lack of land, for land is, of nature bounded, but the seas know no definition, what is sadder than water that is bounded by water, air that is moulded by air, ideas that strain under the weight of other notions, what could be sadder?

For hours you and he had argued, on your bellies before a gravy-stained atlas, you had argued whether the island was shaped more like a dog, lofting an Irish dumpling, or, whether, and this was the view he favoured, it was not more like a fractured pig, slack-jawed in Glamorgan, carrying a thalidomide otter in a plumed hat. He argued that your attitude had, understandably, been tinted by colonialism, the links with Ireland, for who could deny the porcine contour of the Cardigan Bay, the artiodactylic extrusion of Cornwall, and you retorted that the object of this exercise was surely to discover a single object or animal that described the national boundaries, it was that all of Italy could fit into the boot, almost any country could decompose into a minor menagerie, that was cheating, either way, of course, London was clearly positioned near the sphincter.

There was always the National Gallery, he had reasoned, rising from his bench in Russell Square, there was always the National Gallery, he counted his change carefully, for the first stirrings of a massive mid-morning hunger, lithium-lined, had begun to softly glide towards the haunted pit beneath his diaphragm. Eighty-three pence it was, and of course the thirteen pounds, but that he should not eat into, already thick clouds threatened, though there was still enough for a policeman's pyjamas, his grandmother's trusty meteorological adage, there was always the National Gallery, if it should rain, and even if it should not rain, for the wind had scattered the frothy plumes within an instant of herding them together, brandywine sunlight, there was always the National Gallery, the welcome halls that had embraced the two of you in the cold March morning, seven years ago, there was always the National Gallery. Meanwhile, the burning in his insides could be dulled by a large loaf of bread, he would leave a trail of crumbs for you, through the cream corridors of Bloomsbury, down Shaftesbury Avenue, and faceless Soho. In Chinatown the galleons of roast duck dove deep into the recesses of his bread-blunt hunger, but he crammed his mouth faster with hunks of sesame-splattered pumpernickel, and by the time he arrived at the National Gallery all that was left of the loaf was an insignificant sickle of burnt rind that he threw to a passing pigeon. He wipes his mouth, dreadfully dry now, most dreadfully dry, bread-blistered lips seek the rag folds of his damp tongue, momentarily, a quiet dryness invades his cortex, he leans against a stone pillar, the scream of a child slithering upon pigeon shit cuts dry flame between the halves of his mind. Beside him, a woman holding a stuffed otter leaves an unfinished can of Diet Guava Crush trembling upon the rail, Sparrow watches her leave, his fingers inching towards the can. Already the simple poetry of his poverty has begun to please him, and once upon his palate, the tawdry liquid teases a small arc, a micron edge in his quest, the tropical opulence of guava fluid harnessed by his native sweetners, the irony cannot not fail to revive. He tosses the can into a litter bin, is it possible, he wonders, to survive indefinitely, upon the leavings of humanity, not as a tramp, no filthy Beckettsian bum, but in relative style, could one sustain oneself upon the abandoned sandwich, the unfinished drink, change left in vending machines, the odd embossed plastic, unused xerox cards, forgotten Caravaggios? Could one feed forever upon the vast uncluttered dream that squeezed Philip IV and his hunting party into less than a sixth of Velasquez's canvas, this compression of reality has never struck him so full in the face, he turns exhausted to contemplate Martha and Mary, and there again, the curious tableau upon the kitchen wall compensates in dimension for the canvas space it has surrendered to reality, receding far back into the subconscious in dimension for the canvas space it has surrendered to reality, receding far back into the subconscious while the eggs and the fish stand sensuously real, beckoning forth once again the sharp relentless hunger that he had tried to smother under lead balls of bread, this time he invests in fish and chips, on Lower Regent Street, Real British Fish and Chips, the shop sign assures, a quarter of his capital reserves depleted, he makes his way moodily towards the promise of green, past the Duke of York (the grand old duke, who had ten thousand men), perched high, down the trussed steps, and across the Mall, traffic swerving nervously about him and his precious fish and chips, microwave-hot. Waiting for them to cool, he wanders, among the armoured foreheads of the coots and the glassy stares of tufted ducks, until a sunlit stretch, the size of a grave, gives sufficient invitation, the hook of oak root reaches out to hold the carton of chips, what a travesty, they taste of tobacco, he throws them to the clamouring birds.

Tigers, you and he had decided once, must taste like peanut butter, this was the year when Teddy Ginsberg's club had served lion steaks at house parties, there was a concern, it appeared, that catered to such exotic tastes, breeding the animals on large acres of land, somewhere in the Midwest, they had everything,

Teddy assured you and Sparrow, from ostrich fillets to marmoset mcnuggets, but you had wrinkled your shapely nose and pronounced disgust at carnivore flesh, at the iniquity of feeding upon a secondary consumer in the food chain, and later, in the cellar of your own club, while the multitudes gyrated above, you and he had decided that tigers must taste like peanut butter, thick and ammoniac, tigers, you were sure, must taste like peanut butter.

Sparrow, sinking into sleep, catches the curled corner of a gander's beak upon his hair, and sits up quickly, to finish his fish and chips, before the birds eat him alive, not to mention the remains of the cod and the cadaverous fries, they leave his mouth dry, and his whole being racked once more by an incurable thirst.

Behind the dead grass in his grandmother's yard, Sparrow had imagined for many years there lurked an incurious vampire, feeding on the resinate blood of forest rats, pine-spiced rowanberry-red, and when they learnt to flee, he slaked his unwholesome thirst upon the mottled blood of toads, the treacly blood of unwary skunks, the colourless alcoholic fluids of insects. Gradually he became thinner and thinner, his vampire, for he dared not like others to venture forth into the world that changed so rapidly before him, he dared not even to scour the forgotten alleys for an unsuspecting tramp, slumped against a garbage can. For four hundred years he had changed with the times, from his lowly Transylvanian origins he had worked his way across the centuries, across Europe, on the slowboat from Sicily he had feasted upon the olive-scented blood of petrified young girls, the perfumes of restless dreams rising to meet his uneven fangs from the cool salt curve of a bared nape, he had held their hands as the promised land approached, the Statue of Liberty, he had shared their hopes of eternal peace, and yet, upon the bonny Indiana Dunes, he had finally lost his nerve, the vastness of the land resonated ominously with the eternity to which he was condemned, echoed his undeath, and so he had come to cower in Sparrow's grandparents' backyard and stumble, drunk on butterflies, into his dreams, into his first poem. Sparrow's first poem, gathering moss now in the crevices of a useless mind, for the Professor had committed it to memory, the effortless lattice into which were meshed the birthdates of all his students, the call numbers of the entire mathematics departmental library, street maps of obscure unvisited cities. Sparrow's first poem, tremblingly offered, in the cusp of childhood and adolescence, when conversation had veered finally from set theory towards the sublime, the fourteen-year-old Sparrow had unfolded the spidered foolscap, his first work of art, and the Professor's eyes had clouded with a distant laughter that had remained remote to the day of his verdict, to the last desolation, when it had revealed itself as nothing but a shield against pain, the valley of laughter that came to separate, during the Professor's trial, his agony from his disbelief, and broadened with time to engulf him. On the day that they took him away, Sparrow had held the poem, his first poem, to a candle, knowing yet that it would always be secure in the Professor's memory, etched upon voluptuous crests of laughter.

In the thick of a summer storm he burnt his poem, the rat suet hissing and spitting, trickling over the dusty candle stub that crowned the abandoned tree of Sefiroth, laid leafless upon a moth-eaten billiard table that he had reassembled in his room, for before divination became a means of survival, Sparrow had taken to dabbling in the occult, fashioning the ten lights of the Qabalic tree of Sefiroth from venomous tallow, stretching red wool between the emanations to mark the twenty-two pathways corresponding each to the twenty-two Tarot, the twenty-two letters of the Hebrew alphabet. The ashes from his poem spilled upon the vowelless abyss between Kether and Hokmah, drifting over the gangrenous felt towards the lonely stump of Tifereth, the wool stretched taut between Netsah and Hod, juggled by the Fool, or so some said, and the last outpost, Malkuth, dyed in raven blood, nestling against the jagged table edge where in the winter of 1923 his great-grandfather had snapped his ivory cue. Outside the storm wailed, the sallow flame was smothered by a vast seed-soaked wind, the Hanged Man flew from the Tarot pack into an orange patch of light, mocking, once more, the orgy of presentiment that had engulfed him in these past few months of the trial, the Hanged Man, signifying Adaptability, A Desire to Learn, Violent Change, and Sacrifice. He buried his sooty nails into the crumbling felt, he must pare his being of illogic, that which he had gladly embraced as a sure route to that generous wall of laughter that lay beyond the Professor's eyes, a union of number theory with numerology, the Qabalaic total of the Messiah was after all three fifty-eight, three five eight, falling into that unique class of numbers whose first digit is the subtraction of its second from its third. The Hanged Man, strung from a slim ankle, he flung it through the open window, and the others after it, the Empress, the Magician, the Pope, and the Fool, flying out they fell upon the wet washing, flapping in the rain, sticking to the stucco petticoats, the cuffless shirts. But the desire to be free of premonition still vied with the bitter ease, the tantalising dignity of submitting to destiny, that small hollow voice that has refused to desert him since, never ceasing to seduce with the dark beauty of doom, the small voice that murmured this morning, as he woke to your dream-swollen lips upon his arm, the quiet blood web that coursed between the sinuses of sleep, and whispered, this is the last day of your youth, Jon Sparrow, use it well.

Use it to violate, once and for all, the circles of fate that settled within you, ten years ago, with the ripping of the candles from the musty felt, ragged fluff gaping at the ten empty nodes of Sefiroth, the wind raised the row of dusty wicks that hung over the kerosene burner, the twisted candle moulds, the bruised beeswax and the tallow, nasturtium oil and bootpolish. He had lifted the small mottled skull that rested on the deathline between Geburah and Hesed and brought it down upon the row of bottles, festering frogspawn and tincture of iodine, mustard seed and mercury, oyster sauce and antimony, crushed and mingled under the blows of Uncle Fred's cranium. Uncle Fred had not been for sale, so the lady at Rosemary's Mystery and Imagination Store in Herrin had said, but he had slipped a hand under her leather miniskirt, and stayed for a cup of ginger tea, emerging finally with Uncle Fred in a velvet shoebag (and a pack of dead kobolds to grind into the setting wax). With Uncle Fred's trusty occiput he had smashed the remains of his mockery of fate, for fate had appeared not garlanded in the thick mirth of sorcery, but as cold thin steel, binding the inexorable permutations of a vowelless alphabet into grim metaphor. He had trifled with chance, and chance had got the better of him. Ten years ago, he had surrendered with dignity to the idiocy of destiny, the fetters of prescience tightened slowly about his being, that today he is finally about to cast away, the inevitable circle that he has already distorted by refusing to cross the Atlantic, refusing to complete the final arc, he sits up and shakes off the dead grass, a rotting playing card has stuck to the sheepskin, he flips it over, it is the Nine of Spades, reputably the most ominous of the minor arcana.

To reassure himself, he recovers, from within his duffel bag, his travel journal, turns once more to the last page, where, last night, he has made the last entry, this design that he has violated by extending his journey beyond the compass of its thin-lined pages, there can be no doubt, the lead had broken upon the very last punctuation mark, there is no denying that he has, at the very least, destroyed the correspondence between journal and reality, a conformity that had pandered so shamelessly to the principle of order, the essence of fate, and yet the cloth binding creases suddenly to reveal a butterfly of virgin page, ignored in his haste to record the boisterous response of the rabbit, Andropov, to the allegation that his species might swim, but climbed indifferently, what if it were true, he muses, that the creature understood our every word, if he has been bestowed with an intelligence equal, and perhaps more, to that of any man, what if he has, by resting next to an open book, imbibed much of the Roman alphabet, the numbers, simple arithmetic processes, even differential calculus, the possibilities were endless, and the muteness sublime, he grabs for a pen, and begins to write upon the open empty page,

*There were days when he could hardly rise for the weight of the words, the dry swarm of words knocking against the inadequate geometry of his skull. He would sit and sulk by his basket, greedily*

*eyeing the shelves of books where he might have found comfort, if no one would scream and rush to rip the volume from his eager jaws, the moment they closed about the binding. And even if he should succeed in extricating a volume of choice from the tightly packed row, there was still the problem of turning the pages with his manicured claws, not to mention the embarrassment of being found in that condition, one of the servants had fainted once upon surprising him playing a few simple bars on the piano, it was an indiscretion on his part, the family were out, and he could not resist trying out a few notes from the score that lay open upon the music stand, had been there now for several weeks, while the clumsy youngest daughter, ten-fingered though she was, failed to master the succession, he had not been able to resist standing upon his hind legs and quietly in tipping the keyboard cover* (by now Sparrow had decided it would have to be a dog rather than a rabbit, a rabbit was definitely pushing it), *and – the raised black keys were no problem, the sunken keys however were definitely not designed for canine comfort – the maid had tiptoed in fearfully, expecting a ghost, and apparently what she had found was far less kind to her nerves, she who had wiped enough sheaves of HMV records to have become familiar with the faithful ancestor that attended at the curled lips of the absurd gramophone, why should his attempts to play the blessed instrument precipitate such cognitive dissonance, of course no one believed her, least of all she, herself...*

He breaks off, consumed suddenly by an aching resonance with the tragedy of his own childhood, the beloved books that his father would knock from his hands with a swipe of his hairy ogre-fingers, let's go shoot some hoops, he would bellow, I don't want no kid of mine to be a fairy bookworm, c'mon, let's get some air, he would shout, home on leave from Vietnam, why's he look so green, Alice, he would accuse his wife, he never returned from the war, not even in a body bag, Sparrow will never forgive him the tawdry enigma of his disappearance, although it has spared him a lifetime of derision. Jesus, he's reading poetry, he's a fucking freak, Alice, living with women has turned my boy into a freak, ogre-breath streaked with sour mix whistles against the child Sparrow's cheeks, his father tears the book from his hands, *Peacock Pie*, A Book of Rhymes, by Walter De la Mare, Dewey decimals faded on the spine, he begins to read in high-pitched mimicking tones, '"Come!!" said old Shellover, "What?" says Creep. The horny old Gardener's fast asleep.' What is this shit, he exclaims, some goddamn French faggot, I take it, this De la Mare, he flings the book across the floor, *Peacock Pie*, it spins humbly on the linoleum. *Peacock Pie*, he found a copy, riddled by silverfish, on a shelf beneath the broad window of your room in Calcutta, kneeling to unfasten the shutters following an afternoon of rain, he had found himself rummaging through the limbless residues of your abandoned book collection, hiding in the dark recesses of these wall-thick window shelves. *Peacock Pie* he found with its covers missing, several Enid Blyton hand-me-downs sporting tall columns of scratched-out names of previous owners, a French dictionary: school prize for proficiency in a foreign language, *A Brave New World* in paperback, Henry Miller's *Plexus*, ears cuffed, Sparrow thumbed his way through a forest of faded fiction, then lingered upon a peeling flank of natural history, *Guide to Mammals of Britain and Europe*, its spine severed. In his hands it fell neatly into halves, he read an underlined paragraph: *can swim but climbs indifferently*, the rabbit, Andropov, uncurling from his afternoon siesta, stretched open his jaws in long, silent yawn, *can swim but climbs indifferently*, Sparrow read aloud for his pleasure. The rabbit. Andropov shook his whiskers violently and charged for Sparrow's ankle, Sparrow brought the book down as a shield against the sharp, eager teeth. Confused, the rabbit retired to his nook, and Sparrow replaced the book between two crumbling botany texts. Could it be possible, then, that a creature might be born, a rabbit or a dog, better a dog, equipped with the intelligence to comprehend all, but with no means of expression, was it possible? Not that realism was the issue, realism Sparrow has always steered clear of, in art and in life. He looks upon the journal page that he has half filled with his story, and acknowledges, in a sudden stab of incomprehensible emotion, that it is the first time he has written anything since he had abandoned, in disgust, a witty couplet with which he had hoped to charm his mother, thanking her for the typewriter she had sent him as a high-school graduation present. Momentarily euphoric, he had sat down with the new machine, intending to stun her with a coruscating epigram, one in which his resentment would sidle alongside his gratitude, for she had added in her letter, that, to her deep regret, she would not be able to come up for his graduation, your momma'll be weeping buckets, she had assured him, as if it meant anything to him anyway, his high-school graduation, he had attended only for the sake of his grandparents, marched with a carrot-haired cheerleader up the long aisle, delivered the salutatory speech in his own subversive Latin, his grandparents had been proud, why had he never brought her home, they asked of the carrot-head, who clung to Sparrow with such sweet devotion, I only had her once, he longed to say to them, in the Marshall Fields parking lot, no attachments formed on my part.

# IV

# *Luxuries of Fate*

His fingers, clenched white upon the fountain basin, seem to fuse, in colour and texture, with the stone. You turn to Daniel, he is gazing absently towards the Admiralty Arch, you could have been, you think, the two of you, in an earlier time, not too far into the past, just after the War perhaps, you would not be you, but some suburban sweetheart, flowers in your hat, and he would be he, perhaps in his worn Sunday best, nervously twirling his hat in his hands. You have never lost your taste for fantasy, the desperate desire to intercede in the fairy-tales that had gilded your lonely childhood, calling for you to whisper the secret of the treasure into the handsome adventurer's ear, to hold back the golden-haired maiden from the call of the goblins, to urge the Hamlyn councilmen to pay the Pied Piper, how you longed to share their world. Many years ago, while wandering with your father in the mildewed bowels of a Welsh castle, you had found a handkerchief which you have been sure was the same as that which an English child, the Boy who became a Baron, then a Spaniard's slave, had found in the roots of a yew tree, a tree that grieved, like him, for England. Spreading the magic handkerchief on the ground, the first thing, the boy, Harry was his name, had asked for was a glass of English water. You had been sure that the tattered rag you had found was the very same, secreted by Harry in the Edwardian dungeon, so that you might find it, when the time came, oh, the desire for destiny still runs strong in you, and you cannot help feel that the eyes that fall fondly across the pigeon-thick square to the child, encased in pigeon swirl, that these eyes were made for your pleasure alone, that the only purpose of Daniel's insular being is to have illumined your senses for a few hours, why else, after all, would the creator have bestowed, upon these insignificant lips, such richness of smile?

Erika, your father's German tutor, whose car had brought you to the handsome ruin, had made you throw away the handkerchief at once, but not before you had had a chance to make one wish, spreading the tortured rag upon the ragged green, you had wished among the sheep droppings that your cousin Avishek would come to spend his Easter holidays with you and your father, rather than go home to his parents in Africa. And so he did, waking you one morning with war whoops, once again he was to share your tiny blue room in the university flat in Griffin Close. For a month he would displace you from the upper bunk, litter the sill with Matchbox cars, paint moustaches on your dolls, leave thick purple bruises on your arms from sudden scorpion pinches he inflicted upon you, but he would also bring your cereal, in the morning, while you were still in bed, and eat with you, occasionally pinching your toes through the blanket, and then the day would begin. If your father was home, you would venture into the windy spring, and trek across Africa in the grounds of the manor that lay beyond the stream, search the source of the Nile under daffodil banks, you, the flamboyant Burton, and he, the successful Speke, back for fishfingers and baked beans at noon. Your father would tell you stories, stories of great men and their great deeds, stories of civilizations, long faded, stories of people whose history the world no longer cared to know, or stories simply of how it had been when you were both very young and you all lived in Calcutta, or even before, before you were born, how it was during the war, when he was a child, how in the middle of it all, one morning the poet, Tagore, had died, and they had been ordered, at school, to go quietly back home. And even then, even then, there was already a hint of indifference, of irritation, in the way he answered Avishek's eager questions, his dead wife's sister's child, thrust upon him by thrifty parents, the eager child whom he would come to despise later, as the worthless youth who had dragged cheap doom into the clear corridors of his home. He would brush aside his excited queries with a coldness that would run faint glass needles into your child mind, even though the boy remained blissfully unaware of this gossamer tension. Afternoons you spent, for the most part, at home, for your father would leave, with strict instructions not to open the door, not to anyone, and even if he did not leave, the blue skies of the morning were sure to turn dull, dark drizzle would ruin the promise of conquering the South Pole, in the stillness of rain, you would lie upon your belly and read, while Avishek muttered and buzzed with his aeroplanes, he was to grow up into a pilot, a dream he nourished far beyond childhood, even now the trail of jet smoke will stir sweet despair in his veins, the feeling that a large chunk of his time on earth has passed never sinks so deep as with the whirr of wings in the clear summer air, or that firm arc of jet white against the distant blue.

* * *

Avishek, recoiling in horror from an edentate extrusion of used chewing gum, moulded skillfully into the cusp of pillar and rail, observes that the man has left his perch again, and kneels now beside the boy, who has clearly tripped in bird shit and messed up a knee, now you, too, have risen and are making your way across the square. Boldly Avishek descends (on the stairs, a fleetingly familiar gaunt grey-eyed face, rapidly brushed aside, Sparrow? surely not), and walks across the street, until he stands directly in view of the tableau, the tall stranger squatting to wipe his son's knee with a grubby handkerchief, he cannot see that it is soiled, but he presumes it is in keeping with the rest of his accoutrement, the speckled blue jeans, the scarecrow overcoat that drags now in pigeon dust, besides, you have taken the handkerchief from his hands, and proffer, in its stead, a white tissue from your handbag, it must have been a filthy rag, you are stroking the child's head, who are they, how is it that you are here with this unlikely pair, on this autumn morning, in Trafalgar Square?

* * *

You stroke the child's cheeks and find them strangely dry, indeed the eyes, you bend to examine them, are dry, was he not crying? you ask his father. He has a problem with his tear glands, says Daniel, he doesn't produce tears, not much anyway, enough I suppose to moisten his eyes or whatever. You stare aghast at the desiccation of pain upon the red-rimmed hazel. His mother, Daniel continues, wrote to a magazine when he was little, you know, where they give medical advice, and they said it was nothing. He screws the tissue into a ball and flicks it into a nearby garbage can, trust an agony aunt to trivialise his predicament, a boy who cannot shed tears, you touch his cheek in deep pity, a boy who cannot cry, the poetic possibilities make your head reel.

His father lays a rough-shaven cheek, still wet from fountain spray, against the boy's, rubbing wet stubble against the tips of your fingers, you're all right now, he commands his child. Grazing your nails with his smile, he draws away and straightens himself up. You move your hand, once more, up the child's cheek, specked now in spurious dew, shall we go and get some band-aids, you ask the boy, hoping to entice with the sticky strips that had transformed all childhood trauma into pure delight, scabs you had picked at so that they might, once again, demand protection from the germ-laden air, so that you might pry open the bathroom closet and reach for the magic box, and select among the multitude of shapes and sizes that which most suited your wound, and then the delicious petrification of pulling off a mangy strip, studying the discolouration of the flesh, the faint recalcitrant outlines of adhesive. But the promise of gauze and plaster does not brighten the tearless eyes, the bloodless lips remain pressed together in child grimace. His father, however, declares it an excellent idea, pragmatic Dan, immune to the mutilation of flesh, after day upon day of feeding liver into the yawning jaws of mammoth mincers, cold steel spitting blood upon his narrow jaw, he hums to the familiar rhythm of the cracking of sheep skull, ground with chocolate to feed hungry calves, and when the customer asks for ham, he is there always, before any other, lifting the sweaty mass onto the slicer, standing back to relish the smooth clean strokes of the blade, the pale curls of flesh that unwind onto the glazed paper. He gestures vaguely towards the Haymarket, there should be a chemist's up that way, he says, but really, you must have other things to do, I don't want to waste any more of your time.

His eyes pass over his son, still whimpering softly, under the weight of your hands pressed upon his temples, shall we go and get some band-aids? you ask, ignoring his father's polite protestations. You dare not raise your eyes to Daniel, for fear that the silver noose has slackened, that the precarious divertissement has already played its brief score within his weary veins, you dare not meet his eyes, for fear that they are opaque with farewell, a lead weight that might crush your own effervescence, for your inchoate desire has yet to be manacled in language, no citadel of platitudes guards the moist membranes of your neonate lust, and you know well that what is unspoken is as easily undone. And even so, five years ago, one sunswept afternoon, on the mangy roof terrace above your sister's flat, it was you who had advised her to nourish with silence an inscrutable bond that had grown over the year between herself and a neighbour's son, the lanky youth who read his violently anti-establishment plays to her on sombre afternoons, between the gusty snores of her mother-in-law, floating in from the smaller bedroom, your niece quietly tinkering with her toys. The narrow furrows upon the youth's brow behind cheap foolscap had wakened a disturbing longing in your sister to return to the days of her maidenhood, when she might have had the privilege of returning his bold wet caressing glances, and he, fearless youth, had feasted upon this changing landscape of her dreams behind the peeling shutters of her home. You, he held in shy distrust, he did not much care for your poems, he had told her, the irregular contributions that you continued to make to a certain literary magazine, despite having vowed, a few years ago, never to write again, when in attempting to translate your poems to Avishek, you had met a wall of tender indifference that had frightened you far more than the green doom of your love. You had read to your cousin of the bellies of ants that burst with honey, and he had smiled patiently and suggested a game of caroms, eager only for the thrashing of wood upon wood to weave wild harmonies into your young passion, you told him of the red-bordered past of the young lovers in your poem, how they longed, when their love was dying, to taste of a tree's embrace, and he saw only the black of your eyes, your lips softly moving, and the stream of curious words drenched him in the flavours of sleep, it is odd, he told you, how dreamlike a language sounds when you only half know it, a language I did not know at all would just roll off, like hard pastry, but all these words that I almost understand...

The young woman in your poem is working on a jigsaw puzzle of the *Mona Lisa*, you explained, but a section of the smile has been left behind in Calcutta, this unwholesome tragedy is suddenly unbearable to the youth, who mutters something about cigarettes and leaves, forever, wandering through a field of weeds and flowers, he arrives finally at the rural train station, while his lover waits with his tea, growing colder, and colder...

But even in familiar English, your words are just a shell, they flow past Avishek and beyond him, and he is immersed only in the energy of your emotions, the coils of your hair upon the printed page, bearing your name in strange hieroglyphs, an alphabet that had been coarsely ground and force-fed to him once, and hung undigested somewhere in the narrow alleyways of his subconscious.

A handful of salt, your poem ended in self-conscious tribute to Camus, a handful of salt fills the mouth of the garrulous slave, you would remind him, later, in a letter, the last that he threw, hopelessly, into the fermented jaws of the Atlantic, a handful of salt, he had smiled and brushed his hair back slowly with his fingers, I'm very proud of you, he said, let's have a game of carom. You slipped the yellowing magazine onto the bookshelf, and knelt to rescue the carom board, once more, from its cobwebbed nest under the bed, and rubbing talcum into the pitted wood, you thought bitterly, I will never write again, never.

You tousle the boy's hair, afraid to meet Daniel's eyes, afraid that they are tight with a dead sea salt, as dry as the eyes of his tearless child, words have not enchained your newborn lust, but the silence in which it has blossomed might also betray, games without rules will bleed into the wind, and yet it was you that had urged your sister, five years ago, to contain her passions within a storm layer of silence, that words must on no account give structure to this unholy tryst, for how else would the young playwright continue to fill her afternoons with the endearing discomfort of his polite presence, the youth who had held your poems in such contempt. Last year he came pale to her funeral, and sobbed uncontrollably before the black-and-white enlargement that smiled broad against the chubby white wreaths and the incense sticks. The sandalwood smoke rose astringent to your eyes, you were overcome by a sudden treacherous wave of sleepiness, groped your way in a mist to your bedroom, fell asleep, unawares, woke, suffused with guilt, to the sounds of Alexander's pen, scratching upon yellow foolscap, woke to the low poison of smothered argument as a young cousin pleaded permission to attend a Christmas party. I fell asleep, you said, bitterly, how could I have fallen asleep?

Never mind, he soothed, nobody minded, sleep some more, my love, if it is sleep you need, outside the moon, still swathed in memory of night, twisting her bare shoulders in the afternoon sky, how naked was the flesh of the moon in that pale winter sky, you would think she had dropped her clothes, said Alexander smiling, left them on the threshold of dawn, and now she waits, naked, for the passing of day, waits for the night to grace her open pores, sleep, if you must, my love, sleep.

Daniel, you do not dare meet his eyes, for fear that the shadows will be impatient in their hollows, for fear that your ministrations have come finally to be as lead upon his tongue, you keep your eyes upon the boy, shall we get some band-aids, you ask hopefully, defiantly, and then the firm reassurance of his fingers at your elbows, you turn gratefully to him, trembling imperceptibly. He curls his fingers around your arm, his thumb traces a delicate arc across the inner seam of your sleeve, you are very kind, he says, smiling. His smile is a thin river of breath between chaos and order, a sublime negation of all chance, of all other alternative than to lead him and his son through the crowds, gathering thick now, into the antiseptic confines of an apothecary's lair, to indulge in all manner of cotton wool and swabs and germicidal creams, and perforated plasters by the dozen, and then to muse among the multitude of suggested remedies for one that will sooth the child's burning chest, one that will taste also perhaps of warm log fires and old fruit cake, of grandmothers and ghosts, the beloved linctus of your childhood, you settle finally upon one that claims a traditional recipe, reassured that its principal ingredient is treacle, swallowing a capful, the child makes a face, I'm hungry, he whines.

Well, so am I, you tell him, I know a wonderful sandwich shop, you say, we have to cross to the other side, but the prawn salad and the chicken tikka leave the child cold, you promised we'd go to Burger King, he accuses his father, who ignores him and asks for Brie, without bacon. I'm vegetarian, he tells you, at least, I try to be, he laughs a short laugh, you can have your burger, you tell the child, perhaps we can eat in St James's, it is probably the last bright day of the year, and we should make the most of it.

He holds his son's head firmly, tilting it up so that he may read the tempting menu, his eyes, keen now with some laughing fantasy, are upon you, briefly, then back again to the boy. He kneels to take his trembling order, and again his eyes rise to your face, his smile shifts from the boy into the regions of your delight, can it be, you wonder, that you will spend this afternoon, somewhere, in his arms, how can it be, and why? Surely it will be merely an interlude of soundless, sandful pleasure, a silent desire for revenge grown raw, for last night her face had risen sharply to meet you from the entanglements of a delicious narrative, Erika, your father's German tutor, her face had stared at you through heavy chains in a ship's cabin of stone, as you read to your niece at bedtime, it was her face that a young Dutch maiden assumed – Erika. You read to your niece of the young Woman's love for a sailor, how she sold her soul so that he might live, denizen of a lost sea, she had slept under chains and woken with the tail of a fish. Your niece had not stayed awake to hear the extent of the maiden's predicament, and later the girl had screamed in her sleep, you were in Alexander's study across the hall, and so you had heard her, run to her side, fallen asleep holding her, kissing nightmare from her lids, had she been dreaming of a girl, smothered under a pile of chains, woken screaming, who would have heard her scream if we had not been up there, Sparrow had asked you this morning. You had gestured sadly with your hands, and replied that children were always left alone with their nightmares. You, when you were her age, you would wake in terribly guilty sweat from dreams of Erika, you had begun to dream often of his obsession with her, you dreamt that your father wandered through a jungle of mushrooms calling her name, you dreamt that he walked the ocean floor, his hair streaming from his tall forehead, harsh salt bubbles beading upon her name, while you pleaded from the frailty of a rocking dingy above, you pleaded silently with him to return from the translucent depths. From such dreams you would wake with an unfamiliar ink upon your tongue, that you tried quickly to gulp down, chase back into the frightening infinity of your growing subconscious, what other snakes dwell there, you had wondered, nine years old, shivering quietly in the white summer dawn. You would close your eyes to the obscenity of the stillborn morning and try to conjure your mother, the softness of black that had surely been her hair, the quietness of black that had been her eyes, her smell you felt certain was of mint cake, sweet and cold, your mother of whom you never dreamt, instead you had dreamt of the glass smell of Erika's cheek that she would press against your own every time you met, her pale lashes beating violently upon the fringes of your dream, and your father lost in the firm terraces of her laughter, that only the night before you had heard abbreviated by the soft click of the door lock, your father's footsteps returning, he had watched her from his bedroom window, as always, he had waited until the orange Beetle fretted and fumed its way out of the parking lot, after it had disappeared, your father had studied his hands by the narrow light of the street, and then his face in the window glass, running worried fingers down the tall creases of his forehead, and across the thickness of his chin. It was he who refused to marry her, a year later you heard the door bang forever upon the thin metallic frustration of her sobs, you waited, and then fearfully rose, on the pretext of thirst, to tiptoe past the living room where he sat, your father, in your scrutiny, unperturbed, he sat calmly watching *Brighton Rock* on television, did Erika wake you, he asked? Why was she crying, you asked, reluctantly feigning innocence, why was she crying? I said I wouldn't marry her, he replied after some hesitation, suddenly eager to elevate you into his adult world, and so in a rush came your initiation, unclothed in ritual, naked of sacrament, in that one wind, undecorated came your transition, in one stroke, a new language was born between you and your father, into which sex and death and all other taboo wove with ease, you drew the felt tatters of childhood about you, those that were to fall away now in great rough clumps, now that you had been unceremoniously cast into the heady and precarious state of rulelessness, the first fluted chasms of the glassblower's breath. You sat with your father that night, curled against the sofa in your flannel pyjamas that Erika had bought for you the week before, you sat and watched on television the rabid paroxysms of the young Attenborough, feeling proudly the privilege of sharing his bleak anger, now that you had legitimately toed the territories of adult grief, that stark pain of rejection, which you took then to be a woman's pain, only a woman's pain, that your stony-faced father ignored with such supple unconcern. You think often of how it might have been if he had married her, your father, if your sister had been brought across the seas for the two of you to ripen gradually in the England of the Seventies, how might it have been then, if instead of the diseased neon of Hogg's New Market, the Birmingham Bull Ring had shaped your sartorial imagination, if instead of the fallen arches of the dentist's home (who had bequeathed his house to your school), you had learnt your algebra within the platigrade assemblage of Northfields Comprehensive, and your sister, might she still have been alive today, in Stoke Newington perhaps, changing nappies on a gaggle of half-caste children, progeny of some balding academic, who would have loved her, perhaps. Erika would never have let you stumble so harshly into adult awareness, she would have nursed you within the comforting confines of childhood ritual, she would have shielded you surely from the violence of chance, the intoxication of the aleatory that became the nectar of your existence. That night she left, sobbing wildly, from your life, left you to be rudely pushed across the borders of childhood, she left you to the mercy of a heartening anarchy that you came to recognise as life. The afternoon before, you had walked with Erika in the rolling manor park, a quick frost had frozen the pondskin into a sheet of glass, you and she skipped stones on the floating sheet of clear ice, and a primordial reverberation issued, echoing her desperation, your father would not entertain any commitment, you were glad of this then, a chill gladness in the violence with which her stones skimmed over the transparent surface, later that week you came alone in search of the eerie whalesong of the ice, but it had turned a dull white, as if penetrated by cataract, stones settled with a disappointing thud upon the thickness, the ducks sat disconsolately upon a frozen lip, you fed them the remains of your sandwich, and wondered at the treachery of ice, that only the previous week had yielded such music, and now clung like frozen oatmeal to the grassy shores, utterly unresilient, where before it had stretched smooth, as taut as the colourless pain behind Erika's pale lashes, that pure expanse of pain, eyes that would haunt you forever. Even now it is her face that a trembling Dutchwoman will assume, shivering under a pile of chains in the stone cabin of a ghost ship, the Liar's story that you read last night to your niece, the young Dutch maiden who became a mermaid under a blanket of chains, in strange inversion of the Andersen fairy-tale, she will wander the depths of the ocean, through submarine forests, she will wander with Erika's marble eyes, with her bloodless lips she will tease bubbles of air from her brine prison. And when tonight you resume this strange tale, your niece stirring impatiently under piles of down, your mermaid will be embalmed once more with images of Erika, the fading torture of her presence within your father's dreams. You look through a frieze of noise towards the silent movements of Daniel's lips, as he communes with a lack-lustre McDonald's employee, the boy tugging at his sleeve as he orders his lunch, is it a futile desire for vengeance, grown suddenly sharp, that stills your senses to all but the movement of his lips, or is it that the fulvous contours of his smile are chill with destiny, a Moabite vermilion, that was crushed to dull dust, many years ago, when your father had unshackled you, untimely, from the luxury of fate.

• • •

The ducks, branded, enthralled, totter unsteadily away as you approach with Daniel and his son, he holds your sandwiches and a bottle of Chianti you have picked up along the way, the child clutches an enormous patterned cup and his greasy packet. Avishek, who has purchased, while you were in McDonald's, a newspaper, and several bars of chocolate, takes a bench, in quite dangerous proximity, for the heady experience of having you practically brush past, as you climbed out of Trafalgar Square, half an hour ago, has left him eager to hover once more on the edge of discovery, to lurk in the brighter cone of shadow. Perhaps he has begun to hope that you will spot him, introduce him to your curious companion, the long-limbed man who sits by you, an elbow grazing your arm. You produce a Swiss Army knife from your handbag, he uses it to uncork the bottle, splashes wine upon his hands, he laughs and licks them clean, two McDonald's paper cups emerge from the paper bag, he pours, he raises a toast. Is he your lover, years ago Avishek had asked of Jon Sparrow, is he your lover, then, and you had laughed, there are shades of Sparrow about this youth, the dark hair, gaunt cheeks, deep-set eyes, and the filthy clothes. Is he one of your friends then, this dark stranger, although he certainly lacks the intellectuality that Sparrow exuded, even in his carriage, his presence, irritating as it was, then, so many years ago, a dead spring, and then of course, there is the sickly child, who munches in such terrible haste through his oily burger, who are they, he wonders, where have they come from?

The Chianti drapes like ripped silk upon your tongue, you sip it out of the paper cups, and eat your sandwiches in a silence, so comfortable, that you might as well melt into the trees and the grass, a stoic pelican comes into view, a chunk of Brie escapes Daniel's sandwich, why are you vegetarian? you ask.

He waits to swallow before he answers, it has nothing to do, he says, with how cruel we are to animals, though I have nothing against the bastards.

My friend Jon Sparrow, you tell him, went through a phase where he ate nothing but chick peas, but that was only for a week.

Is this the friend who left for New York this morning? he asked, greedy for the opportunity to mention paradise. What is it like, there, in New York, is it like they say it is?

New York, you say, recovering from the wine's sudden swift back-kick, ties with Calcutta for my second most favourite city in the world.

Calcutta, he echoes, a little perplexed, is that where you come from? New York, new heaven, and Calcutta, synonym for inferno, in his media-configured conscious, I was wondering, he says, where you came from, what is Calcutta like? he asks, casually curious about hell.

Calcutta is like New York, you tell him.

He smiles, taking this astonishing answer in his stride, pours another two glasses, and asks, what is your favourite city, then?

Paris, of course, you tell him, throwing back your head to follow the flight of a drunken gull.

On the verge of his second nervous breakdown, your father took you to Paris, a few weeks before you were to return to the subcontinent, where he thought he might make more progress in writing his thesis, you were eleven and a half, almost, and enjoyed the ferry ride, your father seemed cheerful enough, you reached Paris in the evening, in broad daylight, it was August, and checked into an inexpensive hotel near the Sorbonne, I would like to study here, you told your father, hoping to please, hoping desperately to disperse the faint edges of blue that had begun to close about his tall forehead, as he stood against the tall window, staring down at the throngs of happy strangers, he woke you at dawn, told you to dress, we have to leave, he explained. It was best, he told you, if they took the next flight out of Orly. But what of the return ticket, you asked. That can be returned, he said, irritated at the emergence of your dead mother's thrift within you, he had already booked seats on a flight, hurry, hurry, he urged, outside it was blue, and somehow deathly cold, you found a cab, by noon you were in London again, it was raining.

And what about London? asks Dan, what about London, you are leaning now upon your elbows, he folds himself down beside you, what about London, where does London come on your list?

Years later you would go to Paris on your own, Sparrow had claimed to have found a job at a bookshop in the Latin Quarter, you pictured a small attic room, a shower on the landing, waxed toilet paper, you found your way to the bookshop from the Métro station with the help of a young man who very kindly carried your bags. Jon Sparrow, the cashier shrugged, never heard of him, but an Oriental woman, rushing by with an armful of paperbacks, stopped to tell you, oh yes, he was staying there, you could wait for him upstairs. Upstairs? You were shown a narrow set of stairs that led into a dim landing, bookladen, an ancient refrigerator rattled in a short hallway where there was also a metal sink, a cat was licking the slow drops of water that fell from the faucet, it jumped away as you passed. Jon Sparrow, yes he should be here, assured an old woman perched in lotus position upon a soiled velvet divan, you sat at the window, and waited, studying the cauliflower buttresses of the Notre Dame. People, like scraps of coloured paper, floated pleasantly around you, so where was Sparrow, and where in God's name did he sleep, where was the sweet little attic with its chipped washbasin and faded Toulouse Lautrec posters? When he arrived, it was as you had feared, his bed was the little alcove above the divan in the landing, the gilt-edged loft where the rest of the inmates hid their belongings in the daytime behind greasy green velvet curtains, the nights were a little chilly but he had purloined an airline blanket on his flight across the Atlantic, and that did the trick, and where were you to sleep? you asked petulantly, Sparrow concentrated upon the sunset sky, after a while he said, you can stay with Vladimir, you knew that all along, he added wearily.

London, you say, is in a class of its own, it is a city I would say I both hate and love, if the large part of our relationship were not indifference.

I hate London, he says, but you all do, all of you that crowd into the mangy pubs, every evening, day after day, all of you, that wake and sleep under its shiftless skies, and in the hours that separate waking and returning to sleep, produce, consume, and procreate, produce and procreate less than you consume, as is your wont, you all hate London.

When I get tired of London, I go to Paris, you say.

To your brother-in-law's empty apartment near the Pantheon, a few blocks north of Rue Cujas where your father had dragged you awake, fifteen years ago, to catch the first flight back to London, to leave without so much as a glimpse at the Eiffel Tower or the Louvre, you had wanted so much to be able to complain, like him (for he had been to Paris twice before, for his work, apparently, left you with his supervisor and his wife), about how badly the *Mona Lisa* was housed, instead for years you would swallow when friends and cousins asked, what did you see in Paris, you would squirm and smile, oh, this and that, you would say, the usual things, change the subject, until, suddenly, it became easy to speak of how it had really been, how the anguish of coming so close to seeing Paris, and not seeing Paris, became as romantic as having seen Paris, and your father's lunacy, a marvellous family joke, almost on a par with the story of your absent-minded grandmother whom an aunt had found once at the dinner table distractedly raising the fishcakes that she had meant to feed to her puzzled grandson, to her own oblivious lips, the child gaping beside her.

Vladimir, in your dreams his kisses would taste of cream liqueur, and yet, every night you locked your door before you slept, Sparrow snored on the living room cough, temporarily released, at your insistence, from his gilt alcove in the bookshop. Every night, you would return to the flat after midnight, still refreshed, and play Trivial Pursuit until dawn, Sparrow would begin to fade, and Vladimir would rise with you, you might talk for a while, at the door to your room, and then you would smile and yawn, inside you turned the key always in the lock, and yet you would dream in delicious detail of his kisses, and you would wake warm to his smile, proud of his strong shoulders under his thin bathrobe as he poured coffee into your mug. Yet as the day grew, you would harden, until the night, slamming wedges into your Trivial Pursuit chip, you would feel not the slightest trace of desire. By the last evening he had given up, when you woke at noon he had gone, leaving a note that he would be back late, and this put you in a fearfully bad mood, you returned early with Sparrow to the flat, it was empty, stop mooching, said Sparrow, what do you want from him, it's your own bloody fault. It's not him, you lied, I just feel apprehensive, somehow, about going home, and so all night you lay, horribly awake, waiting for his sounds, and when they came, they were wreathed, as you had half expected, in a woman's laughter. In an hour it would be time for you to leave for the airport, you surrendered to insomnia, and unpacking your toiletries, padded your way to the bathroom where you took a long hot shower that left a tin taste of unsleep upon your tongue, you scrubbed your face with Vladimir's mother's Japanese course clay until it flamed red, brushed your teeth vigorously and flossed with both waxed and unwaxed tape, and then retired once more to your clammy chamber to await the dawn. You dragged your bags into the living room, Sparrow would not wake, mumbled farewell and buried his face into the candystripe cushions. You stood for a while in the darkness, and then, upon a windy impulse, tiptoed back and knocked upon Vladimir's door, without waiting for an answer you pushed it open, and treaded across to his bed, leaned over the bare back of the sleeping woman at his side, and kissed his flabbergasted cheeks, thanks for everything, you said, and emerged triumphant, ready to return, for a second summer, to the city of your birth, which you were determined, more than ever, finally to come to know.

That summer, you wandered, armed with your black-and-orange umbrella, you scoured the city for all that had been hidden to you, returned always disappointed, seeking comfort in sleep, only to be mocked by dreams of Vladimir, dreams of his kisses, stiff as beaten sugar. All summer you dreamt of Vladimir, when you returned to university that fall, he was waiting, by the mailboxes, standing there as if he had been waiting all summer, waiting for you to come and check your mail, you unlocked your new mailbox, stuffed with summer mail, trembling suddenly as his eyes came to rest upon the blind movements of your lips, he came nearer, you stood petrified and with his arm around your shoulders, he led you away from a disgruntled Sparrow, still fiddling with his mailbox lock, led you in a trance outside into the green fields, clotted with freshmen. Later you found Sparrow, buried in the bowels of the library, this is a ridiculous passion, he told you, it can only be short-lived, you will soon tire of him, Sparrow presaged, you will soon tire of this mindless lust, and indeed you had, but you have never stopped dreaming of Vladimir, sipping slowly of the overwhelming memory of his love, a deep dark liqueur still lingers at the base of your tongue, and rises, sometimes to drench your senses, in the thickets of sleep, you wake, suffused with guilt, and reach for the shadow at your side, and the day will be spent in the heady incense of a mellow and incorporeal reverberation, ironing butterflies.

The child begins to cough once more, spewing bun and burger, which the more intrepid birds dart in to grab, his father turns to him and slaps his back, then holds his tiny chest once more in his broad hands, you rummage among the paper bags for the bottle of cough mixture. The boy begins to whine, but with a gentle pinch on the nose, his father tips a goodly amount of the medicine between his parted lips. Gasping for breath, when released from his ignominious posture, the boy tries defiantly to spit out the mixture, but it has already been swallowed, he raises his raw, tearless eyes to his father in angry despair. Daniel laughs and ruffles his hair, bet you feel better now, finish your burger then, before the birds get it.

Avishek, munching his way through a packet of surprisingly moreish Maltesers, begins to feel the first thin threads of boredom, of unfulfilment in lurking in the shadow of this mysterious configuration. He starts to wonder whether it is time now to burst in upon you, what a surprise, bumping into you like this, or perhaps it is best that he relinquish the fading pleasure of following you and the unlikely pair until you can be followed no more, until the London masses rise to engulf you, or a sudden treacherous sinew of traffic muddies the spoor, or a quiet curve of empty street even, but as he makes to rise, he is frozen by a bold sweep of the dark stranger's hand, lifting the bottle from between himself and you, to place the obstruction behind him on a precarious tuft of wild weed, the hand returns to the regions of your being, obscured from Avishek by a withered oak branch. He edges along the bench to free himself from the diffracting veil of rotting leaf, and suddenly his heel hits against a soft mass, he reaches down to investigate, it is a mildewed tennis ball, mottled yellow green, he kicks it back under the bench.

You swill the remains of ruby ragwater in your paper cup, a blood-thin drop bloats upon the corner of his lips, catches a sudden flicker of sunshine, a dim capacity for wings degrades your sparkling lust, the old rule trembles, it is in the fields of war-strewn rubble that you are wandering, my love, not a broad riverbend of daisies, a buttercup struggles from under shards of glass, more yellow than a growth of daffodils against fresh green, more yellow than the maleficence of an aimless light, you press your palms upon the knotty oak roots, the grass rises in fierce abbreviation between your fingers, he takes the bottle and swings it in a compelling arc, out of your view, his arm returns, an ominous thickness of shade, it relieves the other of the weight of his chin, so that it may roam free, towards the taut reaches of your consciousness, you let your own arms fall, your head slides onto a burst cushion of leaf, you are consumed by the stealth of his fingers, creeping upon the meanderings of your hair.

The bottle sits behind him, still a quarter full, the bottle, green as mallard wing, he has moved it behind him, the space between you is unobstructed now, his smile will overflow into the crevices barred to his flesh. Avishek watches you, you lie on your back now, staring into the towering cathedral of dying leaves. The stranger is on his side, edging closer, and the boy, staring dully out at the lake, sucking on his exhausted milkshake, and between the man and the boy, the bottle of wine, not empty, not yet, Avishek thinks it is in a nice line from the oak, a gentle spin is all it would take, he searches with his feet under the bench for the ball he has kicked away, the problem of cover still exists of course, but meanwhile, your hair, swelling upon scattered leafpile, begins to flow towards the stranger's fingers, arched upon dead grass, his long fingers seize upon a voluptuous curve of black, and founder within the ripples, the strangulations of crisp leaf.

The ball, which Avishek gingerly extricates, is still light and dry, even though a moraine of spores had accumulated along the trough that divides the green Yin from the yellow Yang, he looks across at you, the stranger's fingers thick in your hair, the temptation is desperate, but the circumstances impossible, he balances the ball upon his palm, lets it roll to the edge of his fingers, catches it again before it falls to the ground.

Spare some change, mister? Startled he turns to face a young girl in an enormous sweatshirt, the oversize sleeves that engulf her hands hanging over the bench like lifeless limbs, give us some change then, mister, the fingers inside the sleeves drew in the soiled cuffs, she sucks the frayed neck, distorting the insignia of the Royal Entomological Society that flaps across her chest. I'll give you a pound, he says, recklessly, if you throw this ball at that bottle, see that man over there, next to the boy, there's a pound in it for you if you can aim it so that it spills onto the man.

A tenner, she says, still chewing on the neck of her shirt, peering through the trees at the improbable tableau.

I'll give you five pounds, he says, but only if you aim right, I'll be there, he gestured towards the water, watching you, and wait till they leave before you come for the money.

A tenner, she insists.

Five, and wait till I've positioned myself before you throw.

She shrugs, is this some practical joke then, she asks, through the ribbed cotton.

He reaches for his wallet, and extracts a five-pound note, waves it at her as he rises, of course, it's a joke, he says, digging into his pocket, here's a pound, for good luck.

She grins, letting the chewed collar fall, a nail-bitten hand emerges from within the sleeve, he hands over the ball, and don't hit the kid, he says, whatever you do, don't hit the boy.

He keeps turning back to check that she has not moved, as he makes his way to the water's edge, he crosses the bridge to the other side. The girl is still there, he leans upon a rail and waits while she moves off the bench, juggling the ball, a flock of geese wander past, gaggle, gaggle, he remembers, a gaggle of geese, and a pride of lions, his mother gave him lessons under the bougainvillaea bushes, before he was sent off to boarding school, a gaggle of geese, the girl is tensing herself for the deed, he can sense it, and indeed, with a sudden flick of her wrist, she sends the ball flying, it makes its mark, the bottle topples, but not against the man, the bottle falls like a proud soldier, and drenches the boy.

He stands frozen with fear as the girl rushes towards you, evidently distressed, apologising, using her long sleeves to soak up the wetness from the seat of the boy's jeans. Avishek grips the pond rails, petrified, ready to run if you should turn your eyes across the water, but you are occupied with the child, and generally more amused, it seems from this distance, rather than disturbed by the accident. The girl stands helpless, ignored, as you gather the detritus of your meal, and leave, she stands there, under the great tree, almost as if humiliated somehow, and continues to stand there, looking at the ground, perhaps she is wondering whether she can claim her money, he rushes back across the bridge, and picks his way through the fowl excrement to where she stands, where, minutes before, you had been rapt in dense and indecorous lust, she stands, groping with her lower lip for the spit-soaked collar of her sweatshirt as he approaches, she sees him and shrugs silently, he holds out the five pounds. I feel rotten she says pocketing the note, I feel really rotten, she says, about doing that to the kid.

Never mind, he says, at least you didn't hit him on the head. It's my fault, it was my stupid idea.

It wasn't a very funny joke, she says, although they found plenty to laugh at, don't see how, poor kid, who is she anyway, your wife?

She's my sister, he says, do you know, he asks eagerly, where they have gone now?

Yeah, she names a department store, your sister offered to buy the kid some new clothes, seeing as they're all wet now.

He hands her another pound, you're marvellous, he tells her, I don't know what I would have done without you.

She does not acknowledge the compliment, continues to kick at the goose droppings, and stoops suddenly to recover the ball, offers it to him, no you keep that, he tells her, eager to leave but not without seeing her satisfied.

Well, I certainly don't want it, she says, flinging it hard and high, it drops behind the nape of a tall elm, well, that's certainly bound to concuss someone, he says cheerfully.

[illegible] the past [illegible]

[illegible]

[illegible] suppose [illegible]

[illegible]

"Yes," he [illegible] you, insisted [illegible] to-day [illegible] new clothes [illegible] her [illegible]

He laughed [illegible] good [illegible] I would have done without you."

[illegible] and [illegible]

[illegible] without seeming [illegible] failed."

"Well, I certainly don't want it," [illegible] behind the [illegible] with that [illegible] bound to [illegible] one, he said cheerfully.

# V

# *Unvowelled Evil*

Sparrow, suddenly stabbed in the shoulder by an intrepid Pinkfoot, turns around to confront the bird, and catches on his left ear the full impact of a mouldy tennis ball, momentarily torn between the two interlopers, he decides there is more satisfaction to be had in avenging himself upon the goose rather than the inanimate tennis ball, but by then the creature has merged into a gaggle of conspecifics, like a leaf among leaves, it has found the most basic of camouflage. He could strangle any one of them, of course, as an example to the tribe, if he could make space for it in his duffel bag, it might even be supper, could one, then, survive indefinitely upon the rinds of a developed economy, the disguised surplus, park fowl and hedge berries, roadside nasturtiums, could the mind feed forever on the residues of metaphor, the excoriations of desire, the careless odours of moulting nostalgia that had come to him, fever-wet, in the festive streets of Calcutta, where, camera in hand, he had roamed, for three nights and three days, gathering the parings of an orphaned lust, dry as bamboo skin upon his tongue.

If he were to reach surreptitiously for one of the raucous flock, and in the cover of thick oak, wring its ungainly neck, would he be able to later find a quiet spot within the five Underground zones to light a fire and roast it, and what if its flesh were as mordant as its call, the shrill blood of geese that his vampire had feasted upon, in Schleswig-Holstein, when he tired of the buttery lymph of Saxon maidens. On a winter morning, a month after you had met, he had told you, much to your discontent, he told you, that within you, he saw qualities of the undead, of a spirit that had travelled vast lengths of time, accumulating experiences that there was none left to share with, a peripatetic vampire, that is what you might have been if your existence were not governed by ordinary considerations of space and time, and at this you took umbrage, for it was an image that was in conflict with your prevailing compulsion to martyrdom, for it was in the time when you still allowed him to tumble, sleep sodden into your narrow bed, relinquished your covers, and sat up through the night, trimming butterflies, so that he might sleep. You had hoped, then, that life might be one massive orgy of mutual benefaction, you endured without resentment, the terrible coughing fits that his foul cigarette smoke brought on, smiled angelic when he raided your change purse, the hard-earned pennies, when he torched your air fresheners. And yet eventually disgust got the better of your beneficence, one morning you sniffed in your closet and pronounced it a veritable crematorium, banged the doors shut and pronounced a ban on smoking, and soon after, when he climbed between your freshly laundered sheets in his sneakers, you laid down the law that if he was to spend the night in your room, he would have to bring his own sleeping bag. Now in the mockery of your plaster-and-gilt home, once more, you had shed these prohibitions, you had tiptoed in, late at night, to lift his leaden head from the pillow of papers on the desk, and guided him slowly to the cold bed, loosened his trousers, unbuttoned his shirt, your fingers faltering only briefly at the collar, stiff with sleep sweat, drawn the soft quilt over his Bombay sandals without a murmur. Through celluloid stretches of half-consciousness, he had seen you smile happily and reach to wipe the dribble off his chin with ivory lace, soft as spangled seaweed. At breakfast you would deliberately serve him on the most fragile Royal Doulton, you who had trembled if he came within a foot of the hideous porcelain rabbits on your college dresser, you now would have cheerfully made chamberpots of the Jasper and Attic Wedgwood, spittoons of the Spode. Over dinner, you would attempt to seduce with thin stemmed gravy boats, sick-making willow-patterned soup bowls. Handing him the artichoke plates, you would watch hopefully for that gleam in his eye, that had inspired such mirth and loathing, years ago, when he habitually tipped your dinner trays out of the window. You and he had taken to bringing your dinner up into your room, for in spring the dining hall seemed all the more unbearable, until the pile of broken china on the roof below and the nightly sound of breaking plates had drawn the attention of the college proctors, who paid a call, but were thwarted by your angelic countenance, and your timid Oriental manner, left, shaking their heads, perplexed, while, in your bathroom, he stuffed his mouth with toilet paper to stopper his convulsions.

If he were to curl his fingers about the neck of the troubled coot that staggers towards its dumpy mate, if he were to tighten his thumbs upon the seam of black upon black, who would know, who would care, but it is an old idea, this, an old fascination for the margins of space, time and emotion, an old reluctance to contribute to the workings of the world economy that had driven him and Vladimir to try and carve their way from Paris to Perpignan in Vladimir's father's station wagon, surviving upon the plentiful degustations and the unsuspecting supermarkets. It was a hot August, five years ago, at night they tossed down the back seat and stretched out in the hatch, putting up into driveways, under the lacquered streetlights, Sparrow would watch Vladimir's great shoulders, glistening with perspiration, heave and ripple, and the cold moon that traced the raw curve of his parted lips. In the suburbs of Clermont-Ferrand, he lost his nerve, the neon blue of the miniature golf sign upon the mighty Slavic features, glorious in sleep, left him dry with fear, he spent the night, sweltering in the coccoon of his sleeping bag, drawn tight about his neck, and the following morning, he left him lathered in the unlit bathroom of a petrol station, left him raising the razor to the majestic curve of his underjaw. Outside he convinced a young woman in a green Deux Chevaux to give him a lift back to Paris, and looking over his shoulder, saw Vladimir emerge, towel slung around his thick neck, still unruffled. Two days later, he strolled into Shakespeare & Co., knocked the pot of yoghurt from Sparrow's hands, his lunch, and demanded, dude, I mean, what the fuck? Sparrow bent down to retrieve his yoghurt, wondering why he had been driven to such rare madness by this insipid immigrant. Anyway, Vladimir continued, I met these amazing Bavarian girls, they hitched a ride in with me, they're staying at the flat, look, man, you can sack out in the living room now that mom's gone, I mean this place is a total dump . . .

Sparrow declined with a resolute shake of his head that shook bookdust into his yoghurt.

Suit yourself, fuckhead, Vladimir ducked his way down the stairs. A week later, after he had hauled Sparrow out of jail, they walked in early morning silence down the river, Vladimir reached out to steady the shaken Sparrow, and the iron of his arm against his back only unchained a curious sadness, a formless nostalgia that sank into the morning mist, unsavoured, dude, you must be starving, Vladimir said, steering him to a nearby café.

Sparrow ate a large omelette, while Vladimir drank four cups of coffee and scoured the *Wall Street Journal* for news of his father's yacht. When his plate was empty, Sparrow raised his eyes to the pale high forehead behind the rampart of newsprint, and said, I'd like another.

A shrill breeze lifted a few strands of black hair that fell with painful slowness over Vladimir's eyes, and the rasp of the green brooms upon the sidewalks began to snowball into a chorus of scratched slate, the second omelette arrived, thick with mushrooms, a woman flung a pail of water into the gutter, and Sparrow brought up the devastation of his first meal, largely undigested.

In the cramped washroom, Vladimir struggled to shove Sparrow's head under the faucet but soon surrendered and commanded him to go ahead and wash his bloody face in whatever way he could, he paid the unsympathetic waiter twice the bill, and guided Sparrow out into the sticky morning sunlight, they sat on a bench by the river while Vladimir finished reading the paper, finally he folded it up and said to the vomit-speckled Sparrow, you should go home, man, you really should.

But it's just a week till when school starts, Sparrow protested, I can't go all the way to my grandparents' just for one fucking week.

Then go stay with my mother in New York, he suggested, she's still angsting over that Yugoslavian poet, so she'll probably love company.

Indeed, the week that followed was one of long late breakfasts that stretched into lunch, while Sparrow munched his way through the plover's eggs and prosciutto, the candied eels and Catalan caviar, Vladimir's mother would lift her long legs across the monkeyskin drums, and endlessly ply him with tales of misery, of the cruel Yugoslavian poet who treated her so badly. If the doorbell rang she would jump, bringing her heels down hard upon the monkeyskin, she was less anxious about phone calls, perhaps because they came so often, and were normally dealt with by the maid. During that week the Yugoslavian only showed up once, and then spent the whole time watching MTV and chewing cinnamon, while she fidgetted behind dark glasses which she had donned to hide an imagined epidemic of crow's feet, but every evening she would disappear into the wide city, perhaps in search of him, leaving Sparrow to his own devices. He dared not, somehow, emerge from the flat, the first two nights were miserable, the white walls, mainly unadorned, seemed to enclose the relentless silence of his suburban childhood, he drank a lot of vodka and flipped through masses of family albums, little Vladimir in sailor suits, watched some irritating television, and fell finally into a strong flat slumber that pinned him down onto the bed despite a gnawing hunger that would begin to tear through towards dawn. On the third night, however, he drank a few vodkas and began to feel better, well enough to settle down with a book, and the evening passed pleasantly, nibbling on Camembert and crackers, the same Vivaldi tape playing itself over and over while he read, by the end of the week he had achieved an unfamiliar peace, which he attributed to age.

And today if he had not courted this pretty defiance of destiny that has brought him, dinnerless, to St James's Park, he might have been once more within those bare walls, jetlagged, stiff-jowled, answering in cryptic monosyllables the questions that Vladimir might throw at him between tortured push-ups, can't believe she's still married to that fucking Eye-ranian, is she happy?

The ball, permanently denatured, huddles among the small change on the broad lip of his knapsack. Sparrow picks it up and grips it firmly, as if there is some message to be deciphered in its pappy texture. He weighs the much abused object carefully, and his fingers curve once more along the rotting clefts to seize it and toss it into the air, and then intercept its graceless submission to forces beyond its ken, the desperate blind descent. He had been a juggler, once, proud prestidigitator, when the permutation of the abstract had become too heavy a burden, he had turned to juggling objects rather than words. His mind had once been a fairground of images, but now only his grandmother's crockery stood in awe of his nimble manipulations, as he perfected the art in the summer before college, he was a natural, the neighbours proclaimed. And although he had refused to join the University Jugglers, scorning their tawdry exhibitionism (juggling was an intensely personal activity, he maintained), his talents had gone a long way towards procuring his fare to England, the following spring, for you had spotted, under the gym arch, a desperate call for jugglers and country wenches, for the Faculty Medieval Feast – no experience necessary – and so, one sunny afternoon he had borrowed your lavender spandex tights and your Kashmiri tunic, while you knotted a fruity pillowcase about your waist with suitcase string, and together you had walked through the grimy slush to the Faculty Club. All evening he had watched you curtsey and bob and spill tureens of cockaleekie soup on the red camaca, while he juggled glass pheasants and wooden geese and then the spicy carcasses of lesser fowl, as a food fight erupted, and jugs of hare began to fly from one corner of the room to the other, he caught them high in the air and balanced them upon his cheesy forehead, and you darted to and fro with steaming copper kettles of coarse cider, plates of toasted peacock paws, he tossed gilt peppercorns into the air and caught them all again between his broken teeth. He imagined a cageful of canaries, released into the pandemonium, wrapping around the proceedings like a long perforated yellow scream. Finally, when the last of the faculty had staggered away, stupefied with unfamiliar liquor and bespattered with offal, you had all assembled, serf-like, the serving wenches and the footmen, the sword swallowers and the madrigal singers, and he, the solitary Fool, solemn jester, you had gathered in the bowels of the great house and consumed, without restraint, the remains of the feast, washed down the game and the gammon with tankards of frothy ale, and then, sated and spent, belching acrid anagrams, you had wandered back through the melting snow. In the darkness, he had wept, as he had never wept before, or ever again, in your presence. He had sobbed and confessed that he had been terrified, all evening, by his mounting indifference towards reclaiming what he had thrown into the dazzling light of the chandeliers, become increasingly reluctant to perform his pathetic contortions in pretty defiance of gravity and only the coarse titillations of the crowds had drowned his growing disgust, smothered his indifference with a shock of imagined canaries, grateful residue of a sentimental education. Between tennis courts bleeding sludge, he had fallen on his lavender knees and sworn never to juggle again, except with your porcelain rabbits, which was an act of pure affection, he hastened to add. You had murmured sympathy, but his outburst seemed to have embarrassed you, he rose and turned towards the streaky dawn, kicked a lingering clump of snow high into the air. Here's to bonny England, he said, to the Ides of March and fair England, Ides of Charm and nobby England, land of corked tongues and Cornish cream teas, calendar Caravaggios and carnivorous coots ... an edgy specimen of the same has crept upon his diet Coke, he flings the ball at its armoured forehead, it misses, rolls away and falls into the pond.

* * *

Hookahface Greedyguts stops at three degrees past midnight, and falls rudely to the bottom of his crenellated dungeon, while your neice still peers anxiously through the lollipop glass of the drier. Last night, Sparrow had absentmindedly used the old teddy to mop up a spillage of the King's Ginger Liqueur, and so he has spent the better part of the day soaking in limejuice, and the maid, before she left, had popped him in the cavernous drier –

this has not been the worst of his tribulations, your niece concedes, besides, it is true, she too, sometimes, has felt the urge to crawl in among the pile of warm clothes, and see what it might be like, to spin, spin within the restless coccoon in spineless harmony with the murmuring bedclothes, to be swilled within that giantmouth, as was Hookahface, now. Hookahface Greedyguts, named after the two-tailed character in the nonsense rhyme, that hapless glumface who spent his days in tortured indecision over which of his tails to use to swat the fly that might land on the very centre of his back. Old Hookahface has been spinning helplessly within his scorching jail, pleading with his one eye, the other having been plucked, untimely, by the cruel rabbit, Andropov. With a hard pinch on the rabbit's jaw you had extracted the eye from the flowery folds of his mouth, but you have never glued it back on, as you had promised then, it still rests in Rima's pencil box, among the butterfly ends and the cigarette foils, the solitary eye. Hookahface Greedyguts comes to a rude halt in half-spin, plops to the bottom of the drier, Rima presses the catch, gingerly reaches in, Greedyguts is terribly hot to the touch, the brass studs in his trousers positively burn her fingers. Bravely, she pulls him out, he has not met her new bear, Sparrow's gift to her this morning, no, Greedyguts has been soaking all morning in raw lime, cheer up, Hookahface, she tells him, rubbing her cheek against his slightly damp hot fur, cheer up, she says in English, cheer up, you have a new friend. She has almost given up speaking Bengali with her toys, so she has heard you mention regretfully to Sparrow, it was something she had not realised, but there was much she had not realised that was becoming clearer and clearer now, especially in the last few months, since her grandfather had left, he had been here for much of the summer, her grandfather, you had marked on her calendar when he would come, a thick red circle around the 7 in June, and later she, herself, had drawn one around the 9 in August though only after he had gone. The day after he left, an odd feeling had come upon her as she gave lessons to her toys, and suddenly the silence had seemed strangely white, she had abandoned the lesson, walked to the window, and leaning upon the ledge, noticed, for the first time in the eight months that she had been there, noticed suddenly how empty was the street, far below, and the desolation of the ragged square, the tired trees. Quickly, she had drawn away and her eyes had fallen upon the calendar on the wall, it was a Garfield calendar that Avishek had brought back for her from America, she didn't much care for it, she had even forgotten to flip it at the end of the previous month. Slowly she took it off the wall and turned the page. August stretched blank, blameless before her, it was already the tenth, yesterday her grandfather had left, she could have marked that, she could still mark it, she snatched the pencil from Hookahface's paw (well not quite, it had been resting, all this while, against his unconcerned shoulder) and drew an unsteady circle about the 9. There, that's done then, she thought, but something about the stark geometry of the rows of weeks still held her, she flipped through the four remaining pages, so this is the rest of the year, the monstrous abstraction suddenly palpable, smooth, cool upon her fingers, the end of the year, always a distant, impossible point in the future, was there now, within the compass of her imagination, and indeed her calculation, and sometime before then, she was to return, for a month, to Calcutta, to her father, and the damp little flat where she had spent the first seven years of her life. She remembered, all at once, the smell of the sun on the peeling shutters as she helped her mother push them open in the dying afternoon, the goblin-faced cat that stood hungrily on the asbestos roof under the kitchen window, waiting for the scraps that the cook would throw her, the fish scales and the stingy offal, she remembered the cemetery of broken dolls and toycarts under her bed, behind the rusty trunk with the moth-balled woollens. She had jumped back from the calendar, as if caught in some terrible act, at the sound of the door, you had entered, your arms full of irises, your favourite flowers.

Holding Hookahface Greedyguts by his mothbitten ears, she creeps out of the laundry room, and tiptoes stealthily down the corridor to the maid's room, it is one of her favourite rooms in this vast house, she likes to sit at the dressing table and watch, through the high window, the lower halves of people as they walk by, the sharp shuffle of the retired men, tapping their canes on the pavement, the short-skirted girls with their blue legs, the resigned dogs that stopped to sniff at the new paint on the railing, once she had been here during a heavy rainstorm, watched in fearful fascination as the rain slashed and spit, at eye level, on the uneven pavement, she had been scared, dived quickly into the maid's arms, who had dropped the sock she had been darning for Sparrow, now look at what you've made me do, she had said good-naturedly.

Rima studies her face in the mirror, is she pretty? everybody tells her so, my god, she's lovely, your friends will say when they see her, lovelier every day, she is pale, she notes, not the colour of the Sri Lankan girl in their class, one of her friend's had pointed this out to her, last week, how come you're not chocolate, she had been asked, how was it she was not the colour of toffee? She had shrugged, somewhat perplexed, and somehow a dim pride had gathered in her, together with a faint disquiet, the same unease that she had felt when their next door neighbour in Calcutta had teased her daughter, you're so dark, no one will marry you, and her own mother had frowned gravely behind the clothesline. Silly cow, she had heard her mother mutter, her teeth gritted around a clothespin, silly old donkey, and the child had rushed behind the billowing saris, to be far far from the wretched notions of the neighbour, lest they should taint her. It was so difficult to tell the good from the bad, the better from the best, what she envied most among grown-ups was this deep secure sense of what to appreciate and what to sneer at, how they would pass judgement with ease upon an afternoon TV film, a pattern of cloth, the face of an actor, the taste of spinach, while she struggled to form an opinion. Her mind, she felt, was like icing sugar, she was always in fear of the shapes it might take.

She clambers onto the dressing table, careful not to upset the pastes and potions, the tree of bracelets, scarlet pincushion puffs, and the brass-framed photographs, she holds Greedyguts up so that he, too, can get a reasonable view of the streets. There are overalled men, trotting to and fro with green garbage cans, a woman carrying a stuffed otter under her arm weaves through them, followed by three pairs of batik leggings, some long African garment of enormous girth (was it a man or a woman? her view stopped at the waist), a man in torn jeans, backpack fronds dangling, two Pomeranians dragging tall stilettos. She sinks back, bored, examines the maid's photographs, she knows them well, the grizzled parents, the solemn-faced brother, his children, her god-daughter, whatever that meant, she is faintly jealous of the chubby child, with her curly black hair, her own hair is dreadfully straight, but they all say it is beautiful that way, what glorious hair, they say, running their fingers through her long ponytail, your fragrant friends. Karin has asked her to be bridesmaid at her wedding, next week, we will put flowers in your hair, she has said, lilies of the valley, I don't care if they are out of season, and you will be the prettiest bridesmaid ever to be seen, said Karin, holding against her neck the almond silk you had chosen for her dress.

She wanders back into the hallway dragging the hapless Hookahface, through frosted glass doors she peers into the cold bareness of the room where your father had spent the summer. His papers lie thick upon the desk, in the corner, by the sharp little window that looks out onto the garden ledge, the subterranean shed where the heavy spades and rakes are kept. In the summer, while he was here, she would come down to watch him work, her grandfather, she would sit quietly at his knee, sucking Hookahface's bow tie, until he demanded a glass of milk, or a water biscuit, and then she would rise, suffused with happiness, rush to the kitchen and carefully pour out a glass of semi-skimmed, add a chocolate digestive, or some savoury morsel left over from lunch, and bring it down to him in his basement sanctuary. Sometimes she caught him in his morning yoga exercises, when he would motion through a tangle of limbs to be silent, or when she descended upon him during an afternoon nap, he would command her to balance upon his rheumatic knees. At night, he would sing to her, in her room, high above, and she knew he sang long after she had fallen asleep, sang late into the evening, at her side, while she slept. And one morning, you had woken her early, pushed her into a pair of dungarees and carried her down into the heavy light, she fell asleep in the car and when she woke, you were on the cross-channel ferry, she could hardly contain her excitement, her first sea voyage, if only Hookahface were there to see! And then that endless length of road, with her grandfather snoring beside her, it was evening when you arrived in Paris, the shady apartment by the Pantheon, where Alexander's mother liked to spend her winters. When she woke, her grandfather was standing at the window, an odd old sadness in his face, Alexander came in, smelling of pine needles, picked her up and tossed her into the air, put on your clothes, he told her, we're going out to get some bread. It was an odd thing, she thought, as she struggled with her turtleneck, it was an odd thing, indeed, for her uncle to want to get bread, not something he would ever do in London. After breakfast, you were off again, and that night was spent among fierce mountains, that swooped insistently upon her dreams, lop-eared, lagoon-lipped, and the day after, the road slipped and curved among the green fangs. Long choking night fell upon her in the tunnel, and then she slept again, until, at long last, you drew up in the narrow driveway of the green-and-white cottage she had inspected so many times in the holiday brochure, Licciana Nardi, in the land of the moon. It was really a holiday she spent with Alexander, for you would leave with your father in the early light of the day to pursue your feverish lust for pyjama-clad cathedrals, bandaged baptistries, while she and he spent the mornings walking to the nearest market to buy cheese and fish. In the afternoons they lazed by the stream at the foot of the orchard, he read and made notes, while she paddled bravely in the cool waters, talking, all the time, to an invisible companion, possibly a large fish by the name of Abdullah. Later, she would help him cook, with the wild rosemary they had picked on their walks, and dried thyme and parsley. You and your father would return, your heads crammed with treasures, to find her laying the table, we had a wonderful day, she would begin excitedly, oh, we had a wonderful time, and your minds still cast in the shadows of stone, you would dismiss her chatterings with a smile, both you and your father, we had a lovely day, she would continue, unperturbed, such a lovely day.

The smell of burning tomatoes comes to her, as she stands, her eyes heavy with small memories, in the small white room where her grandfather had spent his summer, the desk is still heavy with his abandoned papers, the smell of burned tomatoes drifts through the chinks of a summer softly remembered, a rustle among the matte of foliage over the shed roof catches her attention, two wood-pigeons, furiously gobbling berries, their clean white collars bobbing. She climbs carefully onto the table to rest her knees upon the sill, the birds peck away charmingly, their beaks, margarine yellow, clipping deftly across the withered berries. Suddenly, a small crack, like a glass balloon collapsing, and a heavy flutter of wings, one of them flies steeply out of her view, the other lies dead, its coral chest pierced, it has fallen heavily into the small alley between the wall and the shed, it has all happened too quickly, she blinks, trying to cut through the confusion within her, the small filaments of fear, and then the reassuring mossy tones of her uncle's corduroys, he comes swiftly down the steps, sees her in the window and smiles, bends to pick up the dead bird. She slips down from the sill, climbs off the table, and runs upstairs to the kitchen. Alexander is wiping his shoes outside the kitchen door, they're good to eat, he tells her, shaking the dead wood-pigeon, very good to eat, I haven't shot one in a long time, he lays the bird on the kitchen table. The tomatoes are burnt, I suppose, he says, damn the tomatoes, I forgot about them, you don't really want tomatoes, do you? She looks cautiously over the mess of feathers and blood, the bird looks as if it sleeps, hugging its wound. She is overcome by a violent wave of compassion, will we have it for lunch? she asks, unhappily.

Heavens, no, replies Alexander, it's going to be scrambled eggs, I'm afraid. You get to break them.

He lays four eggs out by the dead wood-pigeon, and returns the carton to the fridge. She fetches a mixing bowl from the counter, it is painted with butterflies. Was the other one his wife? she asks, the one that flew away?

Perhaps, says Alexander, but she is glad to be rid of him, for her real love is a very sad king, who lives in an ivory tower by the sea, and feeds her pine kernels and sesame seeds, every evening. He calls her Columbine, which is a very predictable name, but she does not mind. She flies to him every evening, as the sun sets, and stays only until the first stars come out in the night sky.

He lays sausages out under the grill, how many do you want, two or three?

Three, she says, racking her brains for questions to ask about the sad king, she does not want the story to end, why is he sad? she asks finally.

The king? Because once he was a great king, and ruled over a vast land full of white roses, and now he must spend his days in a salty tower, with no one to talk to, but the sea. Besides, he is in love with a wood-pigeon, and that would make anyone sad, let alone a great king, who was born to be sad. In the winter, it is cold, the sea is grey, and the harsh salty wind blows in through the cracks in the ivory, and still he leaves a little skylight open, so that his love may come, and he will feed her rowanberries, and semolina pudding.

Semolina pudding! she cries, disturbed by the sudden intrusion of the prosaic.

Semolina pudding. Of course. She loves semolina pudding. The king orders it for lunch every day, so he can save some for her, she sits on his fingers and picks it off his palm, oh he loves her so much, does the king.

She brings the bowl of beaten eggs to him, he melts butter in a pan, bring me the salt, he commands.

And then? she demands, handing over the shakers.

And then, nothing. That's just the way it is, he languishes in his tower by the sea, and she flies to him, every evening, carrying scraps of newspaper in her beak, whatever she can find, he pastes it all in a scrapbook that he keeps hidden from his captors.

He lifts the pan off the hob and carries it to the table. She rummages in the cutlery drawer for her special fork, one of its tines is crooked, like a double-jointed finger. She has lost interest in the story, it is obviously going nowhere, many of his stories are like that, she prefers your stories, even though the rabbit, Andropov, tends to creep in, thinly veiled as a cat perhaps, always to the rescue, the intrepid rabbit, Andropov. So they eat in silence, Alexander leafing worriedly through a thick journal, and she coaxing Hookahface Greedyguts to live up to his patronymic and share her wholesome meal. The kitchen clock says a quarter to one, there are still at least three long hours to go, three interminable hours before the birthday party. She notices that Alexander is flipping backwards through the journal, and laughs out loud, why are you reading from back to front, she asks.

Many languages are read that way, her uncle answers, Hebrew, for instance, is read from right to left, like this – he writes her name in reverse order, on a napkin, and pushes it across to her, that's how you would write your name, if English words went from right to left.

She studies the assembly of letters on the fuzzy softness, it would be hard to read a book like this, she concludes.

You would get used to it. Alexander tells her, although Hebrew is very difficult to read, I'll admit, especially when it is written without vowels.

• • •

It was your race, Sparrow maintained, that had ravaged the vowellessness of the Hebrews, the purity of condensed consonance had been corrupted by your people, as a stream of whole numbers might be sullied by the infinity of decimals, the spurious continuity of the number line. Prestidigitation is the ultimate recognition of the discrete, Sparrow had asserted, one cannot after all, juggle sand.

But perhaps that is your ultimate dream, to toss up a ball of sand and recover it again in your other hand, while it traces a salt arc between your palms.

You had no right, he said, you had no right, to rob the Primal Tongue of its vowellessness.

Vowels, you contended, are to consonants what form is to content.

He snorted, we all know, he said, that form is merely an excuse for the lack of content. Vowels are the essence of unambiguity, which I despise, vowels are the poor props of thin narrative, vowels emaciate the language, as do punctuation marks, paragraphs, and all other instruments of linguistic torture.

On the contrary, you argued, it is content that is an excuse for poor form. Vowels lend firmness to language, they are the cartilage of thought, of communication, do you wonder how Babel came to be, Babel could never have come about in a vowelled culture. I am sure it was God who denuded the language of vowels during the Fall, and we delivered you of this Lapsarian curse.

And plunged all humanity into the nightmare of the concrete, the definite, the unequivocal?

Yes, to bring them face to face with that ultimate unambiguity, the first and last sound, that universal nasality, OM.

That was many years ago, today, on this October afternoon, playing truant from fate, he encounters upon the Mall, a saffron-robed Anglo-Saxon, who startles the straggling brand of waterbirds in Sparrow's wake, with the very same sound, Om, and then to the fleeing birds, he offers peace, Shanti, Shanti, Shanti, perhaps he is only quoting Eliot, but no, the sleeve of Sparrow's sheepskin coat is pinched rough, a handful of illustrations is shoved under his nose, an aquamarine child floating on a swing, underneath the caption: the Lord, Krsna, unfractured by vowel, in his day they had spelt it Krishna, the curd-thieving deity, had he finally escaped the wrath of vowel? He accepts the wretched print, it is his final proof of the futility of vowel, besides it could well be some parody of Fragonard, could one feed forever the stream of one's literary consciousness from the wealth of free bulletins proselytising pamphlets, the literary overflow of a developed and graphomanic society, could one read one's eyes dry from street signs, advertisements and discarded theatre programs, yesterday's newspapers retrieved from green-wired bins, could one survive undefinitely upon the desanctification of the printed word, the vowelled desecration of language and thought.

Why has man struggled to give definition to language, saddle the infinity between consonants with the cruel measure of vowel, why, when all else has been an obsession with the inconcrete, why chisel language when poetry must remain undefinable, why perfect the human form when all that is truly compelling is its abstraction, in disease and in deliberation, the stark geometry of malnourished limbs, the disks of bone embedded in savage underlip. Why gild your gardens when those that truly haunt the imagination are the many that do not live on land – the swifts who are born, mate, and die in the air, the sea gypsies of Mindanao who spend their lives upon the ocean. It is in the narrow margins of the human condition where life is fullest, and from these realms, language has been dragged into the arid plain of concrete communication, once poetry was language, when the unspoken chasms between the consonants were replete with dream, as now only the hollows between words and images may be, the clashes of metaphor with reality have come to replace the conflict of sound and meaning contained within the single word.

What was civilisation anyway but itself an edge, a space afforded by the absurd, had that not been clear enough, on that fateful day in Paris, a gendarme's firm tap upon his shoulder, and the rest of the night had passed between neon walls, sharing joints with a cheerless young Algerian who had just seen his brother knifed to death. Had it not been clear enough then, between the terror and the disbelief, had it not been terribly transparent that the order that he had come to accept as inviolable was as fragile as the network of elements in his being, of whose impermanence he had been convinced at a more tender age, in much the same horror. Had it not been clear enough that his predicament was neither chance nor destiny, but a vast consuming probability which overhung all semblance of sanity, all experience of order, that any minute now all might crumble, just as at any moment the atoms that constituted his essence might be flung far and wide by a passing vehicle, so the world about him might collapse, the beloved syllogisms, the comforting rituals, disintegrate as suddenly as they had been. For only where civilisation existed without rules could it remain untouched by the necessity of disintegration, in the same way that immortality was only possible outside of corporeal existence, and the loss of vowellessness marked the transition of language across the same boundary that had saved civilisation from the inevitability of disorder. Language had been dragged outside the margin of poetry that bordered the chaos of communication, the sense of spurious order that vowels imposed upon language were as pathetic as the codes of social contract which lend a false sense of security to our lives.

At dawn, he had been woken roughly from deathless dream, and led out of the cell, Vladimir was waiting, his arms folded, leaning against a grey wall, he took him by the shoulders and led him out in silence, into the smoky morning. As they walked down the river, his spirits had suddenly risen like metal vapour to float loudly about his ears, his spirits had risen, but nowhere near as far as he had hoped, the deliquesence of the steel knots in his stomach had come about from a sudden snatch of the first few bars of *The Threepenny Opera*, when an early riser flung open her windows as they were passing below, but the fumes of despair, instead of sublimating, clung in desperate metallic insistence to his skull. Vladimir reached out to steady him, and the firmness of his arm across his sore back released a fleeting nostalgia, which settled, unsavoured, into the mist, dude, you must be really hungry, said Vladimir.

Vladimir, perhaps it was the delicious conflagration of consonants at the hilt of his name that had buried it deep into his tongue, at night he would roll his lips along the darkness, and like a film of blood, that first syllable – Vl – would spread out against his palate, unvowelled evil. You, he complained, mouthed it as if you were stroking a cat, why must you handle all languages, other than your own and that of your sturdy colonisers, with a classical music announcer's radio Italian, he asked in desperation, he's Russian, for God's sake, not Sicilian.

Vladimir Ivanovich, it rolled off your tongue like strips of wet pastry, when you would call to him in mock petulance, and somehow this terrible corruption of his name thickened his desire, his eyes would brighten, lips part in smile, say it to me again, he would plead, I love it when you say my name. And

Sparrow would turn his head to block out your sugary kisses, slurping syrup against his ears, turn up the volume on the stereo to drown out the ecstasies of Vladimir's violent sighs, and then you would be gone, a sudden void behind him, your footsteps fading. He would be left alone to the loudness of Leo Ferre singing Baudelaire, time to light another cigarette and remember those restless shoulders in the cold streetlight, exhausted from scouring the viticultural backwaters for free degustations, he and Vladimir had hoped to make their way from Paris to Perpignan without spending a single franc. For Vladimir, it had been a challenge, man, what a cool idea, I'd be up for that, he had exclaimed, the green of his eyes condensing suddenly under a neutral film of alcohol. To Vladimir it had been a challenge, while to Sparrow, it was only the ultimate submission to the horrifying necessity of existing outside society, outside the money economy, outside the affairs of state – they had vowed not to read newspapers on their voyage – to Vladimir, inveterate informaniac, this additional clause was particularly sweet, a tantalising challenge, for Sparrow it was merely a concession to an unstructured state of being akin to vowellessness, a tribute to vowellessness, and to uninstitutionalised language. To him, it had not been a challenge, and yet it was he who had lost his nerve, in the suburbs of Clermont-Ferrand, he had given up, surrendered to the frightening opacity of Vladimir's shoulders, splendid in the neon blue of a miniature golf sign under which they had parked for the night, the majestic sheen of perspiration upon his neck, his alabaster neck, now territory to your vampire suckings, Sparrow would close his eyes and wait for the burning length of ash to brush his fingers, it was the autumn of your third year in college, an autumn spent in ferrying back and forth from New York to New Jersey, the three of you living mainly in Vladimir's mother's apartment, returning to college only for the odd lecture, or to maintain your job at the departmental library, a responsibility you could never unlodge, much as Vladimir pleaded. Chuck it in, he would plead, perhaps in strange premonition that in the spring, it was to be there, during your late Friday shift, that Alexander would walk resolutely into your life, banishing him to a subtle expanse of your memory from where he would rise only in dream, a cloying liqueur at the base of your tongue, spreading to brush the greedy inversion of your lips. You will never be rid of the lingering mists of his passion, those dark vapours that came to mock Sparrow, many years ago, crushing his French cigarette between his fingers as he strained to be rid of the memories of summer, a hot August night in the suburbs of Clermont-Ferrand, Vladimir Ivanovich, a nervous blue fluorescence lapping at his bare shoulders.

Vladimir, it's a Russian name for Christopher's sake, said Sparrow, you make it sound like a Mafia password.

You are only jealous, you retorted, because your wormwooden Anglo-Saxon tongue can only handle cardboard consonants, not to mention that your unpolished cochlea can hardly distinguish between a sound and its aspirated form.

• • •

The child, in rapt contemplation of her name spelt backwards upon the napkin, does not rise to help her uncle load the dishwasher, normally one of her favourite tasks. She reaches slowly for the pen, lying dangerously at the table's edge, and writes upon the napkin, NEP, pen reversed, and ELBAT, table turned over, EGASUAS, she writes boldly, watching Alexander scrape the remains of her lunch into the garbage, DRIB, she writes, her glance grazing the stiffened wood-pigeon, TIBBAR, she writes gleefully, TAC, GOD, words are playthings, words are plasticine, the lexicon is the juggler's only paradise.

• • •

Words, you said, were anchored in the mind by their centres, the geometric heart, and those that lost control over half their brain invariably read only half of each word, however long the string of letters might be, only the vow of vowel, and yet all of the vowel of vowellessness. The essence of the word then was not a property of its meaning but some chance configuration of the collection of sounds that had come to signify it.

So you had told Sparrow, last Saturday, the final half-twist to a vigorous debate that had dragged its feet into dawn. Placing a kiss upon his papery cheek, you waltzed victoriously out of the room, leaving him stunned, and eager for more. He came to the door, intending to call you back, but drew back when he heard Alexander's heavy footsteps, still awake, my love? Sparrow heard him say, enfolding your shadow in his. Sparrow shut his door softly, and nursed this wound deep into the night, where was the true identity of the word then, if its meaning was slave to its orthography, even undiluted consonance might come under this heavy cranial hook that hangs each word by the seat of its pants, while each side of the brain grabs a leg, oh, the indignity of it all! At breakfast, he asked for proof, you thrust a copy of *Nature* towards him, he read greedily, in 1941, a doctor by the name of Brain (the inevitable rhetorical coincidence, delight of the humorous scientist), in 1941, R. Brain, no less, had discovered that people with lesions in one half of the brain could have difficulty responding to stimuli from the other half of the body, and 'may fail to manipulate objects on that side of the body, for example by pulling on one trouser leg.' This unfortunate predicament extended to the perception of words, but this was not surprising, only suggested that words were read in halves, shared equally between the hemispheres of an egalitarian brain. What was surprising was that it did not seem to matter if the word was written vertically, or even backwards, it was always the latter half of the word that dissolved, which meant that it was in the memory, rather than the conscious, where a word was impaled by its centre point, spatially coded in 'a word-centred coordinate system; that is, a spatially defined coordinate frame whose centre corresponds to the midpoint of a canonical, orientation-invariant representation of the word.' He closed his eyes, and saw within him an endlessness of words spread like butterflies, like folded inkblots around the axis of his brain.

* * *

Sparrow, lips curled in sarcasm, surveys the Lord Krishna, transmogrified into Fragonard cherub, Krsna, fallen foul of the precision of vowel, he who relished form over content to the extent of sacrificing all of good and truth at the feet of the unambiguous inevitable, the stern skeleton of Dharma. He slips the swingborne Krsna carefully between the yawning pages of his journal, against the unfinished story of the sapient dog/rabbit, he would like to continue writing, but a new wind has risen to bite his cheeks, and the crusty batter coils harsh with the tobacco-scented mash within his innards, he could do with some warmth, the flatulent flames of a British gas fire, or the searing ribs of a white radiator, a nest of blankets in which to bury his head, he crosses the turbulent Mall, and comes to stand in the heat blast of the portico of the Institute of Contemporary Arts, but there is no comfort in this dragon breath, only a harsh dryness that climbs into his throat.

They are holding thirty-seven tickets, he hears a young man announce to his companions, as she rapidly divests herself of a red paisley scarf, I'm sorry I'm late, she breathed, thirty-seven, did you say?

Sparrow watches them, from the door, as they approach the counter, commune with the receptionist, and rush towards the auditorium with their complimentary tickets. It is certainly worth a try. He unbuttons the sheepskin jacket, thrusts his thumbs under the collar, and strides towards reception, I believe you are holding thirty-seven tickets.

. . . to the Rufus Stone talk, she finishes for him, reaching under the counter, it's just started, you'd better hurry.

Still jet-lagged, he pleads, yawning naturally, and checking his watch, which reads five past one.

Name? she asks, pen poised, she does not seem to search any list, no need then to descend into the indeterminate.

Dobryak, he says, D, O, B, R, Y, A, K. Thank you.

My pleasure, she says clearly, her eyes, a perfection of studied candour, it's in the Cinema, she adds, pointing beyond him.

A grim youth in black tears his ticket, and then he is in the wholesome gloom, he looks about for an empty seat, pondering the significance of thirty-seven, the magic password, three and seven are ten, and one and zero, one, a single focus in this intangible crucible, this stolen day. His eyes wander to the stage, where the handsome young Rufus Stone begins to read from his new novel, in a lugubrious, and slightly bored, Mancunian public school accent. His heroine is a young woman named Vanessa Vix, she dreams every night that she is swimming, in a lake of black silk. Rufus Stone becomes quite energetic in his description of the dream, how it would be to drown in fathoms of silk, choking softly, silk, drifts like ink into Vanessa's vagina, unwinding into her womb, where her brother's child grows like a fist of stone, her brother, the ruthless restaurateur, Dominic Vix (Rufus Stone's scornful lips twitch deliciously over this name), Dominic Vix, who eats swan's eggs for breakfast, and ultimately, will drown Vanessa, and their child, in a bath of swan slime, a vat of swan droppings, but Rufus Stone does not disclose this devastating denouement, he snaps the book shut as Vanessa Vix wakes, and remembers that the vicar will be coming to tea.

# VI

# *The Glassblower's Breath*

His lips twist in smile, where gladness meets in delicious dissonance with sad scorn, as he surveys his son, the boy fixes his eyes upon the perplexing length of the Ralph Lauren shorts, the heavy hem that loiters against the sticking plaster upon his knee, the grey socks that clamber resolutely up his stick-thin calves, a prelude to the rich grey of the cable-knit pullover, already dusted with the debris of his pale head into which you have combed a side parting, the chin has been wiped clean of raspberry juice, the rainless eyes stare, pleading, at his father, pleading for him to stoop and disperse the confusion within his mind, this new image of himself rubs so silent against the old, the Ghostbusters and the stonewash, the pickled sneakers that you have bundled into a plastic bag that you hand to his father, that his father takes silently, smiling, from your hands. Another cloud comes briefly to blister the sun, it has been a day of racing clouds, windless and yet clouds have scuttled madly across bright autumn skies, and in that spasm of shadow, the boy senses that he had become suddenly peripheral to your being, that your eyes are locked in some sweet debate far beyond his shores. The shopgirl returns with a navy duffel coat, you absently nod your approval, his father's eyes follow you as you walk slowly towards the counter, scribble dutifully, and return, the shopgirl gingerly lifts an arm and eases it through the coat sleeve, and then the other, she buttons him with scorn, and then, suddenly, pats his head, you do look lovely, she says, and then turning to glare at his father, she says, doesn't he look nice, and his father turns his smile, once more, upon the boy, and declares quietly, yes, of course, he does.

From behind a wall of copper saucepans, Avishek watches as you finally descend, you and the stranger, menacingly close, the air between you damp with lust, and the boy, transmogrified by extravagant cloth, following listlessly. He shrinks back behind a row of kettles as the copper gleam briefly catches your eye, you pass, and reluctantly he forsakes his shrine, for this half hour among the cannikins and colanders has been replete with rich recollection, the distortions of his features upon the copper curves have recalled the sarcasm of laboratory glassware, the silence within which he had nourished his ethereal passion in the raw accompaniment of aldehydes, rectified his spirits upon mordant muriatic murk, and Mussorgsky, yes, modest Mussorgsky, and yet, a year later he had filled his letters to you with quotes from popular songs, why, why, when you had appeared in flesh, risen corporeal from the fabric of his fantasies, why had he garlanded you with cheap popular song, metaphors you would struggle to dignify, why had he been content to lure you with boyish fancy, when within him, all along, there had lain the strata of a riper desire. Yet, he knows, it was the innocence of his lust that had giddied you, it was the porcelain paleness of his acid-stained fingers reaching for your hair in the monsoon darkness, to crush between fevered young palms, it was the trembling consonants and the bad spelling that had endeared his writing to you, the adolescent pride of his admission to the pleasures of alcohol that had scattered playful smiles upon your lips, the Sixth Form anecdotes that had caused the soft breasts that he longed to touch to heave with laughter under the swathe of your white cotton sari, as you lay in cousinly companionship upon the enormous bed where you slept at night with your sister, the garment would slip from your lovely neck, sole province of the young rabbit, Andropov, whom you would scoop up, at intervals, from under the bed, to nestle against your chin, and one afternoon, he had dared to reach to stroke between the long ears that twitched against your chin, and for once, perhaps lulled by the stillness of the afternoon, the creature had submitted to his touch, he moved closer, my friend Nick Butterfield, he told you tenderly, kept a lamb in his room for over a week before they discovered him, and that was first when the silence between you, already sumptuous with adolescent nostalgia, was smeared with a thicker layer of blood, the silence between you, already crowded with memories of what had been, bowed low under the weight of what would never be, a silence that he never dared break that summer with words of love, the sorry declarations with which he would fill page upon page in the thick letters that followed, that summer, you had nourished a deep silence between you, that he had not dared destroy even in farewell, when he had reached out to take your hair within his frenzied fingers, wishing that the strands would break upon his palms, like glass.

Through the liquor haze of his smile, you turn and see the boy, dejectedly dragging his new Oxfords across the store carpet, and your heart, watery with lust, melts, you take his shoulders and steer him into a roomful of toys. His father, impatient but appreciative, lingers at the entrance, the boy's eyes brighten, would you like an aeroplane? you ask. In the corner, you see Sparrow's bear, the one he emerged with at breakfast, his present for your niece, you see it, cossetted by its fifty-odd doubles, all similarly unimpassioned by the wealth of plush stegosauri on the shelf below.

Bowed low among an undergrowth of microwave ovens, your cousin raises his eyes to see you disappear with the child into a cavern of toys. The boy's father hangs back at the entrance, leaning against the wood frame, hands in his trouser pockets, his hair, brushed back, is the colour of thick smoke, clouding acrid upon his unwashed nape, and his shoulders stretch firm into the shivering fluoresence. There is a certain tantalising freedom, your cousin concedes, in his narrow form, in his movements as he stretches both arms to span the width of the doorless way, and stands crucified upon air, until a tall young woman carrying a stuffed otter demands to be let through, he obliges, and his eyes linger upon her as she walks past into a bank of refrigerators, and then you emerge, you and the child, in the boy's arms a beauty of an aeroplane, and his father strokes the red wood as he might later stroke your limbs, or perhaps it is the scent of the woman with the otter that is still fresh upon him, an aeroplane, a lovely red aeroplane, perfect undercarriage, this is the ultimate violation of your complicity, an aeroplane as that Avishek, himself, might have gazed upon, many years ago, through shop glass holding your small hand, many years ago, while your father glared from among bags of shopping, come on then, you two, what's this obsession with planes, don't you have enough of them, and you would tug at his hand, plead with him to tear his eyes away from the proud wings, and that afternoon, you and he would sit upon a low branch overhanging the stream, pitching and yawing, you would mimic his angles, scream in rapture at the danger of slipping off into the muddy stream. Later that year, a boy drowned among the festering water weed, the crisps wrappers and the lolly sticks, a boy had drowned in that very spot over which you hung, upon the oak branch, decked in swimming goggles, while he talked of the lands that swept by below, and once, though this you would never know, your father, on his way back from the library, had stopped and been moved by the richness of his imagination, and the pure delight of your laughter, this, your father too has forgot, although in the years to come, when he sits to write the story of his life, he will remember, and he will write of his daughter's laughter, but leave him in the shadow, springtime companion, wind-wild cousin, dastardly protagonist of her childhood dreams.

Who lives in the moon? the boy reads slowly, as silvery letters reluctantly recede, the department store is running a special on man-in-the-moon lamps, who lives in the moon? you echo gratefully, indeed?

The knock-kneed man in striped leggings? Or a kindly old woman, silently spinning moonlight? Or an alabaster rabbit making rice-cakes?

The boy takes in your speculations without a murmur, you laugh, and turn to Dan, expecting curiosity, but he is silent, smiling, savouring your laughter. In his eyes there is only a supreme indifference and this you inhale with pleasure, his fathomless incuriosity wraps you in deep smoky detail.

He reaches to your wrist and lifts your arms towards him, his eyes hover upon your slim faceless watch, it doesn't help, he says, not to have markings, but if it is what time I think it is, Kevin's mum will be wanting to pick him up soon from my flat.

So this is how it is to end then, this impossible interlude, with a tidy farewell in this moonscape of reduced-price wool, this bittersweet cameo, will you treasure it alone or share it tonight with Alexander, and tomorrow with Karin, while you snip and sew, putting the finishing touches on her wedding gown, might you wax lyrical upon his inscrutable smile, between a mouthful of pins and the snapping of thread, or will the young memory of his desire hum deliciously within you while you talk of other things. It will be a bit of both, you suspect, between the skeleton of incident that you will offer to the world, and the substrate of your lust, there would lie an endless expanse of what might have been, for you to feed upon, you offer Daniel the most tender of smiles, well, goodbye, then, you say, it has been a pleasure.

His fingers tightened about your wrist, which he still holds, but I was hoping you would come with me, he says quietly, it's not far by tube, and where a white calmness had begun to grow within you, a blind surge of blood blots out all memory, his smile splinters a wall of mirrors in the back of your skull, his smile, carving deep into your being, you are an old hunger, you dream, you are an old, forgotten hunger, you are my first dream of death.

* * *

Last night the moon came dropping its clothes in the street. I took it as a sign to start singing, falling *up* into the bowl of the sky. The bowl breaks. Everywhere is falling everywhere.

A wall of mirrors shatters beneath the weight of his smile, those lips will surely taste of death, death who had mocked you last winter from the foot of your sister's bed, death who had scorned the softness of your arms, your lips, death had risen, last winter, from the firmness of shadow into regions of raw dream, and yet, starved of mourning, you had drifted into a windless plain where being played charades with nothingness, and the absurd was your only refuge, those lips are certain to taste of death, currents of warm ink clash deeply with a colder suspension, death could never have been ensnared by the old grammar, diced and puréed among familiar vowels, but there in his smile were the makings of a new rule, my love, and this you could not ignore.

• • •

Your niece, hunting near the washing machine for Hookahface Greedyguts's necktie, stumbles upon a jigsaw puzzle box, bursting with photographs. They are all of the rabbit, Andropov, removed on Alexander's command, from the row of leather-bound albums in the liqueur cabinet. The rabbit, Andropov, is fifteen years old, Alexander has told her, he was born in the time of Indira Gandhi's Emergency. A mere five-rupee bribe had secured him from the night-guard at the Children's Zoo by Dhakuria Lake. On your twelfth birthday, you woke to find him calmly munching the pink ribbon that your cousins had tied around his neck, a spreading stain of fresh urine between his back paws. Later he came to be house-trained, although a degree of incontinence has returned with age, the rabbit Andropov is fifteen years old, and has already outlived two of the happy faces that crowded around you that morning, the morning of your twelfth birthday, your sister and the young maid, Bula, are no more. Bula died in childbirth the following year, her unripe hips choked by the struggling foetus, the blind pain of parturition overtaken by keener pangs of death, somewhere the summer sky had been rent by her screams, pond sludge thickening outside the mud walls, these were the images of death for you, these were the dread images that had been wiped clean, last winter, by the soft deathsweet sighs upon your sister's lips as she sank finally into grand oblivion. Last winter, death had wrenched from you the luxury of metaphor, the images with which you had surrounded death for so long, the images that had shielded you from the nakedness of Bula's fate: the mud walls, hot pondscum bubbling, sparrows scattering the crude thatch as they fly on the last note, the last cry that escapes the village maiden's lips, your Bula, doting dogsbody, honorary member of your vast family. You still remember the wistful pride on her face as she would rush from cousin to cousin, helping you dress for parties, she would wave furiously as you tumbled into cars and taxis, but you always returned with some tidbit for her, some trivial object, a rose wrapped in silver foil, a paper napkin printed with the menu, a few dry sweetmeats, your sister would never fail to bring back some morsel of festivity. Your sister had been sewing a dress for the baby when the news came that Bula had died, you threw yourselves into each other's arms and sobbed, and in your brain bubbled the images of heating pondslime pecked by crows, a rustle of sparrows in the thatch, her painscreams floating like smoke across the green paddy fields, death had allowed you, then, to retreat into a world of images, while down below, Bula's father, the family cook, howling with grief, was beating his head upon the courtyard flagstones.

He is still in the family's employ, Bula's father, balder and portlier, even more paranoid, he seals his pots with strips of dough for fear that some jealous servant will slip in and sprinkle salt upon the rice-pudding, or tip asafoetida in the fish curry. Rima remembers fondly how it was he that taught her how to make animals out of dough, little fish, legless birds, it was he that convinced her to put aside the tomato skins in her scrambled eggs for the rabbit, Andropov, for whom he had a particularly soft spot. But you were angry to see him fed the oily residues of her breakfast, it will make him lose his fur, you scolded, and the child had visions of great white clumps rising in the air like cotton, a bald, forlorn rabbit. He was fifteen years old, the rabbit, Andropov, and he had a hundred and eight names, like the Lord Krishna, a hundred and eight names that he had picked up in the course of his long life, names mutating and multiplying, names like M. Ripopet Barabas and Iltutmish and Komalgandhar, an endless string of effable ineffables, many of them forgotten. The rabbit, Andropov, is fifteen years old, he has kept his teeth, which he sharpens regularly on the mahogany feet of the main dining table, where your grandfather and his brothers once ate in heavy western decorum, the six of them, alone, discussing business. Now it has been pushed against the wall and its stained surface covered by a large checked table cloth, hanging long at one end, a perfect shield for the rabbit, Andropov, as he demolishes the antique claws. He has kept his teeth the rabbit, Andropov, but one of his eyes is misted over with cataract, and his sense of smell is not what it used to be, he has lived so long that these photographs of his youth are yellowing among jigsaw pieces. Your niece shakes them out, the pictures and the puzzle-ends, for she has caught a glimpse of mystifying backdrop, she is rooted in horror and fascination as skeletons appear, skipping rope, swinging from lignified entrails of trees. The pieces, she realises, are the flesh that will cover the bone, the bark that will clothe the xylem and phloem, they are the flowers upon the bloodless stalks, and the clouds that will grace the naked skies.

* * *

The grim nudity of the Council flats is an unmistakable advantage to the weary stalker, for by merely positioning himself across the street, your cousin Avishek finds he can trace your movements against the mangy tapestries, the crumbling blue of the naked spaces of sky. With one hand upon the child's shoulder and the other gingerly tapping the rail, you follow your companion, who punctuates the arduous journey with short smiles flung over his shoulder, a heedless Orpheus to your aching Eurydice, long has he dreamt of rescuing you from the dead, your cousin, long has he walked in your shadow, not hoping to turn, nor hoping to turn again. You reach, finally, a long stretch of naked corridor, where the stranger waits, behind a wall of flapping laundry, to take you by the arm towards the vermilion door that will soon bring to an abrupt halt this orgy of scopophilia. Avishek sighs as you disappear and settles down upon a low wall behind him, inadvertently demolishing a newspaper nude with a corner of his heel.

A squat mongrel walks past on a leash and then returns to urinate upon the newspaper. He watches the breasts of the dismembered blonde wilt and blur, and thinks miserably that he might have made a fortune manufacturing nippled buns for a nation of tabloid readers to enjoy with their morning tea. So far the height of perversion they had achieved was the shortbread crucifix, but the geometry had been general enough not to offend, even so it had not sold well, the critics had complained that it was deucedly difficult to balance on a saucer, at the slightest provocation, the rood would snap, and slip from one's grasp.

My friend, Mike, a flash of glasses in the darkness, hello, I'm afraid I can't see you very well. The child pushes open the kitchen door, the afternoon light trickles in. Mike drags a jacket off a thick dungeon pin, I was just about to leave, he tells Daniel, old pancakeface called, she can't pick the kid up now, she wants you to meet her with him at Paddington at half past five, can you hand me that bicycle pump, no not that one, that's grand, cheers.

You struggle to banish visions of flat, pockmarked flesh, you have imagined her in tawny polythene, the boy's mother, you have seen his hands slide upon her thighs as they might take an unruly joint of lamb with cellophane wrap, you do not wish to see her pale and pitted, cowering under the obscure weight of his smile, flinching sadly from the manic tenderness in his eyes. The images dissolve under an assault of colour as he pushes open the kitchen door and your eyes meet a wall, brilliant swaths of spray-paint broken by open shapes of cutlery. A cloud of forks have left their shadow in an electric mire of pink, knives cross like fattened multiplication signs, a row of spoon shapes raise their hopeful faces to a burst of orange. Mike, he says, with an almost avuncular pride, Mike is an artist.

You pause momentarily on the lip of this crater, and then slide into the vast soothing hollow of his confidence, I helped him with this mural, he tells you.

And one dry hot week, this past summer, he had devoted his afternoons to watering one of Mike's sculptures, on display at the Community Hall. It took up half the floor, the enclosure, ribbons of wood twisting around enamel bowls of coloured water, they were the bowls that needed topping up every hour, it was so dry, and Mike was in hospital ... you expect him to tell you why Mike was in hospital, but he will not offer this information as a matter of course, you revel, once more, in his contempt for excess, a mathematician's obsession for the necessary and sufficient. There is no need for you to know, he feels, why Mike was in hospital, it does not become natural adjunct to his offering. His thoughts brush like flowers, large and naked, upon your senses. It was bloody hot, this summer, he says, cupping his fingers around your elbow.

Can I make you something hot? he asks, tea? coffee? – it'll be instant, I'm afraid.

Coffee, you agree, would be welcome, for a sudden dull chill has crept in upon the afternoon. Across the road, your cousin is digging in his pockets for gloves, he finds them, curled together, a warm, weak hedgehog. Through the limp fingers, he catches a glimpse of the ice-hard sun in the window, high above, as it is pulled shut.

Daniel, fastening the window latch, halts briefly at the grainy vision of a man seated on the mossy wall of the facing estate, there is a sinister deliberation in how he pulls on his gloves. A sudden spasm of memory distracts your companion, a childhood bully slowly unzipping his shorts to urinate upon his face. If he were accustomed to metaphor, he might have conjured death, sharpening her scythe, or even a hunter, blowing into the nozzle of his gun, but he is a literal man, your Daniel. Sobered by his sudden recollection, he returns to the task of measuring out coffee, pours hot water and refills what seems to be a permanently boiling kettle.

He hands you your mug, and raises his own in long sweep, halfway to a Teutonic toast. You watch the scalding liquid lap against his lip, blot upon his smile. He has taken you by the arm, once more, he is leading you out of the kitchen to the more sombre scape of a wide-windowed room, richly littered with old furniture. The boy sits wedged between a gate-legged table and a small television, turn that down, will you, his father commands.

When my wife left me, he says, motioning you to sit, I thought I would move out of here, but then Mike moved in, he has the bedroom, and I've moved into here.

You sit, your back straight, upon a church pew, very nice, you say to him, running your hands down the wood.

Employee's discount from the Purveyors of Nostalgia, I got plenty off them, he looks fondly over your shoulder into a jungle of hatstands and carved mirrors, arrayed like a crowd of mourners about a plump, roofless four-poster that must be his bed. A pair of large violet lips stretch across the wall from one tip of naked bedpost to another, Mike, he says apologetically, sitting down, cross-legged, upon the rug. He pulls a mangy violin case towards him, this is full of junk that they were about to throw away, he says, I asked if I could take it home, haven't even looked through it yet, and it's been a year almost. He tips it over the floor, a jumble of brass knobs and dolls' heads and magnifying-glass cases, he begins to laugh, a divine reverberation, rich in mockery, you slide from the pew onto the floor, pick up a velvet beaver, incarcerated within lace, he watches you, silently, smiling now, you sift through the strange rubble and unearth a minute skull missing a millimetre of jaw. You remember the cobwebbed sockets of Sparrow's minion, trusty Uncle Fred, Teddy Ginsberg had painted it blue, a joke that had nearly cost him his life, for Sparrow, in a sudden display of angry strength, had pitched him out of the window, the ground was thick with sludge, Teddy escaped with a bruised tooth, and you rushed with Uncle Fred to the nearest bathroom, which was the men's, held him under boiling water, and dug with your fingernails into the angry blue, and that was how Vladimir had found you, stepping out of the shower to see you struggling with a blue skull. He had tucked his towel about his waist and offered to help, perhaps alcohol, he suggested, will do the job, and so he had followed you, in his state of undress, to Sparrow's room, where Sparrow sat with his head in his hands while Teddy, a bloody handkerchief to his mouth, muttered about the quality of mercy. Leave me alone, Ginsberg, Sparrow said, leave me alone, his voice trailed as his eyes fell upon the unclothed stranger, I'm Vladimir, the youth announced, I think alcohol might help, are you all sophomores?

The only way alcohol might help, said Sparrow, is if it is poured in vast quantities down my throat.

I'm sure we can arrange that as well, Vladimir offered gaily, oh hello Teddy, what have you done to your mouth?

I didn't know you were back, mumbled Teddy through bubbles of blood, how was South America?

What were you doing in South America? you asked. I took some time off to travel, he explained, which is why you've never seen me. Sparrow leaned back against the wall, will you all please leave me alone, he barked, will you all fucking leave me alone.

Well, I'm late for work anyway, you said, setting the sorry skull upon the sill, and when you returned in the evening, having scoured the campus for turpentine, there was a note scrawled upon your door – gone to NY with Vladimir – J.S., the ungrateful wretch, why do these memories return now to disperse your desire, why does the smoke-stale recollection of Sparrow's overheated room vie with the turbulence of the smile that wanders madly now upon your eyes, why does your mind flood instead with the sharp smell of turpentine that had crowded thick in the smoky evening as you set to work, alone, with the abused skull, snow falling outside in sad dense drifts, why do your senses fog with clammy breath of that winter evening, your attention receding suddenly from the hands that push aside the broken pocketwatches and the motheaten egg caddies to reach for your knees. Daniel rests his dark head beside you upon the hard curved edge of the pew, his breath aches upon your ear and yet this precious insanity is fractured by the chalky residues of your past, the blue skull in ominous reflection upon the frozen window pane. At midnight, they had returned, Sparrow and his new companion, Vladimir. Consumed by a desire to see you again, he had dragged the unwilling Sparrow back to the fields of your doom, the ghostly winter spires, Vladimir, who would appear intermittently in your dreams, for the rest of your life, his kisses tasting of orange liqueur, now is not the time to recall your undecided passions, the floating nightmare of your brief physical rapture, for you had returned to your third year in college eager, too eager for the arms you had turned away from in the spring, rejected by your city you sought his relentless desire, I have dreamt of you all summer, you told him, as he crushed your lips under feverish dream. I have dreamt of you all my life, he had answered, but his furious lust had disappointed you, he had waited too long for you, you had become an obsession, his arms would hold you in too deep a possession as you made love, his satisfaction was the long scream of a drowning man as his lungs finally flood with air, only his kisses haunt you still, those that you had dreamt of long before he had touched you, and those that came after, where honeyed fermentations had become frothed with blood, but now is not the time to remember the dry moonlight, his fearless use of the most tragic platitudes of passion, now is not the time. For the heavy silence of this stranger's smile has rekindled a more ancient desire, when these lips move to meet yours, they will taste of death, death who had mocked you last winter from the foot of your sister's bed, death who had scorned the eager softness of your tongue, they will taste of death, surely, these lips that hover now under the hollow of your ear. The boy turns once, between advertisements, blinks and returns to show, it is a black-and-white film, you notice, it is an old Hollywood film, but he prefers it to his father's polite frenzy. Fingers move to lock your neck, rough palms cradle your cheeks, he smiles and reaches down to smother your lips in ribbons of shifting sand, you are my only victory, you fear, you are my last encounter with destiny, you are my final experience of the dignity of fate.

* * *

Last night the moon, the moon buried hard against cork and glass, last night the moon, blistering softly against the bubbled mirrors, I came to the window, last night the moon came dropping its clothes in the street, I took it as a sign to start singing, falling *up* into the bowl of sky. The bowl breaks. Everywhere is falling everywhere. Nothing else to do. But here's the new rule, my love: Break the wineglass, let the shards swallow your palm, fall, fall, gently now, down the everted chute of time, towards the glassblower's breath.

• • •

How could it be denied, when his lips met yours, a new rule was born, how could it be denied, that as the tip of his tongue fed grainy convulsions against your lower lip, how could it be denied that the cathedral windows shattered, and a great burst of colourless light filled the arches, imagine a child, crouched under a pew as the bombs fall, the stained glass breaks, and an unholy brightness bathes the spaces above, you ached to press this new whiteness against your palate, but the fury of his passion bit hard upon your senses, and then the affectless gaze of the child fell upon you like a layer of ice, he sensed your discomfort, drew away, offered his hand to guide you into the hallway, where his lips, drenched with desire, eddied brokenly upon your neck, you felt, against your back, a narrow coolness of wall, why deny that it was a new rule that sliced through the soft links of daylight, the cold raspberry furrows of your tongue rippled in measured agony, the latchkey gurgled, your tongues froze in their embrace, and the new rule, unchristened, mockingly withdrew.

• • •

A monstrous cat, black as night, has entangled herself among a pile of discarded clothes, Avishek watches her with pity as she writhes among the interminable scarves, and the treacherous polyester lace, not sure how he can relieve her of her absurd condition. His relationship with animals has always been tentative, always tinged with embarrassment, his only pet was a West African squirrel that he had once rescued from a Liberian market, relishing the idea of recounting the incident in his next long letter to you, and hoping to probe perhaps the bonds that existed between you and the rascally rabbit, Andropov. It was in the summer when you were about to leave the creature, to desert the oblivious beast for the magic of a foreign land. Of this impending disunion you spoke with more heartfelt tenderness than of your long separation with Avishek, so it was a mirthful jealousy as well that drove him to adopt the forlorn rodent, chirping sadly in the marketplace, awaiting slaughter, it had curled up immediately in the hollow of his palm, he had painstakingly nursed it to health, feeding it from medicine droppers and with mashed banana to lick off his fingertips, until it was strong enough to wander the house alone, much to the distaste of his parents, it built a paper nest under the bed, dragging scrap from out of his waste-basket. He exulted in the deep affection he developed for the creature, for somehow it strengthened your alliance that he too would be stung with the most desperate guilt when he turned the squirrel over to the Swiss taxidermist for safekeeping in his small riverside zoo, for summer had gone as it had come, he was to return once more to Sheffield, and await your letters from the other side of the globe, and as he sat drinking beer in the grass gazebo, the squirrel picking groundnuts from the taxidermist's sunburnt fingers, he watched the solitary leopard, the zoo's single large mammal, padding to and fro in ceaseless monotone. As he reached to tickle for the last time the soft belly of his oblivious pet, a strange hope had nestled against sharp remorse, he stood for a while at the banks of the sluggish river, much has changed, he thought, much has changed. When he returned the following year, bitter in the loss of your love, he had rushed first to the zoo, but he could not find his beloved squirrel among the crowd, she had merged with a dozen others, some of them her own children. Many years later, and not without guilt, he had fallen back upon his tender anecdote of the squirrel whom he had rescued from the jaws of death, he had resurrected this painless memory to inspire affection in Mrigaya, in the few weeks that they had been left alone to discover each other before their marriage, and she, her eyes brimming with devoted compassion, had drunk in the story as the roots of a desert plant, unprepared to flirt with destiny, might receive water. Mesmerised by his halting Bengali, she lost her balance as the rickshaw came abruptly to a stop, her head jolted forward, releasing a smoky river of hair from a precarious topknot, what do you think you are doing? Avishek demanded angrily of the rickshaw puller. It will rain soon, the man replied humbly, I thought you would prefer some cover, he said, drawing a short stretch of tarp across the canopy. Mrigaya raised her arms to fix her hair, releasing an intriguing astringence that mingled with the gathering smell of rain, only to harpoon another few images of you from the ever urgent past, only to sharpen the memory of stormlight upon your downy arms, the baked earth bubbling under the assault of the first vicious raindrops. Avishek closed his eyes and sought to free himself from this inevitable coalition. So you never found your squirrel? asked Mrigaya. A few fat raindrops fell upon his naked toes, peeping outside the tarpaulin, he drew his feet in and opened his eyes. With the mouth of the vehicle sealed off, and rain suddenly descending in sheets, it was like being trapped in the musty insides of an animal, wooden ribcage rattling over their heads, boldly he reached for her hand. No, I never found her, he told the astonished girl, her fingers were cold, pleasantly rough, like familiar wood, he locked them gratefully in his own, would even have touched his lips to them behind the curtain of rain and tarpaulin, if the rickshaw ride had not come to an end, a gentler revolution this time in their seating angle as the man lowered his end, unleashed the tarp, and demanded a full five rupees more on account of the rain. Avishek protested, but only mildly, for he could see it disturbed her. It's just a matter of principle, he explained hastily, lest she should be tormented by notions of his thrift, only a matter of principle. Upstairs his mother was waiting with warm chick-pea curry and potato cakes, they had been to see your sister, she told him, to invite them to the reception, she looks remarkably well, his mother said, for a woman with cancer.

But I thought she was cured, he said, irritated by her tone, it can be cured you know, he said, a little irritated even by the sudden spasm of fear in Mrigaya's eyes at the mention of the dread disease. His mother had been to see her, found her in perfect health, and she had some more news, his mother told him, looking straight into his eyes, news that you were arriving the following week, in time for the wedding, my sister's daughter, she explained to Mrigaya, she lives in London, my sister's daughter. You. He placed his palms flat upon the moist formica, waiting for the news to settle within him, like a man with his back to an oceanfront, suspended interminably in that split second before the waves come crashing upon his head. He waited in fear, and instead a strange wind lifted up from the innards of the past, drenching him in hope, he arched his palms and felt the yolks of old dreams drain into his fingertips. He rose slowly from the table, smiling, and walked out onto the balcony, held his face to the rainspray, and breathed deeply of change. Mrigaya came to join him, cautiously picking her way past the dripping plants, what kind of cancer, she asked fearfully, was it? She is cured, he insisted, she is cured, and in his new condition of elation, this seemed a certainty, she was surely cured, he turned away to shield his mood from the intolerable pity in Mrigaya's eyes. It had shaken him, of course, the first time he was told, this first violation of his past, companion of infancy, your sister, remembered only by yellowed photographs, it had affected him more, certainly, than the news that you had married a Persian and were living in London, for he had drawn no sustenance from the sumptuous probability of running into you on the street, no delicate thrill from the certainty of having been within close proximity of each other somewhere, sometime in the wide city, nor from the presentiment that someday he would find you, when he most needed to, in the crooked hook of a stranger's arm, and follow you through the city, shielded by the exigencies of fate, to this venerable wasteland.

Avishek sits up suddenly as the man whom you would have recognised as Mike, the artist/interior decorator, returns with a pack of young men, all bespectacled and unshaven, carrying several six-packs, they pass close to him, a subcontinental youth among them looks him over somewhat suspiciously. They cross the street and skip over the wall, he watches them as they climb, in clumps, the exposed stairs. They trickle (like cells forcing through a capillary, oh, terrible analogy, but how was one to sluice completely those relentless laboratory images) randomly down the open corridor, once more the vermilion gapes, and swallows them, one by one.

The sound of the latchkey causes him to draw away, not suddenly, like a frightened hare, but with gradual grace, drawing the tip of his tongue down your palate like the final flourish of a sated pianist, taking leave of your blood-swollen lips. Slowly, slowly, he pulls away and smiles, and then peers into the hallway at the newcomers, who are momentarily in conference, but then troop across, hello, hello, you're back then, let me introduce you, Chris, Joe, Jim, Hanif, Ian, you've met Mike. You follow them into Daniel's room, the names swirling about you, as they decide there is enormous pleasure to be had in introducing each other to themselves, Chris, have you met Mike, he's a postmodern ragpicker, ha ha ha, Joe – Hanif, Hanif – Joe, Hanif's a banker, yes, one o' them, capitalist tool, ha ha ha, and Mike, I must introduce you to Chris, he's the local transvestite, Chris lunges forward, splashing the dolls' heads and chipped mustard jars with lager. Their self-absorption is staggering, puts yours and Dan's to shame, even though you still linger firmly in the penumbra of your interrupted physical exchange, he draws close once more, let's leave, he suggests gently, let's get out of here. You shake hands with the pantomime cast. Hanif mentions darkly, his eyes fixed upon your wedding ring, I think your husband might have followed you, there's a bloke outside, watching this flat. You laugh, that's hardly likely, you say, envisioning Alexander within his walls of cork and mirror, my husband's dead, you lie. The child gazes in fear that he will be left behind among the laughing men who have already made fun of his outfit, look at little Lord Fauntleroy here, looks like a Harrods catalogue. He cowers behind a broken gate-leg, and looks pleadingly to his father, who strides to him and picks him up, over the furniture, slings him over his shoulder and takes his farewell. The red door shuts behind you, you look across the road, can Alexander have followed you, there is no one there, for Avishek has wisely removed himself upon the entrance of the horde, to a less convenient spot behind a parked lorry at the corner of a cross street, it is more than absurd that Alexander might have followed you, you muse, as you descend. Is it true, Daniel asks, that your husband is dead.

No, it's not, you reply, he laughs, where are we going now, you ask, I have no idea, he says.

* * *

Last night, the moon, half drowned in cork and dew, turned a bare milky shoulder towards the trees in the sombre square, they took it as a sign to start swaying, moving their limbs to the memory of winter, the heaviness of snow, like the clothes of the moon draped across their boughs, I digress, my love, then the sky split with dry thunder, the bowl was broken, everywhere falling everywhere, nothing else to do.

And the new rule, uncoiling, unborn, could no longer be denied. There was the moon, which you did not see, wrapped as you were, against the gentle swell of your niece under the bedclothes, lulled by her faint nightmare sobs into thunderous sleep. You dreamt, that night, that your sister, instead of dying fresh as a pod of new-blown kapok, had battled long with death, until her skin had charred to black salt, so that the moonstone upon her finger glowed a monstrous milky white, the naked sclera of an unpupilled eye, and you woke, no longer content to live by the old rules, you woke, ready to break the wineglass, and run through the rawness of the vineyards, to hurl yourself, once and for all, towards the heaviness of the glassblower's breath.

* * *

The grass, in vulgar green tufts, swells about the broken glass and the crisp wraps, the outcrops of pumpkin-coloured brick, this is no wilderness for your new passion, you seek a more manicured desolation, a fortress of broken stone, flung to the winds, where you might savour the fullness of this lust that splits your life in half, where before it was only fissured at the level of your dreams. You grope against the blinding green for the threads of your interrupted passion, but a rude curve of steel pipe closes in upon your senses, where shall we go then? he asks you, almost impassively.

A bus pulls up at the request stop, sporting a vaguely familiar number, you climb aboard without knowing why, eager only to be duped by the sorry sense of freedom that any journey affords. You climb to the upper deck, which is empty but for a listless smoker in the back. You make your way to the front, and he follows, perplexed, dragging his exhausted child. He sits beside you and takes your hands, your hands are cold, he says, as if this is a source of profound wonder to him, your hands are like ice, he says in mild delight. You still have the keys, you remember, as you watch his eyes drift aimlessly along the gliding chorus of images without, the knock-kneed houses and spasms of green, the crowds gathering thicker as the bus nears Camden Lock, you still have the keys you remember to an empty flat near Gloucester Road, it belongs to Vladimir's father, Vladimir had sent Sparrow the keys in case he wished to use it, and last week, at the Museum of Mankind, entranced by the blue of haliotis shell on a Maori feeding funnel, Sparrow had dropped them in your bag when they had entangled themselves in his fingers as he reached into his satchel for a pen, he had thrown them in disgust into your handbag, and proceeded to note upon his travelcard that the curious object had been used to feed Maori chiefs while their faces were being tattooed. You had meant to hand the keys back to him this morning, but you forgot. Daniel continues to warm your hands in silence, lost in contemplation. If your paths were suddenly at this moment to uncross, could you have dismissed all that had passed between you as a peculiar infringement of reality on part of some slightly sordid dream? Or would you, in the moment of his leaving, turn to plead as the poet had with love, a love which had lingered in silence, like a dream unfed, until in farewell, the poet had woken to its delicate tune, and followed in desperation that which was by then merely a receding light upon a distant path, a formless phantom folding into the darkness of night, and finally only a blood-soaked mirage, inspiration for one of his greatest poems, evidently mutilated in translation. If we were to sigh now and drop your frozen hands, reach for his son's shoulder and guide him firmly out of your life, you fear that you might indeed barely move your head to watch them leave, you fear that memories of this unfinished afternoon will cling forever about you as bits of dirty glass, a small untidy rip where there might have been a long, taught gash in the fabric, beaded with blood. Many years ago, playing chess in a quiet New Jersey kitchen, this same fear had caught you by the throat, caught you by surprise, for you had expected a warm glow of contentment to surround you, poking at the remains of a coffee milkshake with a chewed straw, you had waited for the dense whisperings of the leaves to stir a deep peace within you, and instead, a sliver of unease lodged itself suddenly in the back of your throat, dissolving momentarily under the weight of rapid emotion brought on by the strains of Simon and Garfunkel, hello darkness, floating in from the porch, David's sister, clicking her strawberry heels to the beat, the afternoon wind, heavy with sweet seed, played havoc with your newly cropped hair. David castled, the music relaxed its hold, and suddenly you felt the disorienting weight of the vastness to the west, the uneven pull of the great mass stretching to the Pacific, and you knew then that cloying peace of this afternoon would rub forever like scraps of candyfloss upon your dreams. Take me back to New York, you commanded David, suddenly ruthless.

Your hands clench under the sudden impact of the vehicle behind you, another double-decker of the same species, nosing the backside of its partner in some lurid mating ritual that forces London buses to always travel in clumps, an affinity that has proved indispensable, however, to Avishek, who sits nervously near the front of the bottom deck, his eyes glued to the orifice of the bus ahead, thankfully still in sight, still there are traffic lights, of course, and the not inconsiderable possibility that this one will try and outrun its predecessor, it will be a nail-biting journey for your cousin, a precarious sojourn through the isthmuses of chance.

Your hands grip each other's as knotted steel, once more the blood beads well against the sinuses of reason, he lifts your palms to his lips, and gratefully fills the icy hollows with the silent swell of his lips, the old rules crumble, crushed to pitiful dust under the rhythm of his breath.

# VII

# *Even the Fish Drowns*

A black lip of cloud edges over the mirthless horizon, Sparrow scrapes the bottom of a small container of yoghurt that he has brought in the hope of comforting both thirst and hunger with a single purchase, an expectant squirrel waits by the foot of the bench, a new park, another stretch of holy green, Green Park, refuge certainly, but not for much longer, for it will rain, most certainly, soon it will rain, the rising hourglass must crack and spill its sand, across the park crowds are folding up their deck-chairs in thousands, his mind is walking a tightrope covered with moths. He scrapes at the plastic whorls of the yoghurt container, in the autumn of your sophomore year, you and he had made your own yoghurt, as part of a scheme to divert your food budget into the travel fund. Solemnly he would perform the daily ritual of filling the jars with milk, small pats of yoghurt nestled inside, rich with the germ that would coax the milk into whey. He told you that the molecular contractions that separated water from the substance of milk were given the very same name as the condensation of two vowels into the absurdity of diphthong, syneresis they called it, the sin of syneresis, he said, was no more than a frantic attempt to rid the language totally of vowel, as was aphesis, he had explained to you, as was aphesis.

Aphesis?

As was aphesis, he explained patiently, the elimination of unstressed (huh!) vowel, as in the transformation of esquire to squire.

You retorted with glee that your race preferred to indulge in a sort of negative aphesis, anaphesis?, by which school became iskul, and station mutated to isteshon. And the yoghurt had been hopelessly watery, a little bitter, after a week of pretending to be satisfied by your experiment, you gave up and gorged yourselves on Salisbury steaks at the Student Centre.

He licks the last of the yoghurt off the abrasive matchstick wood, the small instrument for harpooning battered cod, and the vinegar-sodden chips, the flat-footed spear he had saved from lunch, had rescued him from the ignominy of lapping the yoghurt from the narrow tub, like the fox at the stork's luncheon. For he had found himself spoonless, staring upon a seamless pond of yoghurt, the small yoghurt buds on the shiny inner flap, and almost simultaneously his wandering digits had stumbled upon the stubby fish-fork in his pocket, while searching among the balls of crumpled paper and cat's cradles of dental floss for his lithium. Its potential as a yoghurt spoon only became clear once he had used the fish-fork to urge the medicine bottle to yield its final contents, for some delicate chemistry had materialised between its inner walls and the orange membranes of the last two capsules. He gulped them down with a few slivers of yoghurt, and tossed the empty prescription bottle into a garbage can. The finality no longer frightens him that tomorrow his blood will be free of this unholy brine; by tomorrow the islands of dull salt that cake his nerves will have crumbled, unreplenished, swallowed by his own equilibrating juices. Had they remained buried in salt, would his nerves have transmuted into a delicate network of glass, his body finely threaded with glass nerves, someday might someone lift the cover off his coffin, and find among the dirt and weeds, a glass image of his nervous system, like the skeleton of leaf, all that would remain, perhaps a few worms impaled upon the glass extrusions of his neurons, choked upon the glass bubbles of his synapses, perhaps his brains would be a huge sac of glass, filled with dead worms, who had lost their way within the slippery labyrinth, sucking the soft meat of his crumpled thoughts. For in vain has been this effort to preserve his sanity by steeping it in brine, that relentless salt, lithium, bastard child of the periodic table, tomorrow he will have none.

The last capsules swallowed, the last page of his journal filled, his journal full, but for the sudden island of white, he draws it out once more to continue the story of the intelligent dog/rabbit:

*Perhaps it was when dream ceased to infringe upon reality, when a great divide yawned between the illogic of dream and the tyranny of cause and effect, that curious chill that the March wind brought would never sharpen the fallen furrows of his dream storms, the taste of cold rabbit came only with the tinny froth of a real canned supper, and never in the shapes of dream food, although the hammerings of a dream hunger lingered always into reality, bridging the two worlds. He knew it was he, and only he, among his brothers, that knew of this great divide, for them dream and reality were an uninterrupted sequence of unconnected event. It was true that even in reality, sounds and shapes were shared by more than one meaning. In the summer he had paused to investigate the hum of an electric kettle in a blackberry bush and had found it to be but a circle of wasps, feasting on a bloated carcass of hedgehog.*

*And so he came to fear the illogic of dream, to fear that someday he might never really wake, but remain entrenched within that vast absence of rules that was the fabric of the simple anarchy of the consciousnesses of the rest of his species. To prevent a sudden return to this state of idiocy and logiclessness through the doorway of his dreams, he began to cultivate insomnia, took long walks to fight off sleep, and so came to be captivated by the beauty of dawn, and at the same time afraid that he would lose his memory of dawn – he tried to capture the colours of dawn permanently with ketchup on the living room cream rug, for which he was sent to bed without supper, and thus discovered hunger was the easiest way to stave off sleep.*

Sparrow, running out of paper, resorts to brief notes overflowing into the margins and finally the frothy expanse of cloud on an old postcard of Berlin tucked between pages. Could one compose an entire work of art on blank scraps of paper retrieved from garbage cans, the unused spaces of pamphlets and theatre bills, could he have written his poetry between the crabbed lines of his Latin grammar, in the margins of his Thomas Hardy paperbacks, or merely between the jostling icebergs of his own consciousness, between blind folds of grey matter, untouched by word? Raking through the transparent trash container by his side (which had only minutes before received gladly the residue of his yoghurt), he recovers with glee a leatherbound diary, unlined, scarcely full on a primary reconnaissance. He turns to the first page, eager to continue his story, he turns to the first stretch of white, unmarked but for one delightful memo: February 19 – 7 PM – Cook from Osaka arrives. Sparrow continues his story:

*The ketchup stains faded swiftly from the carpet (consigned now to the nursery) but not his memory of the sunset, nor of the raised outline of himself upon a brass plate upon the gate, BEWARE OF DOG, it said, and this he did not yet know, but the firm shapes of the letters pressed sternly upon his mind, was it his name he wondered, was it his name? The matter was cleared up by the cook from Osaka, who arrived one morning as he was relieving himself upon the carcass of a frog. A small man, he arrived, clad from head to toe in white, Beware of dog, he read slowly, and laughed, I make yakitori out of you, he said, patting him gently upon the head.*

Sparrow turns the page and meets, with dismay, a page-long list of the contents of an entirely chocolate dinner (inspired by a *New Yorker* cartoon, apparently), featuring chocolate-roasted quail, chocolate-flavoured asparagus soup, chocolate cheesecake, and the Estremaduran delicacy of chocolate-covered garlic breadcrumbs. Sparrow, increasingly intrigued, turns the page and faces the constitution of a locomotive dinner: pig's feet, shark's fin, frog's legs, chicken wings – this then is the painstakingly annotated diary of a lunatic gastronome, one who recognises that the mockery of ritual is embedded within its own absurdity, that the more complex the rule, the more fragile, the easier to break the wineglass – that the wine may fill your hand, and vowels be banished, for only then can poetry permeate language, rise from within the banal elegance of destiny, the cloying simplicity of fate, of order, into the infinite devastation of chaos, the breathtaking precipitous beauty of chance. The dog in his story struggles to preserve the order, uncharacteristic of his species, that has pervaded his consciousness, that tongueless order that was his own as a precocious child, with its misery of vicarious emotion, bane of all overdeveloped minds, the dog is a metaphor, of course, for the entire human condition, a precocious species struggling to find order within the intractable universe, and at the end of it all, speechless, dumbfounded, alone.

He turns to the cover page of the diary and discovers the surrealist epicure's name and address neatly pencilled within the provided box, Emanual Forsythe Whitt, and an address in Belgravia, not far, not so very far from where the park tapers onto the ferocious roundabout, hardly a quarter of an hour's walk.

* * *

Does she remember the story of the Oxypycni? Alexander asks softly, kissing the clenched childmouth, the orange-toed Oxypycni who lived under the shadow of the keyed serpent, Ophicleide? I will take you to your birthday party, he soothes her, honey boiling sulphur upon his tongue, choking back his anger he tells her she must dress now, for the clock has struck a half past three, and suddenly she is no longer in his arms, light footsteps recovering mirth in the hallway, and he is alone in the kitchen, a row of partridges gathered in glabrous prostration upon marble prayer slab. His mother brought them around earlier, a good day for game, eh? he had said to the child with a wink, but she had not understood, standing crestfallen at the foot of the stairs, birdchild, abandoned by the moon. His mother blew her a kiss, and flung open the front door, and an unreal stormlight came to bathe her contorted childface, crumpled childhope teetering painfully at the edge of light, she ran to his embrace before the first and pitiful crack of thunder tracked like a mild broomsweep across the skies.

And now the clouds have cleared as suddenly as they came, a tired summer blue paling in the afternoon, a cat stretches upon the sill, neighbourhood tortoiseshell, unfamiliarly smug, what can have kept you from such an overwhelming duty? he wonders, what but your appalling sense of time, your tragic faith in public transport, he sees you trapped in a clot of double-deckered weekend traffic, or sweltering in an Underground coach, caught like a fly in an endless straw, or perhaps even still stretched out upon the grass, engrossed in a book, time away and somewhere else.

Halfway up the stairs, he bumps into the child, racing madly down, she has slipped into the blouse and pinafore that she wore the day before yesterday, when you had driven out to his mother's for tea, he had watched her romping in the garden with Sparrow, watched them from the upstairs study while his mother laid out her plans for an extension to the cottage. He watched her climb onto Sparrow's back, and a strange emotion, mingling magnanimity and jealousy, only the faintest trace of jealousy, certainly, a bizarre emotion settled within the pit of his stomach, and remained throughout the evening. Alexander, you're not listening, his mother protested, and you, quietly surveying the manifold architectural drawings, raised your dark eyes to him in smiling mock reproach.

She wears the same lacy blouse, a little soiled at the cuffs, and the blue velvet pinafore, her hair pulled back into a passable ponytail, but she reeks strongly of aftershave, she must have splashed herself rather liberally with the bottle of Polo he keeps in the bathroom by his study. For quite often he will shave there, especially if he has worked through the night, given sleep the slip. She has doused herself with his aftershave, mistaking the green and gold perhaps for the colours of a more feminine scent she had hoped to wear, he stares helplessly at her anxious face, you look very nice, he manages to say.

She hands him the invitation, the inside pops up with a candy cottage and the wicked witch searing the address into the sky, we'd better hurry, he says to her. Outside, the ice-cream van is chiming, sounds of a summer fleeting, put your coat on, he tells her. At the door, he halts, what about a birthday present, he asks? didn't you get a birthday present? She shakes her head, fear growing in her eyes. What about that bear Sparrow gave you? he says suddenly, what about that bear, it's new, it should do. She hesitates a moment, then disappears. In a few seconds, she is back, carrying a pillowcase, the teddy, it would seem, is trapped between its jaws, snapped recalcitrantly shut, Alexander struggles to unlock the stud and the nipple, gives up and rips the combination out, what was it doing in there? he asks. The pillow was a shark, she explains, in a rough sea of bedclothes, Sparrow's old bedclothes, waiting to be washed, she had seen the maid bury her face in them this morning as she carried them down to the laundry room. The pillow had swallowed the unfortunate animal as he swam ashore from a shipwreck, he is pulled out by his ear, looking none the worse for his visceral adventure, a Jonah among teddy bears, he grins bravely at them, shouldn't we wrap it? she asks. No time, replies Alexander, bundling her through the door. He half expects to see you, running frantically down the street, but it is empty. He takes a small hand and crosses to the other side, there was a man, he begins, who spent a long time in a whale . . .

* * *

Sparrow, strangely excited, rings the doorbell of Emanuel Forsythe Whitt's proud home, and is hardly surprised when it is opened by a footman in livery, a shining black braid between his teeth. The man asks no questions, stands aside, meditatively chewing upon his braid, waits for Sparrow to enter, then closes the door behind him firmly. Sparrow is delighted to find himself in a narrow hall, dominated by a broad staircase angling past his ear, bountifully scarred by built-in bookshelves, overflowing with volumes, old and new, all recipe books, Sparrow notes with satisfaction. He follows the footman through a pair of swinging doors into a large, gloomy room, crammed with furniture. Emanuel Forsythe Whitt at a handsome desk, poring over an old text with a magnifying glass, it is all rather too perfect, perhaps he is dreaming, Sparrow does not care to know. Emanuel Forsythe Whitt is, as Sparrow expected, an old man, immaculately attired in the style of his day, he proffers a bony hand, and greets him in the sort of American accent that Sparrow always imagined T.S. Eliot might have had, are you the new scullery boy? he asks.

I could be, replies Sparrow.

You're from the States? the old man inquires, slightly taken aback.

Jonathan Sparrow, he extends his hand. At your service.

Forsythe Whitt shakes his hand limply. Sparrow, he mutters, I once knew a Sparrow – Samuel Sparrow, that's it – any relation?

I would not know, says Sparrow.

Samuel Sparrow, he invented self-adhesive labels, Forsythe Whitt continues, but it never made him rich, never. Died in a paper factory, Sam Sparrow, had whiskers the size of field voles.

Hmm, says Sparrow.

So what brings you here, young Sparrow?

I found a diary, Sparrow answers, deciding to come clean, I found a diary that you trashed in Green Park – earlier today, perhaps?

My diary?

Sparrow hands across the book, a bit of toffeepaper still clinging to its hide.

Must have been that Japanese scoundrel! Forsythe Whitt declares, I've been looking for it all day.

The cook from Osaka? Sparrow ventures to ask.

The old man glares at him, you have read it?

Only the first few entries, Sparrow replies, almost sheepishly, I thought it had been discarded. I'm afraid I even took the liberty of writing in it – you see, I'd run out of paper, which is why I fished it out of the trash in the first place.

Emanuel Forsythe Whitt sighs, well, at least I have it back, he says. He reads rapidly what Sparrow has added, is this about a dog? he asks.

Sparrow shrugs, possibly . . . though it started off as a rabbit.

Have you ever eaten dog? asks Forsythe Whitt.

Only inadvertently, I'm sure, says Sparrow.

Can you imagine how dog must taste? asks Forsythe Whitt, dreamily.

Astringent, bitter even, Sparrow replies without hesitation.

But spicy, adds Forsythe Whitt, spicy, resinous, and perhaps even a touch of cold cream.

And tigers? asks Sparrow, suddenly feeling tears in his eyes.

Eh? says the old man, distracted.

Tigers must taste like peanut butter, says Sparrow quietly, like peanut butter.

Like soft chunks of putrid memory, invested with sorrow, clothed in the tigerstrips of tender insanity. Algebraic absurdities have freed us of the burden of time; if we did not believe that tigers tasted of peanut butter how would we have lived with the vastness of the universe?

So are you the new scullery boy? Forsythe Whitt asks suddenly.

Certainly, says Sparrow.

The old man reaches across his desk to ring a bell, and almost immediately the footman appears to escort Sparrow back into the hallway and down the stairs into an enormous basement kitchen, many young men intent at various tasks, tonight he will be having an alphabet dinner, really an alphabetical one, with twenty-six courses beginning with Artichoke hearts (in tarragon and honey) and ending in Zarzuela. Can you write? asks the man in black. In a manner of speaking, Sparrow replies, at which he is furnished with a quill and an inkwell and a roll of paper – it is his task to write the menu – Artichoke hearts in tarragon and honey, Bamboo shoots in mustard oil, Cod liver – curiosity overtakes him, he casts his eyes down the list to the less flexible sections of the alphabet, and meets, to his delight, a succession of Veal curry, Whelks in garlic sauce, Xantippe salad, Yoghurt, to pause for breath before plunging into the flamboyance of the Catalan seafood symphony, the fortunate finale, Z is for Zarzuela. But Sparrow does not get that far, between Monkfish meringue and New potatoes, he is challenged in his occupation by a distraught young man who protests that he is the rightful scribe, that if his roller skates had not lost a wheel on the rocky ridge of a Camden pavement, he would not have arrived thus to find his position usurped. He has been without a job for many a week now, he announces with violence, he has an infant daughter to feed, he says to the doubtful Sparrow, who raises his hands in a gesture of peace, calm down, says Sparrow, I was only filling in for you, it's all yours, he says handing him the quill, have fun! He reaches for his sheepskin coat, which the heat of a hundred ovens had compelled him to shed. The row of small dishes on the central countertop is steadily growing, bite-sized morsels of each item, to culminate in the grand fish-fest for which several different hands are stripping squid in a large metal tub on the floor. Sparrow takes his leave of this dream-world silently, passing through a narrow gallery of mirrors into the back-garden, where the footman politely waits to escort him to the road.

* * *

There once was a man, says Alexander, who lived in a whale, lived very well too, for the inside of a whale is commodious, very large that is, and divided by walls of cartilage into many rooms, so it is very much like living in a large windowless mansion really. At first it was very dark, too dark, but once he had settled down a bit, he found a way to trap glowing seaweed that the whale sucked in, wrapped them around the spiny skeletons of sea-urchins and sea-cucumbers, and made very pretty lamps that he hung from the whale's ribs. Other types of seaweed he smoked, in a pipe carved out of a nautilus shell, resting in his armchair, which the whale had swallowed with him, he happened to be sitting in it when it all happened. He used to think that the armchair and the *Nautical Atlas* were all that the whale had swallowed, but one day, he found, hidden between two sheets of blubber, he found a jar of honey, but he never ate any of it, for he knew that if he did, there would not be any of it left for later. In the evenings he would sit in his armchair, smoking seaweed, listening to the whale sing – now whales sing very beautifully, but it is quite something else when you are inside a whale – like being in the pit of an orchestra – it was so beautiful that the man would cry, even though he was a very contented man really, but even happy people cry sometimes. When he cried he would wish that somehow he could talk to the whale, tell him how much he enjoyed the singing, but the whale did not even know that he was there, never felt him wandering around in the vast cavern of his insides, never at all.

* * *

Sparrow, utterly unamused, watches a large stain spread across his pocket as the tin of pickled beetroot that he has purloined from Emanuel Forsythe Whitt's kitchen proves to have already been opened, and gushes cold purple as it is knocked from unstable and unlikely equilibrium inside his pocket by a passing child. The child stops and rubs his head, then giggles to see the spreading wetness, and runs off. Sparrow lifts out the deceiving tin, and drops it into an overflowing dumpster. What might have been supper is swallowed by a confusion of sawdust and rusty hose, a headless rocking horse crowns the pile, some child might still have loved it, muses Sparrow, Teddy Ginsberg would have loved it, Teddy Ginsberg who kept a tea-kettle full of decapitated dolls, where was he now, Teddy Ginsberg, even the fish drowns, he had written in the basement of your eating club, above the beer kegs, even the fish drowns, as if it were some warning against the danger of alcohol. Even the fish drowns, it has a nice ring to it, Sparrow decides, as sorethumbed, he picks his way through a maze of scaffolding, to free himself from the ragged flow of humanity, spreading fast as the throatpulse of the afternoon thickens, in the sudden threat of rainstorm, and more and more people come to fill the streets, victims of an unwritten constitution, they will endure all vagaries of the weather, their blood is cold, Alexander had said of them, their blood is tired under the weight of vaccination, the myth of immunisation, their blood speaks of the attenuation of germ, battles best left unfought, their blood is sealed with the breath of myrrh, embalmed, they are the vaccinated men, hollow men, veins stuffed with old germs.

Can this fractured canopy offer refuge, Sparrow wonders, disentangling himself from an arachnoid extrusion of piping. He gains the foot of the stairs, sits down heavily, picks up a dusty Mars bar, half consumed, and bites gratefully into its mottled flesh. But it only leaves him with a craving for coffee, sorry residue of a month's habit of afterlunch chocolate with you in the park. Inevitably he would linger, walk with you down the ripening Broad Walk, and across Marylebone, onto Park Crescent, the marzipan walls of the Institute of Frenatology, coffee?

you would ask. He would follow you in, up the stairs, pad behind you through the library, into the small sunlit room beyond, your office, where yards of butterflies would be lying on damp blotting paper, that they might be rid of rigor mortis, you would pour a little filtered water on the edges of the sheets, the rest would go into the coffee machine. The afternoon light would fall in clean sheets through the tall windows, you would thrust a warm mug of coffee into his hands. Is it all right, he would plead, if I stay here for a while, and read? He would settle into the corner armchair with a book, alternately doze off and read, filling the room with his quiet chuckles. Sometimes he would find a passage he wished to share with you, stride across and tap you on your shoulder, you must see this, sorry to interrupt, but I must read this to you, he would say. Last week he had upset an entire cargo of Czechoslovakian Clouded Yellows to read from Barthes's *Michelet, the bamboo worm, if you remove the head which is deadly poison, furnishes an exquisite cream whose gentle and sopitive effects, according to the Brazilian Indians, soothe the pangs of love. For two days and nights, a girl who has tasted this cream, sleeping beneath flowering trees, nonetheless dreams that she is running through the depths of the virgin forests, the mysteries of the cool banks which have never seen the sun or the footsteps of human beings – nothing but the solitary flight of a great blue butterfly*.

The pangs of love, you said longingly, who would ever want to soothe the pangs of love?

* * *

Did he ever escape from the inside of the whale? she asks, her small hand in his, did he ever get out? the smallness of her attention shifting back and forth between the jaws of Alexander's narrative and the urgency of their journey, will we be very late? she asks.

But he did not want to leave the inside of the whale, says Alexander, he loved it there, you see, loved the softness of his inner jungle, the cushions of his inner flesh, loved his firm bed of blubber, loved his seaweed lamps. He would begin the day with exercise – work out with the whale's vocal cords, and the whale never minded you see, because his voice got better and better every day with somebody stretching his vocal cords – so that's how he would keep fit, and then he would breakfast lightly on seaweed cakes, and set out for his morning constitutional, walk the length of the whale's gut, which can be a very long walk indeed. And then, for the rest of the day he would think, settle into his armchair and think. You see, he had never had time to think when he was a sailor, because he was busy sailing, and trying to chase rats away from the ship's food, and things like that. But, inside the whale, there was nothing to do but think, to think and think, and think...

What did he think about? she asks, tripping over her shoelaces, he holds out an arm to stop her from falling, kneels to reknot her undone laces, kisses her anxious forehead, well, what did he think about? she asks.

Mostly he thought of the wide ocean, upon whose breast he had sailed for many years, without ever stopping to think about how beautiful it was, except when the beauty of it positively screamed at him, like the beauty of the sunset, or the wild beauty of storm. He tried to remember, instead, the beauty of the calm ocean, the steel of the noontime sea, the endless expanse of depthless water, and the more he thought about the depth of the ocean, the more his mind became like that ocean, bottomless, where other thoughts would weave in and out like fish. By the time they harpooned the whale, and found him inside, he had forgotten how to speak, you see, because his mind was like the ocean, all he could do was smile, and sometimes there would be a few tears in his eyes when he remembered the whale's music, which he missed dreadfully. So they let him alone, because he would never talk, and also because he smelled of blubber, and so he spent the rest of his days in a small cottage by the sea, living on seaweed and honey, staring at the water which had sheltered him for so long, and to which he could never return.

* * *

Yesterday in the country, Sparrow had lifted the child onto the roof of Alexander's car, sticky with chestnut sap, so that she might throw her light legs over his shoulders, and ride against his lopsided shoulder blades towards the overgrown banks of the stream at the foot of the garden, where she would scream "whoa, whoa" as Sparrow made to rush in, rearing and bucking like a mad horse, and finally flopped incautiously upon the ground, with her legs locked about his chin, and her small nails clawing in desperate delight at his meagre hair. He lay for a while with his face in the grass, while she sat pensively rubbing the small of her back, Sparrow heard footsteps, are you all right? he heard Alexander ask the child. Sparrow turned his head to see him crouching by the girl. You might have been more careful how you set her down, he said a little angrily to Sparrow.

Sparrow shrugged, reached to clasp a small grasshopper by its wings, and pop it into his mouth, the child screamed and looked away. They are good to eat, said Sparrow earnestly, better cooked though, in olive oil and garlic.

Has Emanuel Forsythe Whitt tasted of the bounty of insects, he wonders now, watching a stream of bees gush forth from the front-door keyhole of the gutted townhouse. He had finally made his way through the monstrous metallic undergrowth, crawled on hands and knees to the scabby front door in the vain hope that it would be open, and the night might pass between sooted walls, cankered parquet, the singed remains of jam-sodden chintz, for it is still in its early stages of convalescence, this house, its recovery unaided by the sudden downturn in the economy. But the door will not yield to his prodding and poking, instead a stream of bees emerges from within the bandaged keyhole, as Sparrow rips away the plaster, and if the keyhole were to drip thick honey, he wonders, someday will this image not crawl into the viscera of his poetry, someday, for now, it would have been good for eating, to lick slowly off the blackened brass, perhaps he could have lived for a while within these scorched walls, living upon the metallic honey of metropolitan bees, and an occasional feast of beegrubs, fried in the comb, and then there were dark moths to be sure, sootfringed, camouflaged against streaked closet walls, or fat against charred wool, smoked and preserved, all for his picking – if only he could let himself into this oasis of wasteland! And perhaps they would never really come for him, perhaps the owners would let the house languish behind its citadel of scaffolding, wait until the market looked up, perhaps they had set fire to it themselves, for reasons of their own, and he might really survive undisturbed, king of his cinerary castle, he alone with the carbonised family skeletons, the burnt rinds of teddy bear, and the wealth of smoked bedbugs, great cones of ready-cooked silverfish. He could pick his supper from within the crumbling leaves of the burnt books, and someday he might invite Emanuel Forsythe Whitt to an entirely insect dinner, to be eaten off the burnt remains of good porcelain, wipe the wireworm sauce off his lips with smoke-sodden lace napkins, if only he might somehow gain entry to this fertile mausoleum. Sparrow leans his head against the hollow door and remembers suddenly that he might do better, for Vladimir, dear Didi, generous Volodya, Vladimir had Federal Expressed the keys of his father's flat to him, three weeks ago, with it a small note: who knows, dude, you might need some space of your own. Dear Vladimir, Sparrow has the keys to his father's flat, the keys! why did he not think of it before, wandering shipwrecked from park to park, foolishly trying the door to this ghostly gutted mansion, when the day might have passed within the holy bareness of Ivan Dobryak's unused apartment, his head upon his rucksack, there might even be food there, biscuits, raisins, tea surely, rice perhaps, soup cans perhaps if he was lucky, he may delay his departure indefinitely, if it is a comfortable place, how could he have forgotten, he digs out his wallet and locates the scrap of paper with the address, unbelievably convenient, another short walk really, besides the sky has lost some of its menace, he almost feels cheerful, he would certainly have felt cheerful if this fortunate coincidence, like all others in his life, did not reek of fate.

* * *

DOBRYAK, in bold news letters, a little unsettling, is it really empty, this flat? You try the bell, there is no answer, you unlock the front door, and look around for a light switch, and in the darkness his hands rise to the curve of your neck, and you hesitate for a moment to savour the pressure of his invisible fingers, shadowed lips upon your shoulder. Ink-washed, Daniel's smile lofts itself, oh to founder in these various shades of grey, he pushes you gently to a dark wall, and seeks your trembling lips, the darkness is the cusp of two blind galaxies. In this darkness you would gladly remain, but voices part you, your agitated hands stumble upon a light switch, a young woman with a stuffed otter under her arm appears at the head of the stairs, nods briefly as she passes, you turn the key in the lock, it yields without fuss. You push open the door and stare into a desolation of peeled wallpaper, ladders, and paintpots, the boy slips in between you and his father and halts in deep fascination, you follow him, then pick your way through the hallway into a bright bare room beyond, the walls are a relentless white, the wood floor speckled with paint, it was in such pristine space that you had embedded your visions of a life with Alexander, not the jaded mockery of the plaster palace that has since become your home, the beloved image still returns, from time to time, of you and he, in a bare, bare apartment, replete with possibilities, and never so clear as now, in this stark holiness, dense with the smell of new paint. The child, emboldened by your silence, pushes through a pile of garbage bags to inspect the dining room off to the side, where a large table sits under newspaper drapes. What are you thinking, Daniel asks you, running a finger down a dusty doorframe. I was thinking, you answer, that this place has the air of a Buddhist monastery, these white walls seem so ancient. He is unmoved by this unfamiliar image, he walks over to the window, this room, he says, reminds me of where we keep the bulk boneless portions, he looks out into the street, a large moving van has just pulled up outside, whose flat is this anyway? he asks.

The front door creaks, hello, hello, anybody there, it flings open, who should it be but Vladimir's father, greyer than you remember him, he peers through the mess of ladders and peeling paper, my God, it's you, he says, hello, hello. He wades through, his arms flung wide, sweeps you in strong embrace, long time no see, long time no see, the Byelorussian Bronxspeak echoes through the empty apartment, the frightened child scurries back, rushes to his father, who takes his hand.

I knew you were in London, Vladimir's father still holds you by your shoulders, but Vladimir didn't have your address, you look well, you look very well, even more beautiful. This woman, he turns to Dan, broke my son's heart and now she dares to grow more beautiful. He releases you and holds out his hand to your companion. Ivan Dobryak, he announces with the deep satisfaction of one who would want to be no other.

Pleased to meet you, I'm Dan, and this is Kevin, say hello, Kev.

Ivan Dobryak takes them in, father and son, you can sense his suspicion that you have brought them in to squat in his apartment, he has classed them already among the riffraff that his son would regularly bring back to his Manhattan apartment, the homeless addicts that he would find sprawled upon the couch in the morning. He had been glad indeed when Vladimir had gone to live with his mother, who found his vagrants a wonderful novelty – she would be feeding them soup when he woke. There was always the comforting insulation of absurdity in his mother's house, a feeling that you existed on the edge of the world as you lay entwined in Vladimir's room, his mad lust shielding you from the incoherence of existence, the capers of the flood of people that came and went without. Sometimes you would emerge, but remain cocooned, drinking in the chaos through dense meshes of insatiable desire. Sparrow had despised your lipid bliss, your grand passion is a ridiculous anachronism, he would tell you, what is *amour fou* compared with *amour inconnu*, anyway?

I came to return your keys, you tell Ivan Dobryak, Jon Sparrow left them with me by mistake, so I thought I'd drop by to see if I could return them.

He does not believe you, of course, but that hardly matters, well, I'm glad we bumped into each other, he says, rubbing his long hands together. I've got to move some furniture in here, but the bastards haven't finished with the hallway, but maybe we can get them in through the kitchen, there should be some kind of delivery entrance . . .

The windows, suggests Dan, the windows are always the best bet.

That's a great idea, says Ivan, now, that is a great idea.

Your keys, you hold them out to him, it was good to see you.

Give me a call sometime, he calls after you, I'll take you to dinner. The child knocks his knee against a trowel, his father picks him up and hauls him outside. Shut up, Kev, he says as the boy begins to whimper, shut up, will you.

You walk in silence down the street, I'm sorry about that, you say.

He does not smile, so who was this bloke whose heart you broke, he asks suddenly.

I did not break his heart, you say. How can this matter to you, you wonder, how can this matter to you when all else has meant so little?

How would you know? he says quietly, looking into the distance, a hardness in his voice, flecks of ice gathering in his deep eyes. A sharp wind has risen now, coating you in a thick swirl of leaf, is it to be farewell, then, now that the dust has settled upon the afternoon, will he leave you now, in this ripeness of light, laughing ribbons of blood unwinding down the back of your throat, he cannot desert you now, to the ruthless autumn skies, not yet, he cannot leave you parched once more of that ultimate pain, courted long in the silence of the tropical winter, the climax of grief that has eluded you since, the final paroxysm of sorrow that would have left you whole again, if it had come, in the shadow of ice, while others drowned your palms in their easy tears and you sat, hollowed, wiping the puddles from the melting blocks. They had kept your sister on large blocks of ice, on the night of her death, and you had waited by her side for the distant scarlet within you to burst forth in sudden tempest of blood, and only a yellow dawn had come, falling flat upon the arch of your sister's death-soothed brow, only a yellow dawn had come, and your sister's child, asleep in your arms, had stirred and whimpered, and turned to bury her face upon your shawl.

And now he halts, a holy luminiscence escapes from a crack of cloud, garlands your desire in unexpected gold, he takes your hand and leads you towards a wreath of delicate neon. Licorice doors, swung open in trance, close again behind you, as he guides you firmly into the garish foyer of a young blue hotel. You stand aside, revelling in your new helplessness, you run your hands over the dark blue velvet of the walls. In the gilt-edged mirror you can see his tall back as he confers with the receptionist, you can see the child, who has run across to a clump of leather armchairs gathered in front of a television. All this and much more you can see within the mirror but thankfully none of yourself. For this is not the time to look into your own eyes, lest they seduce you, once again, into the orgy of analysis that had come between you and the agony of death, last winter, as you stood, combing your hair, at the old, wardrobe mirror whose attention you and your sister had fought for, often, you and she, as you dressed for a wedding, or straightened your school ribbons. You stood combing your hair, in slow, numb strokes, waiting for the men to return from the crematorium, you stood, facing the cold chipped glass, combing your listless tresses, waiting for the wall of sand within you to crumble and swallow you, and instead you had been engulfed by the irony of light, fettered by the laws of reflection, compelled to create a virtual being that was you, and was not you, and if the mirror had been blessed with memory, would it have held an image of your sister, what binds an image when the being has ceased to exist? You had realised then that for you, your sister's death had been the passing of an image in the mirror, that for you, the truth of her being was elsewhere, firmly entrenched only in the memories that had become the true substance of your relationship since you had left her, eight years ago. That was when the real physical link was severed, eight years ago. There had been more pain then in your parting, you struggled to evoke that smaller sorrow in apology for the numbness that had come to sheath you, but even that was to be denied you, for death had passed by, without raising his cold lips to your proud mouth. Death had left unquenched your need for pain, a rich dry laughter that was the indifference of the universe had come to fill the shell of your being.

The child sits stiffly at the edge of a long couch, his eyes glued to the TV set. His father kneels to pat him on his head, and whisper a few words of comfort. The child nods distractedly, lifts his baleful eyes once in your direction, and then is consumed once again by the moving image. Daniel returns, smiling, takes you by the elbow towards a narrow rake of stairs. It had been a house once, a family home, much like your own, this hotel, you press your backs against the candystriped wall to let by a pair of well-upholstered American women, wearing conference badges. His key opens a door, the first on the left as you reach the landing, inside it is green, the colour of wet moss, the walls are a still watercress, and the puckered chintz curtains sweeping the tufted undergrowth, the green gathers upon the paleness of his skin, fills the hollows of his cheeks. You would have him smell of death, the fermentations of a tropical stillness, green upon his lips. You would have him taste of death, sweet thick green, death, who had surfaced, last winter, from dark caverns of dream to mock your tawdry visions, to mock the tired metaphors in which you had tried to clothe him. You had scattered your dry hair over the glossy curls that fell feckless across the plump pillow, not daring yet to touch your sister's flesh, warm yet, her flesh. You had let your hair sink deep into the sea of lustrous black, until your lips had fallen upon the mingled mass, and moved in bitter haste towards the peaceful forehead, and from the foot of the bed, death had watched, in sad sarcasm, as your lips travelled the length of her hair and came to rest at the smudge of vermilion, poised to encroach upon his ultimate irony, the territory of her tranquil flesh. You had lifted your dry eyes to death before plunging to kiss the uncreased forehead, smooth the lids over the quiet eyes that had risen so swiftly to meet the boatless dark, joking of the smell of festering rodents in her urine, not knowing that it was her insides that had been gnawed to rat foam, or that long before she would find the moonlight unbearable, she would be plunged into indestructible equinox, where her laughter would trickle sandless between a perfect balance of light and shade.

* * *

Paper cups, shining green and gold, rub gently on her lip, the rolled paper rim pressing pleasantly against a newly toothless space in her gum, where a small weak whiteness has made a wobbly appearance already, Rima feels it with her tongue, gluey under the onslaught of sugar. She had come in as they were cutting the cake, the candles blown, still dripping wax, and all eyes had turned to her as she stood in the doorway, so terribly late. Her unshaven uncle stooped to kiss her and then he was gone, leaving a pair of kindly hands to guide her to the table, place a silver hat upon her head, hand her a plate, green and gold, laden with goodies, and the matching paper cup, cautiously filled with strawberry juice. She wrestles with the last few sticky crumbs as the first party game is announced, wipes her hands forgetfully on her pinafore and receives a folded card, sealed with orange tape – you are all to open it together – Jessica's mother warns – and the first person to figure it out, wins. As the rest of the cards are distributed, she studies the edges of her own card impatiently, what could it be, some strange animal? one of the seven Wonders, like the Colossus of Rhodes, perhaps? a fairy-tale character? – Go! – Jessica's mother commands, and the air is filled with sounds of tearing, a string of letters reveal themselves, ominously familiar, but like her tongue, in sticky torpor against her palate, her mind too seems bent under the weight of icing sugar, she knows what these letters mean, she has seen them before, the answer is in her belly, her mother would have said, poking her tummy, in her belly but not yet on her tongue, and then it rises, the answer, cold and clear, like a watery belch, the answer, for it is her name of course, spelt backwards, the answer rises, but her tongue does not yield, frozen under the spell of sugar, her tongue refuses to fashion her thoughts into sound, her tongue cannot be coaxed away from the palate. She watches miserably as another girl raises her hand, Anna Wilson, aided by palindrome, proudly announces that she has cracked the code, bags the prize, a Winnie the Pooh pencil box, and murmurs of respect from all assembled, the maid goes round with the waste-paper basket, gathering the debris of the game.

* * *

DOBRYAK, the name reassures, Sparrow digs into his bag for the keys, the keys? where in God's name are the keys? damn it all and twice round to hell, where are the keys? But before he gives in to despair, there are always the windows, except that now there are faces in them, far too familiar, and before he knows it he is ensnared, Ivan Dobryak, gesturing richly. Well, well, he says, raising the window, this is certainly a day for surprises, come in, come in. So you have been here as well, Sparrow is perplexed, a very strange character with her, Ivan Dobryak hastens to add, face like death warmed over, he says. Had a little kid with him, couldn't figure it out at all, probably some starving artist, except he didn't sound right, you know, sounded, I dunno, kinda working-class, if you see what I mean.

Working-class? says Sparrow with a shudder, working-class? Surely not!

I know you are mocking me, says Ivan Dobryak, magnanimously, and you know I kinda like it. I like it so much that I'm going to take you out to an English cream tea, if you'll wait for me to get my coat.

Sparrow is no stranger to cream tea, thanks to your insistence on garnishing any day-trip with this ritual, he would generally prefer to go with the crumpets and the cucumber sandwiches, although he would always finish the rest of your cream and jam, sucking thoughtfully on his teaspoon between scoops. With Ivan Dobryak, however, he makes no demands, a cream tea it is, within the lavender-and-black interior of the empty restaurant, the scones arrive coin-sized, on a lavender doily, a thimble of cream, and pre-packaged jam, no apologies, Ivan Dobryak drinks deeply of his tea, a wonderful British institution, he proclaims.

He finds himself often in London, he tells Sparrow, now that he travels so regularly to the Soviet Union, that's why I'm setting the apartment up, just so I can spend a few nights there, catch a good show, you know, great theatre London has, great theatre.

So what are your plans? he asks Sparrow, been travelling, I gather.

I have no plans, says Sparrow, I have never had any plans.

Which is why you always fall into the easiest groove, declares Ivan Dobryak, it's the same with Vladimir. All you young people, you think you are defying something, fate maybe, by making no decisions about life, and all you do is play into the hands of fate. Take it from me, life is about defying fate, not just ignoring it.

I had my palm read, recently, he continues, palms I oughta say. He wanted me to spread out both my palms, and he wouldn't touch them, just hovered over them, making funny sounds. He said the left palm told you what the divine plan was, or really had been, what the Big Guy had had in mind for you, and the right hand showed you what you had made of it, and get this – my right hand, this palmist told me, was more different from my left than anybody's that this man had ever seen. For instance, my fate line on my left had is really scrawny, see how much I improve on it on my right palm. Amazing, isn't it – not that I should believe any of it, after all this was just some guy at a party...

You kids have had it too easy, says Ivan Dobryak, if you'd grown up like me you'd know why you have to take control over your fate, because otherwise it's your fate that's going to get the better of you, where would he have been, Ivan Dobryak, still selling insurance in the Bronx, if he hadn't sat up one day and decided to make something of himself? I used to ask myself every morning, he says, how come little me got here, where I am – I didn't even speak English before I was fifteen, did you know that? Fate doesn't like to see you climb, let me tell you, fate doesn't like to see you do better than the next guy, so if you want to get somewhere, you gotta kick the habit, it's a bad habit, fate, just like smoking, it'll bring you down in the end if you can't control it.

Destiny is for the weak, agrees Sparrow sadly.

Destiny? says Ivan Dobryak, destiny, now that's something

else. If you got destiny, then you don't need to fight fate – but only great men have destiny, not you or me, he says.

Even the fish drowns, mutters Sparrow, under his breath.

What was that? asks Ivan Dobryak.

Even the fish drowns, says Sparrow.

I don't get you, says Ivan Dobryak, I don't get you at all.

* * *

Even the sweet clutter of Jessica's room, where they troop in to watch her unwrap her presents, even the gentle disarray unnerves your niece, for the contrast to the stark order of her own room is somehow unbearable. She is a stranger to this casual chaos, the contentment of small anarchies. She must school herself in the art of mess, she decides, for you certainly have not, although your room, admittedly, seems always to be a confusion of rumpled clothing and books, rubbing against lost jewellery, the odd breakfast tray, never recovered. But the rest of the house is always kept in order by the maid, it is not like a house at all, she decides, not like this house, at least, where every corner smells of people and laughter, her home is like a museum, the objects in it, stiff and unloved. She watches Jessica set aside the bear, Sparrow's gift to her this morning, her gift now to Jessica, unwrapped. Jessica sets it aside, with a small 'thank you' to her, then attacks her next parcel with renewed glee. The bear topples off the bed, no one moves to rescue it. Rima looks away in shame, and when they have left, one by one, the other children, eager to experiment with the new toys, she is alone in the room, she picks up the bear, and hugs it to her chest, no one will ever love him, she must rescue him, she creeps out holding him, down the stairs, through the hall, the front door is open, she slips out quietly.

# VIII

# *The Butcher's Arms*

His breath, still swollen in smile, curls around the memory of death upon your tongue, his broken fingernails, lymph-speckled, graze your neck as he pushes you gently upon the green bed. His lips press upon yours with the insistence of heavy raindrops, a smell of damp earth stirs within you, you drink of the paleness of his high forehead, the corpse-green brow that folds and falls into the dark hollows of his eyes. Still smiling, he struggles to master the intricacies of the amorphous garment that you wear under your raincoat, he unswathes the black muslin about your breasts, and throws it over your face, if all is metaphor, you remember from Flaubert, if all is metaphor, you rush to justify the immense uncodable desire that pierces you suddenly, if all is metaphor, what becomes of fact?

What is white dwarf? he asks suddenly.

White dwarf? you whisper, between breathless intervals, why?

He lifts his eyes to your face, you mentioned it earlier, you remember – like a bit of white dwarf you said about the cakes we almost bought at the shop.

His hands are busy at your breasts, what is a white dwarf? he asks, his ignorance unfolding gently about you.

A star, you reply, more composed now. A star that has collapsed under its own weight, the words roll like mercury upon your tongue, precious and fatal. A very heavy star, no longer giving light, you say.

A heavy star, he repeats, mesmerised by this incongruity, stars he still sees as luminous polyps, glittering echinoderms, in an inversion of black black ocean. A heavy star? he asks, smiling.

Getting heavier, and heavier, you say, but he is no longer

interested, he will feast forever on its uneven fate, but the moment it can only feed the blind singularity of his lust, the proudness of your nipples thwarts his curiosity, damn you, he says, unexpectedly, you'll make me miss the appointment with Kevin's mum.

And with his hands he covers your ears, as if to shield you from this innermost thought. Before you can speak, he swoops upon the fullness of your lips, still smothered in light cloth, kisses you through the transparence of muslin, packing it into the wound of your mouth, like some diabolic surgeon, his tongue writhes among the cobweb folds, pushing deeper. Can you take all of the gauze in your mouth, you wonder, this ghostly gossamer, of which once the best weavers of Dhaka could fold a sari's length into a matchbox, can it fill your mouth? But now he has pushed the wet creases away from your palate, tugs at the fabric so that it comes away, ripping a little at your teeth. His unfettered tongue roams, a restless spirit, among dry mouthscapes. The cloth has soaked away your mouthjuices, but in their stead a sweeter flood returns, churned by his tongue, a suspension of immortal honey that coats your senses as suddenly he draws away and rises to pull in the thick green curtains, for a truant afternoon glaze has jerked through the thin window glass, to pull across the room a sheet of white glass, beyond which your face quivers like the face of his grandmother, drowned in her bath water, three years ago.

Before he lowers himself, once more, upon the brocaded whorls, he jettisons his shirt and the black T-shirt beneath, and presents to you his proud, hairless chest, the colour of dingy marble. And as you lift your lips to his collar-bone, succulent ivory, touch his collar-bone to your death-stained lips, you are immersed within the patch of deep green beyond his shoulder, the colour of a dream, dreamt long ago, in the sour stench of a lingering tropical summer, a dream in which you woke, in a climate of ideals, where a man made ready to leave you, and your children, innocently asleep, while outside, in the narrow winding streets, the downtrodden masses marched in heavy silence, the crowds that had called to this unknown man, the father of your children, he stood in the doorway to their bedroom, gazing in mute farewell at those to whom he might never return. Tears gather thick within your eyes at the memory of this dream and wash in smoky rivulets down the broad uncluttered expanse of his chest. For a moment he is still, for he has yet to recover the intensity of his interrupted ardour, for a moment he is still, then swift compassion overtakes the motions of love, he reaches to kiss your forehead, encircle you softly with his arms, hands, no longer frenzied, stroke your salt-scattered hair.

Like a mass of bird feather he holds you, trembling now that the heat of his loins has been suddenly subdued, he closes his rough arms about you, arms that have been deep all week into the carcasses of dead cows, vats of mildewed sheep brain, those arms hold you now in dense embrace, and the smile hovers, once more, within the glorious green darkness. His smile, flecked with forgotten desire, becomes unbearably clear, and mocks, like death at the foot of your sister's bed, your desire to give shape to the incorporeal, to drag from the depths of your dreams, death, as he had appeared, in the chill silence of tropical winter, and weaken him with your dark eyes, as you had weakened them all, death, you had wanted to defeat and possess. From the arc of your sister's brow you had cast your dark eyes to ensnare him, and still death refused to desire you, and so too this smile, hovering above, and stirring within you a mad rush of blood, his smile, refuses to yield to your ripe sighs, he continues to soothe you, the strokes damp, the smile falls, your passion unquenched, he sinks into leaden slumber.

His lips entangle your hair in syllables of sleep, dream-laden fingers stray across your breasts, nipples swell, succubine, under the delicate meshes of drowned desire, fingernails, edged with old sheep blood, curl gently into your neck, and the firm pulse of his breath resonates with the forgotten rhythm of an atavistic passion. You push away your hair, uncover his smile hovering at the edge of the arid chasm of his unconscious. You reach, regretfully, to smother the chorus of swallows that has gathered between your thighs.

* * *

The Butcher's Arms across the street provides a convenient polished counter to set down a tankard of ale and watch, through the swinging doors, the gilt portals of the Grafton Hotel, but three pints later, considerably more intrepid, Avishek drains his glass and walks out through the gathering crowd of college students and bored young professionals, weekend-wild, across the street and through the glass doors into the panelled corridor leading directly to a flight of stairs. Checking the urge to walk up and try each door, he turns into the mirrored blue foyer, ignores the receptionist, and takes a seat next to the boy, whose dry eyes shift briefly from the television screen onto him, and then back again, some miserable cardboard animation that he sucks in like some lurid psychedelic soft drink out of a plastic carton. Avishek reaches into his pocket where the chocolate he had bought earlier nestles, a little soft now with heat, would you like some chocolate? he asks.

What will he ask you when you are face to face, I hope the wallpaper was not too tedious, did you have a room with a view, one that looked across at the spires of the Natural History Museum. Somewhere in that network of alleyways and mews, many years ago, Sparrow had decided to relieve himself, while you waited with an embarrassed Avishek, looking with sad scorn into eyes that trembled in disappointment and loathing, he had come all the way from Sheffield to meet you, and instead was being forced to endure the company of this foul, taciturn youth, who littered the air with bizarre conundrums, and elected to piss, not in the myriad public conveniences, but in a polite corner of the Royal Borough, he was glad to shed him finally at the Wallace Collection, but cringed to see him kiss you full upon the lips, though his saurian tongue stayed put, he had asked you if he was your lover, in a voice as dry as dead reed, he had asked, is he your lover then, this Jonathan Sparrow? You had snorted and laughed and told him, I do not think he could ever be anybody's lover, and even so shadows had sealed fast over his eyes, swept over the carcass of your lust. He did not dare to take your hands, not in the fear that had been there, two summers before, that the meeting of your fingers might be too much to bear, but rather in the bitter anticipation that your flesh would be dry paper in each other's hands. You had wandered through the dispassionate corridors of the city, dragging dead dream, you found yourselves at the Aldwych, where some amusement was provided by a proselytising Christian, who took you for man and wife, this irony sat as tepid steel under his tongue, and he had been disturbed somehow with the confidence with which you answered the pamphleteer's plea to ponder life and death and the existence of God, while Avishek, who had only recently paused to examine his teenage rejection of the divine, stood silent, almost sympathetic. You ducked into a cheap café on Kingsway. Over dingy espresso you told him, you had meant to say, not that you knew the answers, but that it was unlikely that the gentleman would know them any better, as if he cared, as if his mind could comprehend anything beyond the vast vacuum of desire that you had closed about him, and the nonetheless aching perception of your regret that this incident had not been shared with Jon Sparrow, and instead squandered upon him. And when soon (he hopes it will be soon, oh, it must be soon) you descend into this garish hotel foyer, you will, once more, perhaps regret that it is he rather than Sparrow that waits with the child, that it is he rather than Sparrow with whom you must share this absurdity. You had explained to him once, bare arms taunting, that between yourself and Alexander adultery was more a matter of bad taste than taboo, will you be angry then, to find him a witness to your indiscretions, or had you found some way to justify this foray into the uncouth fields of pure lust, had you carved poetry from mountains of kitsch, he looks up at the shimmering plastic chandelier, imagines you in the stranger's arms and burns with desire.

Does he begin to kiss you by taking first your lower lip into the ridges of his smile, glut his pleasure upon its bee-stung warmth, while your upper lip waits, arched back in confident anticipation, like the prettier schoolgirl watching her plainer companion dance, for those are the heights to which his beer-strung breath must aspire, the acid of his saliva will endure the quiver of your upper lip, will it not? Or will his tongue be distracted from this nobler purpose by the intricacies of your teeth, that charmingly crooked fence of enamel that no dentist had dared reduce into the sullen, solemn, marching row of cavities (the truth is, and this Avishek knows, that you refused braces, flatly refused to have your mouth a graceless scrapyard, he had watched silent as you told your father you would have none of it, you were ten years old then, Avishek shivered at your impertinence, looked fearfully at his uncle, but your father only laughed, to Avishek's immense surprise, your father only laughed), will his tongue be lost then in the maze of perfectly individual teeth, those that you had sunk once, in sudden fury, into Avishek's arm, though some of those must have been milk teeth still, a vicious little thing, you could be at times, and Avishek never knew when, never knew when he would have crossed that strange threshold of teasing, when suddenly your delighted shrieks would turn to screams of rage, suddenly you would kick and scratch with unexpected ferocity, you had sunk your uneven teeth once into his arm, the marks still remain, Mrigaya once had asked him what they were, the faint lines, like a scattering of thin iron filings near his elbow, and he had smiled and lied that he did not remember, precious scars of your past, fading every day, every day, his cells conspiring to obliterate the memory of this beloved wound, though it had been no joy then, when it was inflicted, your childfangs had driven clean through his pale skin, drawn blood, he had rushed to his mother, screaming in pain. His mother had fussed over it for hours, do you think he should be taken to a doctor? she had asked, it is an animal bite of sorts, after all? Of course not, your father had thundered, don't be ridiculous, let the boy be. He had sat for the rest of the afternoon, huddled beside his mother on the couch, she dabbed his arm frequently with antiseptic, which stung something awful, and you, quietly penitent, sat smalljawed at the other end of the couch, you're like a vampire, he told you calmly, you're like a little vampire. What's that, you asked. Someone who drinks human blood, he said, that's how they live, vampires, they have bat's wings, and black trousers. You listened greedily, not altogether displeased perhaps at the comparison, they fly around at night, Avishek told you, and are dead during the day, they live on human blood. Like you, he added, flinching again as his mother drenched his closing wounds in Dettol, you must have hurt her, his mother said, feeling a little sorry for you, you must have done something nasty to her, for her to bite you. But how was he to have known that his playful proddings would suddenly unleash such violence in your small frame, how was he to have known when he had crossed the barrier of your tolerance, and is it the same way now, with you, in the act of love, is there some mountainous descent into frenzy, do your nails claw now into the stranger's grimy back, grip his lean buttocks, the weight of his testicles, so happy to be free from their congested denim prison, do your peaceful breasts suddenly rise, in deep fury, towards his ribs, do your soft sighs congeal suddenly upon the roof of his mouth, how are you loving him, my love, you who have never loved me?

• • •

You rise from the custard plush to push aside the thick curtains that he had drawn in anticipation of more violent pleasure, a smaller death than that to which he had succumbed, lulled by your incomprehensible tears. You let back in the afternoon light that had distracted his passion, light raw and thin, light that trembles as if reflected off sad glass, light scattered by tired leaves, light past its prime dressed in youthful song. Last winter, you had risen from beside your sister's deathbed to close the tall shutters against the gathering dark, the mosquito clouds that might drift in to drink of the stillness of her veins, and stagger in the inebriation of death towards the skull-faced ventilators to rest their bloated bellies upon dusty cobweb. But before you drew down the dry wooden slats, you had stopped to remember, the first memory after death, the first small ephemeral triumph, you had remembered how, as a child, you had stood at that very window and gazed wistfully upon a game of hide-and-seek in the vast garden below, games from which you were invariably excluded, for you were too young, too small. Your sister had seen you, clutching the rusted bars, ignored you as always, until she discovered that you, by small subtle inclinations of the head, were indicating to her where the others hid, and thus you had become silent accomplices, your eyes never meeting. You focussed resolutely upon the spot where the monster, Sanjib, had concealed himself. Sanjib, guilty, the day before, of pouring tadpoles down your back, and your sister, sweeping back her hair to carelessly glance at you in the window, would rush towards the tree that hid him, Sanjib, who, a week ago, had dragged street puppies to feed at the teats of an itinerant she-goat, and threatened to cut off your ears if you did not help lift the half-blind puppies out from under a heap of straw and hold their toothless jaws to the underside of the tethered ungulate. You saw him, from your lofty perch, bite his wicked lower lip in exasperation, as time after time your sister found him. He, in turn, would concentrate his energies upon locating her, the game degenerated into a volley between the two of them, and the others, in boredom, dispersed, the game fell apart, and you stood, in the window, elated at your first foray into their world. Yet you would never be part of their world, for the following year you were to leave with your father for England and return in adolescence, intimidating in your knowledge of the lands that lay across dark seas, where the sun never set in summer, and never rose in winter before you were safely at school, you would no longer share their perplexity at the kindergarten chant:

> In winter I get up by night, and dress by yellow candlelight
> In summer quite the other way, I have to go to bed by day
> Have to go to bed and see, the birds still hop from tree to tree.

Legacy of a colonial education, where rhyme rarely met with reason.

Richer nourishment was to be found in indigenous nonsense – they say the skies smell sour, but are sweet to lick after rain – I come, Bycome, in a hurry, Rain come, *jhom-a-jhom*, I slipped and was potato curry – but even much of this was inaccessible to your childmind. How hopelessly alienated you felt sometimes from the absurd, a reluctant recruit to your older cousins' fantasies, clumsy extra in a summer evening's enactment of Tagore's *Land of Cards*, consigned to eternal insignificance as the Nine of Spades. You had spent hours that afternoon cutting spade shapes to paste onto your costume while your sister proudly tamed her satin robes, for she was to play companion to the Prince, sneeze-born shipwrecks who transport desire to the island of yawn-born cards, wreaking havoc in their ranks. Here is the new rule, they say, which is the rule of disorder, the disenfranchisement of chaos. Where the stage curtains had swung once between two mango trees, now a multistoreyed block of flats rears its myopic head, paupering sunlight, and what remains of the garden has been swallowed by concrete. Now Sanjib's wife fills the patch with her potted plants, and trees struggle from within the hardness, in their Caucasian circles of earth, sad fingers of magnolia that you pushed gently away to draw in the shutters, to sit alone, in the darkness, the heavy smell of new whitewash, a ghostly infusion of tattered blue, to sit alone and savour that last few moments of being alone with your sister, before emerging, edged with terrible dark, to kneel at the head of the stairs and take your sister's child into your death-soft arms, hold her silently to your heart, which had only now begun to drum violently upon your ribs, but she had freed herself a little impatiently from your grasp, bent down to retrieve a piece of cinnamon for the rabbit, Andropov, who snatched it eagerly from her small fingers, to fill the darkness again with the fury of his chewing.

* * *

Holy Mary, Mother of God, who came to rank far above the many-limbed images of childhood, the heat and dust of the festival fields, the sandalwood shrine in the mellow alcove, Holy Mary, how much longer this agony, this band of broadening blue in the back of my head, Mother Mary, palanquined in dream, in narrow dormitory cot, oh Mother, why is it that the afternoon light falters, skips a beat, squelched Australian vowels hold the child in solid trance, why is it that three full pints of India Pale have had the time to filter from his blood, leaving him doubtful, ready to try the six-ten from St Pancras, and risk the vast emptiness that is sure to come anyhow, the angels that will lie drowned in suspensions of gold dust, their feathered wings, always too palpable, feathers, home to lice, and other myriad dark infestations, feathered wings shrunken soaked, dripping drowned mites, will compact into the caverns of his being among those very corridors to which he has escaped, so often, even from you, wishing to be alone with his memories of you, the tunnels that have wreathed his desire in marble dark, the deserted carriages, carriages choked with men and women whose lives hung like scraps of muslin about him while he sipped upon dream, carriages, empty but for the darting eyes of a lonely nymphet in the corner, provocations that sealed his mood in such thick honey that he would hunt, almost, often, for a pair of schoolgirl eyes to ignore, perhaps it would be wise to nip across once more to the Butcher's Arms, and attempt to galvanise the fading enchantment of the unreal, that which has sustained him throughout the day, what other would have held at bay the wormwood tide, the flowering gall, that begins now to seep onto his palate, the glass-sheathed despair of that distant spring day, when your lips had met as dry bone in fondless farewell, and he had thanked the gods for revealing to him, once and for all, that he had lost you beyond all hope, that it was only some lingering love of romance in your undeveloped psyche that had drawn you to him in the first place, it was only the murmur of the stoic palm trees that had churned desire in your young veins, his sighs had been music only against the taut parchment of tropical summer, and perhaps if you had not been wrenched from that humid womb, if you had not taken your memories, your desires, your dreams and flung them to harden upon the new winds of a different shore, perhaps, if you had remained among the dust sighs and the sprinkled weeds, among the crow calls and the cart creaks, the mothballs and the mustard fumes, then, he fancied that this obsession would have remained your only refuge, that which was mutely conceived among the daffodil banks of your childhood, where first his blood had coursed to an utterly unknown rhythm, whose curious cadence had only served to startle, is this love then, he had wondered, twelve years old, his knees against the cold wall, drinking eagerly of your stirrings in the lower bunk, but where was the angst, the pain that most spoke of, and where was the lunacy, the rapture, the epiphany of his Shakespearean antecedents, all he felt was a pleasant lightness, desire without violence, that he would savour, through that month, his last Easter holiday in the scurvied Midlands, the first pale edges of flame that he hid in schoolboy harlequinade, from you, his long-limbed companion, whom he found more subdued now though still eager for adventure, still eager to scour the spring fields for the source of the Nile, to swing your long legs, longer now than his, from the apple tree and sight, through palm-curled binoculars, the enraged spittle of the Victoria Falls, Victoria Falls, where he had been the year before with his mother and father, sick with fear Avishek had stood upon the knife-edge bridge, while his father fiddled with his camera aperture, Victoria Falls, where you had never been, Victoria Falls, you would whisper as if it were made of lace.

And where are you now, in what seamy valley of ecstasy, wedged between being and nothingness, in the arms of a shabby phantom, a sorry substitute for death, you who should have been bride of the underworld, slipped through a mirror in wedding white, are ravished now in regions beyond hope. It must be the meaninglessness of it all, reasons Avishek, your disastrous addiction to the absurd. Even with myself, he thinks, oh it is so painfully clear now, even with him, it has been your love of the absurd, always, your craving for the surreal that has led you to indulge his tireless obsession, at sweet distance, of course, at sweet distance, although adultery, you had said, was more a matter of bad taste than taboo, between you and Alexander, more a matter of bad taste, and this he had accepted with pleasure, as the main reason not to indulge in your recovered ardour. For there had been times, indeed, there had been a few fatal moments, when that was all that prevented him from taking you, as he had dreamed once, dreamed for so long, into his arms. The shared dread of vulgarity had balanced you firmly within the comforting patterns of your lives, the reason not to flee to some deserted isle was not so much the pain and anxiety of subterfuge, but the utter crassitude of lolling in some fruity paradise. How infinitely more rewarding to encode your renewed lust in syllables of laughter, to savour its irony, share it freely with the rest of the world, the expansive Alexander, secure in his possession of you, and his own terrified wife, I will soothe you, later, he would promise silently to her troubled eyes. Later, I will take you in my delirious arms and kiss the sweet darkness of your lips, but for now, forgive me this inscrutable passion, forgive me these succulent webs of word, forgive me the forging of my uncreated desire, for it is all I have, save your inadequate, tender devotion which will someday surmount all, but not yet, not while this vernal gamble gathers sweet momentum, not until the last drops drip from the foundered angel wings, and their chorus is a faint drowned whisper, heard only in dream.

• • •

In sleep, he is as disappointing as your first lover, David, who would slumber after love in a colourless circle of security that murmured of after-dinner Scrabble in New Jersey kitchens, of basketball hoops shimmering upon a clear morning sky, of soundless summer evening, white as pain. His sleep had become unbearable to you, in the last days of your love, so unbearable that you would lie, staring into the miserable darkness, prodding his sleeping form with your toes, but he would remain, a fixed shadow, complete in slumber, perfectly in touch with the extent of his limited subconscious. On the night that you left him, no comfort had been more profound than to return to the unadulterated darkness of your unoccupied room, to rest against the richness of solitude, weep grateful tears into the holy night, no longer besmirched by his shallow dreams. All spring you had nursed the aching darkness, and that summer, between humid sheets, you had filled the spaces about you with dreams of Vladimir, and later, when he lay beside you, after your first insane act of love, you wondered, as the evening deepened, what would be the texture of his slumber, but he never slept, not while he was with you, sometimes a tea-coloured broth would swim upon his eyes, but he would shift and wake against the pressure of your shoulder, cover you in warm kisses, then sigh, as you feigned sleep, and sink once more into that light suspension of the senses, so easily dispersed by your touch, who needs to dream, he would explain, who needs to dream, he had said, when I have you? Perhaps if he had felt the need to drown, sometimes, in something more than the shallow waters that sufficed to renew his vigour, perhaps, then, you would not have tired so soon of his indestructible desire, and sought instead the rich dreams of Alexander, whose grave mutterings you had drunk with fascination, the creamy curses, and the laughter, cold moonlight, spiralling deep into the turgid regions of night, the vast winds that rose to inebriate you, stir the dust upon the butterfly wings pinned pale upon stern wax. Even now, in the cold mornings, abandoned by nostalgia you would look to Alexander for comfort, the restless edges of his young dreams, for you have long fallen out of phase, you and he, he will come to bed now in the first silence of dawn, and wake at noon, although, these days, he sleeps less and less. This morning he had been up before you, or perhaps he had not slept at all, you would not know, for you had been encased in the hideous vision of your sister's rotting form, you had dreamt, last night, of how, instead of dying, fresh as a winter creeper, your sister had battled long with death, until the moonstone upon her finger stood a monstrous white against her charred flesh, and the whitewashed walls beside her bed had spread with dark stains of ruined blood, and you had woken, remembering that you had begun to write of her death, long before it had become a reality, you had written of death, not in indignation, or despair, you had written with the disastrous longing that had illuminated the dreams of an abandoned ancestress, companion of the gods, who had called to death to soothe her, to dull forever the uneven flames of desire, the wounded lover who had longed for the blood kisses, called for the cloudy arms to close firm about her, smooth her trembling eyelids, and the endless tears gathering within her, the liqueur of sleep, mesmerised by the permanence of this rapture, this incorruptible bond. The young maiden had called for the ultimate sweetness of his tongue, death, and yet the poet had chastised her haste in courting death, the poet had intruded to proffer a dispirited endorsement of life, naked of metaphor, urging hasty youth to contemplate life's treasures. Is that what marks the loss of youth, you wonder, swallowing chalk as you gaze upon Dan's pock-marked shoulders, this final disenchantment with death? Is life then merely the continuous dwindling of the desire for destiny, that which has given us the manic strength to plow through the universe in search of some all-encompassing abstraction, whether it be god, or the sinuous jaws of mathematics, that peculiar youthful hatred of chance that had conquered chaos, anchored it with simple determinism? Am I, you wonder, about to lose my fascination for order, that which has made music sweet, sweeter, for in music is the desire to tame the untamable most refined, in music, certainly, we have sought to harness our most desperate dreams.

Nicholas Butterfield, Avishek's partner, friend of many years, it was Nick Butterfield who had first interested Alexander in chaos, shortly before it had acquired the trappings of a pandemic, Nick Butterfield had spent an evening scrawling on paper towels, the simplest rules, he had explained to his delighted audience, the simplest rules of change could bring about armageddon, total disorder. At the heart of all stochastic processes, hard determinism lay buried, sometimes deep, too deep, but it was there, so Nick Butterfield believed, and all this he had abandoned to bake bread, and why not, he had asked, darting a quick keen glance at you, all evening he had treated you with the awkward deference of an adolescent meeting, for the first time, his best friend's beloved, indeed his curiosity must have been deep, and you for your part had been overwhelmed, once more, by the realisation of the power you had commanded once, that you commanded once more. Nick Butterfield spoke of chains of uninevitability that bound this universe and Avishek sprawled out on the window seat, gazed every now and then upon him in fond pride, and otherwise fixed his large laughing eyes upon the stream of Sunday-evening traffic outside. Chaos, said Nick Butterfield, can be harnessed to a small degree by predictability, whereas pure chance defies all sortilege, but you were distracted by something in the gentleness of Avishek's voice, speaking in quiet tones to his wife on the hallway telephone. You felt the edges of a soft fear, might there be pain in this, after all, you wondered, might there be pain?

• • •

If you keep the kitchen tap on, Nick had explained, you decouple the two functions, as in that of heating the water, and delivering it to the shower head, partially, at least.

The lease for their Islington flat prohibited showers and pianofortes (and dead donkeys and priests, Nick had added mysteriously) but they had wilfully installed a very rudimentary version of the former, one that could be concealed easily, the problem remained of achieving the tremulous balance, the narrow margin of bearable temperature that the structure grudgingly afforded, for their boiler was of the variety that heated the water as it was used, in some proportion to the force of the flow, this gave you the option of a tepid trickle or a scalding jet. It took four months of burned shoulders before Nick hit upon the solution – if the kitchen tap was left running, the water would heat, and the bathtap could be adjusted without affecting the temperature. You decouple them, he had explained, and hey presto, you are back in the world of linear relationships.

Ten minutes later, he emerged, cursing loudly. Bloody higher education, he muttered, nursing his charred calves. His trick had not worked, the water remained infernally hot. Bloody higher education, doesn't exactly equip you for life's little emergencies, does it?

Easy on the cliché, then, Avishek buried his head upon the mouldy couch, trying to drown out the unceasing clink of the water instrument in the flat beyond, Johnny Anonymous and

Neil Pollution, whose living room was a mess of earthenware, filled to various levels with distilled water, on which they played Serbo-Croatian folk tunes, almost constantly. It had been a terrible year, their first in London, the unrelieved boredom of his laboratory work, the dull conviction that had grown within him in his last year at Sheffield that life would change, that life must change, this watery hope had trickled thin in the saltless stretches of his new existence. A bitter confidence had gathered within him once, in the thought of having lost you, finally to have lost you beyond all hope, you hung like a sweet black dream beyond his other mirrorflecked desires, the finality of this distance had come to enchant, and when that summer he flung your letters, sodden with barracuda curry, into the filthy Atlantic, he still was sweetly stung by the fulfilment of your doom – he had lost you, as all great loves would come to be lost. It was only in London that it grew upon him that you were truly in his past now, that the memories had worn thin like old silk, your face took contours that he could no longer have sworn by, it was over, even the end, even that was over, this emptiness would rush upon him as never before after the occasional act of love that peppered his unwholesome existence, and he would roll away from a woman's sticky embrace to confront the blankness, untempered by the vapid tracklements of orgasm. He would snatch himself quickly away from encroaching fingers, like some toast? he would ask, is something the matter? the girl might demand, and in answer he would fling the tub of margarine onto the rumpled bedclothes, reach over to kiss the bewildered eyes. It was a bad year, the worst yet, certainly, long hours at the laboratory, communing with trypanosomes. He worked obsessively, and without pleasure, shunning all opportunity of distraction, he would return to the flat, late, ignore Nick's note to join him at some juncture in his evening adventures, and settle himself with a baked potato in front of the capricious television set, occasionally he would return to find the flat crowded with Nick's tedious pinstriped Oxford friends, who would chastise him for his devotion to the parasites, and make viscous jokes that slithered over and around each other in his aching skull. When they left, Nick would complain that they bored him. Nick, too, was disillusioned, but found this a source of amusement rather than despair, they had been spat out into the world from their undergraduate cocoons, he maintained, these were the birthpangs of reality, and he embraced them with the gusto of a newborn gulping air.

It was Julie Butterfield that had saved him then from despair, Julie Butterfield, answer to his prayers, she turned up at the flat with her bags, a grown woman, blonde hair tied back into a long shiny tail, I'm staying until I find a job, she announced, I hope you don't mind. From the couch he had shaken his head, he remembered her as a girl, as with you, he had known her for years, but he was far too submerged in a devastating apathy to respond to the familiar lure of nostalgia, he had given up going in to the lab, spent his days reading ferociously, rarely venturing out of the flat. She found his depression fascinating, his African childhood exotic, his public school past amusing, and above all, she could not resist the smell of dry wood upon his breath, their lust had all the qualities of a vast change, the lovely strands of hair upon the pillow, rich in different tints, the reassuring length of her vowels, the black velvet ribbon that she ironed every night, the complimentary theatre tickets that came in the mail, and those bloody cocktail parties that they simply had to attend, and in the middle of this all, her brother, waking him at dawn, put your clothes on, we're going to drink ourselves silly, I've had the most incredible idea, how would you feel, my dear Avishek, how would you react if I told you, our future lies in bread, yes, bread, an endless unexploited expanse for our superior imagination, our cross-cultural talents, bread. Avishek had been angling for some City job, through their parents' connections, some mindless occupation that paid enough for him to marry Julie, but the bread scheme pleased her no end, even though it meant marriage would have to wait. Avishek submitted slowly to the idea, but a strange taste hung upon his palate, a business? bread? what would his father say? His father cursed and this gave him strength, the capital was Nick's, the small business loan, they were the enterprise, and how! No stifling, trifling answer to the Prime Ministress's pungent polemics, five years ago they had set out to create the playground of their most bizarre dreams. But he had not married Julie Butterfield, instead he had taken advantage of a sullen period of silence that followed a trivial argument, to travel after many years to the land of his birth, and return with a wife, doe-eyed Mrigaya, her name walnut-wine upon his tongue.

Chaos, said Nick Butterfield, at a picnic in the Chilterns, chaos encloses only one poetic principle, and yet your modern poet has been scratching, fruitlessly, for blood in that sealed wound, not content to revel in the sweet agony that disorder is no longer merely dissipation, no longer a distant slow dissolution of the exquisite geometry of the universe, but a process inherent within the same rules that create and explain order. Poets, unfortunately, have been trying to milk it for more than that ... his sister slammed shut her book, and unlatched the hamper, laid out an extensive selection of salads and sandwiches, dwarfing Mrigaya's vat of potato curry and the hill of puris (home-made? Alexander had joked), Julie Butterfield dug into the wicker hamper and pulled out an endless stream of pies and quiche, a roast chicken, resplendent with herbs, plump potato cakes, fluted pasties, vol-au-vent with crab, spicy sausage rolls, sambuca naps and fresh strawberry tart, banana bread with ginger butter, fig rolls and frosted knuckles. They stared aghast as she unloaded pineapples, watermelons, cantaloupes, punnetsful of nectarines, raspberries (still a bit frozen, she apologised, they're from Scotland), blackberries, mulberries, dried figs and apricots. Didn't I tell you, her brother asked dryly, didn't I tell you, there would only be six of us.

Mrigaya began to shiver, you put a shawl across her shoulders, she must be crazy, you had said in Bengali, don't take any notice, reaching for a sausage roll, you had remarked loudly, looks delicious ...

Indeed, said Avishek, grimly, you envisioned him weighing petty justice against paltry irony, should he decline every tantalising morsel, or sink blissfully into the yard of strawberry salad at his knees. You watched him waver, and a blunt rusty knife scored your appetite, is there to be pain in all this, you wondered as he reached hesitatingly for the avocado dip, is there to be pain, after all?

He had found himself, later, in a roomful of stale gingerbread houses, he had found himself, wishing he had married Julie Butterfield, for it might have been easier, then, for him to transgress. Sugar dust settled about his nostrils, he let his mind wander, carving images of the four of you at dinner, he and Julie, you and Alexander, the tender fish-knives, clouds of wax light, the pleasantly putrid Chardonnay, no, but your contempt for her would have clouded the tenderness between you, stretched it sour, and yet it all might have been more simple, more patterned. Years later, the fog would have crawled thick about you in the Highlands, you and he, and a gaggle of children, his own and yours, trooping on ahead. The best thing about the fog, he might have said, is that it hides us. How he longed to tell you so, even after the fantasy had crumbled, even after the wet bleats had fizzled into the harsh neon, and his gaze had returned to the stale gingerbread huts, desiccated fairysugar, wizened caramel, fractured candystripe. The entire consignment had been returned, children who had eaten them woke screaming in the night, not from fear that the old witch might get them, but from a terrible tugging at the guts, some mysterious ingredient, which they had yet to analyse. What's the point, said Nick, catching him, alone in the dim store-room, among the forest of gingerbread houses, what's the fucking point, he had said, sweeping back his flour-specked hair. In Japan, they are dusting sushi with gold, and we are making bloody gingerbread houses. Our dreams are spent, he said, his eyes searching the darkness for Avishek's face, our fairy-tales are sunken pits of old old emotion. We are history, and not even that, a cascade of machinery set him scuttling in the direction of the noise, but Avishek stood rooted, enfolded in fantasy. The best thing about the fog, he longed to tell you, the best thing about the fog is how it hides us.

* * *

Daniel, you beg silently, turning his sleeping face in your hands, oh Daniel, wake up, Daniel, please. But he is dreaming of his grandmother, whom he had found three years ago in her bathtub, peacefully drowned. It was not a tragedy for him, more a relief, freedom from the weekly visits to the senile old woman. He had never been attached to her, but as there was no one else to care for her, he had assumed the duty of looking in on her without fuss, it fell on the way to work and so was easily accomplished, he did not mind in the least. He sat for a while at the edge of the tub, wondering whether to pull out the plug. She was clearly dead, wrinkled white, in fetid transfiguration, he decided to let things be and called the police. He is dreaming of the unsteadiness of her shrunken features, under the foul water where, in his dream, dozens of Kissing Gourami float, belly-up, he will not wake while the sewer smell of her death wavers in the wide spaces of his unconscious. You surrender to the firmness of his sleep, perhaps you should leave now, you wonder.

Should you leave now, you wonder, quietly slip away? Leave this interlude in sordid suspension, return once more to the fatuous order of your life, where this day will hang like a mediocre lozenge, half sucked, in your memory? Will you tell Karin, will she not merely curl her sweet lips in distaste, for this has long passed out of the confines of polite lust, will you tell Karin? Will you tell Alexander, will he not merely laugh, hope he had no diseases, he will say, you didn't really fuck him, did you, my sweet? No, of course not, you will tell him, we just messed around a bit, there was some perverse attraction which I couldn't explain, not even to myself, and Alexander will shake his head, and smile, well, don't run away with him, my love, you know I would kill myself. He will kiss you a little longer perhaps than usual, more likely I would kill him, I suppose, he will say, laughing.

You should certainly leave now, you decide, even though your unfinished act of love flaps loose about you, like a fatigued garment, hoping still to be worn to some grand occasion. You should certainly creep silently away, before he wakes, you would go now, but suddenly he shifts to trap your hand beneath his rough cheek, the sourness of his breath circling your wrist.

You wait, and your hand grows numb, your body fills with a motherly tenderness, for he lies, strangely helpless, stripped to the waist, arms flung wide in peaceless crucifixion. You lay your head upon the pillow, beside his head. He stirs a little, opens his eyes briefly, smiles, and reaches to pull you up onto the bed, pinions you to the sagging mattress with his sinewy arm, and falls headlong, once more, into swollen sleep.

His breath rises and falls against your cheek, the blue-tinged nakedness of his closed lids moves you strangely, you kiss the aimless bulge of his iris, and if you were to see him someday, wrapped in old cardboard, a chipped begging bowl at his side, would you stop only to slip your gold earrings into his broken hands, or would you sit awhile silently at his side, worse still if you come upon him on a unicycle, bells on his toes, would he not lose his balance if he were to catch your eye, you might want to hurry on, but your friends will insist that you stay through his act, or your niece perhaps, tugging at your arm, will plead to watch the funny man, would you rather see him beg than clown, my lovely, would you rather see your lover beg than clown?

If you were to extricate yourself now from his sleephold, slip away without farewell, would he return to your life as a manservant at Alexander's mother's home, smile in your startled face as he answered the door, gather your weekend bags from around you, while you stand rooted with fear and delight on the doorstep, and his starched arm would brush yours as he served the soup, for your eyes alone he would take your half-eaten dinner mint and pop it, white-gloved, into his long mouth, all night you would toss and turn and ransack your memory of the new houseplans for secret entry to his quarters, and in the morning, you would wake late, to watch from your window, his bare-chested exuberance, as he washed his mistress's car, and sometime you would find him, through the insanity of instinct, he would latch the barn door, and impale you upon the hay, silent and victorious, cornstalks in his mouth.

But perhaps he is just another writer, searching like yourself for inspiration, and this is all an elaborate ruse, the child is no more his own than the fake Council flat, and you will run into him again over afternoon cocktails, with a different accent, we've met before, he will say to your host, though neither of us could tell you where or when.

You close your eyes and inhale the cidersweet odour of Daniel's dreams, and soon you too will succumb to the vacuity of the afternoon, the firm rhythm of his breath, lapping against your ear. You too will escape the fetters of light, the idiocy of cause and effect, you will escape to reign once more in that region of rulelessness, where your niece calls despairingly to you across a field of gnarled olive shoots, rising like tortured digits from the scarred flanks of an intricate and shadowy world where marriages are solemnised over the bodies of dead donkeys. The child wanders helpless, you wish you could go to her, but you must answer the doorbell, 'tis Ivan, on a visit, tisivanonavisit, and whatever happened to Vladimir, he asks, why did you give him such a raw deal, he was a good man, my son, and he loved you more than anyone ever has, you know that, loved your essence, that very kernel of your being, which you yourself could never come to trust, is this all he receives, then, a few overdecorated lines in this story of your life? Live not on evil, warns Ivan, livenotonevil, and harken to the cries of the moonchild, sifting through her mother's pale garments, the shapes of moonseas pressed against the skimmed white, she wanders the streets, poor child, inhabitant of a strange land, she wanders the streets alone, gathering in her small arms, the garments of the moon, you see last night the moon came dropping her clothes in the streets, we took it as a sign to start singing, and why not, says Ivan Dobryak, how often does the moon come dripping all over the streets, we snorted up the moondust with hundred-rouble notes, wouldja believe it, and we sang, all of us, we sang old Russian folksongs, like my babushka taught me, I thought I was falling up you know, and the sky was a wide wide bowl, that lunar marching powder was fantastic let me tell you, I had the sensation of falling *up*, can you believe that, I wouldn't have thought I was capable of such a sensation, I was falling up into the bowl of the sky, then the bowl breaks and suddenly everywhere is falling everywhere, I can't believe it, everything is falling on something else, let me tell you, it was something else, but I must go now, don't give my son a bad reputation, I beg of you, he was a good man, the best in your life, let me tell you.

Here's the new rule, whispers Ivan Dobryak, tapping you from behind, here's the new rule, he whispers into your ear, break the wineglass, break the goddamn wineglass, and fall, fall, fall if you dare, fall towards the smog of the glassblower's breath.

[illegible]

[illegible]

# IX

# City of Pain

On the plane back to Newark, New Jersey, Sparrow had dreamt that you were dragging Avishek through a swiftly changing landscape of your imagination, your cousin whom he had last seen out of the bus window, long after you had turned away, horribly keen to return to your new life. Sparrow had inclined his head a last time towards the receding bitterness of his smile, and hours later, his head against your shoulder, he began to dream that you had drawn your grim cousin into the territory of your vast unconscious, your shifting dreamscapes, where he fled with you from a gingerbread graveyard into a crowded church, the rabbit Andropov bathing in the baptismal font, and there was Sparrow's own childhood pet, the white-tongued turtle. You ran on with Avishek into a tall brownstone, only to find that this was hell, with knotted sheets twisting down the floorless length, ketchup streaming from the ceiling. You covered his eyes and jumped with him into the void, landing upon the firm green of an Alpine slope, and there, in the sharp sunlight, your cousin buried his face upon the grass and cried from nervous exhaustion, he buried his face upon the sweet-smelling clumps of mountain weed, and pleaded for release, and you, with your cheek against his, your breath warm upon his ear, begged that he embrace the terrifying morphology of your imagination. Don't give up, please, you said, bear with me, you said, tears streaming hotly down your cheeks, bear with me, please. A blinding luminescence woke Sparrow, as you reached over him to pull up the window shade, I need to read, you said, and I don't like the overhead light. He leaned his head against the cold glass, through the chinks in the clouds, he could see the distant ocean, poxed with ice. Hell will freeze over, he mumbled incautiously, and we who have made this will have forgotten.

What does Avishek mean? he had asked.

Avishek? It means coronation, you answered, hugely amused at the translation.

Very regal, Sparrow commented drily.

More divine than regal.

In your country, that is much the same thing, if I am not mistaken.

The white-tongued turtle, his ancestors had borne the weight of the earth while your gods churned the seas for the beverage of immortality, the weight of the universe concentrated upon turtleshell, as an oak table might stand on eggs. The latter was entirely possible, Sparrow's grandfather had assured him, he had seen it himself, the wonder of the arch. Sparrow did not dare experiment with eggs, but the turtle withstood much torture, as the child Sparrow undertook a thorough investigation of the endurance of its carapace, the turtle in revenge gave him mononucleosis, that strange thinning of his blood, which kept him in bed for a year, with books as his only companion, and so Jonathan Sparrow lost favour with the track and field coach, as his wiry form weakened, and instead came into grace with the purveyors of conceptual consistency, Jon Sparrow, poet and mathematician, come softly to his own wake, an unnoticed intruder, shifting the unruly crust from hand to hand, unable to weep for himself.

This flirtatious sunlight, weakens and binds his resolve, the low-cholesterol cream tea has only fuelled his hunger, that grand limitless hunger, hunger of some other being trapped within himself, the aching insensible hunger of some prehistoric beast, dissociated, travelling bodiless through time to find home in his gut. Sparrow senses that he is being watched, and turns around to confront the slightly Oriental eyes of a firm-jawed gentleman in a black overcoat. Sparrow turns in at the gates of the Natural History Museum, the man follows, his dark eyes fixed upon him, searing upon his skull. There is an admission charge, Sparrow fumbles in his pockets, debating whether it is worth the investment. The sloe eyed man is behind him, let me pay, he offers, and without waiting for acknowledgement, shoves a ten-pound note towards the cashier. For both of us, he announces in a tensely groomed British accent, his dark humourless eyes return to Sparrow's face. Will he feed me? Sparrow wonders, will he give me shelter? He sees that the back of the man's head is cruelly shaved, high into his occiput, you shall be anonymous, he says quietly, as they walk into the stiff vaults of the museum. I am Jovanovich, his new companion declares, leading him into a corridor of brightly coloured fish. Within a year, I will be blind, says Jovanovich, so I was told today, which is why I am here to feast my eyes, although perhaps such colourful memories will only sharpen my pain, later, when I can see no more, his voice is a thick whisper, curling like whorls of sugar in the semi-luminous coolness.

I wonder how it will happen, he says, his fingers grazing Sparrow's clenched fist, first perhaps a greyness, do you think, a greyness from which I will be glad to escape into a total dark?

I used to be afraid of pain, he continues, so afraid that I would rather live with an insipid happiness, now I am no longer afraid of pain, that is my only freedom. I look around me, and all I see are people afraid of pain, desperately cowering under the mantle of small comforts, petty illusions. My heart bleeds for them, and how I savour this bleeding of my heart.

I used to be a man of habit, he admits, in pattern I found refuge from pain, as you all do, those of you who shy away from pain, submitting to all the addictions of conformism, and the sorry belief that pain lies outside the narrow path of ritual, which indeed it does.

These fish, he says, pushing Sparrow's face close against the wall, these fish look as if they have just been blown out of glass, and dropped to cool in water, where their motion will be dictated only by the opposing tensions of cooling glass. I cannot imagine an existence more devoid of pain, this submergence, and if man had wanted to avoid pain, he should never have evolved, never struggled out from within the cool ocean depths to meet the tortured rays of the young sun. His hand lingers upon Sparrow's unwashed nape, the tips of his fingers press briefly against a bony protuberance, then withdraw, do you think I will miss any of this flamboyance? he asks, this unnecessary flagrance of colour, or is it shape that I will miss, the shape of neck that I might only feel with my hands, my lips – if one will be so kind – my poor inadequate lips that will never trace the outline of shadow, the changing shapes of cloud, nor the limits of flame.

You remain speechless, says Jovanovich, because I have no place in your scheme, your routine, the little games you have grown accustomed to, even tired of. Admit it, I have destroyed the symmetry of your day, have I not, robbed your petty concerto of its rousing close, how will this day end for you, I wonder?

How can it end, Sparrow wonders, except under the flatulent lighting of an airport lounge, for he will not be able to withstand the onslaught of Jovanovich's dense monologue for much longer, nor can he tolerate the thought of returning, be it without explanation, to the flabby comfort of your home, although it is menacingly close, drawing his senses like a sullen magnet, through the elaborate museum walls. He can feel all paths converge at your door, but surely it is an urge he can resist. How can this day end, that should have ended between soft sheets in an Upper East Side apartment, Vladimir's mother's intermittent address, and less occasionally, his own. Jon Sparrow, itinerant candlemaker, in Brownian motion on Manhattan Island. Your address book will confess to this, the criss-crossing of telephone numbers will trace his history, in grudging detail, from the Greenwich Village basement and Helga's sagging bosom, to a house-sit in SoHo for a travelling professor (she, who stuck her manuscripts in empty vodka bottles, to sail the sea of time, and reach out to some fortunate in another century), and thence to the flatshare on Horatio Street, and always, in between, back to Vladimir, the inevitable nexus, so that his path traces a misshapen flower, as a child might draw, with its many sharp petals radiating from a node at seventy-second and Park (where the pencil will have pushed through the page). Sometimes you will run through the tangled list, your fingernail gathering ink grit, and try to imagine each configuration, attempt to recall the surrounds, the houses and the streets where you had walked, the island that you had abandoned five years ago, promising never, never to return. It is easy to see him in Vladimir's apartment, in that small, bare room, where he had sought refuge from the strains of your passion, many years ago. Bury me in alabaster, he had thought, so that these sounds may never reach me, nor even the silences, that spoke so painfully of the cavernous qualities of Vladimir's desire, bury me in salt, so that only the music of pain will fill the cracks between the granules. I was never afraid of pain, he thinks, I was more afraid of the absence of pain, the worthless density of satisfaction, the molasses of requited love, I was never afraid of pain.

You are still afraid of pain, says Jovanovich, reading his mind, you have run from pain, run long and far – as I see by your baggage tags, you have tried to escape pain, and yet its prison-stripes run the length of your face . . . here, he touches Sparrow's forehead, and draws his ringed fingers down the ridge of his nose and over his lips, the close stubble upon his chin. They are alone in a roomful of mastodons, those beasts whose ancient formless hunger still gnaws at Sparrow's senses, he had carved them once out of velvety wax, the last of his dinosaur series. It had been Helga's idea, and he had crushed them all to pulp on the night that he left, while she stood screaming with despair. Break them all, why don't you, she had said, break them all, you pathetic little wimp, and get the fuck out of here, before I throw you out. She waded menacingly towards him, her enormous bosom heaving. Sparrow flung a last triceratops at the wall, and stalked out into the cold night. Come back, she yelled, you'll freeze. He had to walk through three blocks of filthy motheaten snow before he found a cab, he arrived at Vladimir's as the clock struck four, and was let in by his mother, who was smoking strawberry cigars and watching *A Clockwork Orange*. I'm very glad you left her – she said of Helga – I always felt guilty that I introduced you to her, she is so painfully mediocre. Already he was beginning to feel sorry for Helga, she had expected so little of him, no more than to warm her narrow bed, and mould her used flesh to his strange and unpredictable urges, and the remainder of his passions to inflict upon wax. It was she that taught him the principles of candlemaking, the dipping, pouring, casting, and rolling of wax, those vapourous arts that had diverted him from the wretched condition of graduation, the breaking of the amniotic water, given him purpose in life after college, cemented his links to the island that had not spawned him, yet held him in vicelike parental grip. Two days later, when he went to fetch his things, and saw her in her rococo lair, eyes puffy black, he felt a certain sadness which he mistook for hope. He held her hand briefly behind the till, as Vladimir selected a pair of lapis lazuli armadillos as a birthday present for his mother, beautiful colour, she said bravely, weighing the armadillos in her palm, beautiful blue. Blue, said Sparrow recklessly, is the colour of death. Vladimir frowned, you don't take American Express? You're kidding me, he said to Helga, can I write you a cheque? Sparrow went to the basement to look around one last time, here he had spent the past two years in comparative bliss, already he felt a sweet nostalgia. It was only in nostalgia, he thinks, staring into the open jaws of a pickled coelacanth, it was only in nostalgia that I found any reason for hope.

I have been to more funerals in the past two years, says Jovanovich, than in my entire life, all friends of mine, close friends, yet nothing ever happens to me, it is as if I exist within a magic circle, no virus can harm me, I never even catch a cold. Last week, as I walked into a room, I caught the fragment of a small whisper, stillborn, a small bitter whisper, someone said of me, here he comes, the grim reaper. Tears filled my eyes, it was the funeral of a very dear friend you see, I excused myself and rushed to the bathroom, where in sterile solitude I observed my face, indeed it does have the contours of death, this great jaw, this bony nose, these eyes, my eyes, it was there that I first noticed how my eyes continued to sting long after my tears had gone, as if someone had thrown sugar into them, and today my doctor told me that I would be blind within a year.

My friends were dying, he said, yet I continued to live, my business flourished. I sell glass objects, you know, little animals and gondoliers and the like, and we supply glassware to laboratories, wholesale, a strange substance – glass, not a good business for a sightless man. I gave a party once, some years ago, where the balloons were of a light gossamer glass, and every time a wind blew, they would burst like bubbles and fall about us, soft, thin shards, shower us from above. I had no idea then that I would escape the scourge that was eating through my companions, that I would survive this holocaust, to live until old age, a blind man.

Many miles away, your father wakes to find that the rabbit, Andropov, lying upon his chest, has urinated upon his undershirt. The rabbit, Andropov, increasingly incontinent, twitches his nose in an expression of guilt. He is old, your father thinks, stroking his ears, and the muggy weather does not agree with him. He takes the rabbit into the bathroom to wash his underside, stained pink by his own urine, he has been at the hibiscus flowers again, the offerings your aunts make daily to the gods, the rabbit has crept into the puja room, and eaten the flowers. He brings bad luck to the household, your aunts complain. Your father shrugs, he can hardly deny that family fortunes have never been worse, the businesses finally folding, this old house now sold, and there have been deaths, his own daughter gone, and another far away, but he is glad that you have escaped this decaying city, what did this city ever offer you, he thinks, what but a string of bad allergies, and the meagre advantage of an exotic past which you have exploited so shamelessly in your prose, you must settle down and write a unified work, he told you this summer, handing back the fragments of your literary endeavours, this is all very well, but who will read it unless it is flesh on some kind of bone? An hour later you came rushing down the stairs to his basement haven, flushed and excited, you would write a novel, you announced eagerly, about your friend Jon Sparrow, your college friend Jonathan Sparrow. Who? Jonathan Sparrow? Sounds like a particularly unimaginative pseudonym of Jonathan Swift, your father said.

Sparrow, did he not recall Sparrow? You had spoken often of him in the summers home from college. He was likely to travel to Calcutta in the near future, you assured, for he was teaching English in Thailand. Sounds to me like a typically American thing to do, your father had replied rather disdainfully. To him, your enthusiasm had all the qualities of the childhood fervour with which you would announce your self-conjured projects that had filled your time in Birmingham – a project on clouds, you would announce gravely, rushing to and fro with cottonwool and glue, a project on space, you claimed mysteriously, waving your pen-capped fingers at him, a project on Impressionism, you would say primly, when you were suddenly older, suddenly precocious. Your notion of using Sparrow's doubtlessly hollow Midwestern existence as a substrate for your rich musings seemed to your father just such a half-baked urge, although, last month, when the boy had visited him, he had felt drawn to his taciturn intellect, not to the extent of seeing him as a backbone to any worthwhile piece of fiction, but an interesting young man, his anti-Marxist views notwithstanding. A good-hearted lad, he had won the hearts of all the aunts by presenting them with individual gifts, a nice boy, Jon Sparrow, your father steps under the gusty shower, someone knocks upon the bathroom door, you are not bathing again, at this late hour, are you? It is the voice of his eldest brother's wife, it is ten-thirty, for heaven's sake, she says, you'll catch your death of cold.

The rabbit, he shouts, the rabbit pissed on my chest, do you think I enjoy bathing at this time of night?

That dratted rabbit, she says, anyway, don't stay in there too long, your son-in-law has been waiting to see you, he is eating now with your brothers, go and join them when you are done.

I won't be five minutes, says your father, reaching for the towel, he notices that he has forgotten to let the rabbit out, the creature is grooming itself under the cistern, scratching behind its ears for Vitamin D perhaps: one of your more amusing revelations about his species, a close runner-up to the discovery that rabbits can actually swim, *although they climb indifferently*, you had read from a secondhand book you had picked up in College Street, *although they climb indifferently*, you read amid general laughter. Yes those were happy days, when the house was full of voices, that is now replete only with recycled whispers, laughter rebounding off the edges of a grander past, and soon all this will be dust, pulverised under Marwari bulldozers, and why not, he thinks bitterly, trying the useless flush-handle, everything is falling to pieces, he gives up and begins to fill a bucket. Through the window he can see the moon, listless among the monochrome clouds, it is like a shot from an old black-and-white film, of the sort they used to enjoy in their childhood, any minute now, a flash of lightning will reveal a young sage, undisturbed by demons that seek to break his concentration, or perhaps the camera will pan the heavens until it finds the court of Indra, as some divine dancer loses her rhythm and is condemned to a period of mortality. He tips the bucket of water into the commode, some of it falls upon the rabbit, Andropov, who shakes the drops vigorously off his rump. It will be just him and me, thinks your father, the rabbit and I, in our Calcutta penthouse, watching the lights of the city through the idiocy of glass, for the windows will be shutterless in the tall block that will rise from the ashes of this house, the windows will be of glass, an absurdity in the tropics, your father had declared this morning, but the architect had only coughed and smiled, and moved on to the details of the built-in closets, with your uncles drumming impatiently on the table. It will be just you and I, he says to the impatient rabbit, clawing at the bathroom door, just you and I, at least you need not fear cats, for none will intrude upon our solitude, there will still be crows to be sure, but you have learnt how to handle crows, it was only in infancy that you would emit a piercing shriek at the sight of a crow, our only experience of your voice, for you have been silent, these fifteen years, but for the odd sneeze, when did your race undertake this vow of silence, I wonder, at what evolutionary juncture, when was it that you lost all desire to communicate? Yes, I am coming, he answers to the maid, who taps nervously at the door, tell them I will be there in a moment.

His son-in-law is well into his yoghurt and sweetmeats by the time your father arrives at the dining table, a pile of fishbones by his plate, he has the irritating habit of moving the debris of his meal onto the table, some ridiculous West Bengal tradition, no doubt, your father surmises behind arched nostrils. And if it had been he rather than his daughter who had died, would she have been encouraged to relinquish all manner of flesh in her diet, would she, resplendent in widow's white, have succumbed to the rigours of a widow's diet, to be free of vile whispers, coarse displeasure. Would she, despite your father's disapproval, have embraced widowhood in the same spirit that she had taken up fasting on Thursdays, at the command of her earthly guru, the sage Vidyananda, whose riverside ashram she had visited regularly with her aunts in the years before her death. He had recommended a moonstone, set in square silver, to be worn on the middle finger of the left hand. Life is but a celebration of suffering, he had warned her, however, of the capacity for pain with which the Lord has filled the crude vessels of our being. Would you have the comfort of darkness rather than the blinding of His light?

On the day of her funeral, a car was sent for the Swami Vidyananda, and Alexander, eager to be away from the metallic hustle, had volunteered to accompany the driver, are you sure? you asked him, it's a long and bumpy ride.

At least I will be of some use this way, he had replied, and really, darling, I'd love the chance to be out of this madhouse for a while.

There is something altogether obscene about the commotion, he thought, lowering the window to flick the ash from his cigarette, something utterly unholy, it is the same manic choreography that frustrated our wedding, but at least that benefited from the undercurrent of happiness in the occasion. Grief, you would think, would dignify their actions, but no, grief only lends a raw edge to it all. He rolled down the recalcitrant window again, to throw out the withered butt. The driver looked worriedly over his shoulder, an open window defeated the purpose of air-conditioning, he explained hesitantly in his limited English, producing from the glove compartment a much abused malachite ashtray, a gift from Avishek's parents, no doubt, or perhaps from Avishek himself, strange token of his love, a scooped lump of green-veined stone. Perhaps this misshapen malachite piece was one that the young Avishek had pressed into your eager palm, many years ago, imploring you to remember the texture of his unspoken passion in its smooth whorled green. Perhaps it had cooled the fever of your dream-wet cheeks, this hollow into which Alexander grinds his second cigarette may once have cupped the warmth of your lips, and then you had forgotten it, relic of a greener lust, it had found its way into the glove compartment of this Ambassador. Or was it your father who, in loathful spite, had relegated the object to this ignominious nook? The car turned into Park Street, and his senses were assailed by a fantasy of tinsel and coloured paper, yard upon yard of masks and hats upon the pavement, like the detritus of a Fellini film, the pathos of a post-colonial Christmas, hard sun glinting upon the hasty manufactures, a strange synthesis of traditional motifs with Christian iconography, Alexander tapped the driver on the shoulder, asked him to pull up so that he might divest the tradesman of a quantity of their ill-made, yet fascinating, wares. He would pay more than what they asked, he decided, as he always did, although one of your cousins had rebuked him quite acidly last week for this practice, you foreigners only distort the economy, he had said.

He purchased a selection of masks from the Park Street vendor, and hats for the children, realising only after they had driven off that he could hardly return to the funeral with party hats for the kids, although they had been playing quite a jolly game of cricket this morning when he left, your niece among them, giggling nervously in the paved courtyard. They were playing with tennis balls thank god, even so he was afraid that a misplaced bounce would fracture her delicate skull. He had dreamt the night before that she was drowning in mud, and he was floating books upon the surface for her to hold on to, a bridge of books so that he might reach her, save her, too facile a dream to dwell on, he decided, as the car locked itself firmly into the viscous stream of traffic trickling across Howrah Bridge. Inching along with them, in an identical cream-coloured Ambassador, two young women cast coy glances, laughing between themselves, something in their light movements stirred his blood, so much more eager was his blood in the tropics, he thought, and yet so sated, the curious deep indolence worked by the heaviness of the air, and yet nowhere so much as here did the blood have to meet the challenge of countless impertinent organisms breaking through the useless barriers of skin and gut acid. What strange tension might exist between the alertness of the body's defences and the thickening of blood from the sweetness of heat, he wondered, and the girls in the neighbouring car turned away, disappointed at the sudden portcullis of concentration that evacuated them from his vision.

Swami Vidyananda was still meditating when they arrived, so Alexander spent a half hour on a bench by the banks of the turbid Hoogly, probing the limits of this new irony: the eager blood corpuscles, agitated by the tenacious germs, fighting against the sluggish plasma, could this explain the trapped turbulence of languorous tropical lust? A troop of orphans, clad in much laundered white, marched quietly past. The driver, rubbing robbed sleep from his yellow eyes, came to tell him that Vidyananda was ready. Reluctantly Alexander quit his riverside seat, a few more hours in this peaceful spot was all he needed to organise his thoughts, he felt no desire to return to the funeral. The sage proved to be a quiet man, as befit his vocation, he greeted Alexander calmly, then retreated into a concentrated silence that Alexander found almost as restful as the slothful cadence of the Hoogly. They spent the journey wrapped in their own thoughts, how comfortable it is, thought Alexander, to be in the company of another as jealous of his time with himself, how precious the weight of his contemplation.

Many of the guests had already arrived by the time they drove in through the gates. A strange hush fell on the company as Alexander escorted the guru up the stairs, some touched his feet as he was led across the veranda into the drawing room, where, for his benefit, a white sheet had been spread over the central divan with garlands of marigold pinned along the sides. In one corner, on a heap of flowers, and under a fog of incense, your sister's portrait smiled charmingly at those who came to pay their brief respects, to stand a few minutes before her, their heads bowed, their lips twisted in pain and embarrassment at her untimely death. Your father sat cross-legged under the window, his fingers drifting across the strings of his tanpura, and with him, his sisters, filling the room with song. Alexander decided he would sit with them, hopefully for the duration of the funeral, take the packages to our room, he said softly to the driver.

Swami Vidyananda, perched stiffly upon the divan, had broken his long silence, between mouthfuls of sweetmeats, with a request for a particular Tagore song, it is the day of Christ's birth, he had said sombrely, you might sing the song the poet wrote about him –

What light gave your lifewick flame,
that pain could only run as music through your soul
oh madman, saint and lover?
Disaster smiles sweeter than your mother smiled,
And yet tears come to your fine eyes,
did you still believe that we would follow you
You who disregarded death, and drowned in the ocean of life.

Vidyananda, listening with his eyes closed, shifted a little and let one leg drop over the perimeter of marigolds, until his toes grazed the floor. The rabbit, Andropov, who had spent the morning surreptitiously feasting upon flowers under the divan, shot out and nipped him in the ankle, the sage withdrew his foot quickly, the rabbit slunk back into his hideaway, no one had noticed other than Alexander, who, for once, found himself neither amused nor disturbed by the incident. This equanimity, he reflected, can only be possible in the silence of the tropics, in the discourse within the blood, struggling to forget the pain, and at the same time, seeking salvation through pain, for what is immunity but the memory of pain, in the service of survival?

• • •

Pain, says Jovanovich, running his finger across Sparrow's palm, is not simply there to heighten our perception of pleasure, no more than darkness exists to create the possibility of light, no more than hate sharpens love, all these cheap dualities that you poets cherish. I know you are a poet, I can tell from the shape of your skull.

He lifts his hands to Sparrow's head, like misshapen glass, he says delightedly. You are the best kind of poet, for I can tell you have not written any poetry in years. Your fingers reek of prose, however, he says, sniffing at Sparrow's hands. Like newly mashed garlic, your fingers reek of unguarded prose.

The young man whose funeral I attended last week dabbled in prose, he continues, his eyes were as green as the Welsh hills where he grew up. I still do not believe he is dead.

You never will, says Sparrow under his breath.

What was that? asks Jovanovich, actually he was born and brought up in Cardiff, so perhaps he did not see much of the green hills, only on family outings perhaps, he with his great secret – close, close to his lips, and his lips perhaps against the weak Welsh grass. He took his own life, dear boy, before life became unbearable, a sound choice. Others said he ran from pain, but sometimes the only dignity is in calling it quits, why endure wretchedness, and call it pain?

Not the good, the bad, but the wretched, mutters Sparrow.

You speak very softly, says Jovanovich, and I am a little deaf, yes, a veritable mockery of the five senses, the others are likely to go as well I'm sure, although they say that they become sharper once one is lost, by which they mean sight of course – I have never heard of anyone being able to see better because they cannot smell.

∘ ∘ ∘

The aroma of roasted aubergine rouses the rabbit from his evening nap, he comes to nudge at your father's feet, and receives an oily sliver on a scrap of newspaper. In his youth he would stand on his hind legs to beg for food, but now he is too lazy and smug to perform such endearing gymnastics. Your father tips the last of the fish curry onto his plate, his son-in-law coughs nervously and mentions, we got the contract…

Which contract is this? your father asks, sopping up the remains of the curry with his coarse flour flatbread, the doctors have recommended that he stay away from rice for his evening meal.

For the film set, stammers his son-in-law, for *City of Joy*.

So he would be building a slum, a slum to slum all slums in this city of slum, for no slum had proved slum enough for the *City of Joy*.

It will have to be flooded, his son-in-law declares, we will have to arrange for it to be flooded. Antiseptic sewage, your father learns, will be brought from England for this very purpose. Do you feel no shame? he suddenly asks.

Shame?

Honesty, says your father bitterly, honesty was all we had amid the chaos, honesty was all we were going to hold on to – we had sacrificed order for honesty, for truth.

All art is deception, his son-in-law retorts unexpectedly.

Your father snorts, what you are about to undertake can hardly be classed as an exercise in demystification, he says in English.

I don't understand your long foreign words, his son-in-law answers smugly, but you are hardly in a position to protest, for little in this city is as insulated and false as the comfort of your intellectuality.

The comfort of intellectuality! Name me an activity more painful than thought.

Shitting, for a start, shitting your guts out with amoebic dysentery – I think that might be slightly more painful than musing on art, especially if you haven't eaten anything all day, so that all you've got to shit out are your intestines – these are some of the people who might have half a chance of filling their bellies from working on the set.

One man's bread is another man's circus. But speaking of shit, how do your workers feel about sanitised sewage? Their own shit not good enough?

Such obscene talk at the dining table, an old man grumbles, your grandfather's youngest brother, sole survivor of his generation.

Your father finishes his meal in silence, and leaves the table abruptly, before dessert. He climbs the stairs to his study, where a thin sheet of moonlight falls over the sparse furniture, the bookshelves and tea chests, his cluttered desk, his leather chair, he falls gratefully into its creaky hold, notices that how gladly the moonlight drapes the rusty ceiling hook from which his father had hanged himself, forty years ago. They had not used a ceiling fan in the room since, indeed the room had been locked up and forgotten, until he himself, in his first year of college, had claimed it as his own, dismantling the rusty lock, he had entered boldly, flung his few books onto the table, while the family looked up in awe from the courtyard below. It was not the first time he had been there since his father's death, as a child he had once climbed in through the window, during a game of hide-and-seek, climbed in and perched among the cobwebs and the termite eggs, no one would ever dare look for him there, he knew, but the shame in his knowledge overtook the victory, it was not such a clever hiding place after all. Five years later, he entered openly, wrenching the useless lock from the door, and was surprised to find it had been swept and dusted as regularly as any room, all these years, and he had thought it a rotting mausoleum, for he had crept in only once in the half dark to nestle under the desk, among the soot and the spider offal, and come away with images of great decay, the room had taken the contours of the memory of his father, a whispered abandoned name. Why must a man who takes his own life receive such meagre acknowledgement for the manic courage with which he has knotted his own noose? I am certainly too weak to take my own life, he thinks, far too weak. He, who had come to set his father's memory in order, found only need to dust the spines of his crumbling law texts, and that had been enough, then, for I was satisfied with smaller ironies, he remembers, weren't we all, then, in the mockery of Independence, and before that the mockery of fighting another man's war, aborting our crops to thwart another's enemy, and then dying ourselves of hunger upon an unparched earth, how much simpler then were our ironies.

A slender roach hurries past his finger, of the sort that his maternal grandfather would boil with tea leaves to make medicine for asthma, the summer of '46, soon after his father had died, he had been sent off to North Bengal, to be as far away from the scene of the disaster. And all summer he had caught cockroaches, he and his maternal cousins had scoured their neighbours' courtyards with jars, each roach was worth a fistful of candied puffed rice, for his grandfather sold his asthma remedy in neat brown phials, to supplement his schoolteacher's income. The family had fallen on hard times since the '42 famine, would see harder times the very next year, when their lands would become East Pakistan, and they would join the mass exodus to Calcutta, start over as refugees in the southern fringes of the city, where roaches would be plentiful, but no one to buy the medicine. Though perhaps he would have found a steady clientele now, your father muses bitterly, among the educated middle classes, who had, of late, decided to retreat from the rigours of scientific rationalism, his own poor daughter had treated her cancer with herbs for months. Perhaps she would have been here today if he had put his foot down at the right time, but he had let her have her way, he had always let his daughters have their way, perhaps it is time now to regret this, he should have done more than just scoff at her regular visits to the herbalist, the druid had prescribed some obscure leaf, to be eaten with comb honey, and a pinch of asafoetida, and they dared speak of the 'tyranny of logic' in this world! He should have prevented her, he knows, but he had not known then that it was cancer, he, to whom death should have been an old friend, had not recognised death until poked by a bony finger in his ribs, the fearful biopsy report, and even then, he had refused to acknowledge death's eversmiling presence. He had shut the door in death's face, drawn the curtains against the injustice of night creeping through the shutters to colour the sickroom in cinerary grey. He had insisted, at least, that she return to die in the comfort of her childhood home, that when it came time for her breath to rise for the last time, it disperse among the unbroken shadow of magnolia rather than hover uneasily over the cluttered courtyard outside their dingy flat, her last breath, diluted by dung smoke, fogging the chipped mirror glass over the faucetless basin in the veranda where every morning, for the past ten years, she had brushed her teeth, tilting the water drum to fill her calloused mug. Her movements return to him, etched in the desolation of Tarkovsky monochrome, this afternoon your father delivered the closing speech at a session of his films. The Tarkovsky retrospective had stretched back long enough to overlap with Sparrow's visit, he had taken your friend to see *Stalker* on the evening before he left Calcutta. Sparrow had been deeply affected, your father could tell, for walking home he had been more silent than usual, *not the good, the bad, but the wretched*, eh? was all he had said, *not the good, the bad, but the wretched?* Sparrow had said, with a painful sigh, bringing an unexpected lump to your father's throat, it returns again in this ghostly moonbrine, the unfathomable constriction, your father clears a part of his desk, to lay his head upon the old wood, his heels brush against the rabbit, Andropov, who has crept in to slumber under his chair, he scoops the rabbit out from his insubstantial refuge and lifts him onto the table, strokes the long ears while the creature vigorously licks the salty tears off his cheek.

• • •

*We wasters of sorrows! How we stare into sad endurance beyond, trying to foresee their end. Whereas they are nothing but our winter foliage, our sombre evergreen, one of the seasons of our interior year* . . . that was from Rilke, says Jovanovich, the Tenth Duino Elegy, his paean to pain, my Lord's prayer. I keep it at my bedside, in a velvet menu-holder a friend stole for me once, from a Persian restaurant. We had gone there to dine, you see, and I had admired the menu-holder much, black velvet, unmarked except for a small fish in gold thread in the centre, beautiful! I had not noticed my friend slip his into his briefcase, he gave it to me a week later, for my birthday, my thirtieth birthday, that night I copied the Tenth Elegy in longhand on some good paper. It took a while, for I would throw away the page if I made a mistake, yes it was a fittingly painful labour, and at last, at dawn it was done, perhaps that was when I began to lose my sight, for I was writing by the light of a small, rather exquisite kerosene lamp, a birthday present from my niece. This graceful lamp, she had picked it up in India, where they were being sold by the dozen, my niece told me; also, I was writing in squid ink, another present, and its salty vapours irritated my eyes.

The museum is closing, shall we walk now, says Jovanovich, for I have an hour before I must be somewhere at dinner, and I do not wish to be alone, not on this day of all days, I do not wish to be alone. The sky is beguilingly dark, it will not rain yet, not for a while, I can smell the hour of rain, I did not need to be blind for that. Shall we walk in Hyde Park?

Look around you, commands Jovanovich when they are outside, this is the Leid-Stadt, the City of Pain, always simmering with the mock silence of drowned commotion, these deathless faces, proud concrete, lamentless glass, and yet buried within the chinks of our brickwork, the old elements conspire, the old scourge wakes, to remind us of our true destination, the Land of Pain, Liedlands, where death is a friend, death is merely ripeness, which even the earliest fruit cannot ignore.

*The Duino Elegies*, the professor had lent Sparrow a dog-eared copy once, read only the Third and the Eighth, the professor had warned, they complement each other, for the Third, he had explained, is a celebration of the vastness of our subconscious, that depthless mirrorpool where earthly love can only wet its feet. The Third is the tragedy of that internal hall of mirrors that our fathers have left within us, the diffractions of primal mercury, gorged with our ancestors, that distract us from more immediate passion. The Third is the tragedy of the limitlessness of the subconscious, while the English is of the tragedy of our consciousness, of the external mirror, in which we must always find ourselves, and not another, that we must look not only forward but behind, until face to face with death, when the last looking glass will fall, we may stare ahead, and only ahead, with large brute gaze, only ahead.

I see a child, says Jovanovich, I see a child coming towards us, her eyes heavy with weeping. I hate to see a child weep, says Jovanovich, inclining his head towards the distant figure of your niece, where her blurred form suddenly becomes clear to Sparrow. She is a smudged dot where other movements of people are sharp lines, she is a smear of indecision, caught in a cat's cradle of determined to-and-fro, she is a wavering outline, clutching at a teddy bear that Sparrow recognises as the very beast he had presented to her this morning. His first impulse is to turn away before she sees him, but he pauses as the damp smell of a child's fear reaches him suddenly, her unfocussed movements, small shoulders heaving. He stops still, and waits for her to stumble towards him. Jovanovich, watching him silently, now follows Sparrow's eyes to the child, labouring down the suddenly empty pavement. The child's sobs growing louder, Jovanovich lays an elbow on Sparrow's shoulder, and speaks: *Come away, oh human child! To the woods and waters wild, with a fairy hand in hand, for the world's more full of weeping than you can understand.* The child, very close now, looks up at the sound of his rhyme, a sob stuck in her throat. That's right, my sweet, says Jovanovich, taking her astonished face in his hands, wiping the wetness from her cheeks with his thumbs, this is no time to cry. You are lost, are you? he asks, well count your blessings, for it is not a pleasure you will ever repeat. In a few years, these streets will be etched firmly in your mind, and then you will curse their immobility. How much more fun it would be, you will think, if the same streets did not lead to the same places every day, if every night the streets would draw lots, pick cards that would tell them only their beginning and their end, and leave to them the most creative way of getting from one to the other.

The child notices Sparrow, gives him a look where surprise vies with reproach, a few small threads of relief hang loose along the edges of the look, but they are pulled in quickly, the reproach predominates, why me? Sparrow asks her silently, it is not I that have done this to you. She turns away to look once more into the lemon-shaped eyes of Jovanovich. This is no time for tears, says Jovanovich, holding his hands like a horse's blinkers, filling her entire vision with his hypnotising gaze. Why you are the Pied

Piper! thinks Sparrow. Jovanovich kneels upon the pavement, circles her in his arms, that is a pretty dress you are wearing, he says, you have been to a party, it cannot have been a nice party for you to have left so quickly, how long have you wandered these wretched streets, my child? It must have seemed like hours, and each street the same leading to the same street again. Come we shall sit in that intimate square of green, the Princes' gardens it will be for you, my weary child, a bench to rest your feet.

Jovanovich leads the girl steadily down the street, into the square, Sparrow follows, clutching the bear, which Jovanovich has taken from the child's hands and given to him to hold. Jovanovich guides the dazed child, his hand pushing gently at her head, guides her to a bench, wipes the moisture with his handkerchief, and sits down with the child. Sparrow sits down beside her, holding the bear. Jovanovich smooths her hair out of her face, dark strands stiffened by the salt of her tears, let me tell you the story of a stork, says Jovanovich, the story of a stork who never had any friends, so that when all the other storks left to fly away to sunnier lands, he did not know where to go, for they had left him in the night without telling him. So the stork stayed alone, in the cold waters, that got colder still as the nights dragged on, and how blue his thin legs became from the cold, how lonely he felt, how hungry, and finally, there was a great storm and he could bear it no more, he hopped on his stiff legs to the nearest town. There were lights in the houses, and the smell of good cheer, but the doors were barred fast (for there were a great many robbers in the nearby forest), and besides through the lollipop windows, the stork could see them feasting on roasted birds, which frightened him. At last he came to the church, which was empty and dark, save a few candles burning their last, but the door was ajar, and the stork slipped in, curled up near the altar, and fell asleep. At dawn a priest found him, you cannot sleep here, he said to the stork. But where can I go, said the wretched stork, where can I go in the cold? Through the crack in the door he could see that a thick blanket of snow had fallen overnight. I am cold and I have nothing to eat, please let me stay, begged the stork. All right, said the priest, I have an idea, we will give you shelter if you give us service – you see, our weathercock is old and rusty, last night in the storm, his wings broke off, if you will take his place, we will give you food and shelter for the night. And that was how it was, the stork sat patiently upon the weathervane during the day, and crawled down at night to sleep behind the altar. They fed him well at the cloisters, and soon he found the winter chill quite pleasant. One of the kinder monks even made him a scarf from old odds and ends of wool. Then the weather got warmer, and the stork made a nice nest for himself upon the church roof, for he preferred to stay outside when it was warm, and when his friends came back, they were so jealous, so dreadfully jealous. They would have all liked to sit on the weathervane, and swing back and forth with the wind, the young winds of springtime that would set the stork spinning like a little white top, the calm breezes of summer that would sway him to sleep, the tender winds of autumn, smelling of smoke and scabby apples, and the clean winds of winter swinging him firmly to the south. And perched there, high high above, he came to know much, know of the shapes and colours of land, how they changed with the seasons. He saw how humanfolk loved and lived, and the lives of the beasts around them, those they had tamed and those they had not, but the storks still refused to have anything to do with him, they were so envious. Only the sparrows would come to chat, but their talk was frivolous, and he did not much care for it, and so my child this friendless stork came to find the good solitude, that sweet crust on which you have, I suspect, fed for most of your small life. Do not shy away from this wholesome aloneness, my little darling, for it is all that comes between you and the tawdry awareness of your transience, this illimitable space of loneliness. Save your tears, my child, to wet the grey dough that you know not yet rests in your mouth, death, that you hold so gently, the whole of death, hold so gently, so free from all resentment. Save your tears, child, to soften this dough later, when it will soil your solitude. Do not cry, sweet child, for your tears are too heavy for your light cheeks, so quickly the narrow eye ledge is flooded, come let us think of the happiness of bees, the sandy sleep of rabbits. Let us remember a house without mirrors, or where the mirrors were hung too high for you to peep in them, child, remember the world as it was before you looked into your own eyes for the first time, remember child, and wipe the tears from your eyes. There are many tales that I could tell you, but you have had your fill of tales for the day, tales that came like narrow goblets of glass, through which you could not squeeze your tongue towards the promise of honey at the base. Our stories will hang unsavoured in your childmind, as all good stories must, I would tell you many more, but I am late, says Jovanovich, looking at his watch, I must leave you now, he kisses her cold forehead, kisses Sparrow on his lips, and in a flash is gone, leaving Sparrow alone with the child, who begins once again to cry, shivering now as a sharp wind runs through her clothes. Did he ever really exist? wonders Sparrow, or was he some tormented project of my undernourished imagination? Have we not been sitting here all along, the child and I, since I saw her, crying in the streets? Did she ever stop crying, or was that all a mirage? Was there a man with us? he asks the child, just a minute ago, was there a man? But she only cries harder, digging her chin into her chest. He pulls her to him, and gratefully she sinks her head into his sheepskin coat. Let me put it around you, he says, unbuttoning the garment, you are shivering, here, let me put it around you, get up now, let me put this around you, it will make you feel warmer, get up now, we're going home.

# X

# *The Last Looking Glass*

You push away the covers from Daniel's face to see what remains of the smile, crushed against dense cotton, the lips hang parted, and the smell of birds drowned in cider floats swiftly to your nostrils, how easy it is to disdain flesh, you wonder, enraptured yet by the underline of his lower left lid, and down below, his son looks helplessly upon the first drop of blood that falls from his nose onto the cuff of his new striped shirt.

I've got a nose-bleed, he announces with a sudden jerk of his head, to the stranger beside him, who stares wordlessly as a second drop of blood gathers weight and begins to trickle down the reversed gradient of the boy's upper lip. Then, without warning, he lifts the surprised child out of the armchair into his arms, tips his head back over a forearm, and carries him over to the receptionist. The boy is sick, he says, feeling somehow like a tired refugee, begging with a dying child for administrative mercy. The boy is bleeding all over the place, can you get his father?

Sorry, sir, but what is the room number? It is a different girl, her hands shake as she reaches under the counter for a pile of tissues.

What's your name? he asks the boy.

Kevin, he mutters through his blood-blocked nose.

Kevin what?

Parslow, he says, breathlessly, struggling softly to be released.

Parslow? he asks, the receptionist is already running her fingers down the register, I'll ring him, she says, why don't you lie him down.

And so, he, who had woken to the touch of your finger upon

his eyelid, and reached to hold your breasts, moaning under a sea-seeking lust, thickened by hurricane slumber, he, fell back from your determined lips, and reached for the purring telephone, yes, that's me, you heard him say, and then, I'll be there in a minute.

It's Kev, he said, swinging his legs across you, he's got a nosebleed.

You are downstairs before him, you are there first, as Avishek has hoped, you are there, to be pierced by his eyes, you are there before Daniel has tied his laces, pushed back his sooty locks, you are there to draw your breath sharply as you encounter this tableau: your cousin kneeling by chintz-covered couch, holding the child's head in his hands, tipping it back over the low chair-arm. He looks up at you, he could not have hoped for a more effective ambush. You stand, frozen, as expected, the reckless absurdity of the day's events converging upon you. Your eyes fill with tears, you remember his unfamiliar form, as it had appeared in the summer darkness, when you pushed through the saloon doors, sandals in your hands, look who it is, your sister had said, smiling, hasn't he grown?

Ten years ago, a delightful fury of irrational anticipation that had surrounded you for some days had crystallised in his sudden presence, his happy eyes had given reason to the intermittent gusts of premonition. Something good, you had written in your journal, is about to happen, something good, and yet as stark as pain, you had added, for the sake of poetry.

The boy sees his father and begins to whimper, Daniel rushes past you to the sofa, and pulls his head up, pinching the small nose tightly, the boy howls, we need ice, says his father, holding his hand to the stream of blood, we need ice.

I live, you say, five minutes away, let's take him there.

He throws the child over his shoulder. Thank you for taking care of him, he says to Avishek, who accepts his gratitude with a smile and a nod, the keys, asks the helpless receptionist as he is about to step into the hall, your keys, sir.

They're upstairs, he tells her, don't you have a bloody fridge in this place?

I'm afraid not, but your keys . . .

They're upstairs, the door's open, for God's sake, he pushes past her, you are waiting at the door, holding it open, he passes through. Avishek, who has come up behind him, places a hand upon the brass frame, you walk out into the faltering afternoon, he follows.

You turn down Cromwell Road, are you sure, you ask, that we oughtn't take him to hospital?

Happens all the time, answers Daniel, bit of ice will stop it, how far are we?

Almost there, the striated turrets of the Natural History Museum begin to gleam, you steal a glance at Avishek, he bores you with his eyes, layers of emotion, waiting to be savoured, once the child is taken care of, and yet perhaps, this is the only time that the thickness of the dust between you will settle sweet upon your tongue, will it not, if left too long, shape itself into flat sordid secret, this fortuitous resonance cannot last beyond the death of the evening, your pace quickens.

Hold on, now, Kev, there's a good lad, we're nearly there, he seems to accept Avishek's presence with incurious grace, or is his agitation so deep as to blind him from all else, does he not wonder, Daniel Parslow, who this man might be, mysterious benefactor, faintly but deeply familiar (for he has seen him before, in the course of this strange day, or at least that part of him that records without seeing, his underdeveloped unconscious – or is it merely that he bears an uncanny resemblance to the Hungarian construction worker he met at the video shop last week?), he does not ask for an exchange of identities, ignores and accepts in the same movement of indifference. Look, we're here, he tells his son, as you fumble with your keys, the door opens under pressure from Avishek's hand. Where the fuck have you been? thunders Alexander, appearing in the kitchen doorway, phone in hand, it's Jessica's mother, she doesn't know where Rima is, where were you, I had to take her there myself, and now she's disappeared, where have you been all afternoon?

What do you mean, she's disappeared? asks Avishek, stepping inside, what do you mean?

Within you, an astringent dawn is breaking, one that needs no insomnia to colour it gray. The birthday party, how could it have slipped so completely from your mind? What do you mean, she's missing? repeats Avishek.

Some ice, pleads Daniel, pushing past you with the bleeding child, some ice, but you are transfixed, impermeable. She's not there, anymore, says Alexander, his eyes wet. They said they would get somebody to drop her off here, and now they realise she's left, nobody knows when.

I need some ice, Daniel insists.

Through here, says Alexander, dropping his arm, in the refrigerator, my God, has the boy been hurt?

Have you called the police? asks Avishek. From the kitchen comes a cyclone of screams, the sounds of cracking ice.

Where were you? asks Alexander, where in God's name were you?

You stare helplessly at him, without answer.

Have you informed the police? Avishek asks, grabbing him by the arm.

I just got the phone call.

The child screams, you walk, in deep trance, towards the kitchen, past Alexander, into the warm autumn light, the boy sprawled upon the butcher block, hemispheres of ice pressed to his numb flesh, balls of ice lie scattered on the table. Don't you have any cubes? asks Daniel, in exasperation, these round ones are useless. But the boy has stopped bleeding, drowsily he demands a glass of water.

You take a glass from the drying rack and fill it, tears streaming silently down your cheeks. He takes the glass, but the boy is already asleep, he sets it down and takes you by your trembling shoulders, tell me what has happened, he says. Alexander is dialling the police, he looks up quickly as you back away from the stranger's hands, but they are outstretched in an attitude of quiet possession, Alexander casts a look of scornful dismay in your direction, I don't believe we've been introduced, he says to Daniel.

Daniel Parslow, he says, slowly, softly, for Alexander has been put through to Scotland Yard, the doorbell rings, you hear Avishek stride quickly down to the door, never mind, you hear Alexander say, she has been found, sorry to have troubled you.

You breathe deeply, clutching at the comforting contours of the veined countertop behind you, there is a long row of birds, you notice, uncooked, laid out upon the marble.

The child is in her uncle's arms, sobbing terribly. You realise that you have never seen her cry, save as a mere tot, struggling to comprehend the perplexities of the physical world, a stubbed toe, a tumble from the cot, gravity challenged and denied. You are gathering the courage to face her, when another shadow, stooped and crooked, carrying a teddy, appears, it is Sparrow, Sparrow?

I found her wandering in the streets, he offers by way of explanation.

You didn't go, you say.

I didn't take that flight, he agrees.

He scrutinises Daniel, and the child, lying corpse-like upon the kitchen table. Place looks like a fucking morgue, he says, I'm Jon Sparrow by the way.

Your niece turns away from your outstretched arms, buries her face deep into Alexander's chest, you let your arms drop, let me take her upstairs, he says.

You follow them into the hallway, hesitate at the foot of the stairs, it's best you leave her to me, says Alexander. His eyes break like waves over your lips, wide with the memory of Daniel's kisses, mulberry bruised. Leave her alone for a while, he says, leaning his cheek against the small head, still buried in his shoulder. His hand rises to support the slender neck, you notice the tortured fronds of the velvet ribbon with which she had tried to tie back her hair, the crushed ends hang limply across Alexander's arm, he kisses the dishevelled head as he backs up the stairs. In soft desperation he kisses the tousled hair, and finally turns away from your eyes.

You did not remember to return in time for her party, this will hang as a noose about your neck, forever. Years later she will tighten it about you, she will never forgive you, this child cleaved from your flesh with another's pain. How had it slipped your mind that the maid was taking most of the weekend off, she should have reminded you this morning, of course she had been too sullen, struck with grief that Sparrow was leaving.

You return to the kitchen, where Avishek is suggesting that the boy be moved from the cold kitchen table, where he lies in exhausted sleep, pale as a corpse, trails of blood dried across his face. You lift him off the table into your arms, you hold him in uncomfortable determination, as you once held a diseased beggar child that had swooned in front of the gates to your house in Calcutta, many years ago, your cousins had collared a taxi, and you rushed with the infant and its wailing mother to the National Medical Hospital, and there you had left them, waiting in the emergency room, confident that there was nothing more you could have done, you had rushed across the road to your college, the Lady Brabourne, and scrubbed your arms well in a dormitory bathroom, you were terribly late for your English class, it was the summer of '81, something good is about to happen, you thought as you settled onto the bench under a dyspeptic fan, something good, you had written in your diary that morning, something good, but as stark as pain.

The boy is a stiff bundle of bones in your arms, you take him down into the basement, followed by his father, the bare room by the boiler where your father stays when he is here, you lay the child upon the bed, he wakes briefly, cries out for water. His father soothes him while you wash out a toothglass and fill it in the bathroom, you bring it to him, he drinks greedily and then falls quickly back to sleep. Daniel seizes you by your wrist, his fingers are dry with blood, in the cold half-light he pushes you against a pile of your father's papers upon the desk, notes for an Italian travelogue, they are scattered by the pressure of your rear. Daniel holds your tear-streaked face in his palms, gladly you meet his lips, your tongue gropes upon his palate for the liqueur of death, long diffused, you knead the knotted threads of your father's prose beneath your left hand, the ruined castle well in the Appenines that gave wonderful exercise to your lungs, mountains that had surely never – your father had written –

before echoed the strains of a Tagore song. The page rips, you close your eyes, you are walking within a house of cards, it is an old sensation, but never before physical, you moan under the weight of his hands upon your breasts, you are my new muse, you wish to believe, you are inspiration, cloaked in the shadow of death.

High, high above, Alexander brushes away the child's hair from her forehead, her small frame is racked steadily by sobs, he tries to stifle the convulsions with brief stabbing kisses upon the forehead. How does one kiss a child, he wonders, he has kissed her before, and numerous others, but never to soothe. He has kissed children out of habit, out of affection, from overwhelming love, and these kisses have had more sound than substance, gathering momentum in a long – oooommm – , then the loud smack, and rounded with the – mmmah – , a balanced follow-through, more pomp than circumstance, easily communicated by telephone, can one's lips be allowed to linger on the flesh of a child? He cups her narrow cheeks in his palms, it's all right now, he tells her, everything is going to be all right, everybody loves you, he chokes upon his words, she reaches for his neck, crying for her mother, the phantom finally resurrected. Is this merely the beginning of a delayed misery, this orphan child to whom he has given shelter, agreed to accept as his own, had they not promised that she should never realise how much she had lost, had they not resolved to smother her with their love, swathe her in affection, cushion her from motherlessness with their infinite attention. Where was the value of those long hours in the Natural History Museum, the walks in the park, the country rambles with her eagerly chatting, unaware that the most part of him is immersed in other thought. She will run ahead with his mother's dog, and stop suddenly short of a fork in the path, you will never know which path to take, he had thought fondly, for the fickleness of her attention amused him. Where was the value of the hours spent in his study poring over a colour atlas of parasites, when he had skilfully concealed the diseased horrors of limbs and eyes, and directed her attention only to the kaleidoscope of germs, the blue ridges of mitochondria, the tessellated nuclei, and she had laughed and laughed, the Human Immunodeficiency Virus, she announced, looked so much like the Little Prince's planet, overrun by baobab. He clasps her in his arms, he has never known such pain.

Avishek, finding himself alone with Sparrow, experiences the same discomfort that had sent worms creeping up his vertebrae, many years ago, when they both waited for you to emerge from the ladies' lavatory at the Victoria and Albert Museum, he had not expected to spend the morning chortling over sexually explicit Indian miniatures, which was the entertainment that you and Sparrow had designed for him – at St Pancras station you had announced, we're going to the V&A, as if it was entirely up to him whether he wanted to accompany you, he who had come two hundred miles to see you. He has not changed much, Jon Sparrow, more gaunt somehow, and there might be flecks of grey in his close-cropped hair. He has the air, somehow, of a man awaiting execution, it must be his haircut, Avishek feels a certain tenderness, pity really, what has he made of his life, Jon Sparrow, sometime genius, poet and mathematician, certainly he had heard enough of his achievements in your college letters, but since then, very little, Sparrow, he feels, is cursed both with prolonged youth and premature age. He excuses himself and goes into the hall to telephone his wife. Briefly, he tells her that the girl was missing, and although she has been found, things are very unsettled, he might be late, he tells her not to stay up, she is crying at the other end of the line, the child is fine, he reassures her. Mrigaya weeps bitterly, poor motherless thing, she says between muffled sobs.

How will this night end? he wonders, as the scarlet roar of ripping paper reaches his ears, he stands at the landing, watching your careless shadows behind the frosted glass, how can this night end?

An impulse, undefinable and overwhelming, takes him upstairs, he climbs softly, as if in dream. Whole flights of stairs are swallowed suddenly by the space beneath him, and then he is standing quietly at the door to the child's room. He sees

Alexander bent over her, his face buried in the pillow beside her, sleep sobs come slow from between her parted lips. She sees him and closes her eyes to him, as if she knows that he too has betrayed her. How eerie is her room, bathed in this stormlight, the hellish rocking horse poised fiercely between rhythm and chaos, the one-eyed bear slumped upon the sill, and the saucer eyes of the porcelain doll glittering in the corner. This is her sanctuary, here she must fashion her hopes and dreams. Her eyes open again, this time it is he that turns away from their drowsy discontent. He steals away, pauses briefly to shake his head sadly at the cork-and-mirror walls of Alexander's study, he is propelled graciously down the stairs, into the small white room, where once you had lain, in drugged haze, defenceless against the power of his desire, he had lifted his palm to your burning forehead, with trembling fingers traced the fever upon your lips, and with that gesture he had established a rich sub-text for all further verbal exchange, God knows I have never needed to kiss her, he thinks, sinking his fists into the satin pillows, I have tasted her lips upon every syllable, as each phrase of mine has held her in dense embrace, this gentle lust, our sweet fog, where will it float in this night, how will it curve about the crumbling order of this evening, how will the night end? he wonders, crushing cold satin under his elbows, his head, heavy with dream, in his trembling hands.

Smiling, Daniel whispers in your ear, I have to telephone his mum, she'll be worried, he kisses your jaw. Upstairs, you say, the extension in this room doesn't work. This summer, your father had sent the receiver flying across the room in response to a cowardly editor's refusal to print a controversial article, it has not worked since. You lead the way back up the stairs, gesture towards the gilt-edged antique monstrosity that conceals a miniature touchtone under the dial flap. He picks it up gingerly, you flip up the dial cap, he smiles. His fingers, stark as pain, move swiftly upon the buttons, his fingers, white as death, unfold against the grey evening as Alexander comes down the stairs, outside, the first crack of thunder rocks the skies.

You turn to face Alexander, she is asleep, he tells you. You follow him into the kitchen, where Sparrow sits at the kitchen table eating a mouldy cheese sandwich he has found in the fridge, and Avishek rests upon the bay window, looking out at the gathering clouds.

You hear the receiver dropped, then replaced, you hear his footsteps, Daniel leans against the door frame, and asks, can I call a minicab, his mum isn't home, I'd better take him back to my flat.

Alexander turns around, will you not stay for dinner?

Dinner? repeats Daniel, slightly taken aback.

I insist that all you gentlemen stay to dinner, says Alexander, we are having partridge.

Look, I'd love to, says Daniel, with a smile, but I've got to take the boy to his mum.

Let him rest awhile, Alexander insists, is he your son?

Yeah, he's my son, says Daniel, but he lives with his mum, you see. Saturday's our day out – not that I can always make it, on Saturdays, that is.

So his mother isn't home? asks Alexander.

Well, that's it, you see. I said I would meet her an hour ago. You see I can't often make Saturdays, and then she lets me take him to McDonald's on Wednesday evenings. I don't want her pissed off at me, because she's the one who decides, you know, when I get to see the boy.

But she isn't home yet, anyway, Alexander points out, gently, you must stay for dinner, we have so much food, it will all go to waste.

Partridges, a dozen of them, uncooked, lie in a long row upon the marble slab. What am I supposed to do with these? you ask, perplexed.

Wrap them in bacon, and stuff them with butter, suggests Dan, we sell them ready-trussed with the streaky, although the more finicky types prefer a sheet of pork fat for barding.

Partridges, thinks Avishek, should be stuffed with pears. He remembers how he and Nick had corrupted the old chant, on the ninth day of Christmas, my true love gave me, nine healthy catamites, eight wealthy parasites, seven solemn plebiscites…

My mother sent them, explains Alexander, do you sell game? he asks Daniel.

I work mainly in boneless bulk, he replies, but I had my start in fowl.

There is no bacon, you observe, searching the antiseptic depths of the fridge.

Oh, for God's sake, says Sparrow, why don't we just get some Kentucky Fried.

Can you fry partridges, you ask Daniel.

You can probably grill them, he says, stroking away a tear that nestles still against the corner of your eye. You'd better halve them, though.

Rather a waste, grilling them, remarks Avishek.

You must see a lot of blood, says Alexander, you must see all kinds of blood.

The knife slips and slices into your left thumb, Alexander looks at you, his eyes are thick with sorrow, you leave in search of band-aids, sucking your lacerated thumb. You must see a lot of blood, Alexander says to Daniel.

Yes, I have seen a lot of blood, says Daniel, in my time. My friend Hanif reckons I could fill twenty-two and a half swimming pools with blood every month, standard Olympic size that is.

Does your friend, asks Sparrow, know how many times you could have wrapped around the equator the length of disembowelled intestine that you are responsible for?

I have seen a lot of blood, says Daniel, but I still panic when my son's nose bleeds. Of course, it is only dead blood that I see.

Blood was never the colour of death, says Sparrow.

Nor ever the colour of love, says Daniel, suddenly bitter, I don't believe it's in the heart you know, I don't believe it. There's a writer bloke who keeps coming round for heart, ox heart, sheep heart, pig heart, you name it, he thinks it's all in there, love, you know, but I don't believe it.

You should be a poet, Alexander tells Dan, you should be a poet.

The heart is only the organ of laughter, says Sparrow, the

powerful laughter of bulls, slaughterhouse serenades, he stubs his toes on a spiralling reticulation of images.

The wind howls mercilessly in the square, the skies split with thunder, you search in the bathroom closet for band-aids, but it is empty save for a dusty bottle of elderflower water. This is the bathroom no one uses, the days have passed when this house had so many visitors that a lesser guest might be compelled to bathe within these decorated walls. The willow-patterned tub looks too delicate to bear the weight of sud-soaked limbs, an enormous tureen, perhaps one day you will fill it with the carcasses of butterflies. You return to the kitchen, where they stand in the sudden darkness. He should be a poet, Alexander says sadly, lifting his thick eyebrows towards Daniel.

Indeed, you say, smiling. He stands, your narrow-faced lover, smirking at the array of polished, unused knives buried into willow block, he draws them out, one by one, with the same reluctant flourish with which King Arthur, his only childhood myth, had extricated his destiny from churchside stone. He surveys the glittering array with the same contempt that a pair of designer aerobics shoes might stir within a barefoot long-distance runner, finally he selects an unlikely hatchet and neatly cleaves a partridge in two. You resume your struggle with your first bird, stabbing vainly at its breastbone. Let me show you, he offers, placing his arm upon yours, he grips your fingers, clenched around the knife handle, hold it like this and it's like slicing butter. Blood cloud merge upon your throat where the smell of smoke from his breath, like the burning of dried fruit, brushes wild upon your skin, he should be a poet, says Alexander lamely, looking into your eyes.

He should be a poet, says Sparrow, resting his elbows upon the counter, look at how cleanly he slices through bird flesh.

He has a poet's eyes, offers Avishek, seated on the window ledge.

Clip away the metaphor, suggests Sparrow, waving at the shorn partridge carcasses, shear off the fancy feathers, the crooked clavicles, the seraglio of entrails, pitifully coiled, come clean of the trappings of immortality, emerge as pure flesh.

Dan smiles indulgently, can you season these? he asks Sparrow.

Season them? inquires Sparrow, with the porphyry of autumn, or the sea's summary encrustations?

Salt and pepper, Daniel firmly hands him the silver shakers.

He could move in upstairs, suggests Alexander, mother wouldn't mind.

And write poetry all day, adds Avishek with enthusiasm.

A true poet does not write poetry, says Sparrow, he lives poetry, in the flesh.

He could tell me about blood, says Alexander, he could tell me all about blood.

And the flesh? asks Sparrow, what would he do with his vast experience of flesh?

Mother wouldn't mind, says Alexander, his brow furrowed, she never uses the rooms anymore.

Boneless bulk, says Sparrow, pure flesh, like unvowelled language, yards of flesh, unadulterated by skeleton.

He could stay here, Alexander lays a shaking hand upon your arm as you slide the basted birds into the grill, could he not?

You look away from his eyes, glittering marshes of pain, to the marble slab where Dan's fingers rest, coiled in blood and butter.

I could never have given you what you wanted, says Alexander, not even if I had tried. His hand slips off your arm, he strides to the refrigerator, flings open the ice-box, and extricates from its deep clutches a frosted bottle.

The old potato liquor, Sparrow acknowledges with interest, utterly unfreezable, like most other clichés. Vladimir liked to put it in his bath, perhaps he thought he might imbibe his culture that way – what he never had in his veins.

You remember how Sparrow would crouch against the tub, while Vladimir soaped your neck, Sparrow would crouch in the alcohol steam, and read from the poetry of Jelaluddin Rumi, break the wineglass and fall toward the glassblower's breath, you would stand up, dripping soapsuds, and stare out from the small window onto the chaos of automobiles, twenty-three floors below, on the roof of the building across the road, people were playing tennis, Vladimir would pull you back down into the acid warmth, Sparrow would curse as the thick coverlet of foam that guarded your bodies against his incurious eyes splashed over onto his dog-eared pamphlet, how easy it would have been then to have drowned in the dull vapours, soap and alcohol, bath beads and prisms of salt, the Persian poetry, break the wineglass and fall toward the glassblower's breath, and be smothered by the phantoms of his uncreated visions.

Alexander places a brace of water glasses on the kitchen table, and pours them a quarter full with the viscous liquor, and offers one to Avishek, who shakes his head in refusal, from the recessed comfort of the sill. Alexander shrugs and holds it out to Sparrow, who takes it and the other drink to pass to Dan, and has to wait as he wipes his hands before he can relieve him of the glass. Alexander lifts another pair of tumblers out of the cabinet, will you have a drink, my love? he asks.

You do not reply, he pours himself a quarter glass, and raises a toast, to poetry, he announces, to the endless renunciation of prose!

To the endless renunciation of language, Sparrow says bitterly.

And the total rejection of the future, adds Avishek, his arms folded.

Dan, unruffled, raises his glass, wordlessly, and drinks gratefully of the powerful draught, he turns to you, his smile glistening, you might want to turn them now, he says.

And then you might not, says Alexander, if you do not want to ensure that perfect corruption of the tissues that renders them so succulent to our lips, and so harmless to our juices. If you want one side to char, and the other to remain still smeared with blood ... to the ultimate decay of compromise, he declares, lifting his glass, once more.

To the absolution of destiny, Sparrow clinks chipped crystal.

To the intransigence of destiny, suggests Avishek lightly, rolling his head against the window. The clouds hang heavy upon the thinning treetops, minor threads of lightning leap across the skies, soon it will rain.

• • •

The smell of charred partridge floats crimson in the air, too often has the smell of burning food signalled domestic violence in literature, you cannot let your own existence be consumed by the same pattern, you reach for the oven gloves, the sky clears, bathing the room in that luminescence of disaster that precedes a heavy storm.

You lift the roasting tray out of the grill, the warmth of cooking flesh rises to your eyes, you spin around on your heels, the tray tips, you watch in horror as it slips from your hands, and a fountain of partridges rises and falls.

So much for dinner, says Alexander.

He comes towards you, drains his glass, and draws your head near, how do you see time, my love, he asks, how do you visualise the centuries, is the past a receding line, and the future a blocked mirror, or is each decade a domino, leaning upon another, supported by the undernourished present?

And space? How do you see space? Is it a field full of butterflies, or a limitless lightness? Can the sun rise over a Cauchy horizon? Tell me, love, what elegant thoughts pass through your lovely head?

And love, my dearest, what images speak of love? Not candied hearts and star-swept nights? Teddy bears drizzling stuffing, the twitch of a rabbit's nose? The letters of a naughty cousin, tethered by green ribbon? Or is it the smell of almonds against a sailboat white? Your lips are heavy with kisses, my love, and they are not mine.

He releases you, kicks away a partridge, these gentlemen are hungry, my love, and we have nothing to feed them, my mother shot these partridges that languish now upon the parquet, a good shot is my mother, when she was thirteen her father put her in charge of the Game Book, those heavy ledgers that still line the staircase shelves, Mr Davies, Grouse 2, Woodcock 3, Rabbits 0, Partridges 0, she loved the smell of cold ink, my mother, and the smooth straddled infinity of the Game Ledger, time cupped and doled out into seasons, 1936, 1937, and after the war she met a Persian prince, but I digress, these gentlemen are hungry, if only for your love, and we have little to offer them.

You think perhaps you will leave me now, that it is time to call a halt to this charade, that our passion is resinate, and our tenderness yellowed, the most unoriginal sin has become yours, that most harmless decrepitude, your lips are stained with the velvet of a younger lust, the acid of an immature wine, how it tingles beneath your foretongue, my beloved, if you leave me tonight, what will you remember later of our love? What will you see through the alabaster windows? Will it be merely the shadows of my dreams, the aimless phantoms weaving back and forth in Fellini-esque choreography. Yes, my love, I see you, peeping through stained glass into a candlelit cathedral, where the men and women of my dreams have gathered, they drift back and forth between the sunken pillars, the carven capitals, the floor is bare earth, can you hear Brahms' Requiem in the choir, my love, that blood-salt wind that once fed our passion. With each act of love, we primed each other for death, is that what you miss most, my beauty, that brush with death, faded now into a mere pleasurable surge of blood? Your lips are gorged with death, my love, vinegared green. With whom will you go gently into this rude night? Will it be the butcher? Look into his eyes, my love, can it be he that you will leave with, look into his eyes, they are a poet's eyes, are they not, they are like the moss that seeks to fill the green in a decayed fresco, and his lips, thin and sweetly chapped, how deliciously they twist and tremble against each other, and then the timeless benevolence of his smile, his cheeks are as opaque as death, and his pale hands, my love, if it is an easy encounter with death that you desire, it is he you must leave with, retrace your watery path to the Holloway Council flat, pause, perhaps to nourish your famished selves at the local chip shop, for these gentlemen are hungry, and not only for your love, and the night will pass in slow sweet discovery of a diluted death, the blood will ebb and you will wake parched, stagger into that lurid kitchen of the spray-painted forks, to pour yourself a glass of water, a sweaty dawn will break, barefoot, can it be he that you will leave with? Or will it be your cousin, the baker, there he stands, my love, still in dream, his back pressed against the window, like a wide echo he spirals into the gloom, like a band of laughter, he is waiting to conquer, once and for all, you, in your new condition, he is waiting to take you out into the night where your combined destiny awaits, that which you have ignored for so long, where will you go, in this wild night, with your delicate timeless desire? The daffodil fields are drowned, my sweet, the pollen-packed memories drenched with blood. Your sensations converge upon him, he waits, he has waited for so long, and there is his power, there is the cheap magic, time, the easy draught, fancy mead, nostalgia, the first brush with death, that earliest and most premature of emotions, nostalgia, upon that honeycomb have you endlessly fed, he is the laughing shadow of your past, only he can make death sweet, and strip it of its dignity. Will you go with him into this good night? It may be your destiny, your love has all the trappings of destiny, does it not, my love, how might it be, then, you and he in a small flat in Hampstead, and the child, of course, a consanguinary paradise. But before blood, there was water, my love, and destiny can be tiresome, will you leave, then, with him, dearest, or will it be the candlemaker, after all, Jonathan Sparrow, see him, seated awkwardly at the kitchen table, at the very same spot where this morning he was wolfing down cereal, he broke off to ask for a boiled egg, do you remember, a boiled egg which you denied him, he would miss his flight, you reminded him. Were you in a hurry to be rid of him, my love, he, and why was it that he could not bring himself to leave, enthralled as he was by the reluctant magnetism between you, you are bound by cords of steel, are you not, veins or ore? Unfettered by desire, your spirits clasp and drink of each other, the chain mail clinks, you and he are locked in a lattice of light that only entropy can touch, not mere death, but he is tired, my love, and hungry, he does not relish this non-linearity of his fate. He wishes for it to be as last night, or this morning, he wishes to be consumed in an eternal circle of the events that have made this day, an endless repetition of identical non-ritual. Is it he with whom you are more likely to walk into the night, penniless, homeless, as you had been, in your first evening in this city, many years ago?

He takes your face in his hands, one of them cold from the

glass he has held, what are we going to feed these gentlemen, my beloved, how shall we soothe their hunger, calm their misery, what instruments of succour do we have at our disposal? There is always poetry, but I suspect that of poetry they have had enough, it is death they seek, my beloved. He kisses you violently on your forehead, and moves away, smiling, in this kitchen, my brothers and I took our supper, every evening, for ten years, we would sit around a broken wooden table, the older ones wore their hair long, and their trouserlegs flapped against the wooden knuckles, they spoke business, gold and tapestry, and they spoke of cricket, and the opera, and of the young women they knew and loved, we ate kebabs and pilau, and sometimes fishfingers, when the cook was epileptic, and always behind this broom closet, we kept a well-oiled pistol, and I dreamt, oh how I dreamt, that there was someone, out in the brave world, in a city of sand, perhaps, that craved our blood, this fear kept me awake, many nights, I heard shadows crawl against my window pane, I heard men breathing loudly beneath my bed, and my two brothers slept soundly in the bunks above – and in the meantime, the legend faded, the family curse dried, the killer became senile, time, after all, will heal all, even myth.

It is death they seek, my love, he says, reaching behind the broom closet, and drawing out the firearm, this sorry detritus of my nightmares, that I have continued to tend, instrument of truth. He weighs it sadly in his hands, slips the safety catch, raises it swiftly, a chill whistle divides the charred air, the frothy recoil, look, my love, he still smiles, the Son of Man, Daniel, he clutches at his shattered chest, watch him crumple, my love, he fountains blood upon the greasy floor, he begins to sob fiercely, trails of blood appear at the corners of his mouth, he sinks onto a spray of partridges, he did not deserve this but it is what he was searching for among the cold carcasses, mildewed kidneys, the sheep spittle and the butterfly dew, the sweat of cured shoulder, poor slob, he had the eyes of a poet. And now for the baker, your sweet cousin, hark the small tinkle of breaking glass, he does not protest, my love, for it is indeed what he has been waiting for, for so long, all his childhood heroes have died like this, for your love, all great loves must end like this, the bullet has pierced straight through his precious skull, my beloved, he falls silently, like a summer rain, your first love, he falls gently upon the cold lavender tiles, his toes tangled in the microwave wires, and his last thoughts are of his wife and of how much of an injustice his death is to her, his last thoughts are not of you, my sweet, for he is a man of honour, duty-bound, his last thoughts are of his wife, and of her misery, but for once he is beyond remorse. And your beloved Sparrow, he has risen hastily from his chair, he protests, but only reluctantly, he screams hoarse epithets and catches a bullet in his arm, it burns horribly, but more than any of them, he knows, my love, he knows that this is his destiny, the answer to all his questions, he has stayed back today to die, this harmony is thick honey upon his blood-burst lips as he slips on partridge juices and crashes to the floor, the last two bullets go into his chest, he tries vainly to prop himself up against the dishwasher, falls sideways onto his face.

• • •

That night, you wept upon the kitchen floor, among the drying blood and the partridge juices, the browned butter, you wept ceaselessly, my love, as the evening took on mulberry colours, you dragged them, one by one, across the hall, into the bathroom, the porcelain tub that no one had ever used, you prayed that the children would not wake while you hauled Daniel up by his shoulders, kissed the smoky grey of his hair, the cold cheek, riverrun in blackened blood, the smile, tipping sadly into death grimace, you pulled him across the kitchen floor, the hallway carpet, into the bathroom, where you lifted his legs into the bath, left the rest of him sprawled across the slate-tiled floor, and then you returned for Avishek, unentangled the wires from his feet and pulled him out, under the table, you had crawled with him, once, under furniture that had become mountains and caves and monstrous passes, and if an enemy arrow had caught him, you might have had to drag him out, as you did now, to tend to his wound, you pulled his tall form out from under the table, his trouser-leg caught against an open closet door, you reached over to release it, felt the warmth of his corpse, it was the cleanest of the three, the bullet went into his head, did his entire life have time to reel by, as the skeletons of thought, so painstakingly built, collapsed upon themselves, you dragged him by his feet across the hallway, into the bathroom, panting you release him, and then in a sudden burst of force, held him up, as best as you could, and pushed him forward, he fell heavily into the bathtub, you took his legs and swivelled them around, beyond Dan's blue ankles, and then you reached for Dan's head, which still lay upon cold slate, and lifted him over the lip of the tub, resting his head against the linen closet, now for Sparrow, you hoped, returning, that he would not be there, or that he might speak, croak for assistance, perhaps there was still some way to put his shattered chest back together, but no, his broken body still lay slumped against the dishwasher, you picked him up, he was as light as ever, you carried him slowly into the bathroom, laid him gently across the others' stiff limbs, his arms fell down the sides, grazing the blood-soaked floor. You locked the bathroom door, and returned to the kitchen, where you scrubbed clean the floor, wiped the blood and the partridge fat off the ceramic, the chrome. Splashes of rain came through the broken window where you stood to wipe off the few drops of blood that had spattered the sill. The music had stopped, the house was still, and outside the sound of men digging in the rain, my love, my brothers, digging swiftly, behind the rose-bushes. You heard the rain slipping hard upon their leathery raincoats, my brothers, you heard them throw down their spades and come indoors, splashing raindrops, thick and furry, like the bellies of honey ants. They glided wetly into the night and returned with crates of rum, my love. In icy silence, they unloaded crates of liquor from their black hearse, that thoroughbred that had split the night, when you first came as a bride to this city, my beloved, the family dirge. You hurried past them into the bathroom, where the corpses had begun to slacken their musclehold upon life. You ran your hands along the twisted marble of Daniel's shin. For the last time, my love, you touched your lips to Sparrow's furrowed brow, and with awe you reached for Avishek's stiff hands, to match the whorls upon your fingertips, for the last time, my beloved. For even as you drew away to clench the cruel rim of porcelain, my brothers were emptying the bottles of rum into the tub, the unctuous liquid hissed between their thighs, as you realised that this was no alcohol but only more of that familiar frowst that had once risen harsh against your memories, in the gloom of the high-ceilinged laboratories, this fulgent poison had held upon its dusty brow the markings of death, devil's urine, it hisses against the lobe of Avishek's ear, gathers his dark hair into a slimy knot, fuliginous seaweed. My brothers tip another bottle into the frail architecture of limbs, and gravely, the thin corrugations fade upon Sparrow's badly tended nails, his lips are bleached in anticipation of the lusty liquid that rises to seize them, my brothers break champagne against the tiled walls, Dom Ruinart Blanc de Blancs, 1982, bottles that were turning in their cold vaults as you kissed the soil of your homeland long farewell, bubbles that were gathering as the malefaction brewed in your sister's veins. The soapy spoils shower upon Daniel's ankle, thrust stiff against the wall, my brothers push him down into the seething aroma, a nasturtium of blood issues from his broken chest into the greedy oil, withers fast within the lustrous depths. His bald palms drip colour, like the defiled frenate wings in your bleach baths, that yield their veins to light. His bones appear under his translucent flesh, transfigured marble, the royal water slakes the dim thirst of his smile. My brothers lay their hands upon your arms, guide you outside through the thick fumes. Soon the tub will be a sweet mass of farinaceous broth, thick with the bilge of unravelled wool, buttons of keratin, and the evaporation of flesh, all this my brothers will pour out into the garden grave, already awash in lime, in the thunder and the rain, they will seal the gaping wound, drown it in rose-bushes. There goes the telephone, my lovely, it is your cousin's wife, I tell her he has left, long before. It will be hard, my beloved, to justify his absence, his roots are many, they curl about this earth in confounding sinews, my brothers will have to struggle to hide his tracks, and the secret of his death will fester within you, forever, my lovely. The butcher will be easier, for his inarticulate son, heavy now under drugged sleep, they will return unharmed to his mother's home, leave him wrapped upon the doorstep in warm blankets when the rain lets up at dawn, there are many that will miss him, but none will look too hard for him, for he is the salt, the scum of this earth, my love, he who stained your lips with his smile. And Sparrow, Sparrow will be easy, my love, Jonathan Sparrow, easily erased, who will miss him, who, upon this wide earth, but you?